Other Books By Denise Grover Swank

Harper Adams Mystery
Probable Cause (short story)
Little Girl Vanished
Long Gone
Luck of the Devil
Lost in the Dark
Last Reckoning

Iris Gardner Mystery
It Runs in the Family

Maddie Baker Mystery
Series complete

Magnolia Steele Mystery
Series complete

Carly Moore Mystery
Series complete

Rose Gardner Mystery
Series complete

Darling Investigations
Series complete

LOST IN THE DARK

LOST IN THE DARK

Harper Adams

Mystery #4

DENISE
GROVER SWANK

<hr>

Chapter 1

<hr>

"Get away from the window," James said behind me in a gruff voice.

"Why?" I turned around to face him, letting the heavy curtain fall back into place over the window overlooking the front yard of the property we'd just moved into minutes before. "I thought we were safe here."

"We are," he grunted, dropping onto a worn green sofa.

I grimaced at the dark stain on the cushion beside him. "I'm not so sure we're safe from bed bugs—or whatever diseases live in that thing."

He gave me a piercing glare. "You can't expect the Ritz Carlton."

"I've never stayed in a Ritz Carlton in my life," I said, my tone sharper than intended. But this was the third safe house we'd rotated through in a week, and they seemed to be getting worse with every move. "My expectations aren't that high. Strangely, I thought yours were."

He scowled but kept quiet.

I closed the distance between us and perched on the edge

of the peeling pleather recliner beside him. "Sorry." When he didn't respond, I placed my hand over his. "James."

He turned to look at me, his face blank, neutral in that way I'd come to recognize—he wasn't pissed at my criticism. He was worried.

I'd spent the past seven days with him, 24/7, and I'd started to learn his tells.

"We're safe," I insisted, giving his hand a squeeze.

At least we were safe at the moment.

We were on the run, hiding from Gerald Knox, who might as well be a ghost for all we'd been able to find out about him. All I had were scraps, and the most damning one came from his mother, Nicole.

Nicole had killed *my* mother, who'd learned about my father's work as the Knoxes's attorney. My father had helped Knox—and other shady businessmen—hide, bury, or sanitize money over the past two decades. And she'd been collecting proof.

A little over a month ago, my father had left her. But before he walked out, she told him about the file and threatened to make it public.

So, my father turned around and warned Nicole.

Nicole came to Jackson Creek under an alias and set up an "accidental" meeting with my mother. My mother had few real friends, and Nicole had offered a sympathetic ear. But it was all a play to find out what my mother knew. When Nicole couldn't get it out of her on friendly terms, she'd escalated to threats. But my mother had still refused to hand the information over.

That's when Nicole—helped by her son and his people— had killed her.

She'd staged it to look like an accident; my mother's car had driven off the bridge outside of town. And my father had covered up for Nicole by fueling rumors that my mother had done it on purpose.

The evidence fit. He'd asked their family doctor to prescribe her antidepressants, which had been in her system at her time of death. And tongues were already wagging about the way my mother's neat and tidy life had suddenly turned messy. She was a cautionary tale—a woman who'd taken pride in being better than everyone else.

The town had swallowed the whole story.

James and I did not, and we were able to retrieve the evidence my mother had collected and hidden away.

Before we'd gone on the run, we'd copied everything into a password-protected file on the cloud and locked the original documents in a safe in his office. I spent the first day on the run, digging through the files with a fine-tooth comb, looking for evidence to bring the Knoxes down.

Evidence that strongly suggested the Knoxes had a large-scale money laundering scheme. Was it enough to bring them down? Maybe not, but it would be enough for a law enforcement agency to get a search warrant to start connecting dots.

Once we realized what we were sitting on, we had one brief discussion about turning it over to the FBI, but we'd both quickly dismissed it. At least for now. Getting arrested would be too comfortable for them, not to mention, they were slippery enough to get bail and live their lives until they finally made it to trial years from now.

They needed to pay sooner.

But there was something else that made us hesitate. My mother had paperwork that tied the Knoxes to the purchases of properties James suspected to house criminal activity. One in particular stood out—a warehouse Knox had sold recently. A warehouse James thought played a role in human trafficking.

And apparently, James had been looking for information about a trafficking network in Little Rock. He wanted to pursue this lead, so we hadn't mentioned bringing in the law since.

Still, I wondered if I'd made a selfish decision.

"I should have killed Nicole," I said flatly.

"No," he said. "She was unarmed."

"And look what we're dealing with now."

When Nicole Knox realized we had evidence implicating her son, she'd had his men run us off the road. She'd wanted James alive—long enough to question him before she killed him. We'd figured she probably just wanted me dead.

The crash had left him with a concussion and unable to run, let alone shoot a gun.

When they advanced on us that night, I did what I had to do.

I'd killed nearly a dozen men, but they'd still kidnapped James and taken him to a warehouse.

I'd tracked them down and found him tied to a chair, Nicole seconds away from pulling the trigger.

I took out the guards, who were doing a piss-poor job of protecting her, and then shot Nicole in the arm to keep her from killing James. I'd been ready to kill her after she admitted what she'd done to my mother, but James had talked me out of it. He'd insisted I'd regret killing an unarmed woman.

Only now, I regretted letting her go.

Sure, Gerald would still be after us if I'd killed his mother, but at least I would've had justice. It would have made it a little easier to bear with our current situation—

James was recovering from a concussion, and we were hopping around the state, trying to stay hidden until I was sure James could hit the broadside of a barn with a handgun.

James's gaze softened, an expression I was still getting used to. "You did the right thing."

"*You* would have shot her," I said matter-of-factly.

His eyes clouded. "That's me. We're talking about you."

I let out a harsh laugh. "I'm not Detective Harper Adams anymore. I don't follow the rules she was so obsessed with."

He slowly shook his head. "You're still more her than you want to admit." He grimaced.

"You shouldn't be moving your head. You're impeding your recovery."

James snorted. "It's nothing. I've had a helluva lot worse."

Yet, he wasn't arguing with me that he wasn't a hundred percent. And he sure as hell wasn't ready to go on the offensive.

Concussions were tricky things. James had admitted this wasn't his first—or even his fifth—which probably explained its massive impact. Each concussion made the next one harder to recover from. We'd hoped he'd be better by now, but his progress had been slow. His double vision had disappeared a couple of days ago, but he was easily tired and had persistent headaches.

It felt like we didn't have any time to lose. The Knoxes were hot on our tails, and it would boil down to us or them.

It made total sense to try to find them, only James said Gerald Knox was notoriously secretive about where he lived—or even did business. Which had proved to be true after I'd taken advantage of my private detective license access and spent the last week trying to find anything about his location.

There was nothing.

He had a bank account, no loans, and supposedly no property. But I also knew that property could be hidden by corporations, which I suspected to be the case here. Especially since there was evidence of Gerald Knox selling a Little Rock warehouse under a corporation and that same corporation had recently been dissolved.

James was certain Gerald Knox was the man in charge of the trafficking ring, but I couldn't find anything to tie him to it.

James was also certain that whoever was in charge of the trafficking ring had been doing it for a while. At least three years, based on the fact that James had insinuated he'd worked out a deal with the Feds where he'd have his charges dropped from a previous case if he helped them bring the ring down.

Which meant the ring had been in operation a while. And he'd been running it while I was a homicide detective. The thought lit something cold and furious in my chest.

If Gerald Knox was selling people, then I needed to catch him. I needed to *stop* him.

And even if he wasn't, I needed him and his mother to pay for what they'd done to my mother.

Sighing, I got up and headed for a closed door off the living room.

"What're you doin'?" James demanded, suspicion lacing his voice.

Turned out he could read me pretty well now too.

"I'm finding the bedroom so I can wash the sheets. If there's a washer and dryer, that is."

I pushed the door open and found a full-size bed with a beat-up wooden headboard and a stained, bare mattress—one stain dark enough that it looked like blood. And large enough to suggest the wound may have been fatal.

"Where did Carter find this place again?" I called out to the living room.

"It's one of mine."

"You own this dump?" I laughed. If there was a set of sheets in this place, I had no idea where to find them. And if I did, I'd probably have to burn them.

"It's a safe house. It's not meant to be comfortable."

"At this point, I'd settle for halfway clean."

When I walked back into the living room, he was leaning his head back on the sofa, his eyes drifting closed. Guilt washed through me. He hadn't said it outright, but I knew he felt responsible for us being on the run, not only because of his concussion, but because he was James Malcolm, and Gerald Knox already had it out for him.

I felt guilty that investigating my mother's murder had gotten us into this, but I felt even more guilty that I was grateful he was in this mess with me.

"I'm sorry for complaining," I said, dropping onto the edge of the recliner again.

His eyes cracked open. "You've got nothing to be sorry about. You're right. The place is a pigsty."

"I'm going out to get a set of fresh bedding and some cleaning supplies."

He jerked upright, his eyes flying open. "The hell you are."

"No one followed us here, James. I made sure of it."

"You're not goin' out alone. I'll call Carter and have him send someone."

"The more you involve Carter, the more dangerous it is for all of us." Carter was in hiding somewhere on his own, because he was also at risk.

He started to protest, then stopped.

We'd left the last safe house because Knox's men had found it in the middle of the night. We'd barely gotten away, sneaking out the back door and driving off without our headlights on. So I understood why James was paranoid. It was now mid-afternoon, and we'd parked in multiple places covering half the state and hadn't seen any signs of them.

"I have a hat," I said. "I'll avoid cameras. Maybe I'll curl my hair and put on makeup." I gave him a dark smile. "You know, a disguise."

He leaned forward, then cupped my cheek. "You're beautiful just the way you are, Harper."

I remained still, but inside I was squirming. I wasn't used to compliments, especially from men like James. I knew I wasn't beautiful, and I'd never had a problem with it before. But with him…

Part of me wished I were.

"I'll come with you." He started to rise.

I gently pushed him back down, then straddled his legs before he could argue again. I cupped his cheek, forcing him to meet my eyes. The bruise around his right eye had faded to a sickly yellow-green.

"You need to rest," I said quietly. "We just spent twelve hours in a car or in restaurants."

"I'm capable of ridin' in a car."

"You just rode in a car in bright sunlight."

His jaw tightened. "I got that concussion a week ago."

"James," I leaned closer, dropping my voice. "You need to give yourself more time to heal."

"We don't *have* time." He closed his eyes in frustration.

"We *do*." As long as we could stay hidden, we'd be safe. The problem was, James hated safe when it looked like hiding.

I wasn't happy about it either.

James wasn't the only impatient one. If Gerald Knox thought we were coming after him, he'd be tightening security, covering his tracks. He might even be moving his trafficking somewhere outside of Little Rock.

I needed to get in touch with my contacts sooner rather than later. But every time I mentioned reaching out, James shut it down. I'd gone along with him up to now, but after hitting dead end after dead end online, it was time to switch tactics.

I wasn't sure James subscribed to the *it's easier to ask for forgiveness than permission* philosophy unless he was the one asking for forgiveness.

Oh, who was I kidding? I doubted he'd asked permission for anything in his life, and I definitely didn't see him begging anyone for forgiveness.

"I'll check in with you every half hour," I said. "And if I see anything suspicious, I'll leave immediately and head straight back to you." When he didn't respond, I added, lighter, "I used to be a cop, you know. I was pretty good at noticing people who aren't behaving as they should."

"I don't like it," he growled.

"I know. But you know I'll be fine."

He closed his eyes again, and I kissed him softly.

James Malcolm, ex-crime boss, a man who'd helped take down an international crime organization, had never struck me as gentle. And for the most part, he wasn't.

Maybe that's why I felt the need to be gentle with him sometimes. Not because he was fragile, a word that didn't describe him, even injured. But because tenderness wasn't something he'd gotten much of in his life, I felt a need to show him he was worthy of it.

Even if I wasn't sure I deserved it myself.

"I'm going to take your silence as a yes," I said when I pulled back.

"I still don't like it."

"I'll even pick you up a steak and baked potato."

He cracked a grin. "You're gonna grill a steak?"

"Hell, no," I said, laughing. "I'll find a Longhorn Steakhouse or something."

"That's my girl."

He'd said that phrase a few times since the night Knox's men had attacked us, and it sent a rush of heat through me every time. I wasn't a gushy kind of woman. I'd never been very demonstrative in relationships, but my connection with James felt different. I didn't want to examine why.

"The bed's not made," I said, shifting off him. "So take a nap here on the sofa."

His gaze held mine. "You got the cash Carter left us?"

"I'll grab it on my way out."

"Grab one of the new burner phones too."

"Will do."

When we'd arrived at the safe house, we'd found a pile of cash, two new burner phones, and a couple of bags of groceries waiting for us. We'd left our real cell phones at

James's house and had been living on cash and burners ever since. Anything to avoid being tracked, but they'd tracked us to the last place anyway.

It made me wonder if Knox had a list of James's safe houses, or if James had a rat in his crew. When I'd asked him, he'd dismissed both possibilities.

He held my gaze now, worry flickering in his eyes for a split-second before he locked it down. "Be careful."

I gave him a cocky grin. "Somebody's gotta take care of you."

"Up until now, I've done pretty well on my own."

I wasn't sure how true that was. I knew he'd had a right-hand man and best friend, Jed, three or four years ago. He still had Carter Hale, his attorney and maybe the closest thing he had to a best friend now.

He wasn't totally alone, but I still felt responsible for him. If he hadn't been helping me find the truth about my mother's death, he wouldn't be caught in the middle of it. Even if he'd wanted to be there.

Or maybe it was deeper than that.

And I wasn't ready to name it.

Chapter 2

The safe house was about twenty miles outside of Hot Springs, Arkansas. One of the burners was a smartphone, but I left it and took the flip phone, hoping it would be harder to track me without a data plan. Still, in case I ran into trouble, I had a shoulder-holstered handgun under my jacket.

On the way to town, I checked the voicemails on my real number, since it had been a couple of days. I wasn't surprised to find two messages from my father. But the three from my friend Louise caught me off guard. Louise wasn't supposed to be worried.

My father was desperate to talk to me and begged me to call, just like he had in the other five messages he'd left over the past week. I was supposed to meet him the night we were run off the road by the Knoxes's men, but obviously I'd never showed. The next day, I'd called and told him I'd changed my mind and would be heading out of town for a while.

I had no idea if he knew I was in Gerald and Nicole's sights, but I had no problem letting him stew.

Louise's messages were shorter and more direct.

"Harper, I'm checking in. Call me."

"Harper, stop screening my calls. Call me."

"Harper, we need to talk. ASAP. Call me."

Before James and I had gone on the run, I'd told Louise I was planning to spend some time with my grandparents in Jonesboro and wasn't sure when I'd be back. She knew I'd been estranged from them for years, and that I'd gone to see them the day after my mother's funeral. But I hadn't filled her in on the details.

Not that I could share all of them.

Louise had no idea my mother had been murdered. She believed it was an accident. And she definitely had no idea I'd partnered with James Malcom to find out who'd killed her. She'd seemed satisfied with my explanation of visiting my grandparents—which I'd asked her to keep to herself—but after a week, she was probably starting to wonder when I'd be back.

I drove to a Walmart, which was a lot harder without GPS, but I'd been to Hot Springs a few times and remembered the general location. After I bought sheets, bath towels, cleaning supplies, and food that wasn't the processed crap Carter had delivered, I headed for the checkout, passing the wine and beer section.

I stopped the cart, my gaze snagging on the aisle. It took everything in me not to turn down it.

It had been a week since my last drink, and every day was still a struggle. If anything, the struggle was getting worse. The first few days, willpower had kept me on track. Now, the stress of running was chewing my nerves to the bone, and everything in me screamed for something to soften the edges.

I tightened my grip on the cart handle, fighting my internal war. Other than whatever I had going on with James, my life sucked right now, and for the past six months, drinking was how I had coped.

One bottle of wine wouldn't hurt, right?

Or a six-pack of beer?

If I bought beer, I could drink it slowly—one at a time—instead of trying to pace myself with an open bottle of wine.

No.

I closed my eyes, fighting the pull to that aisle.

It was hard to accept I'd never have a drink again. No glass of wine with dinner. Or a margarita by a pool. No cold beer on a hot summer's day.

No alcohol. Ever.

Alcohol was part of polite society, always there, and knowing I'd never have it again was a hard pill to swallow. No pun intended.

But I was also a realist. And the cold, hard truth was I could never drink again. The sooner I accepted it, the easier it would get.

At least I hoped it would be.

I headed for the checkout lanes before I could change my mind. After I paid in cash, I walked out into the warm spring morning and drew in a deep breath. I'd walked away from temptation. Maybe I'd cave next time, but this morning was a win.

One day at a time? More like one minute. Maybe even ten seconds.

After I loaded the bags into the backseat, I pulled out my phone, facing another temptation. Calling Louise could be risky, but she sounded concerned in her messages. I didn't want to worry her, and considering she was a sheriff's deputy, she might start digging into where I'd gone.

Leaning my butt against the trunk, I placed the call.

"Deputy Louise Brown," she answered in her official deputy-sheriff voice, not that I was surprised. The number wouldn't show as mine.

"Louise. It's me."

"Harper?" Her voice jumped an octave. "Why haven't you answered my calls or texts?"

"Sorry. I've been on a tech detox." It seemed as good an excuse as any.

"Your father is freaking out."

My back stiffened. "What? How do you know?"

"He's called me multiple times, telling me he thinks you're in danger, but when I press him as to why, he won't answer." She paused. "Do you know what he's talking about?"

I did, but I wasn't about to admit it. "He's probably just paranoid after my mother's death. When I left for my grandparents', he and I weren't on great terms. I didn't tell him where I'd gone. Did you tell him?"

"No, you told me to keep it a secret. But he told me you were supposed to meet him last week and you never showed."

I pushed out a heavy sigh. "I already told him that I'd changed my mind. I called him the next day."

"He's about to file a missing person's report on you, Harper."

My father being persistent in tracking me down hadn't been on my bingo card. "I didn't tell him I was going to my grandparents' place, but I told him not to worry. That I needed some space to process."

"Funny thing, that," she said, her voice tight. "I called your grandparents."

I pressed my back into the car, panic swirling in my head.

"No response to that?" she prodded.

"Okay," I said, "I didn't go to my grandparents' house. But I knew if I told you and my father that I needed time away, you'd worry."

"So where are you?"

I hesitated. If there was anyone I trusted in law enforcement, it was Louise. But I couldn't flat out tell her the truth.

Could I?

"Hot Springs," I said. "I'm having a spa week."

"You never struck me as a spa girl." She didn't bother hiding her skepticism.

"It's beautiful here," I said, my gaze scanning the Walmart parking lot. "I mostly spend time outdoors."

"You know what's also funny?" she asked, then didn't wait for me to answer. "James Malcolm hasn't been seen all week either."

My panic flared again, but I was proud I kept my voice even. "So?"

"That seems like a coincidence."

"What are you insinuating, Louise?" I asked with a laugh that sounded almost real. "That I'm having a torrid affair with James Malcolm?"

"Who said anything about an affair?"

I'd walked right into that one.

"Then what are you insinuating?" I asked, my tone still light.

"It's odd timing," she said. "And the day you supposedly first went to your grandparents, he wasn't at the tavern. He's always at the tavern."

"Maybe he realized that all work and no play make a person boring," I countered.

Her silence hung in the air like an anvil.

"And I *did* go to my grandparents' place," I said. "I found out that my mother lied to me and my father about why we stopped seeing them. That's what I was going to talk to him about last week, but then decided it was water under the bridge. It wouldn't change anything."

"She lied?" The edge in her tone was gone. "Why?"

I hadn't planned to get into any of this, but I had to tell her something. "She found out my father was having an affair, and she didn't want her parents to know." Not the full truth, or the order of events, but it was close enough.

"If they didn't know, how did you figure it out?"

"I saw my aunt too. She saw my father with his mistress and told my mom." I swallowed. "So, my mom cut them off."

That one was closer to the actual truth.

"That's messed up," Louise said, disgust curling her words.

"What's even more messed up is she told them I didn't want anything to do with them either." My throat tightened. "They sent me birthday cards for years and she sent them back without ever showing them to me."

"Harper." Her voice softened. "I'm sorry."

"Yeah." My voice cracked. "So I needed to get away for a while to process everything."

"I can believe that," she said, then her tone shifted. "You should know that I also got a call from your former partner, Keith Kemper."

Shit.

"Why in God's name would Keith be calling you?"

"He wanted to know if I knew why you'd contacted the lead counsel for the State Attorney General."

She let the silence do the work.

Keith had called me about the same thing, but he hadn't said whether Mason Deveraux had indicated why I'd placed the call. If Keith knew and had told Louise…

Was she giving me enough rope to hang myself?

She really was going to make a great detective.

Then something else hit me.

"Wait. How does he know we're friends?" I asked. "We weren't friends in Little Rock, and until he called me last week, asking the same thing, I hadn't spoken to him in months."

"I asked him about that," she said. "He told me you'd mentioned it to him."

"Again," I said, "I haven't talked to him since … probably last November."

We were silent for a beat.

"He's having you watched," Louise said.

A chill slid down my spine. I suspected she was right, because how else would he know? "The question is *why* he's having me watched."

"I told you in Little Rock that I don't trust him," she said in disgust. "He was gaslighting you when someone kept breaking into your house. He tried to convince you that you were imagining it. What if he was behind the break-ins?"

I shook my head. "You think Keith broke into my house? Why?"

"What if he was looking for something?" She pressed. "Or, if nothing else, he wanted you to think you were losing your mind." She paused. "Make you question your memory of the shooting."

I let her words sink in. She had a point, only I knew for a fact Keith hadn't been behind the break-ins. That had been a man named Drew Sylvester, who'd been hunting for something of my sister's.

But Louise didn't know about any of that. She didn't know about Drew Sylvester. Or that I'd discovered his brother had witnessed my sister's murder nearly twenty years ago.

There was a whole hell of a lot I hadn't told her, and suddenly all those lies didn't sit right.

"Maybe," I said finally, because I knew for a fact I hadn't told Keith I was friends with Louise. And if he'd lied to her, that meant something.

"Why aren't you calling me from your own phone?" Louise asked.

"I lost mine. That's why I haven't called you back."

"Why not get a replacement?"

"I decided to upgrade to a newer model," I said quickly. "It's not here yet."

"Huh." Another pause. "Where do you suppose Malcolm's taking his vacation?"

Shit. Shit. Shit. She wasn't letting this go.

"How would I know?" I asked with a laugh. "It's not like he'd run his travel plans by me. Why don't you ask Misti, the bartender?"

"I did. She said she wasn't privy to the information." Louise's voice tightened. "Which seemed odd, since he's always acted pretty tight with his staff."

"If they don't know, what makes you think I would?"

"Because, even though he tried to be discreet, I could tell he has a thing for you."

Funny how I hadn't noticed. "You're crazy."

"Am I? He's a good-lookin' man. Mysterious and has a dangerous edge. That's hard for some women to resist."

"Do I strike you as most women?"

"No," she said without hesitation. "But I can still see the appeal."

"What exactly are you insinuating, Louise?" I asked lightly, purposely not giving her an excuse to latch on to.

"Are you sleeping with James Malcolm?" She didn't even bother tiptoeing around it. "I mean, you're not interested in Nate Davis. He's a really nice guy—steady, dependable. But I always knew he wasn't your type. So, I asked myself … who would be the polar opposite of Nate?"

"Why would I run off to Hot Springs to screw James Malcolm when I could just as easily do that in Lone County?"

"That's the part I don't get," she said. "The timing's off. Your mother just died."

"Seems like it would be the best time to run off," I said, going on the offensive. "I mean, I *did* run off."

"But why would Malcolm run off?" Louise pressed. "I asked around, and no one remembers him being gone for more than a day or two at a time. Definitely not a week."

"Then, I guess you'll have to ask him when he gets back."

She was silent again, heavy and deliberate.

"Rumor has it there was a big shootout off BB County Road last week," she finally said. "The night you were supposed to meet your father."

"Wow." I was struggling to keep up the charade. Her questions were exactly how I would have played a suspect. Wear them down. Twist them up. Make it hard to remember the lies. "What happened?"

"Good question. The deputies who went out to investigate couldn't find any evidence of anything except a car fire."

Carter had said he'd clean up the scene, which included the bodies. Several of them.

"How'd the car catch on fire?"

"Good question. The deputies said it was put out by the owner."

James Malcolm was the owner, and he sure as hell hadn't put it out.

"So, then no shootout?"

"That's what they're claiming."

"You sound skeptical."

"It sounds sketchy."

I could let the topic drop, but since she didn't know I was involved, I pressed her. "Which part?"

"The part where you're lying to me."

The lump in my throat turned solid. "About what?"

"That's just it. I don't know. But I know you're not just having a self-care week in Hot Springs."

I leaned my head back, struggling with my conscience. This wasn't how you treated a good friend. But I'd been involved in multiple illegal activities over the last month, and Louise was a deputy sheriff. If I told her too much, she'd be duty-bound to report it. And once she knew, she'd be in trouble right along with me—whether she wanted to be or not.

Still, she could be helpful. Hell, she'd suspected the Little

Rock PD was dirty before I had. Then again, I'd been idealistic and naïve. I was neither of those things now.

"You're right," I said carefully. "But there are things I can't tell you, for your own sake. And if I'm honest, for mine too."

"Are you going after the Little Rock PD?" she asked, breathless.

I blinked. "No."

"Don't lie to me, Harper." Frustration sharpened her words. "Friends don't lie to one another."

"You're right." My throat tightened. "And I've tried to not outright lie to you. I've just made some lies of omission." I drew in a slow breath. "I'm not going after the LRPD. At least, not yet. I'm working on something else first."

"What? Are you working a case?"

I decided to give her a nugget of truth. "Yeah. I was working a case when I went to see my grandparents." I paused. I needed to be damn sure I wanted to do this, but I was tired of keeping so many secrets. I could tell her this one. "My mother didn't accidentally drive off the bridge. And she didn't do it on purpose either. She was murdered."

She gasped. "What? But the report says it was accidental."

"Yeah, the autopsy report was doctored."

"How do you know that?"

"Because I've seen the real one." My pulse pounded in my ears. "She was doped up on antidepressants, and she had a head wound to the back of her head, made by a cylindrical object." I swallowed. "Which means she didn't hit her head in the wreck. Someone hit her in the head, put her in the car, and pushed it off the bridge."

"Why didn't you tell me?" Accusation and pain laced her words.

"I didn't want to put you in danger. Someone doctored the autopsy report, and everyone who's aware of the real one is a threat."

"A threat to who?"

I chewed on my bottom lip, unsure how much to disclose. If I gave her a name, she'd insist on handing it over to law enforcement, and I wasn't willing to do that. I knew there were dirty cops, and I didn't trust this wouldn't get buried.

"I can't tell you," I finally said. "For your own safety."

"Don't bullshit me, Harper," she snapped.

"This is big, Louise." My voice went flat. "My mother uncovered some criminal activities, and they killed her to keep her quiet."

"How do you know that?" she asked skeptically.

"She had a safe deposit box with evidence."

"Your mother wasn't exactly living on the edge," Louise said dryly. "Did she uncover an illegal bridge game in her garden club?"

"No. Worse." I pushed down the grief that caught me by surprise. "And I think she's been collecting proof for years."

"From where? How would she even get her hands on it?"

"If I tell you, you'll be obligated to act," I said, frustration leaking into my voice. "And I'm not ready for that yet."

Her voice went cold. "So you're investigating this on your own? Outside the law?"

"I have a PI license," I said matter-of-factly. "I'm not outside the law."

"But you're *not* doing this alone." It was a statement, not a question. "Malcolm's helping you."

I didn't respond.

"Why would he do that?" she demanded.

"How would I know the inside of James Malcolm's mind?" I said lightly. Too lightly.

"But you *do* know the inside of his pants?" she asked dryly.

I wasn't sure how to answer that. I didn't feel like lying, but I didn't want to confirm it either.

Louise groaned. "I would hope to God that if you trust him

enough to work this with you, you'd know why he's doing it. How do you know you can trust him?"

"I need you to trust *me* on this, Louise."

"*Harper.*"

"I can't take this to law enforcement. I don't trust them. And based on what you told me about the car fire? You don't either."

"That's not fair."

"Isn't it?"

"There's a lot of good people in this department," she shot back.

"I think you're right," I agreed. "But all it takes is one or two who aren't."

"There are a hell of a lot more than one or two rotten apples in Little Rock," she said in disgust.

"That's not my concern right now," I said, keeping my voice even. "Not that I have any plans to notify them of anything. I need to handle this on my own. If I involve anyone, it will likely be the state police and possibly Mason Deveraux."

"So you *did* call him," she said, satisfaction creeping into her tone.

"I did, but by the time he called me back, I already had the answers I was looking for."

"I hope you know what you're doing. And I hope to God you're not placing your trust in the wrong people."

"I'm going with my gut," I said softly. "It's worked for me in the past. I have to believe it will work for me now." Especially since I was beginning to trust it again.

"If you need me for anything, let me know," she said. "I'm guessing you called from a burner."

"Yeah."

"Tell me if you change your number again. I need to be able to get ahold of you."

"Yeah. Okay." James wouldn't like it, but I suspected there

were quite a few things I was getting ready to do that he wouldn't like.

"Promise me one thing," she said, her voice hard.

"What's that?"

"When you're ready to take down the LRPD, you'll let me help you."

I noticed she'd said *when* not *if.* And she was right. A month ago, I'd been ready to crawl under a rock and hide from what had happened. Not anymore. I was going to take down Keith and anyone else who was dirty, but I had to deal with this first.

But I knew this was personal to her too.

"When I decide to go after Keith and his fellow assholes, you'll be the second to know."

"Who's the first?"

I let out a short, humorless laugh. "I don't think you want me to answer that."

She paused a beat. "I really hope you can trust him, Harper."

"I have a small circle, and I trust that circle implicitly."

"I hope I'm included in that circle."

"That's a given."

"Then go get 'em, Harper." She hung up, and I wondered if I'd said too much or too little. Either way, I'd just dragged Louise closer to the fire.

Time would tell.

Chapter 3

I leaned against the car and studied the parking lot, trying to decide my next move. If my father was about to file a missing person's report on me, I needed to get in front of it. The last thing I needed was the Lone County Sheriff's Department putting me into their system as a missing person.

Which meant I needed to pull up my big girl pants and talk to my father.

A shot of whiskey sure would take the edge off.

The entrance to Walmart was only about fifty feet away. I could get a few of those little plastic bottles. What harm would one shot cause?

I shook my head, bitter disappointment flooding me. Would it be this hard to stay on top of my cravings for the rest of my life?

Then again, at the rate I was going, there was a chance my life wouldn't last all that long anyway. Could James and I really take on someone as powerful as Gerald Knox and live to tell the tale? It was the two of us against an organization.

Then it hit me that James had already taken down an

international organization. If anyone could do it, he could. I just needed him to tell me how he'd pulled it off. So far, I'd asked very few questions about his past, trusting him to tell me when he was ready. Maybe I needed to press him on this one.

But first, I needed to talk to my father.

He was probably at his law office, but he didn't have a direct line to his office, and I didn't want to talk to anyone there. I called his cell.

"Hello?" He sounded nervous, likely because it was an unknown number. Or was he nervous for another reason?

"Dad, it's me."

He gasped, and his voice broke. "Harper. Thank God."

"I heard you called Louise asking about me."

"You wouldn't answer my calls."

"Maybe I don't want to talk to you."

"You wanted to talk to me last week," he said, sounding steadier now. "You were supposed to meet me at the park."

"And I told you the next day that I changed my mind."

"I've heard from Nicole Knox."

I was silent for several seconds. It didn't surprise me that she'd reached out to him. I knew they'd been in touch. Dad's partner had seen them together at the park in Jackson Creek. We'd both mistakenly thought she was his mistress.

Hardly. He'd been doling out a warning about my mother.

"And?" I finally said.

"You don't seem surprised."

I let out a bitter laugh. "Actually, I should have known she would contact you, but somehow, it never occurred to me. I must be slipping."

"This isn't funny, Harper," he snapped. "Nicole wants you dead."

"I'm sure she does. I suspect I've given her quite the scar on her arm."

"You need to give her whatever she wants. If you do that, she'll let bygones be bygones."

I laughed again, this time for real. "You really believe that? After I shot her?"

"She's given me her word."

There was no way he could be that naive, but I let it go for now. "And what exactly does she want me to give her?"

"Don't play stupid, Harper. We both know you found the file your mother hid in that safe deposit box."

"I think that's the first truthful thing you've said to me to since I was a kid."

"That's not true *or* fair," he snapped.

"Isn't it?" I prodded. "Why did you ask me to come home this past winter?"

He hesitated. "Because I love you. I was worried about you."

"Yeah." Skepticism dripped off the word. "I'm not buying the *I want to be a good dad* act. Not anymore. It had a good run, but we've moved on. So tell me the truth. Wouldn't that be a nice change?"

"*Harper.*"

"*Paul,*" I said, letting the name land like a slap. "See? I can play this game too."

"You're being immature."

"And you're a murderer. Aren't we a fine pair?"

"I *never* murdered *anyone.*"

"Maybe you never pulled a trigger, but you're guilty all the same."

"Who have I supposedly murdered?"

"My mother."

"I had *nothing* to do with her murder. I didn't even know Nicole had befriended her."

"How did Nicole know about Mom's file?"

He didn't respond.

"You told her," I said, my voice icy. "Which pretty much guaranteed she'd end up dead."

"Just like you will be if you don't give Nicole what she wants," he spat.

"You honestly believe she'll just let me go?" I asked in disbelief. "After I shot her and she spilled blood on her pretty silk shirt?"

"Of course not!" he snapped. "Which is why you need to give her the file and then run and hide."

"If you believe she'll just let me hide, I've got some swampland in Florida to sell you. You and I both know I'm a dead woman walking. The real question is why you care. Because you've never cared about me. Not like that."

He gasped. "How can you say that?"

"You didn't give two shits about me for years. So, I know you had a special reason for bringing me home from Little Rock back in February. Just like I know you have a special reason for wanting me to give Nicole the file." When he didn't respond, I pushed on. "I suspect neither of you know what's in the file. And you really need to know for damage control." I let that hang for a beat. "And since we're throwing around theories, I'm going to add this: I think *your life* depends on me handing over that file. Correct me if I got any of this wrong."

"These aren't people you play around with, Harper," he hissed.

"Maybe you should have thought about that before you got in bed with them."

"I never slept with Nicole Knox!"

"That's not what I meant, and you damn well know it." My grip tightened on my phone. "But since we're on the subject of affairs, I know about yours from years ago. Aunt Hannah saw you screwing a woman in your home office."

I really wished we were doing this in person. I would've loved to see his face.

"That was years ago." He didn't sound as confident.

"I also know you were partners with Dale Ambrose and a man named Richard around the same time, and you and Richard had Dale Ambrose murdered." I let a beat pass. "Funny how his car accident was so similar to Mom's."

"I never had that man killed."

"Maybe not, but you didn't turn in the man who killed him either." I paused. "Here's a freebie for what's in Mom's file— that's when she started collecting evidence against you."

"You're playing a dangerous game, Harper," he said, his voice colder than I'd ever heard it.

"Am I?" I countered. "Who put me in the game?"

"I sure as hell didn't."

"Bullshit. Like I said, you brought me back home for a reason. *That* put me in this game. If I hadn't been living in Jackson Creek, I never would have questioned her death. Hell, I might not have even come home for the funeral."

"It was time you came home," he said flatly. "Besides, you had nowhere else to go."

"You know, I desperately wanted to believe you came because you cared." My voice rose, and a woman pushing a cart past me with a toddler sitting in the seat gave me a stern look. "But that was sixteen-year-old Harper, desperate for her father's love." I swallowed hard. "I know better now. If you really wanted me back, you would've come for me much sooner. Before my life fell apart. Hell, you wouldn't have let me leave home for college without making sure I knew I was welcome to come back anytime." Anger burned in my chest as I spat out, "So cut the shit, *Dad*."

"If you're going to take that disrespectful tone, then we have nothing further to talk about," he said stiffly. "Call me back when you've seen reason, and I'll coordinate a location for you to leave the file."

He hung up.

Emotion churned in my gut, and part of me wanted to scream. I'd thought confronting him would make me feel better, but it hadn't. It had made everything so much worse.

Tears stung my eyes.

Was I really so unlovable that my own parents had thought nothing of using me as a pawn?

No wonder I was incapable of having a healthy relationship.

James popped into my head, and I released a bitter laugh. I wasn't sure what I had with him, but it wasn't a relationship. It was sex and adrenaline and bad timing. We were each other's current fucks, that was all. Nothing more. Nothing less.

But I no longer had alcohol to help convince me to believe my own bullshit.

I wouldn't have killed that many men for a fuck buddy. He was more to me than that.

Still, this was hardly the time for me to analyze what I felt for James Malcolm, who was probably already flipping out about how long I was taking.

I needed to get back.

I got in the car and nearly drove back to the safe house, then remembered I'd promised him a steak dinner. I found a steak house and ordered at the bar, struggling not to order a whiskey to sip while I waited.

I headed outside to escape temptation and leaned against the trunk again, watching the cars whiz by. But being alone with my thoughts was dangerous right now. I was still processing my conversation with my father and fighting the urge to go back inside and get the whiskey I was dying to drink.

I needed a plan. We couldn't afford to sit and wait

anymore, not if my father was going to let Nicole know he'd talked to me. We needed to go to Little Rock.

Before I could talk myself out of it, I called Carter Hale.

"This better be an emergency," he said, all business when he answered.

"What constitutes an emergency?" I said flippantly. Then, realizing he'd never speak to James that way, I added, "And how'd you know it was me?"

"Because Skeeter told me you took this burner phone. And an emergency would mean your life is on the line."

"Does the fact that I'm standing outside a steak house wrestling with my demons over ordering two fingers of whiskey count as my life being on the line?"

I'd meant it to come out as a joke, but it fell flat. Carter knew I'd given up drinking. He was the one who'd gotten me the meds to help me through DTs.

"It's gonna be a struggle, Harper," he said sympathetically. "But you called me instead of ordering it. That means you still have control."

"Maybe so, but it's a sliver."

"Maybe tell yourself a sliver is better than nothing."

I couldn't help laughing. "You're a glass-half-full person, aren't you?"

"I'll deny it to my last breath," he joked, "but I'm guessing that's not why you called."

"Nicole Knox called my father and threatened to kill him if I don't turn over my mother's file."

"What does Skeeter say about that?"

"I haven't told him yet. I'm still running errands."

"You shouldn't be running errands at all," he admonished. "That's what I'm for. Getting you what you need."

"Well, your people didn't check whether our safe house was halfway clean, so I'm getting bedding, towels, and cleaning supplies. Oh, and steak and a baked potato for James so he'd agree to let me go alone."

"You two need to stick together."

"I'm fine. He's fine. And I've only been gone a little over an hour."

"You're not thinking about giving Nicole Knox the file, are you?"

"She'll have to pry it out of my cold, dead hand."

"You'd have to get it out of the safe in Skeeter's office first," he said with a short laugh.

"Yeah, well, this isn't about having the physical file. She must know we'd make copies. I suspect she wants to know what's in it so she and her son can brace for blowback. My father doesn't even know what's in it. He claims if I give it to her, she'll pretend none of this ever happened."

"Do you believe that?"

"Of course not. I don't think he does either. This is only about protecting himself."

"Would you do it for him?"

"The cold, dead hand statement still applies. He made his bed. Now he can lie in it."

He was silent for several seconds, then said, "I appreciate the update, but I'm guessing that's still not why you called."

"No wonder James keeps you around," I teased. "Along with a whole host of other reasons. But you're right. There is something else."

I told him that I'd been thinking of reaching out to some of my old sources in Little Rock.

"Are you asking for permission?" he asked.

"You know how to cut to the chase."

"I don't see any reason not to."

"James won't like it if I do this alone."

"You're right. He won't."

"But he's also not a hundred percent. He got a headache from riding in a car in broad daylight. I know recovery gets harder the more concussions you rack up." I took a breath, knowing I needed to tread carefully. "I don't want to piss him off, but you and I both know we've been hiding too long. I need to do something."

"What exactly are you asking for, Harper? My blessing to defy my boss?"

"No." I shook my head. "I don't know what I'm asking."

"I'm sure you've realized he's protective of the people he cares about. Which means he'll probably fight you on this. Hard."

I laughed. "I'm not deluded enough to think that's why he'll fight me on it, Carter."

"Sounds like maybe you are if you think you mean nothing to him."

My heart skipped a beat. "I didn't call to hand you a *does he like me, check the box* note."

He chuckled. "I should hope not. We don't have the technology to hand physical objects through a phone call."

I groaned.

He laughed again. "I suspect you're asking if he'll forgive you if you defy his wishes."

"I doubt there's any way he'll agree to let me go alone. He could barely stomach me running errands without him."

"So that *is* what you're asking." He paused. "He takes loyalty very, very seriously."

"This isn't about loyalty."

"Are you sure about that?"

"I've proven my loyalty multiple times over," I insisted.

"He's had a history of people choosing their own best interest over his. Once bitten, twice shy."

"I'm not doing this for my own self-interest, Carter," I said in annoyance.

"Are you sure about that?"

A woman walked out of the restaurant, holding up a brown paper bag and heading toward me.

"Our food's ready," I said. "I need to go."

"Whatever you decide, make sure he knows who you're really doing it for. Even if it *is* for you. The only thing he values more than loyalty is truthfulness."

He hung up before I could tell him I already knew that. Maybe that was part of why I respected James so much.

Chapter 4

When I reached the safe house, I called out, "It's me," before I unlocked the door and walked into the living room. It was probably unnecessary. James had likely been watching the window.

He was on the sofa, a handgun beside him. He had circles under his eyes and two-day-old stubble, but it only made him look more ruggedly handsome. "Run into any trouble?"

I shut the door behind me. "No. How's your headache?"

Irritation flickered in his eyes. "It's fine."

"Did you get any sleep?"

"I'm not a goddamned baby," he said in a surly tone.

I could have taken offense, but I was feeling generous after the three calls I'd made on my burner. Besides, I knew his frustration wasn't directed at me. "You and I both know sleep will help."

"I'm fine."

"I know it's early, but I say we eat dinner and then I'll start cleaning."

"You're not the maid," he snapped.

"Maybe not, but I don't see one hanging around, so someone has to do it."

"Carter should have made sure it was clean."

I set the food bag on the coffee table and sat down beside him. "Carter's doing the best he can." I reached for his face, and when he didn't pull away, I pressed my palm to his cheek, turning his head to face me. "*You're* doing the best you can."

"But it's not enough, is it?" he asked bitterly.

I pressed a soft kiss to his lips, and to my surprise, he grabbed the back of my head and held me close as he took over, his mouth hungry for mine.

A wave of desire rolled through me, and for the hundredth time that week, I wondered if sex was slowing his recovery. But every time I brought it up, he shut it down, saying he'd waited long enough to have me, and he wasn't waiting any longer.

I eagerly kissed him back while he reached for the button on my jeans. Moments later, I was naked, and his clothes were on the floor next to mine.

I straddled his lap, my hips resting on his thighs as his hands worked their magic on my body.

"I missed you," he murmured against my lips, before his mouth trailed kisses down my neck, then lower.

It was hard to concentrate on his words. "I wasn't gone that long."

He didn't answer. He just kept touching me, pushing me higher and higher. When he finally slid inside me, I was more than ready. We moved together hard and fast, like neither of us could get enough, and it didn't take long before we both fell apart.

I closed my eyes and rested my forehead against his, trying to catch my breath. Sex had never been like this with any man before him. I'd tried to blame it on our precarious situation—the danger we were living in had heightened our senses—but I knew that was a lie. At least for me.

His fingers trailed down my back, soft enough to raise goose bumps.

I lifted my head slightly and smiled down at him. "You sure know how to make living on the run exciting."

He didn't smile back. "I'm sorry."

I shoved his chest lightly. "Are you serious? At the risk of boosting an already too-large ego, sex with you is the best I've ever had."

He made a face and scoffed. "Please. There's no way Limp Dick Kemper could have satisfied you."

I laughed. "I'm not sure anyone has ever called my former partner that."

He gave me a sardonic look. "Tell me I'm wrong."

"That he has a limp dick or that he couldn't satisfy me?" I made a face. "I never knew what being truly satisfied meant until I had you."

Embarrassed by my admission, I nodded to the bag on the coffee table. "Your steak's getting cold."

He lifted a hand to my face and smoothed back my hair. "Give me a moment."

"To recover?" I teased.

His gaze held mine. "To look at you."

Heat flooded my cheeks. I started to pull away, but he held me in place.

"Don't look away," he murmured. "Why does it bother you that I want to look at you?"

My gaze found his again as I tried to figure out how to answer. "I don't know. A lot of reasons, I guess." I drew in a breath and made myself hold eye contact. "I know I'm not beautiful. You could do so much better than me. Hell, I'm sure you have."

His face tightened. "Who told you that you're not beautiful?"

I tried again to get off his lap. "I need to get cleaned up."

He rolled us, pinning my back to the sofa as he loomed over me.

I could have felt intimidated or threatened, but I knew he wouldn't hurt me. Not physically, anyway.

"You're not gettin' out of this. Why don't you believe me?"

"I've looked in the mirror, James. Many times."

He stared down at me as if I'd spoken a language he didn't understand, then shook his head. "You really don't see it."

"No, and that's okay."

"I do," he said in a husky tone, his thumb brushing along my cheekbone. "Your eyes are—dark and intense. Like you're two seconds away from calling bullshit."

I huffed a laugh, but it caught in my throat when he kissed me, slow and sure, then tugged my lower lip gently between his teeth.

Heat pooled between my legs.

"And your mouth." He kissed the corner of it, then a line to my jaw. "Your hair." His fingers threaded through the strands. "Your neck." He pressed a kiss to my pulse point, and my breath hitched.

"And this." His mouth drifted lower, and I squirmed as his hand slid between my legs. I let out a helpless sound.

"That," he murmured in satisfaction. "I love that sound. I love how you react to me." His fingers kept working, steady and relentless, until I was right on the edge again. He leaned into my ear. "Come for me, Harper."

I obeyed, buckling against his hand as the orgasm rolled through me.

When it passed, I lay beneath him panting, and he kissed me again, softer this time. "You're beautiful, Harper Adams. Don't you ever doubt that's what I see."

I blinked up at him, caught off guard at the intensity of his gaze. "You really believe that."

"I won't lie to you," he said. "Not about something that matters this much."

I released a short, bitter laugh. "About my beauty?"

"No." His eyes held mine. "How I feel about you."

My face heated. He was more open than I'd expected, and I didn't know how to handle it. I pushed on his chest. "Now your steak is even colder, and steak's never good heated in a microwave."

He lifted a brow. "Who said there's a microwave in this dump?"

I burst out laughing, and he grinned back.

I wanted to bottle this moment up and tuck it away for later. I wasn't sure what was in our future, but I suspected once we started digging into this case, we wouldn't find many quiet moments.

"Fine," I said. "Then I'll heat your steak up in a skillet, assuming we've got one, and a stove that won't burst into flames."

I pushed at his chest and started to get up, but he caught my wrist. "It isn't your job to wait on me."

I snorted. "I should hope not. But if I'm heating up mine, then I can heat yours too."

I slipped free and headed to the bathroom, hoping he didn't follow. I needed a minute—or twenty—to get myself together.

Whatever this was with James … it was getting real, and I didn't know how to handle that. I'd gotten good at running whenever things started to get real. But I didn't want to run from him, and that was what scared me most.

When I came out, he was in the kitchen, standing in front of the stove. He'd found a skillet and was heating up the steaks and the green bean sides.

"James, I was going to do that."

"I'm not an invalid."

"I know."

"I need to start doing more. I'm tired of sitting around."

I braced a hand on the back of a kitchen chair. "If you do too much, you'll slow your recovery, not help it."

He glanced over his shoulder, his mouth set in a hard line. "We've sat around too long. We need to take the offensive."

Relief flickered through me, but I suspected our versions of offensive didn't match.

"I'm glad you agree. I made a few phone calls while I was out."

He turned fully, eyes going sharp. "Who did you call?"

"First, I called Louise. She's been leaving me messages. She was so insistent I call her back, I knew something was up."

A scowl pulled at his mouth. "And?"

"She said my dad had contacted her. He was about to file a missing person report because I wasn't returning his calls."

He rolled his eyes. "Like he gives two fucks about you."

"I know," I said. "Which is why I called him too."

The dark look in his eyes confirmed he liked that even less.

"We've got a few problems," I said. "The first, less important one, is that Louise put together that I left town about the same time you stopped appearing at the tavern."

"She thinks we're together?"

"I didn't confirm it, but she's not stupid."

"What does she think we're doin'?"

"Her first thought was that I'm going after the Little Rock PD."

His gaze went darker. "That's next on the agenda."

"I told her that. She wants in when we go after them."

"So she knows I'm helpin' you?"

"I didn't confirm it, but she knew." I held his stare. "And she insinuated she thinks it might not be all business."

He studied me for a long beat. "How do you feel about that?"

"Honestly? I'm not sure."

He gave a short nod, like he'd file that away and deal with it later.

"I'm not ashamed of you," I said, like I was daring him to argue.

He went still.

The truth was part of me was hesitant to admit I was in *anything* with James Malcolm because of his reputation. What would Louise think? What would the good people of Lone County think? The disgraced Little Rock detective screwing a criminal…

I pictured their judgment, and all I felt was cold, familiar defiance. They already thought the worst of me. What difference would it make if they thought I was sleeping with James? Still, I didn't like the thought of those people knowing anything personal about us.

"What about you?" I asked.

Confusion filled his eyes. "What about me?"

"What about the people in your world? What are *they* going to think about you being with an ex-cop?"

"The people I care about already know."

Carter. Misti and his other employees. But I was sure there were others. People he didn't talk about. "What about your FBI handler?"

Surprise flickered in his eyes, gone so fast I almost doubted I'd seen it.

"Who says I have an FBI handler?"

"Come on, James. You didn't get out of prison because the system suddenly grew a conscience. You got out for a reason."

"Why would they bother? What criminal would trust me after I turned on a cartel?" His voice went flat. "I'm a turncoat. No one's gonna tell me anything."

"Then how did you get out?"

"They had a flimsy case."

I believed that, but I also knew he wasn't telling me the whole story. While I could choose to take that personally, I was pragmatic enough to know we hadn't reached that level of trust yet.

"Okay," I said. "I'll buy that—for now. But we still need to talk about how you brought down the Hardshaw Group."

He scowled, turned back to the stove, and flipped the steaks over.

"If you're looking for lessons on how to bring down the Knoxes, then you'll be disappointed. That took nearly a year to gain their trust and infiltrate their group. Which meant doing things I wasn't happy doing to prove my loyalty. The Knoxes aren't going to trust either one of us."

He shifted to look at me again, his eyes hard. "Why did you call your father?"

"I told you. So he wouldn't file a missing person report."

"You could've had Louise tell him you're fine. Or contacted the sheriff's department directly in case he'd filed already."

"You and I both know I needed to talk to him."

The muscle on his jaw ticked. "How'd it go?"

I told him about Nicole Knox contacting my father and threatening to kill him if I didn't hand the file over. And that she'd supposedly forgive and forget if I gave it to her.

"My father suggested I drop it off somewhere for her people to pick up, then disappear. Presumably, far, far away."

"How convenient for him."

"She won't know if she gets the original file. And honestly, I don't think she cares. She just wants to know what Mom had gathered, so she can prepare for any blowback."

"That makes sense."

"But she also wants to make me pay."

"That's a given." His gaze narrowed. "Who else did you call?"

I didn't ask how he knew. "Carter."

He gave a short laugh. "Did you call to give him hell over the safe house?"

"No. I told him about Nicole and my father."

"That's it?"

I hesitated. "I ran an idea by him."

His brow furrowed. "What idea?"

I hadn't planned on having this conversation while he stood at the stove, reheating our food. I'd hoped we'd be sitting down, but stalling wasn't a good idea. Better to rip off the Band-Aid.

"I want to go to Little Rock and get in contact with some of my old sources."

"I'm fine with going," he said, eyes flat. "You and Carter are the ones who keep telling me I need more time to recuperate."

I drew in a breath, steeling myself. "Without you."

I'd expected him to blow up, not the steely silence I was facing now.

I knew from interrogating suspects that responding with silence made people want to fill it. It felt strange being on the other side. It only took five seconds for me to cave. "Hear me out."

He lifted the fork in his hand like a warning. "I'm listening."

"I want to reach out to some of my old contacts and see if they know anything."

His face stayed hard. "What kind of contacts?"

"People who keep their eyes and ears open."

"You think they know something about the Knoxes?"

"Maybe," I said. "Maybe not. But it's a good place to start. My internet searches have been useless, not that I'm surprised."

He studied me for a moment. "So, why do you want to go without me?"

"For one, you're still not one hundred percent, but for another, some of them won't talk if you're there."

"You think they'd shut their mouths because of me?"

I snorted. "Maybe one or two of them, but the others won't talk to anyone but me."

"You're not going to Little Rock alone."

"Are you planning to have one of Carter's hired guys babysit me?" Like hell that was going to happen, but I planned to hear him out.

"Hell no," he said derisively. "I'm going with you."

I wasn't surprised, but I shook my head. "No."

His brows lifted. "No?" he asked incredulously.

"Hanging out in the car for twelve hours gave you a headache. And you want to do another three hours, round trip?"

"We won't come back," he said, turning back to the stove like that settled it.

"You mean we ditch this safe house? We just got here."

"We should be in Little Rock anyway. The Knoxes won't be looking for us there. Not yet."

"You have a safe house in Little Rock?"

"No, we'll stay in a hotel. Somewhere they won't think to look."

"Where?" I asked, skeptical.

He reached for the phone in his pocket. "Let me handle it. But don't unpack anything. We'll eat, then head out."

I wasn't sure he was ready, or that his plan was as solid as he thought, but at least we were finally doing something. And if I were honest, I was grateful I wasn't doing it alone.

Chapter 5

I was sitting at the kitchen table, so I wasn't eavesdropping. It was just impossible not to hear James's side of the call. Carter clearly didn't approve, and I half expected him to call me the second James hung up. Especially after James told him to get us a room in a nice hotel downtown for at least four nights, then followed it up with *I'm the boss*, saying he'd do it himself if Carter didn't comply.

"Nice hotel?" I asked dubiously once James hung up after biting Carter's head off. "Does he call *this* place nice?"

James scowled as he pierced one of the steaks in the skillet with his fork and slid it onto a plate. "I know what you're thinkin', but he knows I mean something with room service."

I stared at him in disbelief. "We're just gonna waltz into the lobby of someplace like The Capital Hotel?"

He turned and grinned at me. "Why not?"

"Uh… maybe because we're trying to keep a low profile?"

"No one will be looking for us there. They'll be checking out the shady motels around the I-30/I-40 corridor."

That made sense. The corridor was a suspected hot spot for

trafficking. And by staying downtown, we'd be close to it without advertising ourselves.

"He'll probably make reservations at The Morrison. It's downtown and close to the I-30/I-40 interchange."

"You told him to get it for four nights. You think we're gonna solve this that quickly?"

"No, but I figure we'll need to move somewhere else by then."

He had a point.

I sat back in the chair and watched as he finished plating the food, then set the dishes on the table.

"No arguments?" he asked, a smug grin tugging at his mouth.

"Would you entertain one?"

He sat down and held my gaze. "Maybe."

I stared at him, surprised.

"We're a team," he said, dropping his attention to his plate. "And while I'm a great idea man, I'm not opposed to considering other options."

Something in my chest tightened at the word *team*. I was pretty sure James didn't do teams. Not unless he was the coach.

"Why do I get the feeling you weren't always open to other ideas?"

He didn't answer right away. Then he said, "I wasn't opposed. I was more … dead-set on bein' right."

"And now?"

"I still believe I'm usually right," he said, glancing up. "But Little Rock is your turf. You might have a better idea or two."

I couldn't help grinning. "Why do I think that was hard for you to admit?"

"Not as hard as it would have been five years ago," he said, like it pained him to admit it. "I'm an evolved man." He picked up a steak knife and started cutting. "Now how does this downtown hotel location work with your contacts?"

"I have three to check in with. One downtown. One south of town. And another out by the industrial park."

"I have a few people," he said, not looking up. "I doubt they'll be eager to see me, but they'll talk."

"We're not going to torture anyone," I said adamantly.

He gave me a blank look. "I didn't say anything about torture."

"I've seen some of your interrogation techniques," I countered.

He returned his gaze to his food. "We'll play it by ear."

We ate in silence for a few moments while I turned his plan over in my head. It wasn't the worst idea … except for one part.

"You're going to need to sit some of this out. You shouldn't overdo it."

He shook his head. "I'm not letting you do this alone." When I started to protest, he held up a hand. "I'm not doin' anything alone either. After dealing with Nicole, you know the Knoxes are ruthless. We need to be each other's backup." His eyes cut to mine. "You have your sources and I've got mine. We'll see what we can find—giving each other space when we need it but remaining close by—then figure out what to do next."

"What's your end goal here?" I asked bluntly, voicing the question I'd been holding back all week.

His mouth tightened. "To bring down the Knoxes."

"And find out who's running a trafficking ring?"

His lips pursed even more. "That too."

"Are you doing this in conjunction with the FBI?"

He scowled. "This again. Why would you think that?"

"That's not an answer, James. It's a deflection."

He held my gaze, his eyes hard. "No, Harper. I'm not working with the FBI."

"What about another alphabet agency?"

He groaned. "Harper."

Another non-answer. Which told me he was definitely working with someone. The *who* probably didn't matter, but the *why* might. "What is *their* end goal?"

"I never said I was working with anyone."

"For the sake of argument," I said in a breezy tone. "Let's pretend you are. What's the endgame?"

"To stop human traffickers," he said flatly.

"But how? Arrests? Elimination?"

His jaw ticked. "You mean murder." It wasn't a question.

"Sure," I said flippantly. "Murder. What's the ultimate goal?"

He held my gaze for several seconds. "Hypothetically, if I were working with an agency—not that I'm admitting I am." His voice went colder. "It would be to end this operation. However I see fit."

"They've given you carte blanche?" I asked in disbelief, then quickly added, "Hypothetically."

"They want it ended," he said flatly. "The least messy way possible."

"Is murder less messy than trials?"

His eyes darkened. "In some cases, yes."

I knew he was referring to the Hardshaw Group. I was pretty sure the founders were dead, but plenty of people beneath them had been swept up in the arrests. And plenty of those people had enough hidden money to bankroll high-priced attorneys. Last I'd heard, there was a fear that a few might walk—and then head right back out onto the street and build their own syndicates with everything they'd already learned.

"I can't murder anyone, James." But even as I said the words, I wasn't sure that was true anymore. He was the one who stopped me from killing an unarmed Nicole Knox. And if I didn't plan to kill him, why didn't I just turn my mother's files over to the FBI? Maybe I just couldn't bring myself to admit it.

He held my gaze again, and I knew he was thinking about all the men I'd killed last week trying to protect us. Trying to save *him*.

"That was different," I whispered. "That was self-defense."

"This might come down to self-defense too."

I could see that, but I didn't think James was counting on that *might*.

"What guarantee do you have that they won't prosecute you for murder?" I asked.

"I never said I was going to murder anyone," he said, taking another bite.

But if he didn't have an iron clad *Get Out of Jail Free* card, then I could be dragged down with him. Arrested and charged. My life and freedom were riding on the details he wasn't sharing.

I trusted him. But did I trust him enough to bet everything on blind faith?

"You don't have to do this," he said, like he was reading my thoughts. "I can handle it on my own."

"What happened to *we're a team* and *we need to be each other's backup*?"

"We can be a team while we investigate," he said. "And when it gets ugly, then I'll handle it."

"You're gonna face Knox and his security team on your own?"

"We don't know what we'll be facing," he said. "I'll figure out a plan once we have more information."

"If your endgame is to eliminate Gerald Knox, why not just assassinate him? Why the dog-and-pony show of digging into the operation?"

His gaze darkened. "Because after the J.R. Simmons fiasco, I learned if you cut off the head of the snake, it grows two or more. Smaller and hungrier. Then they get bigger over time. We need to destroy the whole god-damned thing."

"So what's the plan?"

"I don't know yet," he said, holding my gaze. "I'll figure it out as we go. But I meant what I said—when it gets to the end, I'll deal with it. You don't have to be part of it."

"So, no immunity," I said, not bothering to soften it. "And you don't want me to get caught in the blast radius if you go down."

His jaw flexed. "I never said I was part of anything. Not an agency. Not a deal."

"Then what is this?

"Revenge."

I scoffed. "You said you've been working on this for a couple of years, and you *just* made the possible link to Knox. Where does the revenge come in? You want to take down his entire business because his mother had you snatched?"

His face darkened. "We have history."

"But you don't know for sure he's part of the trafficking ring. Try again."

His jaw tensed. "Knox came onto my radar about fifteen years ago. His daddy was a hard ass, but the son…" He drew in a breath. "Gerald was a spoiled, entitled asshole who thought the world owed him because of who his father was. I heard that when his daddy died, he took over and became ruthless. His father was into gambling and shady business deals, but he was considered a fair man. Then Gerald stepped in. The gambling went by the wayside, and I'd heard rumors Knox Junior was laundering, but I didn't give it much thought. Not until I saw what your mother had. If he's laundering at the level your mother's paperwork hints at, he's funding something massive. Not just profit—protection. Payoffs, properties, lawyers. The kind of operation you build when you're running a trafficking network."

"That still doesn't explain your history."

He held my gaze. "About four years ago, he joined forces with a man who was trying to take over my territory." He took a breath. "I didn't find out until a couple of years ago, but a trustworthy source confirmed it." His eyes went flat. "So, now I consider this an opportunity to take what's his."

I cocked my head. "An eye for an eye?"

"You could say that."

"How certain are you that Knox is the trafficker?" I asked. "The laundering is pretty strong evidence, but do we want to put all our eggs in Knox's basket and focus fully on him?"

His jaw ticked. "Knox fills the whole damn basket."

I nodded. "Okay. Then we go into this with the presumption Knox is behind it until we find evidence that proves differently."

He stood and picked up his now empty plate. "Finish up. We'll leave in a few minutes."

I watched as he dropped his plate in the sink and stalked out of the room.

This was crazy. *I* was crazy. It was downright foolish to follow him into this without more information about who he was working with and what they wanted. Or what the consequences would be if he didn't do exactly what they wanted.

Because the FBI had already screwed him over once.

With the Hardshaw Group takedown, he'd done the dirty work—nearly two years of it. The plan had been for him to be there when the agencies swooped in and made arrests. But he hadn't been there. And since he hadn't followed their instructions down to the letter, they'd arrested him too.

Who was to say they wouldn't screw him over again?

If I was doing this with him, I should make him tell me everything before we took another step.

But...

I also knew he wouldn't let me get caught up in whatever

he was doing. He'd use me to help dig up what he needed, and then he'd cut me loose and take the responsibility on himself.

Only I wasn't just worried about me.

I was worried about him.

Still, I knew if I pushed too hard, there was a chance he'd ditch me entirely and take this all on himself.

A few weeks ago, I would have been furious about his secrets. Now, I understood he was walking a thin line.

I wanted him to tell me. But I didn't want to force it. I wanted him to tell me because he trusted me enough to know the truth.

So for now, I'd bide my time.

And if we got down to the wire, I'd find a way to force his hand.

I only hoped it wouldn't come to that.

—————————————

Chapter 6

—————————————

The sun was beginning to set when I pulled up in front of the Morrison Hotel, where Carter had indeed booked us. I handed the valet attendant the keys to our car, and his quick glance— then the little pause—told me he wasn't impressed. Not that I was surprised. Our car was several tiers down from the luxury cars he was used to seeing.

We hadn't thought through this part of the plan. Or, knowing James, he had and just didn't care.

But why *wouldn't* he care?

A new thought tried to claw its way into my brain—James's low expectations for how all of this ended—but I shoved it back down. He didn't strike me as suicidal. And he would never purposely put me in the Knoxes' path.

He grabbed our bags out of the backseat, rejecting the bell-hop's offer to take them, then strode inside and up to the front desk.

We weren't the only people in jeans in the marble-encased lobby under the six-foot-high chandelier, but I couldn't help thinking we didn't look like we belonged. Then again, maybe I was projecting.

After James checked in using a fake ID with the name Jeff Beachum and a matching credit card, he asked if they had a map of the city. The woman pointed us to the concierge, who was talking to a couple about the best seafood restaurant within walking distance. The couple headed out, arms intertwined and giddy about their plans, and the concierge turned his attention to us.

James asked for the map, and the older gentleman handed him a rectangular paper, then asked if he could help us with anything else, like restaurant suggestions, or things to do.

I expected James to say *no thank you*, but he surprised me by wrapping an arm around my back and tugging me to his side.

"Actually," he said, warm and polite, "this is the first time in ages that my wife and I have had a few nights away from the kids. Are there any type of performances within walking distance? Like a play or musical? Maybe a symphony?"

If the concierge noticed neither of us was wearing wedding rings, he didn't let on. "We at the Morrison are grateful you chose us for your stay. Unfortunately, there aren't any performances tonight, but there's a comedy club a few blocks away."

James looked down at me, all soft and charm. "I know you had your heart set on a musical, but would that be okay?"

I had no idea what he was up to, but I could play along. I gave him a warm smile. "We could watch one of those mindless action movies you love so much for all I care. I'm just grateful to have some alone time with you."

James turned back to the concierge. "Can you get us two tickets? And a suggestion for a restaurant nearby. Something nice."

"Of course," the concierge said. "I can make dinner reservations—"

"That's okay," James cut in. "We're gonna spend some time up in our room, and I'm not sure how long we'll be."

The concierge's smile turned knowing. "Of course. I'll take

care of the tickets and have them waiting for you at will call, sir."

James dropped his arm from my back and pulled out his wallet. "Actually, we'd appreciate it if you had the tickets brought to our room. Just slide them under the door." He handed the man two twenty-dollar bills. "Will that be a problem?"

The concierge looked at the bills in his hand, and his grin spread wider. "It would be my pleasure, Mr....?"

"Beachum," James said. "Room 564. Just charge the tickets to my room."

"Will do, Mr. Beachum. You and Mrs. Beachum have a wonderful evening."

"You too," James said, then took my hand and headed for the elevator.

He rebuffed another bellhop's offer to take our bags before we got on the empty elevator. We rode in silence to the fifth floor, then walked down the hall to our room. The electronic lock clicked when he waved his key card in front of it. He pushed the door open and held it, letting me enter first.

I took two steps inside, then stopped.

This wasn't a hotel room. It was a suite.

"Nice enough?" he asked, sounding amused.

"It's the nicest place I've ever stayed in my life." I turned to face him. "This room must cost a fortune."

"I figure I owe you after all the dumps we've stayed in this last week."

I turned again, taking it all in. A seating area with a sofa and two armchairs framed a marble-topped coffee table. Floor-to-ceiling windows looked out over the Arkansas River. To the right sat a four-poster, canopy bed draped in heavy burgundy velvet. Next to the bed was an open doorway that revealed a marble-encased bathroom.

"I was hoping for an Embassy Suites, not the New York City Plaza Hotel."

He dropped the bags on the floor and stepped up behind me, pressing his chest to my back and sliding his arms around my stomach. "The Embassy Suites was booked."

"Liar."

He pressed a kiss to my neck.

"Why the big show about the comedy club tickets?" I'd waited to ask, knowing there were cameras in the elevator.

"Alibi." He pressed another kiss on my collarbone.

"But we're not going."

"I seriously doubt Knox is going to dig that deep. If he hears a couple who looked similar to us checked into the Morrison, then hears they booked tickets to the comedy club tonight, he's not going to think it's us."

"We can't be sure of that. We should be more careful."

"Sometimes the safest place to hide is in plain sight."

"We should make a plan for tonight." He'd slept for most of the drive, so we hadn't had a chance to discuss it. "I'm not sure if my contacts will know about Knox or be able to tell us how to find him, but they might have heard something about human trafficking."

"It's a good place to start."

"My closest contact is a bartender at a bar within walking distance of the hotel. Hopefully, he's working tonight."

"Sounds good." He dropped his arms and headed for the bathroom. "I think we should take a shower before we go."

I leaned my face toward my armpit and sniffed. "Do I stink?"

He chuckled. "No, but it seems a shame to let a shower like this go to waste."

I followed him into the bathroom, my mouth dropping open as I took in the multiple shower heads.

"Besides," he said. "It seems a little early to contact your bartender source. We should wait a few hours."

"And take a shower?" I asked dryly.

"Unless you have a better suggestion on how to fill the time."

I lifted a brow. "Maybe some room service? I know we already had an early dinner, but I'd sell my soul for a piece of cheesecake."

He reached for the hem of my shirt and started to lift it over my head. "That can be arranged."

Part of me protested that I needed to focus on the case. This was a distraction.

But I'd lived my life for my job and look where it had gotten me—alone.

Maybe it was time to live a little.

Or a lot.

Especially since the odds were against us.

Chapter 7

An hour and a half later, we left the hotel, heading down the stairwell and out the back entrance.

While we didn't need to dress up to go to a comedy club, it made sense that we would have made some effort to clean up if we were really a couple getting away from their kids. James only had T-shirts and jeans, though, and the nicest outfit I had was a pair of clean jeans and a light blue, long-sleeve, button-down shirt. We were both wearing jackets to conceal the weapons we carried. Once we were several hundred yards from the hotel, James fell into step beside me, his freshly shaven jaw catching my attention. It had taken everything in me not to reach out and touch his smooth cheeks earlier.

"Tell me about this bartender," he said.

I cast a quick glance toward him, then turned back to the sidewalk. "He works at the Brass Magnolia. Sometimes he hears things. Illegal things."

"How does he get this information?"

"Does it really matter?" I scoffed.

"How do you know it's trustworthy?"

"Because he's given me information before. It's always turned out to be true."

"Why would he talk to you?"

I shot him a dark look. "When you say 'you' do you mean *me* or do you mean me as a cop?"

"The latter."

I shrugged. "He has his reasons."

"You know the reasons and you're not going to tell me?" The challenge in his voice was clear.

"I don't see why you need to know," I countered with plenty of attitude. "I'm not going to tell you who he is, so what does it matter?"

He came to a halt. "You don't trust me."

I stopped and turned back, dragging a hand over my head. "It's not that I don't trust you, James. I have to protect my source."

"You have to protect him from *me*."

I shook my head in frustration. "That's not it at all. When he started giving me information, I had to swear to him I wouldn't tell a soul anything about him. Even then, he only gave me little pieces at first. Until he decided he could really trust me."

"You didn't even tell Limp Dick?"

I rolled my eyes. "Not even Keith. I promised my source I wouldn't tell a soul, and I meant it." I stepped closer and pressed a hand to his chest. "And unfortunately, that includes you."

His jaw hardened.

But to my surprise, he didn't argue. "You're going to let it go that easily?"

"This isn't easy." He exhaled through his nose. "But I have to respect your promises." He snorted. "Don't look so surprised."

"I'm not surprised." The lie came too easily. "Okay, I'm a little surprised. I thought I'd have to fight you on it."

"I have plenty of my own secrets, and you've respected my need to keep them. The least I can do is respect yours."

"Thank you."

He started to say something, then stopped, then tried again. "Maybe one day we won't have as many secrets between us."

I gave him a skeptical look. "You're going to tell me what alphabet agency you're working for?"

"If I were working for a federal agency," he said mildly, "at some point in the future, I'd tell you."

I wasn't sure I believed him. Or maybe I wasn't ready to deal with what that *if* implied. I lifted a brow. "I'm still not telling you the name of my source."

He laughed, an honest-to-God laugh that caught me off guard. "And as I said before, I respect your promises."

"Thanks, but let's get going because I'd like to hit up my other two sources tonight."

We continued down the sidewalk, and I squashed the impulse to warn him that he was still recovering and that he needed to tell me if all this walking became too much. I knew he'd be lying on the ground, bleeding from his ears, before he'd admit anything was wrong.

Which meant I had to keep an eye on him.

We walked several more blocks, side by side, our fingers brushing every so often. The urge to reach out and take his hand was surprisingly strong, but I resisted. For one thing, we weren't on a date. For another, I suspected neither of us were hand-holders.

Funny, how a week with James had me questioning that.

When we approached the Brass Magnolia, James scanned the exterior of the brick building, then turned to me. "This isn't what I was expecting."

"You thought it would be a dive bar?"

"Yeah," he conceded. "This place looks a little high-class for an informant."

"You'd be surprised." I glanced up and down the street. "You'll need to stay out here."

His eyes darkened. "Like hell."

"James," I said in a warning tone, "if he sees you walk in with me, he won't talk. In fact, I suspect he'd never talk to me again."

"We shouldn't be separated."

"I'll be fine, but if I'm not out in five minutes, text me. And if I don't respond, then you can come in."

He pulled out his phone and started a timer. "I'm holding you to that."

Several seconds had already counted down.

I almost protested but decided it wasn't worth it and went inside.

The bar had once been a bookstore with rich wood paneling and old-school trim, and the current owner had used that to his advantage. The Brass Magnolia had a private-club feel without the rich boys wearing blazers and ascots. Booths lined the walls, and tall-backed leather barstools ran along the counter. The lighting was dim, but not so dark you couldn't see —just enough to make everything feel expensive.

I'd spent plenty of time here over the three years since it had opened.

Nearly every table was full, not that I was surprised. The place had always been popular. I scanned the bar, looking for my source.

Relief washed through me when I spotted Bobby behind the counter, working a cocktail shaker.

An empty barstool sat several feet away from him, so I slid onto it.

"Be with you in a minute," he called, pouring the cocktail into a glass.

I didn't respond. I was too busy fighting the sudden, sharp desire to order a whiskey.

My mouth watered at the thought of the warm burn it would give me as I swallowed the first sip. Why hadn't it occurred to me that sitting in a bar would tempt me? Had it occurred to James? Was that the real reason he'd wanted to come in with me?

I quickly dismissed the thought. He mostly wanted to make sure I was safe. I had to grudgingly admit that if the roles were reversed, I'd want to do the same.

Like any good partner would. There was no reason to read anything more into it. On either side.

A few minutes later, Bobby walked over and stopped in front of me, his face going blank the second he recognized me.

I gave him a warm smile. "Hey. Long time no see."

I'd met Bobby about five years ago while working a homicide case. He'd witnessed a murder, but he'd refused to testify at the trial. Keith had tried to pressure him, but we'd had two other witnesses, so I'd convinced him to let it go. Keith had grudgingly dropped it and moved on.

But I hadn't forgotten.

Unlike Keith, I hadn't wanted to pressure Bobby to testify. I was more interested in *why* he'd refused.

He'd been working at a different bar back then, and I'd stopped by midafternoon on a weekday and seated myself at the counter. The place was mostly empty, so it only took Bobby a few seconds to notice me. And even fewer to recognize me. His face had flushed with anger and he shouted, "Can't you people take no for an answer?"

I'd quickly assured him I wasn't there to try to change his mind. In fact, I was there to make sure he was okay.

His face had paled and he'd looked like he was about to pass out.

"Did someone threaten you, Bobby?"

"Why would you ask that?"

"When people don't want to testify on a case, it's either because they don't want the hassle or they're scared."

Keith had presumed Bobby was an asshole who couldn't be bothered to do his civic duty, and I'd understood why. Bobby was in his early twenties with visible tattoos, six-foot-two, and around two-twenty. He looked like he should be the intimidator, not the intimidated.

But people weren't always scared just for themselves.

"You here to psychoanalyze me?" he'd asked, a vein bulging on his forehead.

"No," I'd assured him. "Like I said, I'm here to make sure you're okay."

"Why would you care?" he'd demanded, his anger rising.

"Because I became a cop to help people. That means it's my *job* to care."

"Tell that to the cop that arrested my little sister," he'd said in disgust.

It took some coaxing, but he'd finally told me his sister had been arrested for possession of pot.

Contempt had covered his face. "It wasn't hers." He'd shook his head. "Yeah, I know what you're thinkin'—*That's what they all say*—but it really wasn't. It was her so-called friend Alyssa's. The cops showed up at a park where a bunch of teenagers were partying. My just-turned-eighteen-year-old sister had been drinking, and she panicked. She knew our parents would lose their minds if she got arrested for underage drinking." He had exhaled hard, like the memory still had him by the throat. "She had a bottle of vodka in her backpack, and she was stupid enough to think the cops wouldn't see her pick it up and toss it into the woods. Only she was also trying to be a good friend, so she tossed Alyssa's too."

"And Alyssa's backpack had the pot," I'd finished.

"Yep," he'd said bitterly. "But the police didn't care. They saw her touch it, so she got charged with a felony. It didn't matter who it really belonged to. They just wanted an arrest."

"They charged her with a felony? It should have been a misdemeanor."

"And it would've been," he'd snapped, "if Alyssa didn't have a big bag of pot and a set of scales in her backpack."

I had grimaced at that news. "They charged her with intent to sell. I'm sorry."

"You should be," he'd said, his voice tight with rage. "We tried to hire a lawyer to fight it, and three different attorneys told us it wasn't worth the risk. They said the prosecutor would plead it down to a misdemeanor and she'd get probation. If we went to court, there was a chance she'd lose and go to prison for five to ten years."

"So she took the plea."

"Obviously," he had said with plenty of venom. "She'd just graduated from high school. My parents wouldn't let her go to the university in Fayetteville and made her stay in Little Rock so they could keep an eye on her. Between her anxiety after the arrest and the way her life got yanked sideways, she dropped out at the end of her sophomore year. Now she works at Target."

"I'm sorry," I'd repeated.

"Are you?" His lip had curled. "You and your lazy-ass cop friends are the reason her life got derailed. She still gets freaked out when she sees a cop."

"Is that why you didn't testify?" I'd asked softly.

Fire had burned in his eyes. "Why should I trust anything any of you have to say?"

"You're right," I had conceded. "Why should you?"

My question had caught him off guard.

"But I'm not like the officers who arrested your sister." I'd leaned forward slightly, keeping my voice level. "I don't look for the easy answers, Bobby. I do the work because I want to get things right. I don't always succeed, but I try my damnedest."

"I'm sure that's what they all say."

"Actually, no," I'd said with a bitter laugh. "Some don't give a shit."

He'd blinked in surprise. "I can't believe you admitted that."

I'd shrugged. "It's the truth. And I believe in telling the truth."

After that, I'd started stopping by every few weeks, partially to ask about his sister's well-being, but mostly just to talk. If I could convince him that not all cops were assholes, then I'd consider it a win. It helped that he was good company.

Less than six months later, he gave me at tip on another murder case I was working. Turned out, he had cousins with criminal ties, and they liked to talk when they got drunk. Bobby's only stipulation was I never reveal where I got my information, and he'd keep telling me what he heard.

And surprisingly, he heard a lot.

Two years later—shortly after he moved to the Brass Magnolia when it opened—he admitted he'd been scared to testify about the murder he'd witnessed. A crime boss connected to his cousins had come around and told him if he testified, he'd "mess up" his little sister.

So it turned out Keith and I had both been right. Not that Keith ever knew. I'd kept my promise, and no one knew where the information I got from Bobby came from.

Now, Bobby was glancing around the bar. His breathing was shallow, his shoulders tight. "Haven't seen you in a while."

He was nervous I was there. Why?

I hadn't been in since the shooting last October. Did he

think I'd murdered that boy in cold blood, just like everyone else? Did he think the past five years had been one long con?

"I moved back to my hometown in the middle-of-nowhere Arkansas," I said. "But I'm back in town and thought I'd reach out."

"You're not a cop anymore," he said flatly.

I wasn't surprised he knew I'd left the force. The news outlets had made sure to let the public know they were safe. "You're right. I'm not. But I am still investigating cases, I just don't have a badge to go along with it."

Bobby didn't look convinced. If anything, he looked more anxious.

"You obviously aren't happy to see me," I said, deciding there was no reason to beat around the bush. "We've been friends long enough that I'm hoping you'll tell me why."

"*Were* we friends?" he shot back with plenty of attitude. But I could see a flicker of hurt in his eyes.

So he believed the news reports and thought I'd been conning him.

I leaned closer to the counter and lowered my voice. "I didn't kill anyone in cold blood, Bobby. The kid had a gun. The department set me up to take a fall, although I have no idea why." I held his gaze. "I plan to find out, but I'm working on something else first. I really hope you can help me."

His posture softened a fraction, but he didn't look eager to resume our friendship.

"Remember when you told me about your sister? And I admitted that some cops don't give a shit, but that I did?" He didn't respond, but I kept going. "Who better to push off the force than the person who cares?"

The words came before I really thought them through, but then I did, and they hit me hard. Why hadn't I considered that before? If there were dirty cops, maybe they thought I'd gotten too close to something. It made sense to not only get rid of me but discredit me in the process.

Bobby's eyes widened. "Oh. Shit."

"Yeah," I said, "Oh shit."

"I told you cops weren't trustworthy."

I wanted to argue *not all cops*, but I couldn't find it in me. "Well, I'm not a cop anymore."

He glanced toward a man who'd stepped up to the bar several feet away. "We're pretty busy tonight."

"I only have a few questions, then I'll take off."

He grimaced. "You're gonna need to order something. Your usual?"

"Just a club soda."

His brow lifted. "Really?"

I'd always come by off the clock, and even though I hadn't been an alcoholic back then, I'd loved a good whiskey. I could almost guarantee I'd never ordered a non-alcoholic drink from him before. I shrugged. "I'm working a case."

His eyes narrowed. "You just said you weren't with the police."

"I'm not. I'm a PI now."

He didn't respond as he filled a glass from the soda gun and set it in front of me.

I placed a twenty-dollar bill on the bar. He slid it toward him and pocketed the bill as he moved down to help the customer.

I picked up my glass and took a sip, bitterly missing the burn of whiskey.

One day at a time.

One minute.

Bobby's attitude had me on edge. Maybe it would soften his demeanor if he had a few minutes to think over what I'd told him. If he believed I wasn't trustworthy, he wouldn't give me anything useful. But even worse—all the time I'd spent nurturing our friendship, hoping to prove not all cops were the same, would be tossed out the window.

He pulled two beers for the guy, then came back to me.

"Why are you here, Harper?" He looked more receptive, but he wasn't the easygoing Bobby I'd known last September.

"Have you ever heard of the Knoxes?"

I studied him for a reaction to the name but didn't get one.

"Who's that?"

"You've never heard of them?"

"Should I have?"

"Probably not," I said. "I've heard they're pretty private."

"Then how would I know who they are?"

Yep, he still wasn't convinced. He never would have talked to me in that tone last fall.

I leaned closer, keeping my voice low. "This is important, Bobby. I'm working a human-trafficking case."

He flinched, his eyes widening.

"Does our agreement still hold?" I asked. "That whatever we tell each other stays anonymous? Make no mistake, it still does on my end. I need to know it holds true on yours."

He hesitated a moment, then nodded. "Yeah."

Relief washed through me, but I didn't linger on it. "Thank you." I leaned in a little more. "The Knoxes are running an operation here in Little Rock. Are you sure you've never heard of them?"

He shook his head. "No, never. I can ask around if you want."

I would love nothing more than to have him talk to his cousins, but I couldn't risk his safety. If the Knoxes were as dangerous as I believed, they wouldn't tolerate anyone asking about them.

"No," I said firmly. "Don't do that. I don't want you popping up on their radar."

"That bad?" he asked.

I gave him a sideways grin. "They have a bounty on my head."

His face went a little green as another customer approached the bar. "Don't go anywhere. I've got to take care of this, but I'll be back. Okay?"

"I'm not going anywhere."

He gave me a worried look as he headed over to his customer.

I wondered if I'd said too much, but I'd always trusted that anything I told Bobby stayed between us. Telling him my life was in danger seemed to have given him more motivation to help.

Out of the corner of my eye, I saw someone approach the bar near the entrance. I did a double-take when I realized it was James.

I checked my phone but didn't see any missed texts. Had my five minutes passed and he'd come in to check on me? Why hadn't he texted first?

Strangely, I wasn't upset. Especially since he'd perched at the other end of the bar, pretending not to know me. In fact, he didn't look my way at all.

The female bartender on his side walked up to him. He must have said something witty, because she released a flirtatious laugh.

Jealousy pricked me, sharp and fast, but I took a deep breath and shoved the feeling away. Either James wanted me or he didn't. I wasn't going to fight anyone over him. Besides, I was pretty sure getting hit on in a bar was a regular occurrence for him. He was just usually on the other side of the counter.

Still, it was hard to resist glancing over at him.

Bobby returned a few minutes later with an apologetic look. "I'm super busy tonight, Harper, not that I think I have anything that could help you anyway."

"You haven't heard any rumors about trafficking?" I asked quietly.

He grimaced. "Sure, I hear rumors here and there, but nothing of substance. More like people presume it's happening."

"Any names tied to the rumors?"

He shook his head. "Nope."

"Your cousins don't talk about it?"

"They're not mixed up in any of that," he said too quickly. "But I could maybe float the topic…"

I shook my head. "No. Don't. If you went fishing on purpose and we used what you got, it might blow back on you."

His brows shot up. "*We?*"

"I have a friend helping me."

Bobby took a step back, fear filling his eyes. "You told them about me?"

"*Absolutely not.*" I kept my voice steady, even as my stomach tightened. "I swore to you I would never reveal who you were, and I mean it. I'll take your name to my grave."

He grimaced. "God, I hope it doesn't come to that."

"Me too, but I swore to keep your identity a secret, and I take that seriously."

Even as I said the words, guilt gnawed at me. James could see exactly who I was talking to. It would take him and Carter less than an hour to find out Bobby's identity, and that was being generous.

The truth was, I'd led James to Bobby. I didn't think James would do anything to Bobby or even tell anyone else about him, but I hadn't been careful. What if someone else had followed us here and was watching me now?

I must have done a good job of hiding my inner turmoil, because relief washed over Bobby's face. "I know you take it seriously. It's just… I spent the last six or seven months thinking you weren't who you said you were. Especially when you didn't come back after all that shit went down. I mean, I knew you'd left the police, but I thought we were friends."

"I *did* stay away." I swallowed. "But it was because I was embarrassed and ashamed about what happened. I was public enemy number one. I wasn't going *anywhere* in public."

His mouth shifted to the side. "I guess that makes sense." Sadness filled his eyes. "It still sucked."

"I know. And I should've come by and told you my side of the story. I'm sorry."

He shook his head. "No, you were dealing with other shit. And it sounds like you're in even worse trouble if there's a bounty on your head."

I grabbed a slip of paper out of my jacket pocket and placed it on the counter. "If you see or hear anything you think might help me, will you call or text me at this number?"

He picked up the paper—a corner torn off the hotel stationery with my burner number scrawled across it. "I'm not sure I'll hear anything, especially if I'm not asking any questions."

"Definitely don't ask questions." I kept my voice firm. "I want you to have as much distance from this as possible. And don't worry. I have a few other people to talk to."

He tucked the paper into his pocket. "Be careful, Harper. It sounds like you're in the middle of something really dangerous."

I grinned. "Dangerous is my real last name."

He laughed. A couple of years ago, he'd told me I was the least aggressive cop he'd ever met, and I'd told him that was because he wasn't a threat. Any threat I faced would see a different side of me. After that, he'd started calling me Miss Dangerous.

His laughter faded. "Seriously, Harper. Be careful."

"I intend to."

Chapter 8

I took another sip of my club soda, then slid off my stool and headed to the entrance, never once looking directly at James. But out of the corner of my eye, I saw him nursing a bottle of beer at the bar.

Outside, I stopped in front of the building next door, a retail shop that was closed for the night, fighting the urge to pace. I worried James would come out too soon and that Bobby would realize we were together. But a good five minutes passed before he finally emerged, his gaze sweeping right to left as he searched for me.

I stepped away from the corner of the building but stayed in front of the retail store in case the bar had cameras.

He strode over. "Find out anything?"

"Nothing helpful. He's heard rumors of trafficking but nothing of any use. And he's never heard of the Knoxes."

His brow shot up. "You told him about the Knoxes?"

"I only asked if he'd heard of them."

His face darkened. "If he tells anyone you were asking—"

"He won't. We have an agreement."

"How do you know he'll stick to it?"

"Because he has no reason not to." I gave his chest a light shove, turning the tables on him. "Why did you come in? You were supposed to text first."

"Walking in was faster. Besides I wanted a beer."

My gaze must have darkened.

His face softened. "I saw you weren't drinking anything alcoholic."

"It could have been vodka."

"It wasn't."

"How do you know? Can you smell by my breath?"

"I just know." He paused. "It must have been hard sitting in a bar and not drinking."

I considered brushing it off, but he'd seen me at my worst when I was detoxing. There was no reason to hide this part of my recovery. "It was. But this afternoon at Walmart was harder, when I walked by the liquor aisle."

His eyes widened. "You didn't tell me."

"You didn't really give me a chance," I said with a laugh. "If I recall correctly, you had my clothes off within about two minutes of me walking through the door."

He grinned. "It was longer than two minutes, but I was off my game." His smile faded. "How bad was it?"

"I stopped myself from going down the aisle, but barely."

"Barely is good enough."

"Then I ordered our steaks at the restaurant bar."

"And you still didn't get a drink." He cupped my cheek. "Those are all wins, Harper."

"I'd hoped it would get easier. If anything, it feels harder."

"You've been sober for a week. It's going to get harder before it gets easier, but you've got this."

I gave him a sideways grin. "Maybe I could kiss you and get a taste of beer."

He smiled back. "I won't argue if you kiss me, but I had water before I left, so you might be disappointed."

"Thanks," I said softly.

"I told you I'd help you through this, and I meant it. I only got a beer because I needed a reason to be in there. I told the bartender I was killing a few minutes before I met friends for dinner, but it still would have looked suspicious if I'd ordered water."

"Agreed."

"So where are we going next?"

"A convenience store, but it's too far to walk. I thought we could take a taxi and pay cash."

He frowned.

"We could go back and take our car, but they'll have a record of us getting it from valet parking."

"A taxi will be fine." He started scanning the street, then waved at a small sedan with a lighted Uber sign that had just turned the corner.

"We could wear disguises," I teased. "You could get a buzz cut or bleach your hair blond."

He gave me a sideways glance that let me know neither of those things were happening. "Maybe *you* should dye your hair or wear a wig."

I made a face. "I'll pass on the wig."

The car stopped at the curb, and the driver rolled his window down. A guy who looked to be in his mid-twenties leaned across the passenger seat. "You guys need a ride?"

"Yeah," James said, "but we don't have an Uber app. Can I just pay you cash?"

His eyes lit up. "Sure thing."

James opened the back door and slid into the back, letting me follow behind him.

"Where to?" the driver asked.

I gave him the intersection of the convenience store, and he gave me a hesitant look. "Are you sure? That area's a little rough."

"I'm sure," I said.

James handed the driver a twenty. "I'll give you a hundred if you'll wait outside for us while we're inside."

The driver took the money, then shook his head. "No way I'm parking alone in that area. One of you'll have to stay in the car."

I shot James a warning look before turning back to the driver. "My husband will stay outside with you."

The guy narrowed his eyes. "You're not gonna rob the place, are you? I don't wanna be a getaway driver."

"No," I said in a reassuring tone. "My seventeen-year-old niece ran away from home, and my husband and I flew in to try to find her. Someone said they saw her working at the convenience store. I want to go in and see if she's there, and if not, ask whoever's working if they've seen her."

Sympathy filled his eyes. "That's rough. You got a photo handy? I could show it around."

The story had come to me on the spot, so I obviously didn't have a photo.

"Let me pull it up," James said, his phone already in his hand. I stared at him in surprise as he tapped on the screen. Seconds later, he was holding up his phone for the cab driver to see.

The man studied the screen for several seconds, then shook his head. "I haven't seen her, but like I said, I'll show it around." He heaved out a sigh. "I wanna help, so I'll drive you around if you have other places you want to check out. My friend's kid ran away too. Got involved in drugs. It was rough on the whole family."

"Thank you…" James said, then leaned closer to the front. "What's your name? If you're gonna be helping us, we should be on a first-name basis."

"Alex," the driver said, putting the car in drive and taking off.

"Nice to meet you, Alex," James said. "I'm Jeff, and this is my wife, Amber."

"Sorry to meet you under these circumstances," Alex said, turning a corner.

"Same," James said, sitting back and nonchalantly taking my hand. "But I'm thankful we have someone as helpful as you on our side."

I glanced down at our linked hands, then back at James, but he was peering out the side window.

Alex asked us a few questions as he drove, such as where we'd flown in from, how long we were staying, and where my niece had run away from. James readily answered them all— we'd flown in from Dallas, we were staying two days, and our niece, Penny, was from Pine Bluff.

James appeared cool and collected, but it made me uneasy that we'd fallen this easily into the role of a married couple. I'd only told Alex we were married because that's what James had told the concierge. It was better to try to stick as close to the same story as possible. I hadn't been prepared for how right it felt to sit next to him and pretend we were a long-term couple. Then again, maybe I was reading too much into it. Maybe it felt right because we worked so well as investigative partners.

When Alex pulled into the convenience store parking lot, I asked him to park to the side, out of view of the front doors. He gave me a questioning look.

"If Penny's in there and sees you waiting out here in the car after I get out, it might spook her and make her run. I'd rather approach her slowly and ask her to come home."

"Good thinkin'," Alex said, pulling into a space at the end of the building. "Jeff, you can go in with her if you want. I'll wait."

"No," I said, giving James a pointed look. "I need to do this alone."

James looked like he wanted to argue, but he sat back in the seat. "Okay, but text or call me if you need me."

I started to open the door, then turned back to him and pressed a quick kiss to his lips in gratitude. "Thank you for trusting me."

When I pulled back, he cupped the back of my neck and held me in place several inches from his face. "Always."

My heart fluttered, and I reminded myself that this was not the time or place to swoon over a man. I climbed out of the car and hurried toward the entrance, resisting the urge to glance back at him.

I needed to get a handle on myself.

When I stepped into the store, I was instantly hit with the smell of pot and BO. I wasn't surprised. It always smelled like that in here. The woman I was looking for stood behind the counter, selling a pack of cigarettes to a boy of questionable age. Not that I would have busted Cassandra for selling to a minor, even when I'd been on the force. She'd been too valuable to risk losing her trust.

She handed the kid back his change, and her gaze lifted to mine, surprise flashing in her deep brown eyes.

I walked to the cooler, grabbed two bottles of water and a bag of chips, then set them on the counter.

"Been a hot minute since I last seen you," she said in a cool tone as she rang up my items.

"I moved down to Lone County."

"I bet you did," she said derisively. "I'm surprised you didn't leave the country."

"So you believe I shot that boy in cold blood?" I asked, trying to keep the disappointment out of my voice.

"Fuck, no," she sneered. "That boy was white. Ain't no way you would have shot an unarmed white boy." I started to protest, and she laughed, waving her hand, her braids bouncing against her shoulder. "I'm just playin' with you.

You wouldn't shoot no one unarmed—white, Black, or purple."

"Thanks for believing me."

"Hell, anyone who knows you knows you wouldn't do such a thing. And even if you did, you would have owned up to it."

"Cassandra, you have more faith in me than just about anyone else in my life."

"Then, honey," she said with a piercing gaze, "you need to get yourself some new friends."

"Yeah," I said with a bitter chuckle. "I learned that the hard way."

"So what are you doin' out this way?" she asked. "Because I know you don't live out in these parts."

"I'm not a cop anymore—"

She waved me off. "That's old news."

"I'm a PI. I'm working a case up here in Little Rock and wondered if you knew anything that could help."

She started to bag up my items. "I'll be happy to tell you anything I know."

"I'm working a human trafficking case. Have you heard anything?"

"Sure, I hear about men pulling teens off the streets and pimpin' 'em out." She made a face of disgust. "It happens more often than you'd think."

"I'm looking for something larger and more organized. I've heard that a big crime family may have used a warehouse in the industrial area."

She froze for a second, then resumed bagging, her movements slower. "What kind of crime family?"

"I'm not sure if you've heard of them. Rumor has it they like to keep their names pretty private."

"Give me a shot anyway."

"Knox," I said. "Gerald Knox, but I hear he goes by Gerry."

"Thought you said it was a family."

"His mother, Nicole, is involved to some degree, but I don't know how much. I doubt she gets her hands dirty at the street level. Then again, I doubt Gerry does either."

She pursed her lips. "Nope. Never heard of 'em."

"That's okay," I said, pulling another slip of paper out of my pocket along with some cash. I set both on the counter. "Can you text or call if you hear anything, okay? I've got a new number."

Cassandra took both, pocketed the paper, then counted out my change.

"Will do, Harper," she said, handing me the bills and coins.

"These people are dangerous, Cassandra," I said. "Don't go searching out information about them."

She laughed. "You know me better than that, Harper, girl. I don't search out nothin'. Everything I know comes to me."

I grinned. "In this case, let's keep it that way."

I grabbed the bag and headed outside. My two best sources had given me absolutely nothing. I had one more to check, but it looked like we were going to have to do some old-fashioned stakeouts.

Chapter 9

I climbed back into the car and shut the door.

"Any luck?" James asked.

I shook my head. "No one's seen her. It was a false lead."

Alex grimaced. "That's rough."

"Where to now?" James asked.

"Another bar." I gave the cab driver the intersection where it was located.

We rode in silence for the next ten minutes until we reached our next stop.

"This isn't a bar," Alex said in a wary tone. "This is a strip joint. You really think your niece might be here?"

"It's on the list of places she might have been seen," I said, then added with a touch of desperation, "I have to check it out."

"I'm goin' in with you," James said, in a tone that told me he wouldn't change his mind.

"I agree," our driver said as he backed into a spot in the back row. "Jeff, you can't let your wife go in there alone. The Velvet Room has a rough crowd."

James gave me a dark look, and I rolled my eyes. I'd been

here several times on my own, but I wasn't going to argue with him. My source wouldn't care if I brought James in with me.

We got out and started across the parking lot, James snagging my hand. This time, I suspected he wasn't doing it for show. He was making sure I didn't ditch him.

"Who are you meeting in there? Another bartender?"

"A dancer, but there's no guarantee she's working tonight."

"Is me bein' with you gonna be an issue?"

"Nope, it'll probably give me a better cover. It always looks a little strange when a woman goes into this kind of place alone."

"So you don't come here enough to be recognized?"

"I usually meet her somewhere else, but I lost all my contacts when we switched phones. She probably won't be able to talk to me here. I'll have to give her my number and hope she gets in touch."

"She's a dancer?" James asked.

"Yeah."

"Then if she's workin', we'll be able to get her alone."

"A private room?"

He shrugged. "Honestly, it's the best option." He turned toward me. "You sure she'll talk if I'm there?"

I gestured to him. "She'll like what she sees and she semi-trusts me. I suspect she might say more to you than me."

"If she's working," he said flatly.

"Exactly."

He opened the front door, standing to the side to let me enter first.

I cast a glance toward our car. Alex's face was lit up by the glow of his phone screen.

"Hey," I said. "How did you come up with that photo of our pretend niece to show Alex?"

"I had Carter pull up a list of missing girls in Little Rock," he said. "I figured they might be tied up in this trafficking ring.

So I opened the file and picked one." Then he added, "Her name really is Penny."

It was a good idea, but it stuck under my skin. When had he asked Carter for the file and why hadn't he shared it with me?

James paid the cover charge, then we entered the dimly lit club. My eyes took a moment to adjust as I scanned the seating area. James seemed to be waiting for my lead, so I headed to an empty table in the back row—not that the place was very large. The rules for adult clubs in Little Rock were pretty strict—topless, but the dancers had to wear pasties, and they had to have some kind of bottom covering, even if it was a tiny G-string. Most people who wanted to visit an establishment like this wanted more skin and they wouldn't find it in Little Rock.

A woman was dancing on the stage, but she wasn't my contact. We'd only been seated about thirty seconds before a waitress wearing barely anything more than the woman on stage came over to take our order.

"I'll take a draft beer," James said, looking up at her face and ignoring the massive amount of cleavage less than two feet in front of him. "And my wife will have a club soda."

"No alcohol?" the waitress asked in surprise.

James made a face. "She's on a medication that she's not supposed to drink with. Sucks. I know."

The waitress gave me a semi-sympathetic look, then walked over to the bar.

"Good call on the medication idea," I said.

"Yeah, most people drink in these kinds of places. It might look suspicious if you didn't," he said, glancing around. "Do you see who you're lookin' for?"

"No, she's not on stage, and she's not out here either. If she's working, she's probably backstage getting ready."

He leaned back in his chair and crossed his arms over his

chest, keeping his gaze on the stage. "That's how we ran things too."

I did a double take. "Wait. You own a strip club?"

"Past tense," he said, still not looking at me. "The Feds took it over when I was arrested. I heard it reopened, but the new owner's an asshole and treats the girls like shit."

I continued to stare at him in disbelief.

"Why is that so hard to believe?" he asked, after turning to face me. "You know I was up to shady shit in my past."

"You say the owner treats the girls like shit. Are you saying you treated them well?"

"If you call payin' 'em a living wage and giving them bene-fits, well, then, yeah."

"Wait." I shook my head. "That's unheard of."

The waitress returned with our drinks and set them on the table. "Want to open a tab?"

"Sure," James said, handing her his credit card with his current alias. "Thanks."

She took the card, then headed back to the bar, turning so that her bare ass cheeks nearly brushed the side of his face.

I frowned in irritation, but I reminded myself that just because we were a couple didn't mean women would stop hitting on him. Especially in a place like this. I picked up my drink and took a sip as James took a long pull from his beer.

My mouth watered at the thought of drinking a cold beer, and I tried to tell myself that a club soda was nearly as good. It wasn't a convincing lie.

"You were saying you treated your dancers well," I said, "Better than most strip club owners. Why?"

He released a short laugh. "Because it was the decent thing to do?" He took another sip. "Look, I didn't run the place. Jed did. I let him have full rein. He wanted to pay them a living wage and give them health benefits, so I agreed."

"Don't do that," I said, "Don't try to pawn off bein' a decent person onto someone else."

"Like I said, it was Jed's idea."

"But being so generous had to cut into profits."

"I'll say." He took another drink. "We lost money on the place."

"So why not cut their wages or benefits?"

He turned to look at me again. "You ever been to Fenton County?"

I shook my head.

"It's one of the poorest counties in the state, and most of the girls workin' there were single mothers. Hell, I'm pretty damn sure Jed set up some kind of daycare system before he quit." He drew in a frustrated breath. "We made sure they made enough to pay their rent, feed themselves and their kids —enough that they wouldn't be so desperate that they'd put themselves at risk by soliciting customers for extracurriculars. Some still did, but most were just tryin' to get by."

"What happened after Jed quit?"

He shrugged. "I got a new manager and told him to keep the same rules, but he wasn't as respectful. And shortly after, the Feds took over." He took another sip of his beer. "I still think about those women sometimes."

I knew, deep down, James was a good person—I saw how he treated his staff at the tavern, but what he was describing was above and beyond. He'd gone out of his way—to the point of losing money—to help those women. Sure, they'd still stripped to make a living, but at least he'd made sure their basic needs were met.

"You say it was all Jed," I said, "but you had to approve it."

He shrugged. "They were his ideas."

"But you're the one who lost money."

"I made enough legit money. I needed the tax break."

I frowned. "Don't do that."

He turned to face me, one brow lifted. "Do what?"

"Don't downplay what you did. I need you to be real with me, James."

He shifted in his seat to face me fully, setting his bottle on the table. "The truth is, Harper, I never thought of a single one of those things. They were all Jed's ideas. So I'm sure as hell not gonna take credit for them."

"At least take credit for letting him do it and providing those women with enough money to take care of their kids."

He shook his head. "It wasn't enough. I was trying to do more for the county, and the agreement I made with…" His voice trailed off, and he drew in a shaky breath. "Is that her?"

The song had ended, and a new woman walked onto the stage.

"No."

But my mind lingered on what he'd just said. He'd wanted to do more for his county and he'd made an agreement with— who? The Feds? The Hardshaw Group? I wanted to ask more questions, but this wasn't the place. Still, as far as I was concerned, this conversation wasn't over.

Which led me to my next topic.

"When did you ask Carter to pull files on missing girls?"

He looked at me in surprise. "When you decided to come to Little Rock. I sent him a text and asked him to pull 'em. They came in shortly before you pulled up to the hotel."

"Why didn't you tell me you'd done that?"

He blinked. "You don't think it's a good idea?"

"It was a great idea. I'm asking why you didn't tell me."

He studied me for a moment, then rubbed his eyes with his thumb and forefinger. When he dropped his hand, he covered mine on the table. "You're right. I should have told you."

"Why didn't you?"

"Honestly? It never occurred to me. I'm used to takin' the lead. Bein' the one with all the information."

"We can't work like that, James," I said, my tone firm. "We either work as true partners, or this won't work. At. All."

"You're right," he said, holding my gaze. "It's not that I purposely held it back. I just didn't think to tell you. I'll try my damnedest to be more forthcoming, but there's a good chance I'll slip a few times before I get used to our new rules."

The man was forty-four years old, and as far as I knew, he'd kept most of his life close to the vest. Jed had probably known more than most, but I also knew James had kept secrets from him.

"I can't do secrets," I said, leaning closer. "I know you have things in your past you can't share, and there are things from cases I've worked I'll never be able to share with you. But from this point on, it's all truth, no secrets. Deal?"

He met my gaze, hesitating. "I've never had that kind of relationship with *anyone* in my life. There've always been secrets."

I could have taken that to mean he still wanted to live by that code, but I heard it as a confession—an admission this was new territory and it wouldn't come easy.

"I know," I said, looking into his deep brown eyes. "I've never had that kind of relationship either. I've always kept everything bottled up, but the only way we're gonna work— both professionally and personally—is if we put it all on the line." When he didn't respond, I wondered if I'd gone too far. Asked too much. We were barely a couple, and we both had trust issues. But the only way I saw this working was if we shared everything from here on out.

He lifted his free hand to the back of my head, his fingers threading through my hair and pulling my face close. "Do you know what you're askin' of me?" His husky voice sent chills down my spine.

I gave him a half-grin. "Do you know what I'm asking of

myself? I've never been totally open with *anyone*, let alone a lover."

His eyes darkened. "Why does you calling me your lover turn me on?"

"Maybe because you're hornier than a man with a concussion has any right to be?"

He grinned, his whole face lighting up. I'd rarely seen this side of him before we'd started sleeping together, and I couldn't get enough of it. "All I can promise is to do my best. This is all new territory for me. I've got a lot of things to unlearn."

"How did you manage previous relationships?"

"I was never in an equal relationship. Ever."

His admission made sense. Even his best friend had been an employee. It made me realize how special what he was offering me really was.

I wanted to ask more questions, but he kissed me so thoroughly, every question dissolved into the ether.

The song onstage ended, and the DJ's voice boomed over the speakers, announcing the next dancer. "Get ready to set your night ablaze with the intoxicating beauty of Ruby!"

I broke the kiss and pulled back, turning to face the stage.

The spotlight swept across the small platform, stopping on a woman in sparkly heels and a sequined jacket.

I glanced back to James. "That's her."

Chapter 10

The men seated around the stage whooped and hollered as the music started and Ruby began to dance, then provocatively slid her jacket over her shoulder.

"I presume she dances, then comes out and serves drinks after?" James asked, glancing at the stage before turning to me.

"Yeah."

He gave a curt nod, then sat back in his seat and focused on the stage again.

Ruby—Dani's stage name—was a talented performer. Then again, she'd been dancing for a decade, so she knew exactly which moves drew the most attention, and in turn, the most money. Sure, she was grateful for the cash the men stuffed into her G-string or the other few strips of fabric left on her body, but her real goal was to entice them into paying for lap dances and back-room meetings.

The now familiar burn of jealousy filled my chest. James's full attention was on Ruby as she stripped off her layers, but I reminded myself he needed to look interested, or a private room request would seem suspicious.

I sipped my club soda, everything in me screaming for a

drink. I took a deep breath, trying to release the tension in my shoulders. I didn't *need* a drink. I only wanted one. Badly.

James reached over and took my hand, setting it on his lap. I gave him a questioning look. He leaned in close to my ear.

"I don't know what you're thinkin' right now, but you're the only woman I'm interested in seein' strip. And I know you would probably kill for a drink, but you've got this." He pulled back and studied my face. "Do both of those cover your thoughts?"

I lifted my chin. "I'm not jealous, Malcolm."

His grin spread. "Good, because you're all the woman I need."

I scoffed, shaking my head, but he leaned over and kissed me again. This time I registered the taste of beer on his lips, making me crave it even more.

He pulled back slightly and cupped my face, his thumb tracing my jaw. "Whatever happens from here on out, just remember you're the only one I want."

I drew in a breath, my heart racing as I gave a small nod. He was smart to look interested. This was how we'd get Dani to talk.

Ruby's set ended and she went backstage. Our waitress sidled up to James, asking if she could get him another beer.

"Yeah," he said, "but what I really want is to get a private audience with Ruby. Do you know when she'll be out?"

Our waitress scowled. "She's gonna be a few more minutes."

James pulled a bill from his wallet and stuffed it down her cleavage. "That's for you if you tell her I'm willing to pay double the normal rate."

The woman batted her eyelashes. "You lookin' for a threesome? Because I can join you and Ruby. We both know how to have a good time."

"My wife will be roundin' out that threesome," James said

gruffly. "But you can get me that beer and close my tab. I'll be payin' Ruby in cash."

The waitress pulled the money out of her bra, her eyes widening at what looked like a hundred-dollar bill. "I'll get right on it." She set her tray on the empty table next to us and hurried to the back.

"Someone's a big spender," I said in a dry tone.

He gave me a sardonic look. "Money talks, and Alex is outside waitin' on us."

He had a point. Plus, after Bobby's reaction, I wasn't sure what Dani would do when she saw me. Had she heard about my shooting? I wasn't sure she even paid attention to the news. She'd never been too thrilled to see me in the past, but she'd trusted me. Would she trust me now?

James leaned in close again. "Fill me in on what you know about her. Why didn't we come see her first?"

I should have filled him in while she was dancing. Before, I could have blamed it on being half drunk. Tonight, I had no excuse. "I met her about seven years ago, soon after she started dancing. She got busted for solicitation. I suspected she knew something about a case I was on, so I got her charges dropped in exchange for information. Every so often, I'd meet with her if I thought she might have some something, but she usually doesn't know much."

"But it seems like an exotic dancer might be privy to trafficking information."

"Agreed. She hasn't offered any information about it in the past, but you might be able to get her to talk. I know she gets taken in by pretty faces fairly easily."

His brow lifted mischievously. "Are you telling me I have a pretty face, Harper?"

"You know damn well you have a pretty face, Malcolm."

"That's twice you've called me Malcolm in the last few minutes. Is that my clue that you're pissed at me?"

"I'm not pissed."

He gently grabbed my chin, holding his gaze on mine. "What happened to your no secrets rule?"

"I'm not keeping secrets."

"Lyin' is the same thing."

"I'm not pissed," I said, less forcefully. "But you know you're good looking. I don't know why you need to hear me say it."

His voice turned husky. "Maybe because a man likes to know the woman he's sleepin' with finds him attractive."

A wave of heat washed through me. "Would it help you to know that you are, by far, the most attractive man I've ever slept with?"

He dropped his hand, and a grin spread across his face. "That helps a little."

I shook my head. "You're incorrigible."

"Keepin' you on your toes."

The waitress walked up behind James. "Ruby's agreed to meet you. If you'll follow me."

James stood, then held his hand out to me like he was Prince Charming asking me to dance at the ball. I took his hand, resisting the urge to roll my eyes. When I stood, he wrapped an arm around my back, his hand resting on my hip. We followed the waitress through a curtain in the side wall and down a dark hallway to a curtain-covered doorway.

"You can go on in," she said. "Ruby will be with you in a few minutes."

James ushered me into the dimly lit room with a bench seat along the back wall. I couldn't help wondering how often they cleaned the velveteen cushions.

The waitress lingered in the doorway, and James held out a folded bill. Grinning, she pointed to her cleavage.

James slowly slid the bill down the center of her bra, saying softly, "What's your name, sweetheart? Next time I'll be sure to request *you*."

A grin spread across her face. "Breezy."

"Until next time, Breezy…"

She gave him a saucy grin, then let the curtain fall and disappeared.

James turned back to me, and I lifted a brow. I knew he was doing what needed to be done, but I couldn't help the irritation building in my gut.

"You must love that so many women are eager to drop their panties for you."

His expression turned serious. "I know what I can have and what I want, Harper. Make no mistake—I want you."

He definitely knew the right things to say, but he had a point. He had chosen to be with me, and I needed to trust in that. James Malcolm was an extraordinarily attractive man, and unless we moved to some remote location, women would always show their appreciation.

I walked over to him and held his gaze. "I need you to make me a promise."

"If I can, I will."

That was fair. "If you lose interest in me and want to be with another woman, I need you to tell me. Don't cheat on me. I'm a big girl. I can take it."

"I swear to you, I will never cheat on you," he said in a low growl. "Is that promise enough for you?"

"Hello, sexy," a woman said from the doorway.

I dropped my hold on his face, and James turned to face her, partially blocking her view of me. "Pleased to make your acquaintance, Ruby."

A lacy robe hung from her shoulders, barely covering a sparkly bra and G-string. "Such a gentleman," she cooed, stepping into the room and letting the curtain fall behind her.

I moved out from behind James and stood at his side. "Hello, Dani."

Her face froze, and she glanced from me to James, then back again. "You're into threesomes?"

"Why don't we all have a seat?" James said, motioning to the bench.

Fear filled her eyes. "Am I in trouble?" she asked me, remaining rooted in place.

"Absolutely not," I said firmly.

"So you really want to have a threesome?" she asked, confusion covering her face.

"We just want to ask you a few questions," James said, then held out several hundred-dollar bills. "But why don't we sit first?"

She looked at me again, fear still in her eyes.

It occurred to me that she wasn't going to volunteer information without something to compel her.

"You're not in trouble, Dani," I said. "In fact, I'm not even with the police anymore. I'm a private investigator, and I'm looking for a missing girl. We were hoping you could tell us if you've seen her." I glanced at James.

He picked up on my cue and pulled out his phone. "Her name is Penny," he said, showing her the photo after he pulled it up.

She studied the photo for a moment. "She looks young." She shook her head. "I haven't seen her, but the owner's pretty careful about makin' sure the girls are legal. Last thing he wants is gettin' busted for havin' underaged girls."

"We think she's been trafficked," I said. "Do you know anything about a trafficking ring?"

She bit her bottom lip, hesitating. "Nope. I don't know anything about any of that."

"Are you sure?" James asked in a honeyed tone, taking a

seat on the bench. "Maybe you've heard some whispers or rumors."

"We all hear rumors," she said, softly, the tension in her shoulders easing. "But they're just rumors."

James patted the seat next to him, and Dani walked over and sat beside him.

"What rumors have you heard?"

"There was a dancer here," she said. "Wilhemina, but her stage name was Nova Lux. One night she didn't show up for work, but that's not all that uncommon. But the night before, a super creepy guy was interested in her. He refused to pay for anything extra—no lap dance, no private room, nothin'—but he kept staring. He only ordered one drink and stayed for about an hour and a half. We all talked about him after he left. How he was a cheap weirdo who couldn't afford us. But then Willy didn't show the next night, or the next. Her roommate said she just disappeared. Left her stuff and everything."

"You don't know who the guy was?" James asked.

She shook her head. "But one of the girls heard him talkin' on the phone while Willy was dancing. He said somethin' like, 'She's perfect. Just what the client ordered.'"

I shot a glance at James. His expression was grim.

"Do you know if anyone reported her missing?" I asked.

Dani rolled her eyes. "Why bother? It's not like the police are gonna do anything about it. Willy's no one. Just an exotic dancer with no family and no money."

As much I hated to admit it, she had a point. Even if it was undeniably wrong.

"How long ago did she disappear?" I asked.

She made a face. "About a month or so ago?"

"Did she have a boyfriend or maybe an ex?"

She shook her head. "No. We teased her about not having a man in her life, and she said the men oglin' her were all the men she needed."

"And she hadn't mentioned anyone watching her or stalking her? Maybe waiting outside the club after she left?"

"No."

"Do you have a photo of Wilhemenia?" James asked. "We can look for her while we're lookin' for Penny."

Dani started to shake her head, then stopped. "Wait. There's a photo of her on the wall by the entrance. She's the redhead."

James gave a curt nod. "And what about the creep who was interested in her?"

"No one got a photo of him, if that's what you're askin'. It's not like we have pockets to carry our phones." She gestured to her skimpy outfit. "Speakin' of which, I can give you a lap dance while we chat," she said, running the back of her fingertips over his cheek.

"I appreciate the offer," he said, giving her an expressionless look, "but any information you can provide is worth what I'm already payin'."

"Consider it a bonus," she said with a sly grin, then glanced back at me. "It might help shake something loose."

I wanted to say, *like your boobs out of that skimpy top*, but was smart enough to keep my mouth shut. I only hoped I looked unbothered.

"Go for it," I said dryly, leaning my shoulder into the wall. "Whatever helps us find your friend and the teenage girl we're lookin' for."

I'd hoped my comment would help her reevaluate, but if anything, it incentivized her more.

She straddled James's lap, resting her hands on his shoulders.

Great.

"What about security cameras?" James asked in a bored voice as she began to dance on his thighs.

"In this room?" she asked, then stood and turned around, shaking her ass in his face. "Or the club?"

"Inside and outside of the club," James said, acting like he was making idle conversation. "A place like this must have cameras."

"Sure." She settled back on his lap, her back to him, and started humping his crotch. "But I don't know nothin' about that."

"Someone has to," he said.

"Sure, the manager and the owner. Oh, and Tony, the head of security, but he's not gonna pull it up. Not for a missin' girl."

Because they were replaceable. A dime a dozen. They wouldn't waste their time on a girl they barely saw as human.

"What about some of the other women who work here?" James asked. "Surely, they want to help find your friend."

"She's not my friend," Dani said as she grabbed his hands and put them on her hips. She carefully arranged her hands over his.

"You do realize there's a no-touching rule," I said dryly, crossing my arms over my chest.

She glared at me in defiance. "Only if I don't want it."

It occurred to me that she must have heard me ask him not to cheat on me, so she was doing this to get to me. The question was why she was pissed at me. I tried to remember our last interaction. I'd dropped by her apartment and asked if she knew anything about a man who spent time at the club. I'd shown her a photo, and she'd denied knowing him. She'd been short with me, but I'd chalked it up as irritation that I was bothering her. I hadn't thought I'd *actually* pissed her off.

James kept his hands on her hips, but his fingertips didn't dig in, and it didn't look like he was putting much effort into holding her.

She glanced down at his hands, a scowl flickering over her face.

"If you could get a photo of the guy, we'd make it worth your while," I said.

Her gaze snapped to mine. "How do you plan to do that?"

I'd expected James to jump in and make an offer, but he remained quiet. I considered offering anyway, but I couldn't see his face to gauge his thoughts and it didn't feel right to offer her his money. "What do you want?"

"I want my new solicitation charges dropped," she said, venom in her eyes, "but you're pretty worthless there, aren't you?"

So, she knew I'd left the force? Had she wanted me to help her sometime in the last five months and realized I couldn't act on her behalf?

"Yeah, I guess I am," I said matter-of-factly as she began to dance again, James's hands still resting lightly over the strings covering her hips. "What else do you have in mind? More money?"

"I want my damn charges dropped," she spat out, her body going still. "Those and the possession charge."

I frowned. "What kind of possession charge?"

"I got busted with some ecstasy when they picked me up for solicitation."

My brow shot up. "That's new for you."

Her glare deepened. "The guy was in his forties and had just gotten divorced. He asked me to get him something to make it a memorable night."

"And you couldn't rely on your skills?" I asked dryly. I shouldn't be provoking her, but I felt helpless to stop myself.

"That's your price?" James said flatly. "Your charges dropped? Both of them?"

She glanced over her shoulder at him.

"And if Harper makes that happen, you'll get images of the guy?" he asked. "Inside the club and outside with his car?"

"Harper's not a cop anymore," she spat. "She can't make that happen."

"Don't worry about that part," James said. "I'm more concerned about whether you can hold up your end of the agreement. How long do they keep the security footage?"

His request was pointless. Most systems didn't store longer than fourteen days before recording over themselves.

"Maybe a month," she said.

"Let's be clear," I said, my tone firm. "Your charges won't be dismissed until I know you've got images." Because she had to know the images were gone. She was stringing us along to get what she wanted.

She turned her glare to me. "I'm not handin' anything over without knowin' they've been dropped."

I was about to tell her that wasn't how we did things, but James spoke first.

"Then how about we work out an agreement?" James dug in slightly on her left hip, making her flesh pucker. "You get the images, then let us know. Once we're sure they're helpful, we'll get the charges dropped."

She released a soft gasp, and I preferred to think it was because she thought she might get her charges dismissed, not in response to his touch.

Still, I wasn't going to waste our time on her bullshit.

I propped my hands on my hips. "Why would the manager keep the footage thirty days?"

She gave me a look of surprise. "What?"

"I'm not stupid, Dani. I know most places only keep their tapes for two weeks, so don't bullshit us."

"Shows what you know," she sneered as she slid off James's lap. "The owner keeps them for at least a month. There were some drug deals goin' on out in the parking lot, and he had an arrangement with the narcotics department. If he gave them the footage, they'd look the other way with things goin' on inside the club."

If that was true, it still didn't guarantee the footage existed. Dani had said Wilhemina disappeared about a month ago.

"Well," James said, "if he only keeps the tapes for thirty days, and your friend disappeared about a month ago, then I'd say you better not waste any time lookin' for the right footage."

She took a couple of steps toward the door, then turned back to him. "Don't I get credit for tryin' to get the video? It's not gonna be easy."

"This isn't high school English class," he said in a lazy tone. "I don't hand out extra credit or participation trophies. I reward results."

Her upper lip curled with disgust. "You're a real asshole."

"That's a known fact," he said, a menacing look covering his face. "Name's Skeeter Malcolm, and I have *quite* the reputation."

Her eyes widened slightly. "*You're* Skeeter Malcolm?"

I stared at her in shock. Dani knew who he was? Sure, he'd made national news three years ago, but she wasn't much into current events.

"How do you know about me?" he asked in a lazy, seductive drawl.

She hesitated, then said, "Razor."

He leaned back, stretching an arm along the back of the bench. "And how do you know Razor?" He appeared utterly relaxed, but the gleam in his eyes was lethal.

The name meant nothing to me, but it appeared James had heard of him.

She shot me a nervous glance, her previous belligerence gone. When I gave her a cold stare, she turned back to James. "He comes around. He likes private dances."

"With you?" James asked, tilting his head in challenge.

She drew in a shaky breath. "Used to be with me, but he prefers the new girls lately."

I suspected that meant younger.

"And how did my name come up in conversation?" James asked.

She glanced at me again, this time addressing me. "Razor doesn't like people talkin' about him."

"Most people don't like to be talked about," I said, "but you can't drop that you know Skeeter Malcolm's name and not tell us how you've heard of him." I used the name he'd gone by in his previous life. No need to give anything else away.

"The real question is why *you're* with him," she said, looking me up and down. "Little Miss By-the-Books who doesn't do nothing wrong. Why are *you* with a murderer and weapons dealer?"

The weapons dealing caught me by surprise, but thank God I'd entrenched myself in interrogation mode and gave away nothing. "I told you, I'm not a cop anymore."

"So you turned to the other side?" she asked in disbelief. "You're the last person I thought would go dark."

"I haven't gone dark," I said flatly. "I'm just working from a different angle, trying to find missing girls who have been trafficked. Skeeter Malcolm has a similar goal, so we're working together."

A haughty look flitted over her face. "From what I heard when I walked in, sounds like you're screwin' him."

I shrugged slightly, still keeping my bored expression. "What can I say? A girl has needs and he's a good lay." I paused. "But we're getting off topic. How did you find out that Skeeter Malcolm is a murderer and a weapons dealer? I can't imagine Razor just dropped that in polite conversation. Or pillow talk, for that matter."

She glanced over at James, who still had his arm slung over

the bench like he was enjoying a day at the park, but the look in his eyes remained deadly.

"I heard him tellin' someone else over the phone."

"What was he saying?" I asked.

"I don't know," she said in frustration, running her hand over her head. "He said something about Skeeter Malcolm was a dead man walkin'."

"When was this?" I asked.

She grimaced. "A week ago?"

"A week ago, he said Skeeter was a dead man walking because he was a murderer and a weapons dealer?" I countered. "Must have been quite the unbelievable conversation."

"I already told you, he didn't tell me that stuff. I heard him on the phone."

"Maybe it would help if you tried to recall how the conversation went," I said. "Maybe set the stage with where you were and what you were doing."

Venom filled her eyes. "You want me to tell you he took a phone call while I was ridin' his dick?"

"If that's how it happened," I said flatly.

"Well, he did, fuckin' prick. He said it was an important call, and he had to take it. I started to get off him, because I've learned that guys like him don't discuss business in front of the hired help."

That was one way to put it.

"So you were still fucking him while he took his important call?" I prodded. "Maybe you pretend you're Razor and tell me how his side of the call went?"

Her jaw clenched. "He answered with his name and was quiet for a few moments, then said, 'So, Skeeter Malcolm's a dead man walkin'. He listened to something on the other line and then said he was busy at the moment, and he'd be by in an hour. That was it. he hung up."

"So... where did the murderer and weapons dealer part

come in?" I asked. "Because you don't seem like the independent research kind of girl."

She shot me a dark look. "I asked him."

I didn't hide my surprise.

Dani released a bitter laugh. "You've taught me that knowledge is power."

I suppose I had, but asking questions of the wrong people could also get her killed.

"What exactly did you ask?" James asked, still using his lazy tone.

She turned to him, her body going still. "I asked why Skeeter Malcolm was a dead man. He said you'd pissed of the wrong person. I asked him why he was so happy that you were a dead man, and he said, I shouldn't be cryin' over you, because you were a murderer and a weapons dealer. Then he said it was too bad you'd stopped sellin' weapons, but you still aren't to be trusted."

"Did he say why I'm not to be trusted?" James asked with a hint of edge.

"He said you're a liar and snitch."

James gave a slow nod. "While it's true I hold my own special interests above all others, I'm not a liar. When I make a threat, I can guarantee I mean it." He dropped his arm and sat up straighter. "Since you know who I am, then you've probably figured out I'm not a man to double-cross, because I promise you, I'm bigger and badder than Razor ever thought of being." James paused, holding her gaze. "Either you get the tape or you don't. If you can't get it, let me know, and we'll part on good terms. But if you bullshit me…" His voice trailed off, letting Dani's imagination fill in the rest.

Based on the way her face paled, she had a healthy imagination.

"Harper, give my new friend your number," he said, keeping his gaze on the dancer.

I pulled one of the slips of paper from my pocket and held it out to her.

She stared at him for several seconds, then turned to me and snatched the paper. "How do you plan on getting my charges dropped if you're not a cop anymore?"

Good question, because I had no idea how that would happen either. I'd never made promises to informants I couldn't keep. I didn't plan to start now. "Actually—"

"We have our ways," James said, getting to his feet. "You get those videos, and we'll take care of the rest."

She started to leave, and James called out, "Dani."

She turned back to him, her hand gripping the curtain.

"Don't try to pass some other guy off as the guy watching your friend. Trust me, I'll know if it's not him."

She stared at him for another second, then let the curtain fall as she left the room.

———————————————

Chapter 11

———————————————

I wanted to rip into James for making a promise we couldn't keep, but I wasn't going to do it in here. I had several other questions too, but they would have to wait. I strode out of the room, letting him follow behind. We passed through the main area and then past the bouncer. I glanced at the photos of dancers on the wall and spotted Wilhemina. She was the only redhead in the bunch. I stopped short, James nearly running into my back. I pointed at the photo.

"That's her."

The bouncer gave me a dark look, but James pulled out his phone and snapped a couple of shots.

"No photos," the bouncer barked.

James ignored him and, gripping my elbow, steered me toward the door.

Once we were in the parking lot and several feet from the door, I yanked my arm free and turned to face him, barely reining in my anger, "*What were you thinking?*"

He gave me a wry look. "You'll have to be more specific."

"At the moment, I'm talking about you promising to get her charges dropped. I can't do that, James!"

"There are other ways for it to happen, Harper," he said simply. "What else is bothering you?"

"You can't just tell me there are other ways and leave it at that," I snapped. "You'll have to be more specific than that."

"Have I ever not followed through on something I've promised you?" he asked, his voice ending on a husky note as his hand rose to lightly cup my upper arm.

My breath hitched and I chastised my body for reacting to nothing more than his voice and the light touch of his hand. My body's addiction to him wasn't what we were discussing.

Truthfully, he always followed through on his promises, which meant he likely had a plan. But the dynamic of our relationship had changed—I needed to know what that plan actually was. "We're partners now, James. You owe me more concrete answers. Is this something you expect Carter to work his magic on?"

"My name carries a lot of influence."

I narrowed my eyes. "So *you're* going to get her charges dropped?"

"If she gets the videos."

"How do you plan to do that? Bribes?"

"I have a few ideas, but I'm not sure which direction I'll go. We don't even know if she'll get the footage."

I could have pushed for more specifics, but I'd let it go— for now.

His brow lifted. "What else?"

"Who's Razor and why does he hate you?"

"That's a conversation that'll take longer than we've got."

"You're not going to tell me?" I snapped.

"I suspect you have other questions regarding Dani's conversation with Razor, but I'm not going to tell you standing in this parking lot. I'll tell you when we get back to the hotel."

My anger cooled to a simmer. "Why not tell me that straight off? Why go with the dramatics?"

"Good point." His brow ticked up. "Anything else?"

I knew what he was thinking. "If you think I'm upset about the lap dance, you're sadly mistaken."

He grinned. "Good to know."

I gave him a dark look. "Just don't be following up with Breezy."

He laughed, then winced.

"Is your headache back?"

"That would suggest my headache ever left."

"Come on," I said. "Alex probably thinks we're having a disagreement."

We both glanced over at the car, but Alex was bent over his phone. If he'd been paying attention, he was pretending he wasn't.

I headed over to the car, and James fell in step beside me, his hand settling lightly at the small of my back.

I shot him a wry look. "Worried I'll take off somewhere?"

"Maybe I just like findin' a reason to touch you."

Another wave of warmth rushed through me, leaving me disconcerted. I wasn't used to a man affecting me like this. It wasn't the ideal time to start.

Alex glanced up as we approached the car, unlocking the doors just as James reached for the back handle. James gestured for me to get in first.

When we were inside, Alex looked over his shoulder as James shut the door.

"You were in there for a bit. Did you find out anything about your niece?"

"Possibly," James said, settling back in the seat, a slight grimace pressing his lips flat.

"Where to next?" Alex asked.

We'd been in the club for longer than I'd expected. The clock on Alex's dash said it was close to eleven.

James gave me a questioning look.

I didn't have anyone else to check with. It also wasn't lost on me that James had done more tonight than he'd done since the accident—and the club had been loud, the stage lights had been bright, exactly what he didn't need.

I shook my head. "I don't have anything else. Let's go back to the hotel."

James nodded. "Okay."

"I picked you up outside the bar," Alex said. "Where're you guys stayin'?"

James paused for a moment, then gave him the name of our hotel, sat back, and closed his eyes. I stared at him in surprise.

We rode in silence, and I berated myself for not checking on him sooner. Hell, he probably shouldn't have been out at all tonight.

When we neared the hotel, I expected James to tell Alex to stop a block away so we could sneak in through the back, but he let him pull right up to the entrance, then handed him two folded bills.

"Thanks for your service, Alex."

Alex took the money, then handed James a card. "If you need a driver during the rest of your stay, just give me a call."

James thanked him and opened the door, holding out a hand to help me out on his side.

I wasn't used to a man treating me like royalty, and my first instinct was to refuse, but maybe it wouldn't hurt to let myself be spoiled a bit. Besides, our cover was that we were a married couple. Letting him help me out went with the act.

We were silent until we reached our room. James locked the door behind us, then headed to the sitting area as he took off his jacket.

"You did too much tonight," I said, toeing off my shoes next to the bed.

"It needed to be done," he said matter-of-factly. He tossed his jacket onto a chair, then removed his holster and gun and set them on the coffee table.

"I could have gone on my own," I said as I removed my own holster and gun.

"Like hell," he growled. He sat on the sofa to remove his boots.

I wasn't offended. He knew I was capable. He was just worried about me going alone. Just like I would've been worried about him.

"You need to go to bed," I said as I left my gun on the nightstand and crossed the room to him.

He patted the seat next to him. "Sit with me for a moment and enjoy the view." He stretched his arm along the back of the sofa.

I sat, not surprised when his arm slid down to settle across my shoulders. I wasn't used to this either. Keith had never been a cuddler, and before him, I'd made sure to steer clear of men who were touchy-feely. But this didn't feel like cuddling. It felt deeper, like we both needed the physical touch to know this was real. Or at least that's how it was for me. Since James didn't seem like the cuddly type, I could only presume it was the same for him.

I settled into his side, reveling in the warmth of simply being with him, alone, after sitting next to each other in the car with Alex, then at the club.

We sat in silence for several minutes, looking out at the lights of North Little Rock across the river and the glow of the pedestrian bridge.

"Do you think Dani will come through with the videos?" he murmured against my hair.

"I don't see how," I said, disappointment settling in the pit of my stomach. "Most places don't keep tapes that long."

"I keep mine for ninety days. At the tavern and back in Fenton County."

"The strip club?"

"That too. I also had a pool hall."

I turned around to face him in surprise. "How did I not know you had a pool hall?"

A smug grin twisted his lips. "Your investigation of me must not have been very thorough."

"I guess not since I didn't know you were a weapons dealer," I said dryly.

He brow lifted. "You knew I was in organized crime. What did you think I did?"

"Drugs. You were working with an international drug cartel."

"I was working to bring *down* an international drug cartel." He made a face. "I didn't deal with drugs."

"You're telling me one of the poorest counties in the state didn't have drugs," I said dryly. "That kind of situation is ripe for drug activity."

"Someone else in the area ran drugs, then he was arrested and eventually killed. Another guy took over." He sighed. "You're right. People who are poor and without hope need an escape. Denny Cartwright gave it to 'em."

"And you condoned it?" I countered.

"Who am I to tell people how they should escape their shitty lives," he said with a hint of arrogance. "Nature abhors a vacuum, and when Daniel Crocker's organization fell apart, Denny took over."

"Why didn't *you* take over?" I asked, trying to understand.

He held my gaze for a moment. "Just because people wanted to escape didn't mean I was going to give them the poison to do it."

"But you provided guns and bullets to people who likely had no business with them."

He sighed, closing his eyes again. "You know I'm not a saint. Maybe I'm not proud of all the things I've done, but there's no changin' the past, and to be honest, I wouldn't change all of it. Everything in my past is what got me here today." He squeezed my shoulder. "With you."

He had a point about all of it. I knew he'd been a crime boss. And sure, I'd figured illegal activity and murder had been part of that, but I'd lumped it into his involvement with the FBI to bring down the Hardshaw Group. How could I have forgotten that he'd had decades of criminal behavior before that?

"How are you feelin' about me now?" he asked, his eyes still closed.

"It's complicated," I admitted.

"You can change your mind about us at any time," he said softly. "If you realize the gravity of who you're with."

"You're not that man anymore."

His eyes opened and he held my gaze. "I'll always be that man, Harper. I may not be doin' the things I did, but I'm still him."

And yet I wanted him anyway. What did that say about me?

I was too tired to reason it through.

I settled back into him and returned to what had sidetracked our conversation. "Why'd you keep the tape for ninety days? It must have taken up massive amounts of cloud storage."

"Same reason the owner of the Velvet Room probably keeps his for at least thirty days. To cover my ass."

I cocked my head. "You mean like turning in people committing crimes on your property, like the guy here?"

He chuckled, then grimaced. "More like to make sure I had an alibi when something happened that law enforcement wanted to pin on me." When he saw my confusion, he said, "I ran my business out of the pool hall."

"Oh." That made sense, especially since he'd said Jed ran the strip club. "What other businesses did you have?"

"Those were the only two in my name. The rest are under aliases and LLCs to keep my name out of it."

"Which is how you knew about corporations wanting anonymity filing in New Mexico when we worked the Hugo Burton case."

His mouth ticked up in acknowledgement, but his eyes looked strained.

"You need to go to bed, James," I said, patting his chest.

He stared into my eyes. "I don't want to go to bed yet."

"Then let me give you a neck and shoulder rub. Maybe it will help with your headache."

A wicked glint filled his eyes. "Maybe I want you to rub me somewhere else."

I cocked my head and said wryly, "I already did that twice today. I thought a man your age needed more time to recover."

He burst out laughing, but just as quickly grimaced.

"If you're not going to bed, then I'm giving you a massage." I nudged the coffee table toward the chairs with my foot. "Sit on the rug."

"I don't let many people boss me around," he grunted, but he was already sliding off the sofa and onto the floor.

"You've bossed me around plenty the past couple of months, so now it's my turn."

He rested his back against the sofa, and I crossed my legs in front of me, placing both hands on his shoulders. His muscles were tighter than I'd expected. I gingerly kneaded them, and he let out a soft groan.

A wave of heat washed through me, but I ignored it. "This will probably be better if you take off your shirt."

"Tryin' to get me naked," he teased as he pulled his shirt over his head.

"Get your mind out of the gutter," I teased back as he tossed the shirt to the floor. I pressed my fingertips to his bare skin, focusing on easing the tension from his muscles.

"That feels so damn good," he said with another groan.

"I should have been doing this all week," I said, guilt pricking me.

"You were doin' more important things."

"Not twenty-four seven." And it hadn't been all that productive anyway.

"You're doin' it now," he said softly as I continued to knead. "That's what counts."

"Let me know if I press too hard."

He didn't respond, but I could feel his muscles loosen as I worked over his shoulders and the back of his neck. I wanted to ask him about Razor, but he'd just relaxed. I didn't want him to tense up again.

"You don't have to keep doin' that," he murmured, sounding half-asleep after I'd massaged him for at least five minutes. "Your hands have to be gettin' tired."

"I'm good." I didn't want to admit I liked touching him. That I liked feeling him. Hell, I barely wanted to admit it to myself. "When was the last time someone rubbed your shoulders?"

"I can't remember anyone ever doin' this for me."

My hands stilled. "No one?"

"Don't sound so surprised," he said with a sigh. "What about you? Did Limp Dick give you shoulder rubs?"

I couldn't help grinning at his nickname for my ex. "No, he was too self-centered."

"Did you give them to him?" he asked, a hint of menace in his voice.

His tone caught me off guard. "Yeah, a few times. Are you jealous?"

He turned his upper body slightly to face me. "Jealous? Fuck no. I just wanted confirmation that he's as much of a prick as I suspected."

I grinned. "I already told you he's a prick. Now turn back around."

He gave me one last look, then turned to face the chairs.

I resumed his massage, and it only took a few seconds for him to relax again.

"Why has no one done this before?" I asked gently. "I know you said you didn't do girlfriends, but there must have been women in your life who meant something to you. Women you dated for at least a few months."

His breath hitched slightly, and he stayed quiet for so long that I didn't think he was going to answer.

"There was one," he finally said, barely loud enough for me to hear him. "She caught me by surprise and slipped through my defenses."

I expected to feel jealousy—especially after the way it had flared up several other times tonight—but the sadness in his voice smothered it.

"How did you meet her?" I asked softly.

"She wasn't from my world. She was an innocent, and I fell hard for her, even though I had no business thinkin' about her that way. I kept it to myself for quite some time, until she started to feel something for me. Even then…" His voice trailed off. "I knew it was wrong, but I'd wanted her for months, and when I had the opportunity…" He drew in a sharp breath. "I couldn't stop myself. It's my deepest regret. I nearly ruined her life."

A pain stabbed my chest. Not jealousy, but sorrow. "She was a grown woman. She could make up her own mind."

"She had no idea what she was gettin' herself into."

"She knew what you did?" I asked. "She knew who you were?" I couldn't imagine how he could have kept it from her.

"Yes."

"Then she had to know what she was getting herself into."

"She was naive." He sounded bone-weary, and I knew it wasn't from his concussion.

I couldn't argue that point, since I didn't know anything about her. "If she wasn't from your world, then how did you meet her?" I asked, repeating my earlier question.

He paused. "The first time was at my pool hall, but then I saw her about six months later." He stopped again, like he was cutting himself off.

"You were interested in her, but you kept it to yourself. You must have kept running into her if you saw her often enough to fall for her."

"We did." He left it at that, so I didn't push.

"How long were you together?"

He released a short laugh. "Ironically, not that long. And even when we were together, it was a secret." He glanced back at me. "I'll understand if you decide to keep us a secret."

I arched an eyebrow. "I'm no one's dirty little secret, James Malcom."

He looked surprised.

"What?" I challenged. "Once this is done, you either openly see me, or this will be a short-lived tryst."

He gave me a pointed look. "*Tryst?*"

"Fine, affair. Friends with benefits. Whatever you want to call it."

He studied me for a long moment. "You want us to be linked together in public?"

"I don't plan to rent a billboard announcing that I'm screwing you, but yeah. If I see you at the tavern, I'm not going to pretend we're not together. Besides, your staff already knows."

"They won't talk."

Before I got to know him, I would have presumed they wouldn't have talked out of fear of retribution. But now I knew better. They were loyal to him. "I don't care if they talk." I paused. "Do you?"

"It's *you* I'm protectin'," he said in exasperation.

"That doesn't answer my question, does it?"

Still watching me, he let out a heavy sigh, then turned back around.

"Your reputation will probably be ruined," he said softy.

"News flash. It's already ruined. I don't give a shit what people think about me."

"Liar," he scoffed lightly.

I drew in a breath. "Okay, fair. But I'm tired of worrying about what people think about me. I just want to live my life." I let my fingers glide over his shoulders as I began to massage again.

"Did someone find out about you two?" I finally asked. "Is that why you ended things?"

He was silent for several seconds, and I was pretty sure he wasn't going to answer the question, but then he surprised me.

"It ended for a lot of reasons. For one, we only saw each other a few times a week at my house. For another, she wanted a husband and a family. My life wasn't conducive to either of those things."

"They could be now," I said, almost regretting the words as soon as I said them. "Your life is very different than it was."

"Is it?" he countered.

"As far as I can tell, you're not running a crime ring, so yeah, I'd say it is."

"I still have a reputation. My name precedes me. Like tonight. That makes me dangerous." He was silent for a moment. "Do you want those things, Harper?" His question hung in the air. "A husband? Kids?"

"I never saw myself having kids," I said thoughtfully. "I was a workaholic, and I swore if I ever had kids, they'd never doubt my love for them. Seems to me the surest way to make your six-year-old question whether you love them is to miss their dance recital or T-ball game because you're close to cracking a case and you can't tear yourself away."

"Your situation has changed too," he pointed out.

"Maybe. But I don't know that I have it in me to be a good mom. So it's probably best I don't become one."

He absorbed that, then asked, "And a husband?"

I shrugged, belatedly realizing he couldn't see me. "I never thought I'd get married. I was married to my job."

"Again, your circumstances have changed."

I laughed. "If you're worried I'm gonna try to drag a marriage proposal out of you, you have nothing to worry about."

He chuckled.

Silence hung heavy in the room.

"You loved her," I said. Not a question.

He was silent, then let out a soft, "Yes."

I let that sink in.

"What other reasons ended the relationship?" I finally asked.

"Who says there's another reason? Seems to me those two are reason enough."

Something in his voice told me there was more, but I didn't want to admit that. "I just know. What was it?"

He took in a breath before he said, "I'd already cut Jed loose, and I was playin' a dangerous game. While I wanted nothin' more than to keep seein' her, I knew she was in danger." He paused. "And then she made a decision that made the decision for me. So I cut her loose."

His words ended on a bitter note.

I was glad I wasn't facing him so he wouldn't see my shock.

I'd presumed this woman had been in his distant past, when he was young—not as recently as three or four years ago.

"So, not an amicable breakup?"

His shoulders tensed. "She would have fought me on it, so I made it so she wouldn't."

"You hurt her?" I asked in surprise.

"Not physically," he snapped. "I'd never hit a woman."

"I wouldn't be sitting here if I thought you would. But we both know that emotional pain can be just as bad. Sometimes it's worse."

"Yeah," he said, his voice going gravely. "I was hateful. I made damn sure she wouldn't want me back."

"So you sacrificed yourself for her." A statement, not a question.

"Don't do that," he said in disgust. "Don't make what I did out to be noble."

"Fine," I said. "I won't. But let me ask you this—she was a grown woman. Why couldn't she decide whether she wanted to be with you or not? Why did you get to make that decision for her?"

He turned and looked out the window. "Because I'm a controllin' asshole."

I let out a short laugh. "I already knew that. Surely, she did too."

"She did. But she has this habit of seein' the best in people and believin' they can overcome their shortcomings."

I considered that. "Maybe you needed her to see the good parts of you."

"Who said she saw any good parts of me?" he asked in disgust.

"Because I also wouldn't be here if there weren't any."

He bent his knee, drawing it up. "Like I said, she made a decision that was the nail in the coffin of our relationship. And I'd be lyin' if I said that everything I spit at her was a lie."

I wanted to ask what her decision had been but didn't want to press my luck. I doubted she'd betrayed him. If she had, he wouldn't have any trouble saying so.

But I heard the pain in his voice, and I had to ask the question that had me on edge.

"Do you still love her?"

"No," he said softly. "I still care about her and think of her fondly, but I'm no longer in love with her. I don't regret breakin' things off. She wouldn't have been happy with me, and now she's with a man who can give her what I couldn't." He paused. "She's happy."

"What about you?" I asked.

He slowly turned to look at me. "Are you askin' if I'm happy?"

"You have your tavern, your crew who adores you, and Carter. Are you happy?"

"For the longest time, I didn't think I deserved to be happy," he said, pain filling his eyes.

"And now?"

"Now, I'm starting to think that maybe I don't deserve it, but it's okay if I am." Something in the way he looked at me suggested he was talking about me, but then, I couldn't let myself believe it. I was still stuck on the fact he'd loved a woman only three or four years ago. A woman he'd loved deeply enough to give up his own happiness for.

I reached up and cupped his cheek. "Make me a promise, James Malcom."

"You're demandin' a lot of promises tonight," he grumbled, but there was fondness in his eyes. "I will if I can."

His readiness to offer me assurance peeled a protective layer off my heart. "Don't ever make a decision for me. If we do this, we're partners, so you don't get to decide what's best for me. We make decisions together."

He reached behind my head and pulled my face close to his. "I promise," he said, earnestness in his eyes.

I kissed him tenderly, letting my thumb trace his cheekbone. "Come to bed with me, James."

His mouth quirked up on one side. "For the record, in the future, if you want me to go to bed, that's the way to make it happen."

Chapter 12

Once we were in bed, James fell asleep within minutes, making me kick myself all over again. He truly had overdone it tonight. Tomorrow, we needed to take this slower and in shorter stretches.

I lay on my back, listening to his soft, steady breathing, thinking about what he'd told me. I was still surprised he'd opened up so much. Sure, he'd held things back, but I understood why. Some secrets weren't his to share. It made sense that if the woman he'd been in love with wasn't from his world, he'd want to protect her.

The more I thought about it, the more surprised I was he'd told me at all.

I couldn't help wondering who she was and how he'd kept running into her. He'd met her at his pool hall, but they'd crossed paths often enough that they'd eventually fallen for each other.

Someone who wasn't from his world…

An icy dread washed through me.

He'd called her an innocent.

One woman's name kept surfacing when I'd dug into

James's recent past, a woman who didn't make sense in his orbit.

Rose Gardner.

And every time her name came up, James turned defensive, like he was protecting even the mere mention of her name.

I knew in my gut that it had to be her.

James had been in love with Rose Gardner.

I took a moment to take that in. I wasn't sure why I was so shocked. From the first time I'd heard her name linked to his, I'd wondered if there'd been something romantic between them. I'd decided it was too preposterous, but she was a stereotypical good girl, and he'd played the role of the bad boy. It was a tale as old as time.

And yet it still felt like a gut punch.

What decision had she made that ended their relationship? What would have pissed him off—or cut him so deeply—that he'd not only ended things but lit the bridge behind him in a blazing inferno? Had she sided with Jed? Had she fought him on working with Hardshaw?

Maybe both.

There was a photo on James's fireplace mantel of Jed's little girl … along with Rose Gardner's daughter.

Her daughter was four years old.

My breath stuck in my chest. No. My imagination was running wild.

But I couldn't ignore the fact he had a framed photo of both girls on his mantle. And the timing of the little girl's age fit too well.

Was *that* the decision Rose had made that had officially ended their relationship? Had she gotten pregnant and decided to keep the baby? James said he didn't want children. It could have been a deal breaker.

It was a huge leap—I was making assumptions, but that

was how I'd solved a lot of my cases: seeing scattered pieces and figuring out how they fit, even when no one else could.

This felt like a flashing neon sign.

I slid out of bed and moved to the sofa, trying to figure out why this bothered me so much. Rose was in his past, and he'd said he didn't love her anymore. Maybe it was the fact that her name kept popping up, or the possibility that he might have a kid. I didn't think I had it in me to be a stepmother. Then again, from what I could tell, James didn't have contact with the girl. She had Joe Simmons's last name.

Still, there was every chance I was wrong about Rose's daughter.

But there was also a chance I was right.

I grabbed the laptop. I'd done some searches on Rose Gardner a few weeks ago, but I typed in her name again. The articles about her business and her kidnapping by J.R. Simmons came up, but I ignored those and studied the photos instead, reconfirming what I already knew.

She was the complete antithesis of me—wholesome, girl-next-door, with a sheriff husband and a house full of kids on their family farm. She ran a nursery and landscaping business, for God's sake. You couldn't be more homespun than that.

Was that what he wanted? Even if he said he didn't? Was I putting my heart on the line just so it could get broken?

I wasn't sure I could handle that.

This is only a fling. You've told yourself that since the moment you first went to bed with him.

Only, after spending the past week with him, I *knew* it wasn't just a fling. James was everything I needed in a man.

But was I everything *he* needed?

A deep thirst burned in my chest. I wanted a drink so badly I dug my fingernails into my palms. My mouth felt dry, and the minibar across the room taunted me.

One drink wouldn't hurt. It would take the edge off so I could get some sleep.

But I'd told myself that when I'd started to drink last fall, right up until I finally quit. Just one drink, which turned into two, and before I knew it, I'd downed a pint of whiskey and half a bottle of vodka I'd hidden in my water bottle.

Just one drink was a slippery slope I couldn't afford.

Still, I needed some kind of release or I was going to crawl out of my skin. I grabbed some clothes and headed to the bathroom, changing quickly into leggings and a T-shirt, then pulled my hair into a ponytail. I turned off the light before opening the door, making sure James was still asleep. Then I grabbed the key card, my phone and earbuds and crept to the door, snagging my shoes on the way out.

Thankfully, the exercise room was open and empty. I pulled up my fast-paced playlist and hopped on the treadmill.

I started out slow, then pushed harder until I was sprinting. I hadn't exercised in ages, and the wall hit fast, but I kept going, reveling in the burn. I locked onto the lyrics, determined to stop thinking about the woman he'd loved.

It stung that *I'd* never loved a man.

Focus on the music.

I wasn't sure how long I ran before I saw him enter the room. Long enough that I was breathless, drenched in sweat, and feeling like I was going to puke.

He stopped a few feet away and said nothing. He just watched me, dark circles carved under his eyes.

A standoff.

I considered ignoring him, but that would be punishment, and he didn't deserve that. He hadn't done anything wrong. If anything, I was grateful he'd trusted me enough to open up. The problem wasn't him. It was me.

I slowed the treadmill to a walk and pulled out my earbuds.

He still didn't say anything.

"I couldn't sleep," I finally said.

"You should've told me."

"I didn't want to wake you. Besides, I figured you'd either talk me out of it or insist on coming with me."

"You didn't even leave a note. I woke up and you were gone."

"Sorry," I said, guilt washing over me. "I was craving a drink, and the mini bar was too tempting. This seemed like the best way to deal with it."

He nodded once. "You still should have told me."

"I know," I said, meaning it. "I'm sorry."

"Do you need to run more?"

I eased the treadmill to a snail's pace. "No. I just need to cool down."

He crossed to the glass-front mini-fridge in the corner, grabbed a bottle of water, twisted off the cap, and handed it to me.

I drank half of it in a few gulps. He watched until I set the bottle in the cup holder, then handed me the cap. I screwed it on as he sat on a weight bench a few feet away.

He looked exhausted, and it was my fault.

"You should be in bed," I said. "Asleep. I should have just pushed through it."

"You need to work through your demons how you see fit." His gaze held mine. "Did it help?"

My burning insecurities had faded but not disappeared. So had my craving for a drink. "Yeah."

"That's good. Now you know something that can pull you out of that pit. I'd call that a win."

"At your expense."

He slowly shook his head. "Nope. Your success is my success."

"Were you this nice to her?" I asked before I could stop myself.

He looked momentarily stunned, then he sighed. He knew who I was talking about. "I don't know. Was I as attentive to her? No, I don't think so. But I'd like to think she taught me a thing or two about being in a relationship."

His answer surprised me, but I pushed on, asking the question that had been eating me alive since I'd figured out who she was. "If she showed up at your doorstep, begging you to give her another chance…would you?"

A frown creased his forehead. "That would never happen."

"Maybe not," I said, my voice catching. "But what if it did?"

His jaw tightened. "You're asking hypotheticals, Harper. It's a dead end."

That was my answer. A sudden urge to cry burned behind my eyes.

He saw the shift in my face, got to his feet and stepped closer. He hit the stop button on the treadmill, then tugged me off until I stood in front of him.

"I'm a practical man," he said, his voice low. "You've figured that out by now. I haven't spent years replaying the possibility that she'd change her mind and come back."

He cupped my face, and I cringed. I was soaked in sweat. It had to be gross. But he didn't flinch. He just held my gaze, steady and unblinking.

"But if she came to me today," he said softly, "if she walked through that door right now and asked to be with me … I'd say no."

"You have to say that," I whispered, hating who I was right now. Hating that he could see how much this hurt.

His mouth tipped up into a small, humorless smirk. "You know me well enough to know I'm not compelled to say anything I don't mean." He leaned in, close enough that his breath warmed my cheek. "Honesty. Remember? I meant it when I made that promise. I need you to believe me."

"I do," I whispered, desperate to look away but afraid it would feel like losing.

"It's *you* I want, Harper Adams." His voice roughened. "Someone who understands me and my world. A partner who isn't afraid to get messy." His mouth tipped. "And last week, after we were run off the road? That was pretty damn messy."

Messy was one word for killing nearly a dozen men.

"No one's ever fought for me like that, Harper," he said, almost a whisper. "Do you have any idea what that means to me?"

"It wasn't a decision, James," I said. "I just … did it."

"You could've run off into the woods and saved yourself." His gaze held mine. "But you knew I couldn't run. You stayed and fought for me."

We'd promised honesty, so I forced myself to be vulnerable. "Yes," I said, my voice fierce. "And I'd do it again in a heartbeat."

His eyes burned. "I want *you*, Harper."

I closed my eyes and dragged in a breath, hating that I was becoming so damn needy. "I'm sorry."

"Hey." He brushed my check with his thumb until I opened my eyes.

"Don't apologize," he said softly. "We're both workin' through a tangle of things we're not used to feeling." One brow lifted. "And you're lucky I know Limp Dick never really meant much to you or we'd be dealing with a whole different mess right now."

I snorted, shaking my head.

His expression sobered. "I'm not sorry for my time with her. I learned things. I'd like to think it helped get me where I am now."

"We both have a past," I said, swallowing hard. "And it's weird that I'm thirty-six years old and have never been in love.

Your past loves shouldn't bother me." I met his eyes. "I just worry I'm not enough."

"You're everything I need."

"You need an alcoholic with major insecurity and mommy-and-daddy issues?" I asked wryly.

"If that comes with the package of the sharp, stubborn, tough-as-hell woman standing in front of me, then yes. That's exactly what I need."

"I need you too," I whispered.

A slow grin spread across his face. "How hard was that for you admit?"

"Harder than it should have been."

"We'll work on that." He kissed me, tender and steady. "Do you need to run more, or are you ready to go upstairs?"

"I'm ready."

He dropped his hands from my face, then grabbed a rolled towel from on top of the refrigerator.

I took it and wiped my face. "You must have it bad for me if you still want me after seeing me a sweaty, red-faced mess, not to mention, I must stink."

He pulled me close, wrapping his arm around my back. "I want you bad, Harper," he said in a husky tone that sent shivers down my spine.

And in that moment, I believed him, mess and all.

I wondered if I should tell him that I'd figured out who his girlfriend had been, but if he wanted me to know, he would have told me. No need to lay it out. Her identity didn't change anything.

We headed upstairs and showered together, then climbed into bed, no sex involved. As I drifted off, it hit me that this was more intimate than if we'd gone three rounds. Moments like this were the foundation of a relationship.

And, at least for now, I let myself want one with him.

Chapter 13

When I woke the next morning, James was still asleep. I lay in bed with him for about ten minutes, going over what had happened in the exercise room, feeling like I'd hallucinated it in an exercise-induced delirium.

But it had been real.

He was real. What we had was real.

I was self-aware enough to realize that I had trouble believing he could care about me because my parents had discarded me so easily. When we finished this case, I needed to find a therapist to help work through this. Otherwise, I'd forever be questioning James's feelings for me.

Presuming we had a future. But he talked like we did.

One day at a time. Just like dealing with my need for a drink.

One day at a time.

I grew restless and started to slide out of bed.

"Are you runnin' off again?" he teased from behind me.

"If you call getting up to pee running off, then yes." I got up and headed to the bathroom, completely naked. I didn't need to look behind me to know he was watching.

After I peed and brushed my teeth, I grabbed one of the plush hotel robes hanging on a hook and walked out to see him sitting up in bed, shirtless. I knew he wasn't wearing anything under the sheets either.

"I'm about to order room service," he said. "What are you in the mood for?"

"Coffee. Copious amounts of coffee," I said, walking over to the window. The way I'd behaved last night looked different in the daylight, and I was utterly embarrassed. I'd never been needy. Ever. And James was the last person I wanted to be needy with.

"What about food?"

"Whatever you're getting."

I heard him place a call for a double order of pancakes, bacon, eggs, orange juice, along with a carafe of coffee with creamer.

"How's your head today?" I asked, still not looking at him.

"It's still attached to my body, so I consider that a win," he said dryly.

I turned to look at him.

He tilted his head slightly. "There you are."

"Sorry about last night."

"Runnin' off? You should be." But his grin let me know he wasn't pissed. "About the rest… the only way this open shit will work is if we're honest about all of it."

I wanted to ask if he'd learned that from her too, but was smart enough to bite my tongue.

"I told you I have a therapist," he said as though reading my mind. "The past month or so we've been discussing rela-tionships."

Month or so? The timing of when we'd started working together couldn't be coincidental. Then again, when he'd been out of it with his concussion, he'd told me he'd been interested in me for much longer than I'd realized.

He climbed out of bed. "We need to come up with a plan for the day. I figured we'd track down some of my contacts this time." He walked into the bathroom, leaving the door open. "We'll start after breakfast."

"How happy will they be to see you?"

"About as happy as a cat in a bathtub." His voice was faint from the bathroom.

"Then what makes you think they'll talk to you?"

"I have my ways."

I knew he did. The question was how far he'd go to make them talk.

"Do you want to drive our car or call Alex?"

"I say we drive ourselves today," he said. "Carter has another car parked for us at a parking garage a few blocks away, so we can slip out the back door. Maybe save Alex for another time."

"If we're going to do some questionable activities, then it's probably better to not involve him anyway," I agreed.

He poked his head out of the door, his toothbrush in his hand. A twinkle filled his eyes. "Who said we were going to do anything questionable?"

I lifted a brow and gave him a pointed look.

He grinned and disappeared into the bathroom.

I was relieved things weren't awkward. We had work to do. Feelings would only get in the way.

When he walked out a few minutes later, he wore a pair of grey sweatpants and no shirt.

"So, who are your contacts?" I asked.

He sat down beside me and slung an arm along the back of the sofa. "I want to start with Miguel Herra. Last I heard, he owns All American Autobody. It's a body shop in south Little Rock."

"How do you know him?"

"He did a few jobs for Simmons over the last couple of decades."

I gave him a questioning look.

A dark look crossed his face. "He made a couple of cars disappear after the owners vanished."

"And you had a part in making the cars disappear?" I asked cautiously.

He gave me a sardonic look. "Allegedly."

"What about their owners?"

He shrugged.

I really didn't want to think of the implications of that.

"What do you hope to get from Miguel?"

"He got busted about ten years ago and served a few years in prison. He's out now and running a new shop. Supposedly legit. But he was the go-to guy back in the day, and I'd bet money he knows Gerald Knox or did some jobs for Gerry's father. I'm hoping he can give me the name of someone who currently works for Knox."

I took a moment. "And if he has a contact, we follow that lead. But what if he doesn't?"

He pursed his lips. "I have several more people I can track down, but I want to start with Miguel and see where it takes us."

"And Razor?" I asked. "How does he fit into all of this?"

"He's an enforcer. He did work for Simmons in the past, but last I heard, he was workin' freelance."

"If he was excited to hear there's a hit on you, then you must not have parted as friends."

"I wouldn't have called us enemies either. More like cautious acquaintances."

"You think he's done work for the Knoxes?"

"Maybe not in the past, but if I were Gerry Knox and knew I was comin' for him, I'd want the best of the best protecting me."

"And this Razor is the best of the best?"

"He used to be. He's always been a hothead, too quick to anger. But the last time I encountered him, he'd grown a little paunchier and liked his liquor a little too much."

"Don't we all," I muttered.

He gave me a surprised look, then the hint of a grin tipped up the corners of his mouth. "Unlike you, I hear it's dulled his usefulness."

I wasn't so sure my usefulness hadn't been dulled, but I saw no reason to point it out. "Why start with Miguel first and Razor second?"

"Because Razor can be unstable, depending on how drunk he is. I'd rather start with Miguel, who will probably shit his pants when I walk up but is unlikely to throw a punch or pull out a gun."

I frowned. "It sounds like these two guys could have some valuable information. Why didn't we start with them?"

"I wanted to see where your contacts took us." He shrugged. "I couldn't see Miguel until today, and I figured as late as it was, Razor would be drunk off his ass. Besides, I'd rather track Razor down in the daylight."

"So what's our overall plan?" I asked. "Sure, we're trying to gather information to pin this trafficking ring on Knox, but what are we planning to do *with* the information?"

His lips pursed together. "I haven't decided."

"Our goal is to stop Knox. But if he's eliminated, we both know someone will step up to take his place," I pointed out, not dwelling on what 'eliminated' would mean.

"That's why we're gonna bring it all down," he said matter-of-factly.

I did a double take. "That seems ambitious." Especially since these kinds of investigations typically took weeks or months.

He didn't respond.

"Let's say we get the evidence, don't you need to turn this information over to your contact and let them take care of it?"

He scowled. "I told you yesterday that they're leavin' it up to me."

I leveled him with a look. "And then you'll be free of them?"

He was still before he said, "That's the plan."

"You don't trust them?"

"I've been fucked over before. So, no."

"Then we need to come up with a plan that makes sure you're free of them," I said.

"We need to see what we can find before we can come up with a plan," he grunted.

That made sense, but I was still frustrated. "You know, I might be able to actually help with the plan if you'd tell me who gave you this assignment."

He didn't respond.

Frustration roiled in my gut, but I bit back the urge to argue with him. It was obvious he wasn't ready to share this part. Not yet, at least.

"Fine," I groaned, getting up off the sofa. "Keep it to yourself, but you'll have to tell me at some point." I started to walk past him, but he snagged my wrist, pulling me to a halt.

His gaze held mine. "I need you to be patient with me."

The tension in my shoulders eased. "I wouldn't be here if I wasn't. But you know I'll need to know at some point."

"I know."

I gave a nod and then grabbed a change of clothes from my bag. I headed to the bathroom and shut the door, needing a moment alone to sort through my feelings. His initial plan for the day was solid, and it made sense for us to see what he could find from the autobody shop owner before we planned our next steps.

Room service showed up soon afterward. James ate a

hearty breakfast, but I only had two cups of coffee and a few bites of eggs and pancakes. James changed into jeans and a short-sleeve black T-shirt, then we both strapped on our over-the-shoulder holsters, donned our jackets, and left the room.

We headed out the door, down the back stairwell, and out the back entrance. I let James take the lead, heading the opposite direction we'd gone the night before.

After we walked several blocks, James dipped into a parking garage, then climbed the stairs to the top level. It was mostly empty, so the dark sedan was easy to spot. He reached under the trunk and pulled a key fob out, and a couple of minutes later, we were driving out of the garage.

"How long have you been working on this?" I asked.

He shot me a quick glance, then turned back to the road. "You'll have to be more specific."

I glared at him. "You know what I'm talking about."

His lips pressed into a thin line. "It depends on how you look at it. I made a few half-hearted attempts the first year after I was released. I told my handler I had to get settled into my new life and that no one was gonna trust me fresh out of prison. The second year, I made a little more effort. My handler was makin' noise that they were gonna toss me back in prison and reinstate my charges. Over the past six months or so, I've gotten a little more aggressive."

"Why the last six months?"

He hesitated. "I'd put out a few feelers the two years before and asked a few people to contact me if they heard anything. A couple of them started pingin' me last fall."

An uneasy feeling settled in my stomach. "When last fall?"

"Late September, then it intensified in early October." He turned to glance at me.

I didn't respond.

"One of my sources said he heard that there was a shipment arriving early October, but he wasn't sure where or who was even runnin' it. I tried to check into it, but it was vague enough that I couldn't find anything of substance. Then he turned up dead a few days later."

"Someone killed him?" I asked, unsettled.

"The official report was drug overdose, but he'd been clean for a good five years. It seemed mighty suspicious."

"And the other source?" I asked.

"He disappeared."

"Shit."

"Yep," he said with a grimace.

"Are you worried something might happen to the people we talk to today?"

"It's crossed my mind."

"So what do you want to do?" I asked, wondering if I'd endangered my own contacts.

"We talk to 'em anyway."

I studied him to see if he looked as okay with that as he sounded. The expression on his face confirmed he wasn't.

"It took you nearly two years to bring down the Hardshaw Group, between infiltrating them and working with them?" I said.

His hands tightened on the steering wheel. "Yep."

"We don't have nearly two years."

"I know," he said, sounding exhausted.

"Okay, best case scenario," I said. "In your opinion, what do we need to take this operation out?"

"Best case?" He seemed to consider my request for a long moment. "Solid evidence to tie this to all the key people involved."

"And then we turn it over to your handler?"

He was quiet again before he said, "I'll tell them what I've got, then see how they want it handled."

I couldn't believe he was finally admitting to working with

the Feds. "You said they were giving you a lot of leeway on how to do things."

"True, but I learned from the first go-around with the Feds that you have to read between the lines."

"What does that mean?"

"It means I don't trust them worth shit, so I'll make a moment-by-moment call."

"What kind of evidence are you looking for?"

"Guess we'll know it when we see it," he said solemnly.

"So we're shooting in the dark?"

"I'm a pretty good shot. Even in the dark." He gave me a pointed look. "So are you."

While I was sure the latter part was in reference to my shoot-out last week, I suspected it had a double meaning. James couldn't have gotten to the level he'd reached without trusting his instincts, and we were following those at the moment.

Because, right now, that was all we had.

Chapter 14

All American Autobody had a couple of beat-up looking cars in the parking lot, and several more behind a four-foot chain link fence. James shut off the engine and reached for the door handle.

"Do we have a plan?" I asked.

"Nope. We'll just wing it and see how it goes."

"Okay."

He gave me a questioning look.

"You gave me full leeway with my contacts," I said. "I'll do the same with yours."

He gave me a slight smile, then opened the door.

When we walked through the entrance, a twenty-something guy greeted us from behind the counter. "Hey, guys. You got an appointment?"

"We need to talk to Miguel," James said in an ominous tone.

The employee's eyes widened, and he glanced between James and me. "What about?"

"That's between me and Miguel."

The guy swallowed and took a step back. "I'll see if he's here yet."

James shot a glance at me, and I got the message loud and clear. With a nod, I walked out of the front door and around the side of the building, skirting the six-foot chain-link fence that circled the back. There was a solid chance Miguel would run. I didn't know what Miguel looked like, but I suspected it wouldn't be hard to figure out—he'd be the guy running.

Sure enough, about ten seconds later, the back door burst open and a middle-aged man with dark hair ran out, heading for a vintage baby blue Mustang convertible.

"Going somewhere, Miguel?" I called over to him.

He stopped in his tracks and spun to face me through the fence, about thirty feet away. Shock covered his face. "You're still workin' with him?"

He'd heard of me? Maybe he did know something about Knox.

"Haven't you heard?" I asked good-naturedly. "Women are just as capable as men."

He ran for his car and started to open the door when James rounded the corner of the building with purposeful strides.

"He's running," I said dryly.

"Is that so?" James asked as he smoothly drew his gun from beneath his jacket and faced the fence. He held the gun at his side, pointed at the ground, but the threat was clear.

Miguel froze. "You're gonna shoot me, Malcolm?" he cried out in disbelief.

"Not you," James said. "But I *was* thinking of havin' a little target practice with your car."

"You wouldn't dare!" Miguel cried out.

James shrugged.

Miguel stood next to his open car door, presumably weighing his options.

"We only want to talk," I said, hoping I wasn't encroaching on James's plan.

Miguel's face reddened and his voice shook with anger. "The last time Malcolm just wanted to talk, I walked away with a broken nose."

"That's not true," James said conversationally. "I've seen you at least twice since then, and we both know you had it comin'."

"What if I guarantee you won't have any broken bones?" I said.

Miguel kept his gaze on James. "There's a whole lot he can do without breakin' bones."

I tossed James an expectant look.

He ignored me, keeping his focus on Miguel. "As long as you cooperate, there won't be any need to touch you."

"That's the problem," Miguel said, still hovering next to the open car door. "Your definition of cooperation and mine are usually different."

"Is that your decision?" James said, lifting the gun at his side. "We've escalated to the point where I convince you to cooperate by shooting at your pride and joy? Because we both know you're gonna talk to me. It's just a matter of how much damage I cause before it happens."

Miguel's face scrunched with rage before he slammed the car door. "Fuck you, Malcolm."

James waved to the padlocked fence. "How about you open the gate?"

"I don't have the key," Miguel said, still standing next to the car as though he still might change his mind.

"Then how were you plannin' on leavin'?" James asked. "Plowing through the fence?"

Miguel scowled at the proof that he hadn't thought his getaway plan through. "Go around the front. We'll talk in the waiting room."

"Your office seems more suitable," James said.

Miguel took several slow steps toward the fence. "I don't know shit, Malcolm."

"You don't even know what I want to talk about," James said smoothly.

"Whatever it is, I don't know."

"I'll guess we'll see if that's true." James grabbed the gate and rattled it, making the padlock clang against the metal. "Now open the gate, because there's no way in hell I'm walking around front to play this game again."

Miguel walked over, holding the set of keys in his hand. Obviously, he'd been prepared to leave in a hurry. He reached for the padlock and inserted a key, his hands shaking slightly, then took off the padlock. He gave James an expectant look.

"You gonna invite us in?" James asked, nodding to the latch holding the gate closed.

"For fuck's sake," Miguel grumbled, then lifted the latch and pulled the gate open.

He cringed as James strode through, as though he expected to be physically assaulted, but James just said, "Lead the way."

Miguel shot me a look, obviously curious about my involvement. I suspected James had worked solo since his release from prison, and Miguel had made it clear it was out of the ordinary for a woman to be accompanying him.

After Miguel closed the gate—not locking the padlock—he stomped toward the back door, leaving us to follow. Inside, three cars were in all three bays, in various states of bodywork. James had shoved his gun back into its holster, but his persona still reeked of intimidation. Two of the workers sent us nervous glances, but the third kept his face buried under the hood of the car he was working on. I suspected it was purposeful.

Miguel opened another door, and we followed him down a short hall into a small office.

An industrial metal desk was pushed against the wall to the

left, with an office chair shoved underneath. A cheap metal bookshelf lined the back wall, perpendicular to the desk, full of what looked to be schematic manuals for cars and trucks. A metal chair with a cracked vinyl seat sat next to the end of the desk.

"Have a seat, Mig." James motioned to the desk chair. He nodded for me to take the other one.

I sat, but Miguel was more hesitant to move.

"This is just a chat," James said in an amicable tone. "It can be as friendly or unfriendly as you like."

It was already off to a rocky start, but no doubt it could get a hell of a lot worse.

Miguel pulled out the desk chair, his hands shaking even more, and took a seat, casting a glance at me. "I heard you wore all black."

I narrowed my eyes in confusion. Did he know who I was? And while my clothing choice ran on the dull side, I'd worn a lot of gray and navy.

"We're not here to discuss her wardrobe choices," James barked.

Miguel started to say something, then stopped, his whole body shaking now.

"Mig, why're you so nervous to see me?" James asked, leaning his shoulder against the wall in a relaxed pose.

"The last time I saw you—"

"The last time I saw you, we parted on friendly terms," he said. "So try again."

Miguel swallowed. "Word on the street is you're a dead man walkin'. I don't want to get caught in the crossfire." He hesitated. "Or let people think we're workin' together."

James's eyebrows lifted in a barely perceptible movement, as though he was only slightly interested in this information. "You don't say. Who made the threat?"

Miguel inhaled sharply. "Dunno."

James tilted his head. "I call bullshit. Try again." His tone was deceptively friendly, making his order more ominous. "I mean, if you don't want anyone to think we're workin' together, you'd definitely know who you're hopin' to keep the information from."

Miguel shook his head, looking like he was about to be sick, but kept silent.

James's eyes stayed trained on the man in the chair. "Try again." His voice took on an authoritative tone.

"I don't know!" Miguel shouted, beads of sweat breaking out on his forehead.

James crossed his arms over his chest. "Then how do you know there's a hit out on me?"

"Rumors."

"And where did you hear these rumors?"

Miguel swallowed hard. "I don't wanna get anyone in trouble."

James stared him down. "If the person who told you didn't put the hit on me, then neither of you have anything worry about. At least not from me."

Miguel's gaze shifted to me.

"She's not a threat either," James said. "Unless you become a threat to either of us."

Miguel gave me a questioning look, but I didn't react, unsure if I was the good guy or bad guy in this scenario.

"Don't make me ask again," James said in a low growl.

Miguel jumped. "I heard it from Stewie a couple of days ago."

"The Stewie who used to work for you? How'd he find out?"

He took a deep breath. "He's working for Dave Birch at his shop now. Birch Autobody."

I'd heard rumors that Birch Autobody was also a suspected chop shop, but I'd never had any contact with the place.

"And Stewie just called to tell you?" James asked. "Like a hot piece of gossip?"

Miguel's face paled. "No, Dave hosts a weekly poker game. He and Stewie both knew about it, but I don't know any details."

"You're tellin me that Dave Birch and Stewie Crimshaw told you there's a hit on my head, and you weren't the least bit curious about who'd taken it out or why? No questions asked? They just dropped the info, and you played your hand as if they'd told you the weather forecast."

Miguel swallowed.

"Okay," James said with a heavy sigh, pushing away from the wall. "Let's try again."

Miguel shot me a pleading look.

I lifted a brow and said firmly. "I didn't tell you who ordered it, so don't look at me."

Miguel's chest rose and fell.

James took a step closer to him. "Remember the part where you cooperate and I don't touch you? This is an example of *not* cooperating."

"This is gonna blow back on me," Miguel spat out. "And I don't want any part of it. I'm legit now, Malcolm."

"If you're legit, then the guy who ordered the hit won't suspect the information came from you, now will he?" James asked.

"You're not gonna tell him?"

"I plan to make the asshole sorry he dared to cross me," James sneered. "All I want is his name. He'll never know how I found out, because unlike you, Dave, and Stewie, *I'm not a goddamned gossip*." His statement ended with a menacing tone.

Uncertainty filled Miguel's eyes, quickly followed by fear.

"And since you all are a bunch of fucking gossips, *I know* you know who ordered the hit. So don't for one fucking minute believe I'm going to walk out of here without a name."

Miguel's breath started to come in quick pants.

"And let's be clear," James added. "If I find out you gave me the *wrong* name, I *will* be back to make you pay for your lack of cooperation."

Miguel looked like he was about to shit his pants. "Dave said it was Gerry Knox."

It wasn't a surprise, but it still sent a chill down my back.

James gave a slight nod. "Why does Gerry Knox want me dead?"

Miguel vigorously shook his head. "I dunno."

"And what is good old Gerry up to these days?"

"I don't know shit," he said, panicking. "I only know what I heard about the hit, and now you know too."

"You expect me to believe you or your dad never worked for Knox or his daddy when he was runnin' things back in the day?"

"You never said nothing about Gerry's daddy," Miguel grumbled.

"Read between the lines, Mig," James said. "You're very familiar with the Knox family."

"Rutherford Knox, sure," he said, a bead of sweat dripping down the side of his face. "But that was before I went legit. His son had moved onto Birch by the time I got out of prison."

James gave another nod. "Who told Dave and Stewie about the hit?"

"I don't know," Miguel said in a rush, "but you could talk to Dave. He'll tell you."

James gave him a dubious look. "So I'm gonna roll up to Birch Autobody, and Dave's gonna tell me more about Knox?"

Miguel looked like he was about to be sick. "I guess."

"And when I leave here, you're just gonna go back to work and pretend this never happened?"

"Yeah," Miguel said, shaking his head vigorously. "I swear."

James made a face. "Why wouldn't you call your buddies, Dave and Stewie, and let them know I'm on my way to pay 'em a visit?"

"We're not that close," Miguel said, a panicky look filling his eyes.

"But close enough for them to fill you in on the hot gossip. At your weekly poker game."

Miguel swallowed again.

"Maybe you could give him a call now," James said in a deceptively calm tone, motioning to the phone on his desk. "And put it on speaker."

Miguel started shaking again.

"What's got you worried, Miguel?" James asked.

"I don't wanna get Dave or Stewie in trouble either."

"No one has to know we got *anything* from 'em," James said. "That's the beauty of you makin' this call. Your friend will be none the wiser, and Knox'll never know where I got the information."

Miguel's gaze landed on the phone. "What am I supposed to say? It's gonna be weird as fuck if I call one of 'em up and ask about the hit on you."

James shrugged. "Then I guess you better think of something creative, so you don't look weird as fuck."

Miguel seemed to consider it for a moment, then patted his jeans pocket. "I need my cell phone. That's where I have the shop's number."

James slipped his gun out of his holster and trained it on him. "Go ahead."

Miguel kept his eyes on the gun as he stood slightly and tugged out his cell phone. He sat back down and tapped on his phone to wake it up and open his contacts.

"Let me see the contact's name before you place the call," James said in a demanding tone.

Miguel pulled up the contact, then turned the shaky phone to show Birch Autobody in the screen.

"Set it on the desk and place the call, puttin' it on speaker," James said. "But if you tip off whoever you talk to that I'm standin' here listening, our cooperative agreement will be null and void and I won't hesitate to *touch* you." He leaned closer and lowered his voice. "And you'll wish all you had was a busted nose."

Miguel gave a slight nod, then pressed the send button. The phone rang several times before a man answered. "Birch Autobody."

"Dave?" Miguel said, his voice quivering slightly. "It's Miguel."

"What's up? You needin' a part?"

"No… I was telling my guys about the hit on Malcolm."

"What the fuck, Mig?" Dave snapped. "I told you that was confidential information."

"It just slipped out," Miguel said, shooting James a glare. "One of 'em was tellin' me how much he hates Skeeter Malcolm, and I told him he might not have to worry about him for much longer."

"You still shouldn't be spreadin' it around," Dave said, calming down a little. "Razor'll take my head off if he finds out I told you."

I tried not to show a reaction to his mention of Razor. Maybe the criminal world was smaller than I'd thought. But now we had a direct link to Knox.

"They don't even know I got the info from you," Miguel said. "You and I both know there's not a lot of love for Malcolm out there."

"That's the truth," Dave groused.

"But as much as a bunch of us want the bastard dead," Miguel continued, "I'm wondering why Knox has a hit on him. Last I heard, Malcolm was layin' low. Doesn't he have a bar down south?"

"Word is Malcolm insulted his mother."

James grabbed a paper and pen off the desk, then scratched, *How does Razor know?*

Miguel glared at the paper, then asked, "How'd Razor hear that?"

"What does it matter?" Dave shot back.

Miguel glanced up at James, then dropped his gaze. "Just want to make sure it's accurate. Don't want to get our hopes up over nothin'."

"Razor did some jobs for Knox and heard it from one of his guys."

James wrote *Name?*

Miguel looked like he wanted to murder James himself. "What guy?"

"What the fuck, Miguel?" Dave demanded. "Why're you askin' so many questions?"

"Because everyone was sure the bastard was gone when he was locked up in federal prison several years ago, but he slunk out like a cockroach out of the shadows. I want to know that you have a reliable source."

"He's one of Knox's drivers."

James tapped the word *Name?*

Miguel swallowed again. "Was it Tate?"

"Tate? I don't know Tate. Razor said it was Nixon. Nixon called to hire him as reinforcement with a delivery for Knox, and while he was on the line, Nixon told him to be on the lookout for the asshole, and if he sees him, shoot first and ask questions later." Dave released a low chuckle. "That is, if one of Knox's guys doesn't get to Malcolm first."

Miguel's finger hovered over the end call button. He gave James a questioning look.

James wrote *who took the job?*

Miguel shook his head, but James stabbed the sentence with this index finger.

"Knox hired it out?" he said. "Who took the job?"

"How the fuck would I know?" Dave spat out. "What's up with all the questions?"

"I just want to make sure I'm out of the line of fire," Miguel said.

"That shouldn't be a problem since Malcolm's down in southern Arkansas."

Miguel glanced up at James, who slowly shook his head in warning.

"Yeah," Miguel said. "He's down south, but if he comes up here, I hope Nixon offs him and gets a bonus." Then he ended the call.

James stared down at Miguel. "Who's Tate?"

"I don't know," Miguel said. "I made it up."

"So why didn't Dave call you on it?"

"Dunno."

"Bullshit. What do you know about Knox's deliveries?"

"I'm tellin' you I don't know shit about nothin'. Not since I came back and went legit."

A vein in James's forehead began to throb and he said through clenched teeth, "This is uncooperative, Miguel."

"I don't know!" Miguel shouted, his eyes wide. "I swear to God! Rumor has it that Knox is movin' girls, but I swear I don't know shit about anything."

And there was Knox's link to trafficking. But if this had been hush-hush before, and James had trouble getting any information last year, why did someone like Miguel know about it now?

James lowered his gun and patted Miguel on the cheek with a hard smack. "Good job. Sorry you won't get your wish to see me dead."

"The day's young, Malcolm," Miguel spat out with a

defiant glare.

James cocked a brow and gave him a hard stare. "Am I gonna have to watch my back on my way out, Mig? Should I eliminate any threat from you now, so I don't have to give you a second thought?"

Miguel's face paled. "My guys saw you walk in. If you kill me, they'll know it was you."

"But will they tell the cops it was me?" James asked in a dull tone. "Or will they claim they don't know anything?"

Miguel swallowed.

"That's what I thought." James reached for the doorknob behind him, still keeping his eye on the man at the desk. "I have no beef with you, Mig. Let's keep it that way."

Miguel gave a sharp nod of agreement, but he didn't look happy about it.

James opened the door and backed into the hall, keeping his eye on Miguel. I got up and did the same.

"Have a nice day, Miguel," I said cheerfully as I rounded the corner, not waiting for a response.

We headed to the waiting room and then outside. Once we were in the car, James started the engine and pulled out of the parking lot. Frowning, he said, "I'm waitin' on your critique of my interrogation methods."

I turned to him in surprise. "Are you expecting me to blast you for your threats? You don't have a badge. Miguel needed an incentive to talk. You threatened him, but you didn't hurt him. He bought your bluff."

"Nothin' I said was a bluff, Harper," he said in a dark tone. "I would have followed through on any of it."

I took a moment to let that sink in, trying to determine how I felt about it. I didn't believe in torture, and as far as I was concerned, harming someone during an interview or interrogation was torture. Not to mention it was unreliable. Still, I knew James was capable of getting results, which meant I needed to let him do as he saw fit. Then again, I hadn't witnessed him hurt anyone other than the man who had killed my sister nearly twenty years ago. Yes, he'd killed men since we'd met, and if I believed in vigilante justice, they had all deserved it.

I suppose I'd become an accessory.

But I was already a perpetrator of several murders, and even though I'd shot those men in self-defense, I doubted law enforcement would see it that way. Especially if they learned who my companion had been. To be honest, when I was a detective, I probably wouldn't have let myself off either.

I held his gaze. "As long as you don't hurt any innocents, for now, I'll follow your lead."

Surprise flashed in his eyes. "Okay."

"You expected a lecture?"

He made a face. "I expected you to set a line you refuse to cross."

"It sounds like we just got confirmation Knox is selling and abusing human beings, and from where I'm sitting, we're the only ones trying to stop him." I paused. "But if I get recognized—or you for that matter—we'll have to make some decisions."

The corner of his mouth tipped up, and an amused glint filled his eyes. "Like which non-extradition country we're movin' to?"

"Know anyone who makes fake passports real enough to get us out of the country?" I teased.

"Got it covered," he said.

My grin fell. "Wait. I was kidding."

"I'm not."

I considered what he'd said. Would I really run, if it came down to it? Or would I turn myself in?

What did it say about me that I leaned toward running?

Chapter 15

"Is our next move finding Razor?"

"Not yet. I have another idea."

When he didn't volunteer the information, I asked sarcastically, "Care to enlighten me?"

The corner of his mouth twitched. "Sorry. I'm used to working alone."

"Or bossing people around," I said in a dry tone.

A hint of a grin lifted his lips. "That too." He slung one hand over a steering wheel as he turned a corner. "I want to drop in on an accountant."

"An accountant?" I asked in surprise, but it actually made sense. If we were collecting evidence, we could possibly get racketeering or tax evasion charges brought against Knox. "So you *are* turning this over to your handler."

He pushed out a heavy breath. "I'm not sure yet."

"Is this about covering our bases?"

"Yeah."

"I'd feel more comfortable if you laid all your cards on the table."

His hand twisted on the steering wheel, indecision on his

face, before he said, "I'm working with someone in Homeland Security. That's all I can tell you right now."

I took a moment to process that. Homeland Security. Most people associated them with immigration enforcement, but they covered so much more. Like human trafficking. It actually made sense.

"How'd you get hooked up with Homeland Security?"

He grunted. "What part of *that's all I can tell you right now* did you not understand?"

I ignored him and asked, "Did you work with them on the Hardshaw takedown?"

He shot me a dark glare.

"I'm gonna take that as a yes," I said in a smug tone.

His glare turned icy.

I considered everything he'd told me about what he was doing for them. Things weren't adding up. "I can't imagine HSI would let you decide whether to eliminate the organization or turn over the evidence to them."

He was silent for several seconds before he said, "Does it matter what we do with it? All that matters is the end result."

Funny, half a year ago, I would have completely disagreed with that. Now, I wasn't so sure. I still didn't buy his explanation, not totally, but I wasn't sure how to handle it. I decided to let it go for now.

He drove in silence, his body rigid with tension. About ten minutes later, he pulled into the parking lot next to a brick house that had been converted into an office space. The sign over the entrance read Morrow and Crowe, Public CPA.

I turned to James as he put the car in park. "Who are we meeting?"

"Natalie Crowe. She used to do J.R. Simmons's books."

I stared at him in surprise. "And she didn't get caught up in the mess when he was arrested?"

"She wasn't his only CPA. She mostly handled his illegal

stuff, and Simmons took a lot of secrets to his grave. Still, the Feds seized most of his bank accounts and his properties, so it makes sense they'd know about Natalie. She was never arrested, though, so I wonder if she worked out some kind of deal."

"Will she recognize you?"

He made a face. "Most likely. We've met before."

"So I should expect some hostility?"

"Animosity is more likely, but I guess we'll find out soon enough." He opened the door and got out of the car.

I did the same and then followed him to the entrance.

He walked up to the receptionist's desk, and a woman who looked to be in her thirties glanced up at him with a bright smile. "Can I help you?"

"I need to speak to Ms. Crowe."

She frowned and glanced at her computer screen. "I'm sorry. I don't see that she has any appointments right now."

"We're a drop-in," James said good-naturedly. "I suspect she'll want to see me."

The receptionist didn't look as certain. "And your name is?"

"Jonathan Wiseman."

She picked up her phone and punched in several numbers. "Natalie, I have a Jonathan Wiseman here to see you." She was silent for a long moment before she hung up. "She says to go on back. It's the third door on the right."

"Thanks," James said, then glanced back at me before heading down the hall, leaving me to follow.

Where had that name come from? His tenure with Simmons? He must have known it would work.

He stopped outside the room and knocked. To my surprise, he waited for a faint "come in," before he opened the door.

I followed him into a bright office with multiple plants in front of two windows on the far wall. A woman who looked to be in her late forties sat behind a dark wood desk. A desktop computer was arranged on one side of the L-shaped desk, while a stack of folders waited on the other.

The woman's gaze narrowed on James as he entered the room and sat in the far guest chair in front of the desk. She stared at him as though he was a specter from her past.

He probably was.

I shut the door behind me and sat in the chair next to him. Her gaze shifted to me with a look of surprise, then back to James.

"*Jonathan*," she said in a tone that made it clear she knew it wasn't his name. "I never expected to see you again."

He sat back in the chair, resting both his forearms on the chair arms. "I suppose you didn't."

"Our mutual friend is long gone. There's no reason for you to be here."

"That may be true, but I still have a few questions."

She shook her head. "I don't have any answers. I told the FBI everything I knew. If you want answers, get the case file."

"Not about Simmons."

She went quiet, her eyes shifting as though she was trying to jump two steps ahead of him. "I left that life behind, and we both know I would have parted ways with him years before he died if he would have let me."

"I'm not here about Simmons," James repeated, but to my surprise there was a gentleness in his tone.

"Okay," she said, sitting back a little, but her body was tighter than a bowstring. "What are you here for?"

"I want to know if you've heard of Gerald Knox."

Her face remained blank, but her breath became a little more erratic.

I wasn't surprised that James picked up on it too.

He leaned forward slightly. "Natalie, I don't think you're mixed up in anything. I know you wanted out when Simmons was using you. But I also know you had contact with other accountants—"

"I don't know anything, James," she whisper-hissed. "I purposely stay far away from anyone in that world."

He nodded slightly and sat back, his face softening. "Has anyone approached you, asking you to do their books?"

She released a harsh laugh. "Like anyone would trust me after the Feds got a search warrant for my computer."

James cracked a knowing smile. "We both know they didn't get everything."

Her gaze dropped to the desk, but she didn't respond.

"You played it smart, Nat," he said approvingly.

Her eyes lifted, suddenly filled with fear. "Maybe not smart enough."

James lifted his hands in surrender. "I'm not here about that. I swear."

She didn't look like she believed him.

"I'm looking for Gerald Knox's accountant."

She shook her head. "I never did Gerald Knox's books. I never did his father's either."

So, she knew about Knox and his father. If that was a surprise to James, he didn't let on. "I'm sure you had your hands full with Simmons. But sometimes professionals are connected with one another." He turned his head slightly as he watched her.

"I haven't talked to those people in years, James. And when I *did* talk to them, it was never by choice."

"I know," he said softly. "And I wouldn't ask this of you, but I found out Knox is trafficking girls. Teenagers. And from what I've gathered, it's not a small operation."

Her eyes widened and turned glassy.

"I'm not asking you to reach out to anyone," he continued. "But I know you know names. Tell me who reached out to you in the past, and I'll find out the name of Knox's accountant myself."

"Why his accountant?" she asked with a hint of defiance.

"You know why," he said softly. "Look at what the Feds did to Simmons's money."

"Simmons was dead by the time they got to me."

"It doesn't matter. I know you wanted out, but Simmons made it impossible. Maybe Knox's accountant feels the same way. Maybe he or she will be willing to cooperate so they can be free too."

"You think his accountant will be free?" she asked sarcastically. "The only reason I'm free is because Simmons is dead."

James sat back in his seat. "What if Knox was dead too?"

She stared at him like he'd announced he was the new pope. "How is that going to happen?"

"You don't need to worry about that part," James said. "And this is all hypothetical. I'm just sayin' … would the accountant be more willing to talk if Knox wasn't an issue?"

She shook her head in frustration. "I have no idea. I don't know who they are or if they feel threatened. But I know it was easier for me to cooperate with the FBI knowing the boogeyman wouldn't be waiting around the corner to get me."

James gave a slight nod.

"I hear Knox is big," she said in a near whisper. "Bigger than J.R."

"I don't know about that," James said nonchalantly. "I know he's up to worse shit, but I don't know about bigger."

"Knox is more dangerous."

James pushed out a sigh. "I don't know about that either. Simmons committed quite a few crimes he never took credit for. He didn't approve of his son's girlfriend, so he hired someone to kill her in a pretty brutal way. He had his daughter's boyfriend killed too."

Natalie looked like she was going to be sick.

James sat back in his seat. "So J.R. *was* dangerous. He just didn't flaunt it like Knox does."

"All the more reason for me to keep quiet," she said. "If I play a part in finding Knox's accountant, when he finds out, he'll make an example out of me."

"If he's out of the picture, he won't be able to come after you either."

"You're saying you're going to kill him?" she asked in disbelief.

James held his hands out. "I never said any such thing. But you never know when someone's going to meet with an accident."

Natalie rested her face in her hands.

"I know this is scary," James said gently. "And I really wouldn't be here if it wasn't important. And believe me, I know me bein' here puts you at risk." He paused. "If you're really worried, I can have a detail watch over you until this is over."

Her head jerked upright. "Why would you do that?"

"I have no beef with you, Nat. I always knew you got suckered into working for J.R. You weren't the first to fall under his spell, and you weren't the last. Hell, I fell for it too."

"You?" she scoffed.

"Yep. I fell for his bullshit hook, line, and sinker. Until I wised up."

"I took too long to wise up. He had me doing legit stuff in the beginning, and then he gave me something questionable— but insisted everything was on the up and up. By the time I realized what was really going on, he told me I was in too deep to quit. That he'd ruin me." Her breath caught. "I have two kids. I couldn't risk ruining my professional reputation, so I kept doing his books."

"He wouldn't have stopped at ruining your reputation,"

James said. "He would have had you killed. He wouldn't risk his secrets gettin' out."

She inhaled sharply.

"You didn't realize that?" he asked.

"I'd always suspected, but I told myself I was over-reacting."

"You weren't," he said flatly. "But Simmons is gone. He can't hurt you. And I'll make sure Knox won't hurt you either. I'll have a team watching you within the hour."

"You mean for a price," she said bitterly.

"No," James said, holding her gaze. "I've possibly put you at risk, and that's not fair to you or your family. I'll make sure you're protected until this is all said and done."

Disbelief covered her face. "That could be months … years."

"But if you can get me the accountant's name," James said as he stood, "this will take days. You have my word."

"You can't guarantee that," she said in a bitter tone.

I had to agree with her there.

"You hold up your end, and I'll hold up mine." He started for the door, leaving me to follow. "My attorney, Carter Hale, will be in contact with you within the next half hour about your security detail."

"I don't know that I'll be able to get the accountant's name." Panic filled her voice. "What happens if I can't get it?"

He paused, his hand on the doorknob, as he turned to face her. "Are you asking if I'll pull your detail if you don't get it? No. But like I said, the sooner I get that name, the sooner the potential threat to you is gone."

He opened the door, and she called out, "Why are you being so nice to me?"

He gave her a sad smile. "Because J.R. Simmons put you in a difficult situation that wasn't your doin'. By showin' up here today, there's a chance I tossed you back in it. You didn't deserve it before, and you sure as hell don't deserve it now. But I wouldn't put you at risk if I didn't think you could help."

"And if I get the name," she said. "What do I do then? How do I contact you?"

"Carter's gonna give you his contact info. You pass the information on to him and he'll tell me."

Then he left the room.

I started to follow, but Natalie called after me, "Who are you, and why are you with James Malcolm?"

I realized neither one of them had addressed the fact I was there, and James had never introduced me.

"We have the same goal—to shut Knox down."

She squinted at me. "You look familiar. Who are you?"

"I'm Harper Adams," I said, preparing myself for her potential disgust. "You probably saw me on the news."

Surprise flickered in her eyes. "The police officer who shot that boy. Did you really shoot him?"

I drew in a breath. "Yeah, I shot him, but he really did have a gun."

She nodded, pressing her lips together. "You must have really pissed one or more of your coworkers off to get them to set you up like that."

"You believe he had a gun?"

She made a face. "I know how some of those detectives work."

I did a double take. "What do you mean?"

"Simmons had some on his payroll. He had state police on his payroll too." When she saw my look of disbelief, she added, "Honey, I wrote the checks. We called it donations or some other nonsense, but I knew exactly what they were—bribes."

I stared at her in shock for a few seconds before I came to my senses. "Do you remember any of the detectives' names?"

She shook her head. "No."

I didn't believe her, but I couldn't bring myself to threaten someone who'd been caught in a mess that was out of their control. I started to walk out the door.

"What did you do to piss them off?" she asked.

I turned back. "Why do you think I pissed them off?"

A grim smile twisted her lips. "I may just be the accountant, but I've heard things. They had cops on the payroll to look the other way or help things along, but every so often, there'd be a cop who asked too many questions or refused to go along with what Simmons wanted." She paused a beat. "They usually didn't last long."

"He got them fired?" I asked.

"Or killed."

I stared at her, then shut the door. This wasn't a conversation that should be overheard. "I can't see how they could get away with killing a cop in the line of duty."

She released a bitter laugh. "Harper, that would be too suspicious. They usually took care of it when they were off the clock. A heart attack or a car accident. I'm pretty sure one guy 'accidentally' fell off a ladder." She used air quotes around accidentally. "When I heard about your case, I instantly thought you'd pissed someone off. Maybe it wasn't planned, but they sure saw an opportunity and took advantage of it."

While I'd come to believe that I'd been set up, Natalie Crowe's evaluation threw me.

"What?" she asked with a bitter laugh. "You don't believe me?"

I shook my head as I came back to my senses. "No. I believe you. I'm still trying to wrap my head around it."

"This seriously never occurred to you?" she asked in disbelief.

"Not the way you put it."

"Girl, you better watch your back," she said. "As big as Gerald Knox is, he's bound to have cops on his own payroll—probably the same ones Simmons used. If they find out you're trying to bust the source of their bonus money, they won't stop until you do."

A shiver ran down my spine. "Thanks. I think."

She folded her hands on the desk in front of her. "I'll see if I can dig up some of the cops' names, but it might take me a while. I hid Simmons's involvement with the police from the Feds. That information may not be readily accessible now."

"Why didn't you hand it over?"

"Because there was every chance the agents I was dealing with were dirty. Maybe they weren't on J.R.'s payroll, but they could have been on Knox's or someone else's. It's hard to trust anyone with a badge when you realize how many cops are working for drug czars and crime lords."

I grimaced. "How many are we talking about?"

"Depends on if you're talking about street cops or detectives. The higher level? I'd say five to ten percent."

I gasped. "No."

She made a face. "I'll try to get access to those records. We'll see if you recognize any of the names."

"Thanks," I said, still shocked at her admission.

"Yeah. I'll pass this info on to Carter too."

I nodded in acknowledgment, then left her office to catch up to James, my mind still reeling.

Chapter 16

I found James on the sidewalk in front of the building, his phone pressed to his ear. He glanced up at me with a frown and said into the phone, "Keep me updated." He lowered the phone and ended the call.

"Was that Carter?" I asked.

"Yeah. He says he'll have two guys here within the hour, with twenty-four-hour surveillance. They'll be unobtrusive, so they shouldn't hinder her movement, but she'll have a panic button to press should she need them in her office or home."

"That can't be cheap."

He made a face as he shrugged. "I'm not gonna toss her to the wolves."

"Do you really think she's being watched?"

"Honestly, probably not, but I'd rather be safe than sorry. Especially if she starts asking questions and makes someone suspicious." He glanced toward the door. "Let's get out of here and reduce the risk of anyone realizing I paid her a visit."

I couldn't ignore the difference between the two visits. He hadn't been above physically hurting Miguel to get what he wanted, but he was going to great lengths to protect the accountant. I suspected he was doing it because she'd been dragged into the situation unwillingly. That only verified what I already knew about him—while he didn't suffer assholes, he did his best to protect the innocent or mostly innocent.

We headed over to the car, and he didn't waste any time pulling out of the parking lot.

"What took you so long to come out?" he asked with a slight chill in his voice.

"Natalie stopped me. She asked why I was with you."

He cast a sidelong glance in my direction before turning back toward the road. "What did you tell her?"

"The truth. We're working together to bring down Gerald Knox and save a lot of girls." I waited for a beat. "She knew who I was."

"And?" he prodded.

"She said I must have pissed someone off or gotten in someone's way for them to set me up like that."

His head jutted back in surprise. "She believed you?"

"Yeah, when she heard about the shooting, her first thought was that I'd pissed someone off. She thinks they used the situation to their advantage. She said I was lucky. She claims other cops who have gotten in the way or didn't cooperate have been killed."

"How do you think they got away with killin' cops?" He glanced at me again. "Did you notice a pattern?"

I shook my head. "No. I never suspected a thing. She said the cops were killed off duty, and it sounds like a lot of their deaths were made to look like accidents or natural causes."

"What do you make of it?"

I drew in a deep breath as I considered it. "Honestly, I don't know. She said she wrote checks to guys on the force who worked for J.R. Simmons. Yet she claims she doesn't remember any of their names."

"You don't believe her?"

I shook my head. "No. If I were an accountant writing checks to pay off cops, you can bet I'd remember all of them. But she said she might be able to dig up the records. She's going to let Carter know if she finds anything." I tilted my head as I turned to him. "What do you make of that?"

He pursed his lips. "She's holdin' out for something."

"Yeah, my thought too. But what?"

"To see if I follow through with protecting her?" he mused. "To see if she can find someone willing to pay to find out Harper Adams is looking into dirty cops?"

"You really think she's up to the latter?" I asked in surprise.

"If I were a bettin' man, I'd say no. But we'd be fools to not at least entertain the possibility."

A new thought occurred to me, and I gasped. "Oh… your guards will provide double duty, protecting her and watching to see who she contacts. That's part of the reason you're giving her a detail. To spy on her."

He made a face. "Like I said, I'd be a fool not to consider that she'll go to someone after my visit."

"Will your team surveil her phone calls? How will they get access?"

"Unfortunately, we're probably out of luck with the phone calls, but someone from the team will likely go into her office to introduce themselves and give her a panic button. If they're worth their salt, they'll find a way to install a camera in her office and possibly even the public spaces in her home. They might suggest it, and if she refuses, it's an additional reason to suspect she's gonna sell me out."

"Is that a real concern?" I asked in surprise. "I thought she was an innocent."

"She was an innocent when she got dragged into Simmons's world. But by the time he was killed, she was deep in it. I believe she wanted out, but I'm also sure the job came with lots of perks. Perks she likely doesn't have access to now."

He glanced at me. "Like I said to her, I suspect the Feds didn't get all the money."

"Yeah… do you figure she hid it for his family?"

"I thought so too at first, but I know Betsy Simmons is living much more frugally than she used to as J.R.'s wife. Once the Feds seized their property and bank accounts, she went to live with her parents. She's since remarried a lawyer in Little Rock, but their home is more modest than the mansion they had in El Dorado."

"And his son?" I asked hesitantly.

"Joe Simmons never got a dime. He was living with his mother when the Feds showed up and was pretty much kicked out of the house. He went back to Fenton County. He's currently married and living in a farmhouse that needs updates while employed as the sheriff of one of the poorest counties in Arkansas. He didn't get any money."

"Are you sure he's not hiding it? Maybe it's his retirement plan."

He shook his head. "Neely Kate says he doesn't have it."

So he'd asked. "Maybe she doesn't know."

"Trust me. She knows."

I wanted to ask more questions but let it go. "So you think Natalie kept the money for herself?"

"That's my suspicion, but I just asked Carter to look into her spending habits over the past decade."

"Decade? Simmons was killed four years ago."

He shot me a grin. "He's lookin' for any changes in her spending habits. I'm surprised you didn't think of that, Detective."

I made a face. "I would have looked for changes. I just wouldn't have gone back that far."

"You were also constrained by things like search warrants."

He had a point. "Do I want to know how you're going to get access to her bank records over the last ten years?"

"Probably not."

I sat back in my seat, once again evaluating my integrity. Maybe it was better if I didn't know how he accomplished some things, but willful ignorance wasn't necessarily a good defense in court. Not that this would ever find its way into a courtroom. None of this would be obtained legally, and James's HSI contact would be a fool to try to use any of it in court.

"So where do you want to go now?" I asked.

"I was thinking we head up to some of the truck stops at the I-30/I-40 interchange."

"Really? During the day?" I wasn't surprised he suggested the truck stops, just the time of day. They were known as a hot spot for prostitution.

"Might as well get the lay of the land for when we go back later."

"Are you hoping to get a name from Razor?"

"I don't know yet," he said. "If we press him for it, he could set us up or alert Knox's guys that we're comin'."

"Or both."

"Exactly," James said.

"You don't want to go see Razor?"

"Not yet. It's still too early for him to crawl out of his hole."

"Do you know where to find him?"

"I suspect he'll be at his usual haunt." He shot a quick glance at me. "I saw him there back in December."

I narrowed my gaze. "Why were you lookin' for him in December?"

"Funnily enough, I wasn't lookin' for him. I was talkin' to another source. Razor just happened to be there."

"When you were lookin' for leads into the human trafficking?" I asked.

His mouth pursed. "Yeah."

"So, you laid low the first year you got out, then made

tentative attempts to figure out who was involved over the last two years?"

"That's sums it up."

"And you never figured anything out?" I asked, my skepticism creeping in.

He turned and studied me for several seconds. "You don't believe that?"

"Why did you have trouble finding out anything, let alone linking Knox to it last fall, when Miguel happens to know Knox is trafficking?"

He shook his head, frustration washing over his face. "The hell if I know. Maybe I talked to the wrong people. Maybe Knox is getting sloppy."

"I need you to tell me the truth, James," I said in exasperation.

Some of the tension left his body. "I am. Knox had his own people who—as far as I know—didn't interact with my sources. Or maybe I didn't try hard enough."

"On purpose?" I asked, my tone softer. I could only imagine how hard his federal leash had to chafe.

"There's some truth to that," he conceded. "But Knox was never on my radar. I guess he should have been. I'd heard he was laundering. I just didn't make the connection." He gave me a grim smile. "Maybe I'm getting sloppy."

I didn't believe that, but I did believe he'd only put out tentative feelers.

"You made the first connection to Knox when you saw the paperwork for the warehouse," I said. "But he sold it, so where's he taking the victims now?"

"I plan to find out from Razor. He obviously does work for Knox."

"You think he's gonna tell you?"

"Honestly? No. But once I tell him I know he's part of it, I'm sure he'll run off to talk to someone. I plan to follow him."

"But what if it's a phone call?"

"He's usually too paranoid to talk about important things over the phone. He'll run to them and confront them in person."

"What if we cover both potential possibilities?"

He squinted at me. "How do you propose to do that?"

"I say we enter the bar separately. I'll find Razor and sit close. You come in and confront him, then leave, and I'll be there to see what he does."

Indecision wavered on his face.

"You want to tell me no," I said with a little laugh. "But you're struggling to find a reason that will convince me."

He shot me a sardonic grin.

"I was a cop, Malcolm. I can handle myself. Besides, I'm not stupid. I'll be careful."

"I know you're not stupid. But Natalie Crowe recognized you. What if he recognizes you too? He won't be up for a chat."

"Then I'll get a disguise." I shrugged. "Maybe it's time for that wig."

"You're gonna wear a wig?" he asked in disbelief. "I thought you were against using one."

"I don't want to wear one all the time, but I'm up for wearing a disguise for an undercover mission."

He didn't say anything.

"What bar does he frequent?"

"I don't know that he still goes there."

"You were certain enough that you expected him to be there later today."

He scowled.

"What bar, James? What type of clientele?"

"It's a biker bar."

He didn't give me a name, but I'd let that go for now.

"I'll need to dress the part. I'm thinking … skin-tight leather pants—"

His scowl deepened. "I don't like it."

"You know it's a good idea."

"I still don't like it."

I laughed. "Sorry. It's happening. We'll drive through the truck stops, then go shopping. What time do you expect he'll show up?"

"Late afternoon, but I don't want to get there when he does. I want to give him time to get sauced."

"But not too sauced."

"Exactly."

I nodded, but then it occurred to me that we'd be at a bar, with plenty of alcohol. And I'd be playing a part—one that would likely require drinking alcohol.

"You don't have to do this," he said with a forceful tone. "We'll just follow him."

"We don't know that he'll go anywhere."

"We don't know that he'll make a call either."

"True, but what harm is there in trying both options?"

He glared at me.

"I'll be fine. I'm not worried about you confronting him." I lifted a brow. "Or should I be?"

"No," he grunted.

"Then you shouldn't be worried about me, because I don't plan on talking to him at all. I'll just blend in."

He didn't respond, and I knew I'd won. He just wasn't going to admit it.

I was okay with that.

Chapter 17

We spent the next hour staking out several truck stops in the interchange area, getting the lay of the land before we came back that night. I knew it was highly suspected that trafficked girls worked the stops, but as a homicide detective, I'd never had any investigations related to trafficking, so I didn't know any details. We made note of where trucks were parked as well as the locations of the restrooms and showers in the buildings, then took off to get lunch.

We grabbed sandwiches at a sketchy deli and ate in the car to go over what we'd seen.

"Do you know the Nixon that Razor was talking to?" I asked.

"No."

"So, we have to hope Razor leads us to him," I said. "But we need to set him on edge enough to run *to* him."

He frowned. "Yeah."

"I know you don't want me coming, but it's a good plan, James. Besides, if I get a couple of wigs, I can get around Little Rock unrecognized."

"Again," he said in a growl, "I thought you were opposed to wigs."

"I was, but I'm not stubborn enough to ignore how beneficial they could be. Right now, I look pretty much the same as I did when I made the news last fall. But if I change my hair and how I dress, I'm pretty sure I'll be unrecognizable." I gestured to him. "You on the other hand… there's no hiding who you are. A wig won't hide that build."

He turned in his seat, his face lighting up with an ornery grin. "You like my build?"

I shrugged, fighting a grin of my own. "I'm not complaining."

He leaned over the seat, slipping a hand behind the back of my head and pulling my lips to his.

When he pulled back, I laughed. "What was that for?"

"It was my way of showin' you I like you exactly as you are. But you're right about a disguise." He pulled out his phone and began tapping on the screen.

"What are you looking up?" I asked, shoving my trash into the paper bag our sandwiches came in.

"A wig shop." He cast me a glance. "Unless you know of one."

"I can't say I've ever been in one."

"Not even in an investigation?" he asked absently as he tapped on the screen.

"I've never had an investigation that led me to a wig shop," I said with a chuckle. "But I guess I can now say I have."

We drove to the shop, and when we walked in, a younger woman with purple streaks in her long dark hair greeted us. "How can I help you?"

"My wife would like to buy a couple of wigs," James said before I could say anything.

So… I was his wife again. I resisted the urge to shoot him a questioning look. Then again, it made sense for us to keep the same cover for all situations.

She turned her attention to me, scanning my hair with a discerning look. "Are you wanting to try out long hair in your natural color or change colors?"

I resisted the urge to squirm under her scrutiny. "Different colors."

"And the length?"

"Long and short," James said. "As for color, we're thinkin' blond."

The woman gave James an appreciative glance and nodded, before turning back to me.

"Yeah," I said. If I was looking for different, blond was definitely it. "Blond."

"Got it," she said with a bright smile. "Why don't you have a seat in front of that mirror in the corner. I'll be right back."

She headed into the back, and I sat in the chair, feeling uncomfortable. James gave me an ornery grin.

"You're having too much fun with this," I said. "Maybe we should get you a wig too."

He gave me a look that made it clear that wouldn't be happening.

"Okay," the woman said a few minutes later as she emerged from the back carrying several large boxes. "I've got a few places to start. I'm Megan, by the way."

"I'm Jeff and this is Amber," James said.

Her smile spread. "Pleased to meet you both. I think we're gonna have fun!"

I sat in the chair, and she put my hair up, talking me through how to do it so my wig would fit better. Then she put a thin wig cap over my hair before opening the first box.

Megan pulled out a long blond wig and moved over to me. "I pulled this one because it's a honey blond, which will work well with Amber's skin tone. And I chose the length carefully, because while it's long, it's not *too* long." She tugged it over my head, scooting it around to get it straight.

I gaped at my reflection. "I look completely different," I whispered.

The ends of the hair hit about six inches past my shoulders, and fringe bangs lay against my forehead.

"I had a feeling you could pull off bangs," Megan said in a satisfied tone. She glanced over at James. "What do you think, Jeff?"

He didn't say anything for several seconds, then seemed to come to his senses. "You do look completely different."

That was the goal, obviously, but the way he was looking at me made the words sting.

Megan froze. "Is that what you were going for?"

"Yeah," James said, tearing his gaze from the mirror.

"Good!" Megan said, beaming. "The beauty of this wig and the length is you can wear it a lot of different ways. It's made with human hair, so you can wash it, dry it, and curl it."

I jerked my head around to look at her. "Human hair?" That had to be extremely expensive.

"It's the most natural-looking wig," Megan said. "Synthetic hair looks so fake."

"We want real," James said in a tone that let me know he wasn't budging. He had to know I would balk at the price.

"You can style it just like natural hair," she said as she gathered it up on top of my head. "You can curl it. Wear it in a ponytail." She twisted it into a knot. "You can put it in a messy bun. What do you think?"

I glanced up at James, and he nodded. "It looks great."

"So we'll keep this one in mind," Megan said cheerfully. "Let's take a look at the next one."

"Yeah," I said.

She had me try on two more—a long brunette wig with golden highlights, and a shoulder-length auburn one. When the third wig was on my head, Megan squealed. "I knew it," she exclaimed, holding her hands against her chest. "You were born to be a redhead."

They all made me look like a different person, and I wasn't opposed to what I saw. If anything, it made me realize I'd been phoning in on the whole femininity thing. Now I had to figure out which one to get.

"We'll take all three," James said, giving me a look in the mirror that told me it was pointless to argue.

While I took off the wig cap and pulled out all the pins, Megan repackaged the wigs and carried them to the checkout counter, talking in an excited rush about how happy we were going to be with our decision.

She rang up our purchases, and I nearly had a panic attack thinking about how much James was about to put on the credit card he'd pulled out of his wallet.

I stepped out of the store before I could hear the total, already feeling guilty. They would be useful—my notoriety made me recognizable enough that the wigs would come in handy for my work as a PI—but I didn't feel right letting James pay for them. I'd pay him back once I got my mother's inheritance. Whenever that turned out to be.

He walked out of the store, carrying three heavy white paper bags with white cord handles. "What happened in there? Why'd you leave?"

I gestured to the bags. "We should have just gotten one. Three is too many."

"I disagree. Once I saw you in the first one, I knew a wig was a good idea. And three gives you options."

I nodded. "I'll put on some dark eye makeup, and no one will recognize me at the bar."

His gaze darkened as he moved toward the car. "I'm having second thoughts about this plan."

I moved in front of him and he nearly collided with me.

"Are you suggesting I can't handle myself?" I asked in a sharp tone.

His eyes narrowed. "It's not about handling yourself."

"You realize you're being a chauvinist right now, don't you? It's okay for you to go in alone, but not me?"

"I'm six foot two and two hundred and thirty pounds, Harper," he said in frustration. "You're five seven and about one forty. I can throw a punch and knock someone out. You—"

"Can take a guy down too, James. Do you know how many male suspects I've busted on my own? Some of them aggressively?" When he didn't answer, I said, "Neither do I, because there've been too many to count." I stabbed his chest with the tip of my index finger. "I. Can. Take. Care. Of. Myself."

He took a step back, his face softening. "I know you can, but you have to understand, I'm used to being the protector."

"In those woods last week, I think I proved I'm good at being a protector too."

His face softened even more. "You're right."

A triumphant grin spread across my face. "What did you say?"

"I'm not gonna repeat it." He rolled his eyes, then looked pained at the movement.

"You need to rest," I said, pissed at myself for not checking on how he was feeling sooner.

"I'm fine." He moved around me toward the back of the car and popped the trunk. "We need to get you some clothes for tonight, but I also want to take you to a gym."

"We have a gym at the hotel," I said. "I probably ran five miles last night."

"I want to see you spar," he said as he placed the bags in the back, then shut the lid. "That is non-negotiable."

"I have no problem showing you I can spar," I said defiantly. "Especially if it will make you trust me more."

"It's not a matter of trusting you, Harper." He paused, indecision flickering in his eyes.

"I'll be fine," I insisted.

"I need to make sure you are."

———

We spent the next two hours shopping for clothes for both of us—clothes that would help us blend in grungy situations, as well as some nice clothes in case we needed to look professional.

Carter had sent James texts, telling him the team protecting Natalie was in place. One of the bodyguards—a woman—had gone in to introduce herself to Natalie and given her a panic button. She'd also covertly placed a camera on a credenza across from Natalie's desk as she'd walked around the room under the guise of making sure it was secure.

I felt slimy at the thought of watching her without her knowledge, but it was ultimately for her own protection. If someone confronted her before she could reach her panic button, James's team would be in her office in less than thirty seconds.

By the time we finished, I pushed for going back to the hotel so James could rest, but he refused, saying I needed to train more than he needed to rest.

"I'm not sparring with you, James," I said in a flat tone.

"As much as it pains me, I agree. Which is why we're meeting someone else."

I narrowed my eyes. "Who?"

"Tex, who I think has what you need."

"What does that mean?" I asked suspiciously.

"Tex fought MMA for a few years."

"You think I need MMA training?"

"Let's just say that Razor fought MMA, so you need to be prepared for anything."

I wanted to ask when he'd arranged this, but I'd spent enough time in several dressing rooms for him to make a few texts or calls.

"Does Tex know who I am?"

"Yep," he said in a flat tone, keeping his gaze on the road.

"It's killing you that you can't fight me," I said with a smirk.

"If you're suggestin' I wish I could get physical with you on a mat, no doubt." He turned his head to give me a wicked grin, but the strain in his eyes told me his head was throbbing.

"But I think Tex will actually be a better fit for our purposes today."

"Great," I grumbled. "Let me guess—Tex is bigger and badder than you."

His grin spread wider. "Guess you'll find out for yourself."

After a few minutes, he pulled into the parking lot of a beat-up looking building. The sign, which read *Bernie's Gym*, was faded and hung over the single, frosted door entrance.

"Is this place even open?" I asked in surprise. "It looks abandoned."

The parking lot was empty with the exception of an older red pickup truck.

"It's a working gym, but it's closed for us for the next hour or so."

"You paid to have the gym closed?" I asked in astonishment.

"Let's just say Tex owed me a favor."

James got out and walked to the back of the car, opening the trunk. While I was nervous about facing Tex, I wasn't scared of a challenge. I got out of the car.

He closed the trunk and handed me a bag with leggings, a workout bra, and a loose-fitting T-shirt, items we'd purchased on our shopping trip.

The door was unlocked, and we walked straight into a dark interior. It took me a second for my eyes to adjust to see mats on the floor in the center of the room.

"Glad to see you could finally make it, Skeeter," a deep voice called out from the back of the space, echoing around us.

My gaze shifted and I was surprised to see a woman at the far edge of the mats, wrapping her left hand.

She shot me a look full of contempt. "Don't just stand there, princess. Get changed."

Chapter 18

I glanced over at James, who was wearing a shit-eating grin.

"Tex is a woman?" I asked, my eyebrows raised.

"She'll probably kick your ass," he said, "but she'll also show you a few things you don't know."

I lifted a shoulder in acknowledgement, pretending like this was no big deal, but I was even more nervous than I had been before. When I'd thought Tex was a man, I'd suspected he'd hold back for fear of pissing off James. I doubted Tex would show that same restraint. This woman had fought MMA, and she looked the part.

We walked closer, and James said, "Harper, this is Tessa Morales, but if you call her Tessa or Tess, she'll knock your ass flat on the ground." He grinned. "Ask me how I know."

I shot him a look of surprise. "She took you out?"

"Only because he wasn't payin' attention," she said dryly. "And I'd like the chance to even the odds to prove I could do it when you *are* payin' attention."

James laughed.

"Any other time, I'd be happy to see you knock him on his ass," I said. "But not today. He's still—"

"I'm just watchin' today," James interrupted, shooting me a dark look.

He didn't want her to know he had a weakness. Which meant he only trusted her to a certain extent.

"Fine by me," she said, eyeing me up and down, and her expression suggested she found me lacking. "I'm here to knock *you* on your ass, Barbie."

"Barbie?" I asked with a laugh. I'd never been called Barbie in my life, and my current attire of jeans, plain T-shirt, old jacket, and athletic shoes didn't do anything to earn me the title, not to mention my lack of makeup or hairstyle.

"Are we gonna stand here gawkin' at each other or are we gonna spar?" she asked as she started wrapping the scar-covered knuckles on her other hand. She was wearing faded black compression shorts and an old T-shirt that had likely once been black, with a distressed white graphic of a snarling pit bull in a circle and the words *Red River Fight Night Champion* around it. Beneath the logo, in smaller lettering, was *2019 Champion*. The armholes were cut wide to reveal a black sports bra underneath. Her feet were bare, and her dark hair was slicked back into a long braid.

She was going to kick my ass.

But I wasn't going to let her know she intimidated me. I lifted my hands in surrender, then took the bag into the locker room behind me. It only took me a few minutes to change, and I walked out in bare feet, steeling myself for anything.

Tex and James were having a quiet conversation that abruptly stopped when James saw me.

"Don't stop chatting on my account," I said, as I walked closer.

Tex gave me a dark look. Was she pissed that James had asked her to do this? Had he coerced her?

"Okay, princess," she said with a sneer. "Let's see what you've got."

I held her gaze. "Ready whenever you are."

She walked over to a table and grabbed a couple of jump ropes and tossed me one. I caught it before it hit me in the belly.

"Let's warm up," she said, then started to swing her rope and jump.

I followed her lead, starting off slow. I hadn't jumped rope since I'd been in the police academy and that had been a fluke. My toe caught on the rope a few times, which made Tex smirk with derision. But I soon found my footing and picked up the pace.

Tex picked up her pace too, then started some fancy twists and turns of her rope, never once stumbling or breaking her stride. I wasn't fool enough to fall for her goading. This was a warmup, not a jump-rope showcase.

She was watching my feet and my breathing, which admittedly had become labored. I'd already proven the night before that I was out of shape. I recognized that she was assessing me.

After about five minutes, she stopped her rope and said, "Okay, let's move on."

We did some neck and shoulder rolls, then moved down our bodies, with arm and then hip rolls, her watching my every move. After we finished those, she said, "Let's see your fighting stance."

I put my left foot forward, my right foot back, both knees slightly bent. I settled my weight over my back foot, keeping my front foot light. My hands hovered loosely in front of my tucked chin. My elbows were at my sides, my back straight.

Tex walked around me, assessing my stance. I remained on alert, ready for her to pounce.

Sure enough, seconds later, Tex's right hip rolled and her leg started to swing.

I immediately registered it as a low kick. Instinctively, I

lifted my right leg, swinging it outward, prepared to block the kick with my shin.

But Tex pulled back the kick at the last moment, her foot nearly brushing my leg. She returned to her circling as she said, "That's a Thai move. Where'd you train Muay Thai, Detective Adams?"

My blood ran cold, and I jerked my gaze to James, furious. "You told her—"

I didn't finish. Tex slid into my blind side, her foot hooking around my outside lead leg just as I felt a hard shove to my chest. My right foot slid out from in front of me, and I fell forward, pushing my hands out to help break my fall as my knees slammed into the mat.

"So I didn't knock you on your *ass*," Tex said in amusement. "But we're just getting started."

I stared up at her, more pissed at myself than her. I'd suspected she'd be sneaky, but that's what I needed. If I had to defend myself from Razor or some other burly dude, they wouldn't fight fair. And neither would I.

We spent ten minutes with Tex testing my defenses, then she moved on to combat, knocking me on my ass more times than I could count, but toward the end, I'd knocked her down a few times too.

We took a water break, both of us breathless. James had watched us without commentary, but now he said, "What do you think, Tex? Can she hold her own?"

"Depends on who she's dealing with. Is she ready to enter a cage match? Not a chance. Can she deal with someone bigger than her? Hard to say since we're so evenly matched in height. But I'd say she has a pretty good chance. I'd suggest having her fight someone bigger. Someone as big as you."

"I'm not fightin' today," he said.

She laughed. "Not you *any* day. She needs someone who's not afraid to hurt her."

"I never said I was afraid to hurt her," he said in a deep voice.

"You didn't have to," she said, her hands on her hips. "But she still needs to work with someone else who's bigger than her."

James gave me an indecisive look.

"That sounds great," I said, wiping sweat off my face with a towel. "But we'll have to schedule that for another time. We have plans tonight."

Her gaze shifted from me to James, then back again. "Hence the sparring brush-up."

"What makes you think Harper needs to brush up on her fighting skills for a date?" James asked good-naturedly.

"Please…" she drawled. "I've seen some of your dates, Skeeter."

I shot James an amused look. "That's a story I want to hear."

"Maybe another time," James growled. "It's time to head out."

Tex watched us both, taking in our conversation. I suspected not much got by her. Then she turned to me and said, "You weren't half bad. A little rusty in the beginning, but it came back."

"You taught me a few things I didn't know before and helped refresh what I did know. Thanks."

She walked over to me, holding out her still-wrapped hand, knuckles out. "If you need a sparring partner in the future, give me a call."

I bumped my fist into hers. "Thanks. And maybe you can tell me about what happened on James's previous dates."

Surprise filled her eyes when I called him James, but she quickly hid it, mischief dancing across her face. "You've got it."

Chapter 19

I took a quick shower to wash the sweat off my body, dressed in my old clothes, and then we headed back to the hotel. Since we hadn't taken our car, we parked at a garage down the street, then carried the packages to the back door of the hotel. We waited for someone to walk out the back so we could walk in without using our key card.

Now, more than before, we needed to be cautious. For all we knew, Knox hadn't yet realized we were in Little Rock. But given the people we'd talked to, he'd definitely know soon enough. By the time we reached the door to our room, James was dragging. I took the keycard from him and opened the door, dropping my packages on the floor inside the room so I could take his.

"You need a nap."

"I'm not a damned baby," he grunted.

"Trust me, that's the last thing I'd accuse you of being, but you're still recovering and you need to rest."

He reluctantly headed over to the freshly made bed. "What are you gonna do?"

"Look into Razor. You got a legal name for him?"

"Timothy Ransor."

I cocked a brow. "*Timothy?*"

He chuckled. "Why do you think he goes by Razor?"

"Touché."

He slid onto the bed, tugging the pillows on his side of the bed to get more comfortable, then closed his eyes, his hands over his stomach.

I moved to the sofa, casting a glance back at him. "You don't look comfortable."

"What are you?" he grunted. "The nap police?"

"You usually sleep on your side," I said as I took a seat and grabbed my laptop. "Take a nap. Don't just rest."

His eyes cracked open. "You plan to always be this bossy?"

"You think this is bossy?" I asked with a snort. "You ain't seen nothin' yet."

He grunted but kicked off his boots and turned on his side, facing the wall.

Satisfied he was really getting the sleep his brain obviously needed, I booted up my computer and pulled up one of my PI sites, inserting the name Timothy Ransor.

Timothy had been a busy boy.

He had multiple arrests for assault, but the majority had been dismissed. The victims either vanished or refused to cooperate with the DA.

His mug shots looked pretty similar across his many arrests —deep-set, dark eyes, closely shorn dark hair, with a hint of stubble on his face in half the images. His arrest reports said he was six feet even and varying between two-ten and two-fifty at his last arrest in November. He was forty-eight but looked like he was in his mid-fifties. His face was doughy, but he still had a vicious look in his eyes.

Timothy "Razor" Ransor was a killer. He'd just never been caught.

An hour later, I didn't have much more on him. He didn't

own any property. His car was a late-model black Ram 1500, crew cab with dark tint, and it still had a lien on it. He had accounts at two different banks, a couple of recent alcohol-related arrests, along with his mostly dismissed assault cases. The two that weren't dismissed had been pled down to misdemeanors. There was also a recently dismissed protective order.

James said alcohol had dulled his senses, but he was obviously still capable of doing real damage.

I lifted my gaze from the laptop screen to check on James. He was still, and I could hear his slow, steady breathing. Relief settled my anxiety about him overdoing it. At least he was sleeping. I still thought he was doing too much, but now that we were in Little Rock, I doubted I could convince him to take it easy.

I reexamined our loose plan for tonight. Having James walk in and confront Razor felt risky—especially with James nowhere near peak condition. There was a good chance Miguel had already told people James was in town, and Razor would definitely sound the alarm. He might even try to jump James in the parking lot so he could collect Knox's bounty.

I was starting to reconsider.

Sure, I'd be there as backup, but Razor spent his nights in a biker bar. He wouldn't be alone. He'd probably have buddies with him who'd be happy to help with James's takedown. And sure, I'd brushed up on my self-defense that afternoon, but I couldn't take on a group of men.

I also couldn't assume Razor was dumb just because he looked and acted like a meathead. He might decide to end things the fast and efficient way—with a bullet. Then again, if he and James had real beef, Razor seemed like the kind of guy who preferred his fists. He'd want to make it hurt.

Either way, one thing was certain—once James made his presence known at the bar, we were fair game.

Releasing a sigh, I set the laptop on the coffee table and

stretched out my sore muscles. If we were really doing this, I needed a decent shower to wash and dry my hair before I stuffed it into a wig cap. I stood, gathered a few of my packages, carried them into the bathroom, then turned on the shower.

As water streamed over my head, I ran through our options.

There was no cavalry coming. We were on our own.

Which meant I needed to stop thinking like a cop and start thinking like a private investigator.

But I still wasn't sure how to handle this. If our plan was to turn everything over to HSI, we needed to make sure whatever we found was usable—even if only for a search warrant.

Finding the Knoxes' accountant still seemed like a good idea.

If I had time, I'd go undercover and get a job at the firm, then work my way in and try to get access to their files. Or at least find something concrete. But that would take weeks, more likely months. Or longer.

What if we didn't try to build a prosecutable case?

What if we skipped finding evidence of trafficking and went straight to eliminating the threat?

What if we really did take out Knox?

Sure, we'd talked about it, but this was the first time I saw it as a truly acceptable solution.

I was talking about the cold-blooded murder of a man.

You murdered men last week.

I sucked in a sharp breath. I hadn't processed what had happened. I was handling it *too* well. Shoving it into a box and telling myself it was fine to not have an emotional reaction because it had been self-defense.

But the truth was, I'd killed nearly a dozen men. I'd *ended their lives*.

And sure, it had been done in self-defense, but they'd still been sons. Maybe husbands. Fathers. At least one of them had left behind a woman he loved. Their lives were over, and the lives of the people who loved them had been irrevocably changed by what I'd done.

That wasn't nothing. It was a weight I'd been pretending not to feel.

And now I was considering murdering someone else.

Someone I likely wouldn't be shooting in self-defense.

Who was I becoming?

I finished my shower and dried off, no closer to an answer than I'd been before. I still wasn't convinced seeing Razor tonight was a good idea. Sure, I'd been on board earlier, and if James was at one hundred percent, I'd be willing to see it through. But he was still recovering as evidenced by the nap he was currently taking. Could he handle being attacked by a bar full of bikers?

But if we didn't find Razor, we needed a new plan. Something solid enough that James might consider giving up the old one.

So what the hell was it?

I was about to get dressed when I noticed a missed call from a number I didn't recognize and a voicemail. I clicked on the voicemail, surprised when it started playing because it was from Cassandra, the convenience store clerk.

"Harper, this mornin' I was thinkin' about what you said about trafficked girls, and ... well, I think one might come into the store on the regular. She shows up at around eight or so, always gets an energy drink or two and some candy, then she hops into a car with an older guy who's sittin' in the driver's seat. I thought he might be her father, and said something once about her dad, and she got nervous and said he wasn't her dad. It might not be anything, but... I thought I'd let you know. If you wanna talk to her, and she follows her pattern, she'll be in tonight."

My breath caught. This might be the break we needed. There was a good chance this girl had nothing to do with Knox, trafficked or not, but it was worth checking out.

Surely James would be willing to ditch the Razor plan for something less dangerous.

I got dressed, and when I emerged from the bathroom, James was sitting up in bed, talking on his phone.

"Yeah. Let me know if they notice anything unusual." His gaze shifted to me as I entered the room. "Keep me updated on everything else." He lowered the phone and hung up.

"Was that Carter?" I asked, crossing to the bed and sitting on the edge.

"Yeah. The security team has two cameras in Natalie's office, and they didn't have any issues placing them in her home either." His mouth flattened. "She's worried enough that she asked them to come through and make sure it's secure."

I made a face. "But she didn't agree to them planting cameras."

His expression stayed grim. "This isn't much different than a police wiretap."

He had a point, but it felt skeezy. Still, I wasn't bothered enough to tell him I didn't agree with him—it was just enough to make me unsettled.

"Why's she so nervous?" I asked. "She says she's not working with anyone in the criminal world. What are the chances Knox is watching her?"

He grimaced. "I've considered that myself. The only thing I can think of is she's worried Knox'll watch her because of our shared connection to Simmons."

"It still seems like a stretch," I said. "I think she knows more than she's letting on."

"Could be," he acknowledged. "Maybe we can visit her again tomorrow and press her harder."

I nodded, then said, "One of my contacts came through with information."

The corner of his eye twitched. "The bartender?"

"No, the convenience store clerk." I told him about her voicemail, then said, "I think we should go see if the girl shows up."

He glanced at the clock on the nightstand. "It's a little after six. We need to see Razor sooner rather than later."

"I don't want to go see Razor," I said flatly. "I think we should go see if the girl shows up."

He didn't respond.

"You're not going to argue with me?"

He studied me a beat longer. "Are you nervous about seein' Razor? You don't have to go at all, Harper. I can handle it myself."

My jaw dropped. "Are you seriously insinuating that I'm scared to *eavesdrop*?"

"It's not an insult." His tone stayed even. "It's more than simple eavesdroppin', and you know it. You *should* be nervous."

"I'm nervous, but not for me." I leaned forward, my frustration rising. "I'm nervous for *you*. You're talking about going into a biker bar and confronting a guy who will probably shoot you on sight to collect Knox's bounty."

"He's not gonna shoot me in a bar."

"Fine, he'll wait until you're in the parking lot."

Irritation flicked in his eyes. "I can handle it," he grunted.

"Yeah, you probably can, but you're still not on top of your game, and if you show your face tonight, every person who thinks themselves a bounty hunter or a hit man will be searching the city for you." My voice turned sharp. "It'll make it a hundred times harder to find what we need to bring Knox down."

He frowned but didn't answer. He wasn't arguing, which probably meant he knew I was right.

"For what it's worth," I said, "I think we should still talk to Razor. We just need to put it off for now and hopefully get more information first. And maybe find a better place to confront him. Like his house while he's sleeping it off."

"Fine." He sounded irritated as he reached for the hotel landline. "But I'm ordering dinner from room service."

"Cassandra said the girl shows up around eight, so we should be there about a half hour early."

"All the more reason to get our order in now," he grumped, glancing at me. "What do you want?"

I ordered a chicken and rice dish while he asked for a steak and baked potato, then told them if they got the food to our room in under thirty minutes, his tip would be "extremely" generous.

When he hung up, he still looked irritated.

I placed a hand on my hip. "You don't agree with my plan?"

He exhaled and shifted toward me, some of his frustration bleeding away. "Harper, I wouldn't go along with a plan I didn't agree with."

"You sure don't act like you're happy about it."

He sighed. "I'm not pissed about your plan. You made good points. I'm pissed that I'm not at a hundred percent. I'm takin' too long to get over this damn concussion."

"It's okay."

He scowled. "It's not. It makes me a liability." His expression softened slightly. "As you pointed out."

"I wasn't accusing you of—"

"Stop." He paused a beat to make sure I was listening. "You were right."

My heart sunk. I knew that had to be hard for him to admit. "I'm sorry."

He gave a soft chuckle. "For being right? Or for callin' me out? Because you shouldn't be sorry for either." He slid off the bed. "What do you need to do to prep for meetin' the girl tonight? Do you want to wear a disguise?"

Did I? I hadn't planned on it, but it wasn't a terrible idea, even if it made me feel weird.

"I suppose I should," I said. "I don't want to be recognized." A new thought hit me. "And Knox might have told his people to be on the lookout for me too."

James had been walking around the end of the bed, but he stopped and turned to face me.

"What?" I asked when he didn't say anything.

"Miguel said Knox has a hit out on me," he said slowly, "but he didn't mention you."

I shook my head. "Maybe he didn't think it was important."

His brow lifted. "When I have a woman fitting your exact description sittin' in a chair in his office?"

He had a point. "Okay, so maybe Miguel didn't know. But then again, maybe he did. His comment about me wearing black was also odd."

He shook his head, slow and deliberate. "No way. If Razor is talkin' and he knows all the facts, he'd include you."

"But Razor heard it from the driver—Nixon. Maybe he didn't know."

He gave me a pointed look. "Harper. If Knox had hits out on two people who were last seen together and expected to still be together, people would know."

I took a second to consider that. "So… what does that mean? That Knox doesn't have a hit out on me?"

"I don't think he does."

My brow furrowed. "That doesn't make any sense. I'm the one who shot his mother. I was the one who took out all his men. Not you." I released a dry laugh. "If anything, he should be on the hunt for me, not you."

His jaw tensed. "Exactly."

"What do you think it means?" I asked again, a chill running down my spine.

He studied me for a beat. "Nothin' good."

With that alarming prediction, he headed to the bathroom and shut the door.

I got off the bed and walked over to the windows overlooking the river.

Did this mean Knox wanted me alive? But, if so, wouldn't he have told his people to be on the lookout for me? Or did he assume they'd find me when they found James?

Unless there *was* a bounty on my head and Nixon knew it … and had chosen to keep that part to himself. If that was true, then the bounty on me was a hell of a lot bigger than the bounty on James.

My blood turned to ice.

I'd killed Gerald Knox's men. I'd hurt his mother.

Gerald Knox wanted James dead, maybe because of past grudges, maybe because James had been a thorn in his side in the past. James said he'd been part of a group who'd tried to take over his territory. That had to have caused bad blood.

But me…

I was guessing Gerald Knox wanted revenge.

He wanted me alive—and once he had me, I'd probably wish I wasn't.

I went numb for several seconds, trying to wrap my brain around the fact that a crime boss wanted to hurt me in ways I couldn't even imagine. Because I knew what men like him were capable of.

Other than James, I had nothing tying me to Arkansas. My mother was dead, and my father … he might as well be. After everything I'd learned last week, I never planned on having any kind of relationship with him. Sure, I had my grandparents and my aunt now, and I wanted to reconnect with them, but

I'd gone this long without a real family. I could walk away from them and my aunt.

If I were smart, I'd run. Far, far away.

But I guess I wasn't smart.

My fear started to shift to anger, then it caught fire and turned into a blaze.

Gerald Knox and men like him thought they could take whatever they wanted at the expense of everyone else, never giving a damn about the lives they ruined. People were pawns on a chessboard. Inventory. Product.

Gerald Knox was a sociopath, and the world would be a better place without him.

In the end, I suspected it might come down to him or me—and I sure as hell wasn't leaving this world without one hell of a fight.

Maybe I wouldn't have trouble pulling the trigger after all.

The bathroom door clicked open and James walked out.

"I think we should leave Little Rock," he announced in an authoritative tone.

I crossed my arms over my chest, keeping my gaze on the river. So, he'd come to the same conclusion I had.

"Why?" I knew what he was going to say. I wanted to hear him say it.

"He plans to kill me, Harper." His voice dipped. "But he plans to torture you. I should have realized it sooner."

I still didn't turn around. "And if the positions were reversed, would you run?"

"This is *my* world," he said, his voice going dark. "I've done things that Detective Adams wouldn't have hesitated to lock me up for and throw away the key. You're used to playin' by the rules." His eyes pinned mine. "Men like Gerald Knox don't play by any rules."

"I don't know if you noticed," I said dryly, letting my arms fall to my sides, "but I stopped playing by the rules a while back."

He shook his head. "That's patty-cake compared to what Gerald Knox does."

A humorless laugh escaped me. "I'm not running, James."

He closed the distance between us and grabbed my upper arms, keeping a couple of feet between us. "As you pointed out, I'm not a hundred percent." Pain flashed in his eyes. "Which means I'm not on top of my game enough to protect you."

I glared up at him. "Who the fuck says I need protecting?"

"Do you think that makes you weak?" he demanded. "Because I guaran-damn-tee you that Gerald Knox doesn't see you that way."

"I don't need protecting," I repeated, sharper this time. "If the roles were reversed, you wouldn't back down."

His hands tightened on my arms and his voice rose. "That's because I never thought I had anything to lose!"

His words pierced my defensiveness, but I still couldn't make myself believe him. "So you're saying if Knox wanted to torture *you*, you'd run away." My eyes narrowed. "And don't you dare lie to me."

His jaw set, but he didn't respond.

"Exactly," I spat, yanking free of his grip. "I need to get ready." I brushed past him, headed for the bathroom.

"If we retreat, it doesn't mean we won't come back," he called after me, anger sharp in his voice.

"*You* wouldn't retreat," I countered, not looking over my shoulder.

"*Because I'm a goddamned idiot!*" he shouted.

I stopped and turned.

"I'm stubborn and hotheaded," he went on, his chest heaving, "but damn it all to hell, Harper—if the roles were reversed right now, I'd consider pausing."

I tilted my head, my eyes narrowing. *"Pausing?* But not running."

He speared his hand through his head, grunting in frustration.

"You. Wouldn't. Run."

"You are not me!"

I froze.

I knew he meant it as a compliment, but in the moment, it landed like a cut. Like he was telling me I was weak.

"No," I said quietly, my throat tight. "I'm not you. But I have my own tools to work with."

I went into the bathroom and shut the door, then sat on the side of the tub and covered my face with my hands.

What the hell was I doing?

James was right. He wasn't a hundred percent, and if Knox was gunning for me, I needed backup. Protection.

We should regroup. We should wait and make a plan more concrete than chasing an accountant who probably wouldn't talk to us, and a girl at a convenience store who may or may not have been trafficked. And even if she was, she wasn't likely connected to Knox's network.

Moving forward was insanity.

But deep in my gut, I also knew I couldn't back down. Because Knox would see it as a weakness, and men like him only respected strength. If I ran and came back, he'd see me as smaller than him.

But… was that so bad?

I could play into that belief. Let him underestimate me.

Was I this adamant about staying because I feared Knox would see me as weak, or because *I* would?

I drew a deep breath, held it in, then let it out.

Staying was foolish. I knew that. But after the shooting last fall, I'd let myself get beaten down into an alcoholic mess, with zero confidence and nothing to live for, because I'd played it safe. Followed the rules. I'd let Keith and all the higher-ups destroy my reputation, *destroy me*, and I was *fucking done* with letting men steal anything else from me.

I wasn't backing down.

And before I started berating myself for my stupidity, I thought about the girl I hoped to meet at the convenience store tonight.

Who was fighting for her? Or the other women Knox was trafficking? What about Wilhemina from the Velvet Room, who had likely been kidnapped and trafficked, all because she fit some man's sexual fantasy? The police sure as hell weren't looking for her.

Who was going to save *them*?

I stood and moved to the sink to get ready, but what I saw in the mirror stopped me cold.

I'd been hard and no-nonsense before, but the woman staring back at me now … there was fire in her eyes.

I'd been looking at this all wrong. I'd started out wanting to bring Gerald Knox down because his mother had killed mine. Because he'd threatened both James and me.

I needed to change my motivation. I needed to stop making this about myself and make it about them. I needed to save those girls. Nobody else gave a shit about them. But I knew what that felt like, because other than James and Louise, no one gave a shit about me either.

I didn't have a badge anymore, but maybe that wasn't a bad thing. I could do things a cop couldn't.

The rules had changed.

Before, my job was to find evidence to arrest the monsters, with the ultimate goal of getting them off the street.

But what if I skipped the tedious part and focused on the end goal?

That would make me judge and jury, something I'd always sworn I wasn't when I wore a badge. But I'd never needed a judge or jury to tell me the truly evil ones were guilty. And I'd watched too many of them hire high-powered attorneys and walk free.

If Gerald Knox got arrested, he'd probably do the same.

And then more girls would be at his mercy.

I drew in a breath, and a steely resolve settled in my bones.

Knox wanted to destroy me in retaliation.

Which was why I was going to destroy him first.

Where did that leave James and his deal with his handler? I'd sort that out later.

Chapter 20

I put on some light makeup and dried my hair. My wigs and the wig cap were in the other room, so I was ready for James to continue our fight when I opened the door.

Room service must have just come, because when I left the bathroom, he was setting a tray on the coffee table. He glanced up at me, but I didn't see the animosity I'd expected.

"Are you hungry?"

"Not particularly," I said, still defensive.

"You need to eat before we go out. You had a thorough workout today and you need to refuel."

I almost snapped at him that I could decide when I ate, but I knew this was his way of showing me he cared. That he *still* cared, even after our fight.

"Okay," I said, moving to the sofa, and to make amends, I teased, "Couldn't get a suite with a dining table?"

His mouth lifted into a half grin. "You gave me short notice."

He had a point.

We sat down on the sofa, and he handed me my plate, then picked up his own and set it on the table.

"So you're bound and determined to see this through now," he said, picking up a set of silverware. "Not later."

"Yeah."

"What's your plan for the night?" he asked. "What are we doin'?"

I stared at him, surprised by the question, and he flicked a glance my way. "It was *your* contact who came through first. We'll follow the lead and see where it takes us." His voice turned practical. "But if it's a bust, what do you wanna do?"

"I'm not sure," I admitted. "I haven't thought that far ahead."

He cut off a piece of his steak. "You *need* to be thinkin' that far ahead. Ten steps ahead." He didn't look up. "What you're gonna do if she has usable information and what you'll do if she doesn't. What to do if her handler interrupts. What to do if he has backup." He glanced over at me. "You need to be ready for anything."

"Are you suggesting I'm not cut out for this?" I asked, my defenses flaring.

"No." He lifted a bite to his mouth. "You're not a cop anymore, so you need to stop thinkin' like one." He took a bite, then started cutting another piece.

Funny how I'd given myself the same damn speech minutes before.

"I'm guessing that's how you plan things?"

He finished chewing before answering. "Not always. Not in the beginning. Funnily enough, I learned it from J.R."

I gave him another look of surprise.

"There was a time I practically worshiped him," he said casually, like he was discussing the weather. "He was everything I wanted to be. Rich. Respected. Lived in a big fancy house and drove a big fancy car. It made an impression on fourteen-year-old me the first time I met him. It stuck, long after I started working for him."

I gasped. "You started working for J.R. Simmons when you were *fourteen*?"

He chuckled. "No. That's when I met him. He was filling up at a gas station outside of Henryetta. I was impressed with his car, and for some reason, he was impressed with me." He lifted a shoulder. "He gave me his business card and told me to find him when I turned eighteen. Said he'd give me a job."

"And you did."

"You bet your ass I did." His voice went matter of fact. "I was dirt poor. Our family was looked down on. Even if I'd wanted to go to college, I couldn't have afforded it, and I sure as hell wasn't qualifying for scholarships with my grades." He cut another bite. "And truth be told, while most kids were planning on going to college or getting jobs in their family businesses, my goal was working for J.R." He let out a snort. "It was a stupid plan. He was probably humoring me."

"But he wasn't," I said. "He gave you a job."

"Even if he hadn't meant it, I suspect he would have given me a job just for having the tenacity to show up at his house." His gaze went distant. "But when I walked in, he gave me a knowin' smile. Like he'd been waitin' on me."

"You said you worshipped him," I said carefully. "I take it he was good to you."

"He was, at first. He said he saw potential in me and was going to help me become a *man of importance*. My own father was a piece of shit who only found potential at the bottom of a whiskey bottle." He swallowed. "For a man of J.R.'s stature to see something in me…" He drew in a breath. "Let's just say before him, I'd never been treated as anything other than a waste of air. I would have done anything for him." He paused. "Well, almost anything."

I knew what he meant. He'd stopped working for J.R. because J.R. had asked him to kill a child who'd witnessed a murder. James had refused, and J.R. had seen it as a betrayal.

"Did you know he was a criminal when you first started working for him?" I was surprised he was opening up to me, but if he was sharing, I wasn't going to waste the opportunity. "I mean, everyone else thought he was a prominent business-man, right?"

"Yeah." He gave a short laugh. "That's what the good, God-fearin' Christians of El Dorado thought. He made a good show of it too." He speared another bite. "And that's who I thought he was too, at first. He had me doin' above-board scut work, not that I complained. He paid me well enough that I didn't have to worry about my next meal, and that was a first."

"James…"

He snorted and turned to me. "Don't go feelin' sorry for me."

"No child should go hungry."

He shrugged, then took another bite of his steak, and I couldn't help thinking it was in defiance of his past.

"After a couple of years, J.R. started me on small question-able jobs," he said. "Probably to gauge how far I was willing to go. What I was willing to do for him … turns out, it was quite a bit." His voice went flat. "He gave me more and more work, and I followed through every time. I earned a reputation with his other men. Before long, I was taking the lead, not following orders."

He cut another piece of steak. "Then one day he called me to his office and told me he was sending me back to Fenton County." His mouth tightened. "I thought he was jokin'. Or that I misunderstood and he was sending me to do a job. But no. He was sending me back to live there." His gaze went distant. "He said he wanted me to get a foothold in the county and take over. To become one of his Twelve."

"That had to be hard to hear."

"I thought it was a test. And I still worshipped the guy, but it's fair to say I wasn't happy about it. And he knew it. I think he got off on me bein' unhappy about it." He set down his fork. "He gave me seed money and told me to go out and make my way in the world."

"As long as it was in Fenton County."

"Yep." He paused. "So I went back, opened the pool hall, and hired Jed to be my right-hand man. We'd grown up together. He was younger than me, but we both understood what it was to be poor and hungry." Emotion flickered in his eyes. "I knew he was a hard worker, and he felt a loyalty to me that I exploited."

I narrowed my eyes. "Why did he feel a loyalty to you, and how did you exploit it?"

"His sister…" He dragged in a deep breath. "We had a pond near where we lived. Us boys fished there, always hoping to get something to fill our bellies." His gaze went distant. "One time, Jed and I and a few other boys were fishing. Jed's little sister was there too, and she fell in." He swallowed hard. "I jumped in and got her, but it was too late." His voice broke. "I didn't save her. But as far as Jed was concerned, trying was almost the same."

He turned to me, his eyes glassy. "His parents were shit parents too. And just like I had my little brother Scooter, Jed had Daisy. Until he didn't."

My breath caught. Jed had named his daughter after his sister.

And James had a small daisy tattooed under the tree on his chest.

"After she died," he went on quietly, "I kind of adopted him as an honorary brother. But it wasn't the same. Not by a long shot."

"You blame yourself for not saving her."

"She was six. Practically a toddler. I should have been watchin' her."

Six wasn't a toddler, but it was too young for her to have

been playing unsupervised next to a pond. It also wasn't James's responsibility. "How old were you?"

"Nearly a teenager."

"James, you were a kid yourself."

He snorted. "Trust me, I hadn't been a kid for some time by then." He rubbed his jaw. "But I *had* seen her playing on the bank of the pond. I'd been keeping an eye on her. Then Jed caught a fish and we all got distracted."

"It wasn't your fault."

"It wasn't Jed's either."

I suspected they'd both spent their lives blaming themselves for her death.

We were silent for a moment, James probably reliving that horrible moment in his past, and me trying to process it.

"You said you exploited Jed's loyalty," I said finally. "How?"

He shook his head slowly. "By askin' him to work for me. By givin' him a job when he was just as desperate for a way out as I had been when I went to J.R."

"Wait," I said, cocking my head. "You can't be comparing yourself to J.R. Simmons." I said in disbelief. "You are *nothing* like that man."

"You have some delusion that I was playin' Candyland back then," he said derisively. "I was there to make a name for myself. I may have been back in Fenton County, but it didn't mean I was the automatic king of the land." His eyes went hard. "Where you find poverty, you find crime, because desperate people are willing to do desperate, stupid things to survive."

He took a breath. "A man named Daniel Crocker ruled the roost back then. He wasn't happy when I showed up in town, and he had no love for J.R. He didn't have proof I'd been workin' for him, but he'd heard rumors."

I took a bite of my untouched food, worried I'd distract him and he'd stop talking, but thankfully he continued.

"We had a few skirmishes in the beginning." He grimaced. "He had an established outfit, and I had Jed and a few other guys. There was no way I could take him on, at least not by force. So, we reached a truce. He ran his chop shop and dealt drugs. I stuck to my pool hall, where I ran a bookie operation —which was more profitable than I'd imagined."

He gave me a devious grin. "Turned out I was good with numbers." His tone sobered. "I took my earnings, then opened the strip club. We coexisted."

"And you invested in legit businesses too," I said softly.

"Yeah." He scooped out some of his baked potato. "But after a bit, J.R. wasn't happy that I hadn't taken over the whole county. He told me the seed money was an investment, and so far, he wasn't seeing a return. And because he wasn't, he started giving me odd jobs every now and again to pay for the interest." His eyes flicked to mine. "Jobs to make sure I was still loyal."

"Killing people," I said.

He held my gaze. "Believe it or not, I still had some scruples. I made sure they were truly deserving of it."

A week or two ago, I would have been horrified. But after my bathroom TED Talk, I understood.

I wasn't sure whether that was a good thing or bad. Maybe it was just further proof we belonged together.

He gave me a long stare, his face expressionless. "I wanted you to know who you were risking your life with and for. I understand if you need to end this."

I gave him an incredulous look. "End this discussion so you don't have to tell me more, or end whatever this is between us? Because...sorry, if this was your way of trying to make me stop working with you—" I shifted on the sofa so I could look him in the eye. "You're stuck with me, Malcolm."

He stared at me for a long moment, like he wasn't sure he believed me.

I leaned in and placed a gentle kiss on his lips, then pulled back. "I understand you better than you think."

"What does that mean?"

"It means, I'm not a cop anymore," I said softly. "And you're right … I need to stop thinking like one." I swallowed. "Sometimes an arrest shouldn't be the goal." I paused, letting the words land. "Sometimes a more permanent method might be."

Understanding flashed in his eyes. "You plan to murder Gerald Knox."

I couldn't bring myself to admit it. "Will that hurt your position with your HSI contact?"

"Don't worry about that," he said gruffly.

"Of course I'm going to worry about that." My voice grew tight. "I'm not going to do anything to get you in trouble. The plan is to get you free of them."

"I told you, I can handle this how I see fit."

I knew he wouldn't lie to me, but it was still hard to believe anyone would condone him killing a suspect. Then again, the Feds ran plenty of covert operations that never saw the light of day.

"Do you want to turn him over to your contact?" I asked.

He didn't answer.

"If Homeland Security wasn't involved," I pressed, "what would you do in our situation?"

His eyes glittered with something dangerous. "The motherfucker would already be dead."

I hesitated. "Is that what you want to do? Find him, kill him, and let the trafficking operation fall where it may?"

He drew in a breath. "No. I want to destroy that too." His face turned to stone. "For now, we keep doin' what we're doin'. But if I think he's close to homin' in on us, then we move to Plan B."

"Take him out."

"Yes."

I held his gaze, something settling in my gut. "If it comes to Plan B, I want to be the one to kill him."

He watched me for a long moment, as though weighing the cost of saying yes. "Okay. I'll let you have it. But if I think he's going to hurt you, then I'll pull the trigger without an ounce of remorse."

"Fair." I swung a leg over and straddled his lap, my hands resting on his shoulders. "You have no idea what your protectiveness does to me," I said in husky tone.

His mouth ticked up. "If this is any indication, I don't have any complaints."

"How about I show you?"

"Talk is cheap," he grunted as he lifted his hips, grinding into me.

"Then maybe it's time to put my money where my mouth is." I reached down and started unfastening his jeans. "And I have plans for where my mouth should go."

He groaned, leaning back as he stretched out. "You're gonna be the death of me."

Not if I could help it.

———————————

Chapter 21

———————————

A little over an hour later, we pulled up behind the convenience store. I wasn't confident I'd secured my blond wig well enough, but I wasn't anticipating anyone grabbing my hair and yanking.

I wore jeans and a T-shirt with a jacket to cover my shoulder harness, my gun strapped in. I also had a backpack with supplies I might need. I wasn't used to long hair and kept wanting to pull it back into a ponytail, but I needed to look as different as possible—and I definitely didn't look like myself.

The plan was for James to stay behind the building while I walked around to the front door. Once I was inside, I'd let him in through the back door, and he'd wait in the storeroom.

We'd made contingency plans: what to do if she screamed —run out the back. What to do if she wanted to leave her trafficker—we'd bring her with us and figure out where to take her later. What to do if her handler came in—alert James, who would help me disarm him if necessary, then run out the back. What to do if he held me at gunpoint—alert James, and he'd shoot the bastard.

One thing I refused to plan for was walking away with a

big, fat nothing. I'd told him I wasn't going to allow that negative thinking into my head.

After I headed around the building, I walked into the store and spotted Cassandra at the counter. She glanced up when I came in but didn't give me more than a millisecond of attention. When the customer she was ringing up walked out the door, I approached her.

She flicked her eyes over me, curious. "The bathrooms ain't locked, honey. You don't need a key."

"Cassandra, it's me," I said.

Her gaze snapped to my face with confusion, then recognition. Her eyes widened. "Oh, my God. You're undercover."

I grinned. "Good to have confirmation it worked."

"Girl, if I hadn't planned to see you tonight, I never would have guessed it was you. Even if I checked you out at my register."

"I take it your girl hasn't been in yet?"

She shook her head. "Not yet, but if she follows the usual pattern, she should be here within the next ten minutes."

"I'm gonna try to talk to her and make sure she's okay." I leaned in a little. "Would it be okay if I take her to the back?"

Cassandra pursed her lips. "Honey, you can try, but she's as skittish as a bass at a fish fry. I doubt she'll agree to talk to you, let alone go to the back."

"How likely is it that she's been trafficked?" I asked.

Cassandra nodded as the bell over the door clanged behind me. She lowered her voice. "I should've realized it last night, but she's a regular, you know? And I thought most of those girls were older. And kept better guarded. She comes in alone, but a man sits in a car and waits for her."

My heart skipped a beat. "How old do you think she is?"

Cassandra's gaze tracked the customers behind me, and her mouth tightened. In the convex mirror behind her, I saw two guys by the beer case.

"Dunno. She wears a lot of makeup to cover it up," she murmured. "But I'd guess her to be about fourteen. Maybe fifteen."

My blood ran cold. I wasn't sure why the information about her age had caught me off guard. I *knew* young girls got trafficked—I wasn't naïve. Maybe I'd gotten thrown off by Wilhemina from the Velvet Room. She wasn't underaged. But runaway teen girls, or girls from rough homes were easy prey. Desperate for somewhere to sleep and something to eat. They just didn't know they'd traded one prison for another.

Now I really wanted to help this girl.

"I guess we'll see what happens," I said. "For now, I'll wait by the bathrooms, so I don't look suspicious to anyone outside."

She waved a hand. "You do you, girl. If this child is really bein' pimped out, then I'll do anything I can to help her. Lettin' you stand by the bathrooms is no big deal."

"Thanks."

I headed to the back, opened the back door, and found myself face-to-face with an angry James Malcolm.

"What the fuck too so long?" he growled under his breath.

I let him in and made sure the door was shut behind him. "I was talking to Cassandra. Letting her know I was going to hang out back here while I waited."

His eyes narrowed. "You didn't tell her I was gonna be back here, did you?"

"What do you take me for?" I grumbled. "An amateur?"

"No." His voice stayed low. "A rule follower."

It felt like a judgement, not a statement. "Not anymore, I'm not," I said, bitterness slipping out before I could stop it.

"Hey."

I turned to face him, his face inches from mine.

"You can change your mind about any of this at anytime," he said, his voice rough and insistent.

I shook my head. It was obvious he'd misunderstood. "I'm okay with not following the rules."

"Then what are you pissed about?"

That was a good question.

Why *was* I bitter? Because I was furious that I'd lost my badge and was being forced to handle all of this outside the law? Or because I was angry I'd waited so long to color outside the lines?

I decided to ignore the question and tell him something more important. "Cassandra says she thinks the girl is about fourteen or fifteen."

A hard look filled his eyes.

"Hey, girl," Cassandra called out, louder than I'd ever heard her. "You in for your nightly treat?"

I shot a glance at James. "She's here. And early."

"Be careful," he ground out.

"I've got this," I whispered, and headed to the front.

I did *not* have this. In fact, the more I thought about it, the more I realized there was almost no chance she'd talk to me. I was a complete stranger *and* a woman. Even if she wanted help, she'd probably assume I couldn't protect her.

When I emerged from the hall into the store, I paused and flicked a glance at Cassandra. She nodded toward the far back corner, her eyes wide.

I headed that way, pretending to browse the coolers as I closed the distance. I stopped about six feet away from the girl, opened a cooler door, and ran my fingers over the bottles like I couldn't decide.

Then I stole a quick look at her.

She was a few inches over five feet, though her worn black ankle boots added a couple of inches. Her legs were covered in sheer black tights with a few small holes, topped by a black micro-mini skirt. A denim jacket covered her top. She was blond with a quarter inch of dark roots. When she opened the cooler, she turned slightly, and I caught her heavy, dark eye makeup and bright red lips.

Cassandra was right. She looked young. Maybe even younger than fourteen.

I shoved down a wave of horror and fury. If she thought I was angry, I'd scare her off.

She grabbed two energy drinks from the cooler and turned toward me. Under the denim jacket, she wore a low-cut black tank top. A sliver of her red bra peeked above the plunging neckline, too deliberate to be accidental.

She saw me looking and dropped her gaze.

How the hell was I going to approach her?

Cassandra said she usually got candy too. I took a bottle of water and drifted to that aisle. After snagging a Snickers bar, I hovered like I was debating something else. She followed but kept her distance. She was skittish, like she'd been coached not to interact with anyone in the store. We had a product stand between us and the window, but it was low enough that anyone outside could see our heads.

As if to prove it, she glanced over her shoulder toward the door.

I followed her gaze to the white, older Buick parked just to the left of the entrance. A dark-haired man sat behind the wheel. I'd peg him to be in his mid-to-late thirties.

"You gettin' somethin' for your dad?" I asked, keeping my tone light and conversational.

Her eyes flew wide. She snapped her gaze to mine, terror washing over her face.

"Hey," I said, softening my voice. "Are you okay? Do you need help?"

I took a single step toward her out of pure instinct, but she took one back, clutching the energy drinks to her chest as if they were a shield.

I cast a glance at the Buick again. The guy was looking down at his phone.

I dropped to a squat, putting myself out of his line of sight. "I won't hurt you," I said quietly. "I want to help."

She stared at me, frozen.

Fight or flight … and this girl wasn't a fighter.

Then again, a trafficker didn't want a fighter. They'd cause too much trouble. But girls like the one in front of me—small, scared, easily controlled—they were easy pickings.

My stomach roiled. I felt like I was going to be sick.

"You don't have to go out that door and get in his car," I said gently. "I can make sure you're protected."

She shook her head, tears filling her eyes.

"Do you want to go with that man?" I asked. When she didn't answer, I tried a different route. "How old are you?"

She lifted her chin. "Sixteen."

"How old are you *really*?" My voice went softer.

Surprise spread across her face. Then, to my shock, she whispered, "Thirteen."

My stomach dropped and my resolve to save her doubled down. "Do you want to go with that man?"

She gave a slow, terrified shake of her head.

"Harper," Cassandra called out, a sharp warning in her voice. "He's comin' in…"

Panic exploded over the girl's face. She bolted for the door, still clutching the cans to her chest.

I stood and watched as she collided with the driver, who'd been approaching the entrance.

He grabbed her upper arm and shook her hard enough that the cans slipped from her grip and clattered to the ground. His free hand lifted like he was about to strike her, but then he glanced at Cassandra through the window and dropped it. Instead, he shoved the girl toward the spill. "Pick up those cans and get your ass in the car."

I didn't think he saw me, but I couldn't be sure.

Cassandra's gaze snapped to mine. "What are we gonna do?"

I knew exactly what I was going to do. I was furious I'd just stood here and hadn't done it sooner.

I rushed to the end of aisle, ready to bolt for the exit, when a hand snaked around my upper arm and locked me in place.

James.

"You're gonna let her go," he said low.

I glared up at him, fury boiling over. "The fuck I am. *Let go.*" I tried to jerk free, but his grip tightened, hard enough I'd probably have bruises tomorrow.

"We're gonna get her," he said through gritted teeth, holding my gaze. "Just not yet."

"In two weeks when we figure out where they're stashing her?" I spat out, yanking again but getting nowhere.

"Tonight," he snapped. "After we follow them to wherever he's takin' her."

I stopped fighting.

He was right. It was the better plan. And I felt like an idiot for not thinking of it myself.

I turned to Cassandra, who looked like she was about to call 911 on James.

"He's with me," I said. "About her drinks—I can pay—"

"Go!" Cassandra shouted. "The guy's backin' out."

Sure enough, the guy was looking over his shoulder as he reversed out of the space. I didn't see the girl in the front seat.

James released my arm and sprinted for the back, and I was right on his heels. We jumped into the car. He backed out within seconds and shot toward the road.

The white Buick had just turned right onto the street. James pulled out behind it, leaving several car lengths between us.

After about a half minute of silence, he said, "I understand.'

"Understand what?" I asked, still pissed at myself. "Why I threw common sense out the window and almost blew everything?"

"Why you wanted to rush out there and beat the shit out of that guy."

I shook my head. "I was being stupid. I wasn't thinking like a cop."

"That's bullshit," he said flatly. "You were thinkin' exactly like a cop. If you'd had a badge, you would have done the same thing. Only instead of beating the shit out of him, you would have slapped cuffs on him and read him his rights."

"I'm not sure that's much better," I grumbled. "We just established less than two hours ago that I need to stop thinking that way."

"Why did you become a cop?" His tone demanded an answer.

"Fuck you, Malcolm," I sneered. It was the last thing I wanted to talk about right now.

"Why did you become a cop?" he repeated, shooting me a dark glare.

"Because I wanted to help people," I said bitterly. "Like a goddamned Pollyanna."

"Don't do that." His tone softened. "Don't shit on yourself for that. Because I know you were a good cop, before you became a damn good detective."

I snorted. "And how do you know that?"

"Because you care about people," he said. "The ones who can't help themselves."

Some of my anger bled off. "How would you know that?" I asked, my tone still sharp.

"I saw the way you tracked down that missin' girl two months ago. And I knew you weren't just lookin' for Hugo

Burton because it was your job. You wanted to give his kids closure."

I breathed in and out a few times. "So?"

"Don't you get it, Harper?" He shot me a steady look. "That's why we work so well together. You're the heart of the two of us."

I cracked a sardonic grin. "I suppose that makes you the brains?"

"No," he said, deadpan. "It makes me the muscle. We're both the brains."

I considered what he said. "You have heart."

"Not as much as you," he scoffed. "And I'm not saying you're all heart and I'm all brawn. I saw you hold your own with Tex, and I've seen her wipe the floor with plenty of well-trained fighters."

"She was going easy on me."

He barked a sharp laugh. "She doesn't go easy on anyone, which is why she offered to spar with you again." He glanced at me. "What I'm tryin' to say, and apparently doin' a shitty job of, is that we balance each other out."

"But I still fucked up back there," I said. "You're right. I was missing the bigger picture."

"You were thinkin' like a protector," he said, "Don't apologize for that. I'll pull you back when your protective instincts override the plan, and you'll be there to rein me in when I want to go scorched earth."

I turned in my seat to look at him. "What if I want you to go scorched earth?"

"Then grab a flamethrower and join me," he said, "And when I think you're doin' the right thing protectin' someone, I'll be right there, kickin' ass next to you."

A flood of emotion rushed through me. What I had with James felt too good to be true.

But I was also thinking about that girl—who was probably in the backseat of that white Buick, two cars in front of us.

"I think I made things worse for her," I said, my voice breaking. "I think he hurt her."

"And I'll make him pay for that," he said, his voice low and dangerous. "We're gonna save her, Harper. But by lettin' her go for just a short while, we can follow him back to wherever he plans to have her work and get her there. This way, we can save a bunch of other girls too."

He was right, which made me feel like even more like a fool for trying to run after her. "Do you think she's going to tell us where they are? She might not even know."

"Maybe not, but the asshole drivin' the car in front of us sure does, and he's gonna tell us where they are and a whole lot more."

"You're gonna…" I wasn't sure how to finish that sentence.

"Capture him?" he asked, then shot me a dark look. "Get information out of him? You bet your ass we are."

"Information gathered through torture isn't reliable," I felt obligated to say.

"The fuck it's not," he grumbled, then nodded to the car in front of us. "He's gettin' on the highway and heading for the interchange. He might be part of Knox's crew after all."

If only we could get that lucky.

But I was stuck on the fact that James planned to beat information out of him … and the reality that I wasn't as horrified at the thought as I should have been.

Then again, he was forcing a child to have sex with men in truck cabs. I wasn't going to lose any sleep over him getting exactly what he deserved.

Sure enough, the white car pulled off the highway and into a truck stop, driving to the back lot. He found a spot behind several rows of trucks and backed in, probably so he could watch the girl as she worked the trucks.

James parked on the side of the store, the handler's car within view.

"Do you think he'll recognize you?" James asked as he turned off the engine.

"No. If he noticed me at the convenience store, it was brief, and I doubt he'd think a blond woman in her thirties would follow him to a truck stop."

He shot me an evil grin. "To his detriment."

Something fluttered in my stomach, heat blooming in my core. "You need to stop saying things that get me hot when we're in the middle of a stakeout."

Surprise filled his eyes, then he laughed. "*To his detriment* turned you on?"

I laughed too. "It was more like the way you looked at me as you said it," I pushed out a frustrated sigh. "It's beside the point. What's our plan?"

"You're gonna let me handle this one?"

"You probably have more experience with kidnapping than I do. I have none."

If he was offended, he didn't let on. "I'll take the driver, get him in the trunk of his car, and knock him out. I'll drive his car to a secure location, then ask him a bunch of questions." He nodded to me. "Your job is to convince the girl to come with you."

"And then?"

"Then you figure out where she can go, even if it's temporary. If she knows where other girls are bein' kept, *do not* go without me."

"Why would I go without you?"

"Because I'm going to be tied up for a while with our friend over there, and you'll be making sure the girl doesn't bolt."

"You plan on questioning him by yourself?" I asked, unease crawling up my spine.

"I'll be fine. He'll be temporarily incapacitated."

"No." I shook my head. "I don't like it."

"I'll be fine," he repeated. "I'll have Carter send in some backup. You focus on the girl." He lowered his face to mine. "And just the girl. Promise me you won't go after more girls if this one knows where they're kept."

"James…"

"You have to trust me on this, Harper," he said tightly. "Even if you successfully roll in and save half a dozen girls, we both know there are more out there. If Knox knows we're on to them, he'll move them, then the information I get out of *Creeper* over there will be worthless."

He had a point. We were working with limited time. When Creeper and the girl didn't show back up, his boss—Knox or whoever else—would be on high alert.

"Okay. I'll wait for you. I'm not taking her back to our room, though. Who knows what her mental state is. I can't have her knowing where we're staying in case she changes her mind and decides she wants to go back to Creeper and his crew."

He gave me a dark look. "I suspect Creeper won't be around to go back to, but you're right. You still got the credit card you used a few days ago?"

I ignored the statement about Creeper. "Yeah. In my bag." It felt like my trip to the Walmart in Hot Springs had been a few weeks ago rather than yesterday.

"Text me when you figure out where you're goin' tonight. But don't send the address in a text or voicemail. Wait until I call."

In case things went south.

My heart began to race. We'd done questionable things together, but this was by far the most dangerous.

He held my gaze. "You good?"

I nodded. "You?"

He smiled, an honest-to-God smile that lit up his entire

face. "Never been better." He leaned over and kissed me, slow and soulful. When he pulled back, he said, "Don't leave with the girl until you see me sitting in Creeper's driver's seat."

I nodded, swallowing hard to steady myself.

He pressed the keys into my palm. "Time to get some answers." Then he opened the driver's door, climbed out, and walked around the front of the building.

I suspected his plan was to walk around the other side of the store and use the shadows to hide him as he crossed to the back of the parking lot, then sneak up on the driver from behind. Was he feeling up to it? Would his concussion throw him off? I had to trust he knew what he was doing … and hope to hell I could uphold my end of the bargain.

The girl still hadn't gotten out of the car, but the guy remained in the front seat, his phone to his ear.

Great. Was he alerting someone that the girl had taken too long inside and run out of the store? What excuse had she given him? Had she told him the truth?

I wasn't worried about myself. I was worried about the girl. Trafficked young people were trained to avoid questions and stay within sight of their handler. Even if he hadn't seen me, he could have realized she was talking to someone.

What if she hadn't told him I'd approached her, and he thought it was the other way around?

Stewing about it wasn't going to do me any good. And neither would sitting in the passenger seat of this car.

I considered moving the car closer to the trucks, but I still didn't know where Creeper planned to have her work. There were three rows of trucks, and she could be going to any one of them. Besides, I wanted to see what he did when she got out of the car.

I didn't have to wait long. Less than ten seconds later, the back door opened. She climbed out slowly, then shut it behind her.

The guy got out and stepped up beside her, speaking to her aggressively based on the hate on his face.

Her entire body trembled as she nodded.

He grabbed her arm and dragged her closer until their faces were inches apart, his mouth moving, still threatening or berating her. Then he gave her a vicious shove. She stumbled back, nearly falling, but caught herself and took off toward the row of trucks closest to his car.

He stayed planted in front of the car, watching until she passed the front of the truck on the end before he got back in.

If I headed that direction, he'd see me, which meant I needed to move my car. But would he notice? Or, more to the point—would he see me as a threat? An innocent-looking blond woman alone in a car. He probably figured I wasn't likely to notice anything. Still, he might get twitchy if I drove in that direction seconds after she walked that way.

But if I went inside the store before I left, he probably wouldn't think twice about it. If he was paying attention to me at all.

I got out of the car and walked to the front of the store, putting myself out of his line of sight.

The trucks were parked at an angle away from the building, so I couldn't see the girl, but the driver's side window on the first truck rolled down and the trucker leaned out as if he was talking to someone. Seconds later, the window went up and his head disappeared. When I didn't see the door open, I realized he must have sent her away.

Thank God. Because if I saw her get into a truck cab, the driver was going to wish he'd never met me.

I couldn't see her, but I suspected she was heading to the next truck. It felt too soon to move my car, but what if the second truck driver took her up on her offer? I couldn't stand the thought of one more pervert putting his grubby hands on her.

I hurried back to the car, slid into the driver's seat, and started the engine.

Creeper was still in his car, his attention fixed on the trucks, which meant James hadn't made his move.

I backed out of the space and headed between the first and second row of trucks, although the second and third row had fewer trucks. As I drove past the second truck in line, I saw her standing on the running board, looking up as she spoke to the drive through the open window.

Feeling a sense of urgency, I parked in an empty spot in the third row, several spaces away from the last truck. Someone might say something to me about parking in an eighteen-wheeler spot, but I didn't plan on being there long enough for it to matter.

I got out and jogged along the back row of trucks. When I was a few spaces from the end, I cut across to the second row, crouching to see if I could spot her legs beneath the trailers. She'd made it to the third truck.

I'd planned to just intercept her, but Creeper was watching too closely. He'd notice if she started lingering between trucks. But if she got in the cab? He'd be less suspicious. It would be like business as usual.

Taking a chance, I slipped between two rigs and moved toward a cab two trucks down from the last one I'd seen her approach.

I climbed up on the running board and knocked on the window. The seat was empty, but I could see a light on in the sleeper section in the back. I knocked again, and a few seconds later, an older man leaned forward between the seats. He saw me and made a face.

"I ain't interested, honey," he said from behind the glass. "Besides, ain't you too old to be turnin' tricks?"

Compared to the girl who was now one truck over, I probably was.

"That's not why I'm here," I said, keeping my voice low. I was pretty sure he couldn't hear me, which is likely why he climbed into the front seat and lowered his window, looking like he already regretted it.

"See that girl over there?" I kept my head angled down in case Creeper was looking this way. "She's been trafficked, and I'm trying to get her out."

His eyes flew wide. "Did her family hire you to save her?"

If only.

"Something like that," I said, because sadly, he'd probably think she had greater worth if someone was willing to pay me money to bring her home. "But her handler is over there in that white car watching."

He glanced in that direction, his jaw tightening. "What do you need me to do?"

"I need you to let her into your truck."

His mouth fell open, and he shook his head. "What? No! I'm a happily married man, and I ain't into that stuff."

"I know." I kept my voice even. "That's why I approached you." Total lie. "But I need you to let me in first. Then, when she approaches, you let her in and I'll convince her to come with me."

His face pinched. "Why wouldn't she want to go with you?"

I did *not* have time for this. "Because she doesn't know me," I said. "I'm a PI who was hired to bring her home, remember? But who knows what she's been through. Maybe even brain-washing. It's going to take some convincing to get her to leave with a complete stranger."

Through his side window, I could see she was still talking to the driver of the rig next to this one—a rough-looking guy in his late twenties or early thirties. The way he was eying her told me everything. She was going to get into a truck cab, but it wasn't going to be this one.

Dammit.

The older trucker frowned. "I don't know about this. Maybe we should just call the police."

This was getting worse by the second. "No police. By the time they get here, her handler will know something's up, force her into his car, and take off." I took a chance and lifted the edge of my jacket. "I'm armed and can handle him if I need to, but I'd rather do this quietly and avoid a scene."

He still didn't look convinced, but thankfully, he didn't seem spooked by my gun.

The guy in the next truck was opening his door.

"Fuck me," I muttered and hopped off the running board.

"Such vulgar language!" the older trucker called after me as I ran to the front of the truck and peeked around the corner to see if James had taken care of the handler.

Creeper was still in the driver's seat, his gaze focused on the truck the girl had climbed into. If I tried to get her out, Creeper would see. But there was no way in hell I was going to stand here and let that girl have sex with yet another pedophile.

"Dammit, James," I muttered. What was taking him so long?

Then I saw him lurking by a dumpster about ten feet from the car.

Maybe James needed a distraction. Letting Creeper see me might not be such a bad thing after all.

I stomped around the front of the truck, making sure Creeper saw me as I walked up to the driver's door of the truck and jumped up on the running board, noticing the elaborate artwork of a dragon on the side panel.

I didn't see anyone in the front seats, so I started pounding on the window with both fists. When there was no response, I slammed my fists against the glass again and shouted, "I saw that girl go into your truck! If she's not out in five seconds, I'm calling the police!" I beat on the window again.

Creeper had noticed the commotion. He got out of his car and stalked to the front of his car, looking like he was about to head this way and confront me.

James snuck up behind him until he was about a foot away. Creeper stiffened, and seconds later, James steered him toward the trunk, following closely behind him.

Time to get the girl out of here.

I pulled my gun and held it up to the window, hoping the trucker could see it. "Asshole, I've got a gun and you don't send that girl out here, I'll use it!"

"You can't shoot me back here," he shouted from the sleeper section, his voice muffled by the glass.

"Maybe not," I shouted. "But I can shoot your fancy paint job! Or I can run this barrel down the side and add a little artwork of my own."

"I'll call the police, lady!" he called out.

"And I'll tell them you're trying to have sex with a thirteen-year-old girl," I shot back. "Maybe I should call them myself and give them your license plate number. That way they won't have any trouble finding you."

He scrambled to the front, bare-chested, but thank God, still wearing pants. I wasn't sure what I would've done to him if he'd already molested her.

"I didn't know she was thirteen, honest to God!" he shouted, his eyes wide with panic. "She told me she was seventeen!"

"That's still underage, you fucking pervert. Where is she?"

He shot a disgusted look over his shoulder. "She's freakin' out in the back."

"Open your door," I said, my voice full of menace.

"No way!" he barked. "You've got a gun!"

"I just want the girl. Send her out, and I'll leave you alone." I hated that I was letting him off, but what could I do? Actually call the police? They wouldn't do anything without proof, and besides, after Natalie's news about all the dirty cops on the force, I couldn't trust them.

The truck driver turned and snarled at the back, "Get the fuck out of my truck! I'm not gettin' shot over you!"

I leveled the gun, pointing it at his face through the glass. "If you talk to her like that again, my no-shooting-you rule will fly right through this fucking window."

He held up his hands, fear washing over his features.

She suddenly appeared behind him, mascara tear streaks tracking down her cheeks. Thank God, she was still clothed too.

I swung my glare back to him. "Did you hurt her?"

He shook his head hard. "I didn't touch her, lady! We just got started, then you were bangin' on the window!"

Her eyes widened when she recognized me. Then they dropped to the gun. She shrank back.

"Roll down the window," I said to the driver, rapping the butt of my gun on the glass. "I need to talk to her." When he looked like he was going to say no, I leveled the gun on him.

The window started to lower, but only halfway.

That was all I needed.

She was still between the seats, frozen with fear.

"It's okay," I said softly. "You're safe. But we need to go. *Now.*"

"Go where?" she asked, her voice shaking.

It occurred to me that she might come easier if she thought she was doing what she was supposed to do. "Back to the house," I said, praying she was kept in a house.

She seemed to relax slightly. "What happened to Buddy?"

"He's indisposed," I said. "I've been sent to bring you back."

She shook her head. "I don't know you."

"I know. I'm new—from another house. There wasn't time for me to meet all the girls. But we really need to go."

"But we just started," she whispered, tears spilling again. "I haven't hit my minimum yet."

The trucker shoved his door open, and I slid sideways before it knocked me off the running board. "I'm not getting in the middle of this." Then he turned back to her. "Get out!"

I'd jumped to the ground. I was about to climb back up, but the girl scrambled over him and nearly fell out of the cab, face-first onto the pavement. I caught her with my free hand and held her arm until she found her footing.

She pulled free and rushed to the front of the truck, eyeing the Buick, then froze when she saw James sitting in the driver's seat.

"Where's Buddy?" she asked, shaking like a leaf.

"I told you. He's indisposed. We need to go. *Now.*"

She pivoted to look up at me, terror in her eyes. "Are the police really comin'?"

I suspected her fear of law enforcement would get her moving. "Yeah. Which is why we need to go. But not with that guy in Buddy's car. You're supposed to come with me."

Her gaze dropped to the gun in my hand. When she nodded, I struggled to hide my relief. I led her to the row behind the truck, moving fast. Thankfully, she kept up.

"I don't understand what's going on," she said, crying again as we made it to the lane and walked quickly toward my car. "I don't want to get in trouble."

"You won't be in trouble," I promised. "I was sent to get you. We just need to hurry."

When we reached the car, she automatically reached for the handle of the back door. I suspected she always rode in the back, staying out of sight.

I slid behind the wheel, slipped my gun back into its holster, and started the engine. Seconds later, James pulled the white Buick up beside me, facing the opposite direction so the driver's side windows lined up. We rolled down our windows at the same time.

"Good thinkin' with the distraction," he said.

"Thought I'd speed things along," I said, keeping my voice down.

His gaze flicked to the backseat window, then back to me with a questioning look.

"We're good," I said. "I told her Buddy is indisposed."

He gave a slow nod of understanding. "Be careful."

"You too," I managed, pushing down my nerves. Things had gone well up until this point. I had to trust they'd keep going that way.

He gave me a grim smile, then rolled up his window and drove off.

Chapter 22

"Are you sure I'm not in trouble?" the girl asked from the backseat.

"Positive."

"Why were you at the gas station?"

"That's a really good question," I said, scrambling for a believable excuse. "I was there to take over for Buddy. He knew he was in trouble, and when he saw me, he freaked out and made you leave. He thinks he's getting fired."

"Is he?" The hope I heard in her voice nearly broke my heart.

I glanced up to meet her eyes in the rearview mirror. "I promise you that you'll never have to worry about Buddy again."

She held my gaze for half a second, then dropped it to her lap. "What about Savannah?"

"What about her?" I asked, filing the name away. Was she another girl? Or a handler?

"She's the one who usually takes over for Buddy."

I'd heard it wasn't uncommon for trafficked girls to age up

and start taking on some leadership positions. Was that who Savannah was?

"She's busy with something else the boss is dealing with." I kept my voice steady. "I'm Amber, by the way." I used my alias on instinct. "Sorry—I forgot your name. Things happened fast."

"Lexi," she said. Silence stretched for a few seconds. Then, softly she asked, "Is Nixon mad at Buddy? I heard him say Buddy isn't bringin' in enough money." Her fear-filled eyes lifted to mine in the mirror. "Is he mad at me too?"

My heart kicked hard. Nixon. A direct connection to Knox.

"I didn't make my minimum tonight," she continued, sounding panicked. "We just got started. I only made the fifty from that guy, and I hadn't even done nothin' yet."

"It's okay," I said firmly. "I promise. There's something big going on, so Nixon pulled us. He told me we need to lay low for a bit."

Her face was a mess, so I leaned over, grabbed my backpack from the passenger-side floor, and pulled out a pack of wet wipes. I handed them back to her.

She took them, gave me a questioning look, then pulled out a wipe and started to wash off her face.

"Are we goin' back to the other girls?" she asked in a small voice.

I considered telling her the truth, who I was and what was happening, but it felt too soon. I needed her to feel comfortable with me first. "No, not yet. It's not safe. We're worried the police are about to raid the house." I watched her reflection to gauge her reaction.

Her eyes widened with fear, confirming my suspicions. They'd probably told the girls that if the police ever got hold of them, *they'd* be the ones in trouble.

Fresh tears streaked down her face. "Are Maya and the others gonna be okay?"

If I were her handler, I'd put the fear of God into her and use it to keep her obedient. I wouldn't be doing that. "Yeah. That's what Savannah's doing—moving them somewhere else. They'll be fine." But I had to wonder how much time we had before Knox realized Buddy and Lexi were missing and then tied their disappearance to me and James.

"How old is Maya?" I asked gently, figuring it made sense I wouldn't know. I was "new" after all.

"Fifteen."

I nodded slowly, then lied. "But if they do get raided before the move, she's young enough that the police will take her into the station, then release her. And one of the others would be there to get her."

She nodded, looking torn between relief and resignation.

I wasn't sure how long I could keep up this ruse, but I needed to wait until we were holed up in a motel room before I came clean and, hopefully, got information from her.

I'd already merged onto the highway, heading west on I-30, putting Little Rock behind us. The more distance I put between us and Knox, the better.

Even if it meant putting more distance between me and James.

Then again, maybe he had the same idea.

After about ten minutes, she glanced out the window and stiffened. "Where are we going?"

"The police might be looking for us," I said gently. "I'm trying to make sure we're safe, which means driving out of Little Rock a little bit."

She went still, then started shaking. "Are you moving me somewhere else?"

"You mean to another house?"

She slowly shook her head. "Another city. Maya said they were probably gonna move some of us to Memphis soon."

I fucking hated these people. "No, Lexi. I promise, we're just going to hide for a bit. We're leaving Little Rock, but we're not going far."

"Okay." She relaxed at that, sinking back into the seat.

"Are you hungry?" I asked.

Her gaze flicked up to mine in surprise. "Buddy says I shouldn't eat before I work."

I lifted a shoulder into a lazy shrug. "We're done workin' tonight, right? We might as well pick up something to eat. What sounds good?"

She looked even more stunned. "You're lettin' me pick? Buddy never lets me pick unless I had a really good night."

Buddy was a fucking prick, and I hoped James gave him what he deserved. And more. "Well, I'm hungry and I'm having trouble coming up with what I want," I said. "So, I thought you might have something in mind."

"I can pick *anything*?" she asked in a small voice.

I wasn't a hugger, but every part of my being wanted to pull over, wrap my arms around her, and promise her those people would never hurt her again. But I couldn't do that yet, so I kept my tone light. "Anything. You may not have made your minimum, but you did exactly what you were supposed to tonight, so consider this a reward."

Her face brightened, confirming what I'd already suspected: she'd been trained to please her captors, likely because they rewarded her when she did.

She seemed to mull it over for a few seconds. "Can I have some fries?" she asked, still tentative.

Fries? That's all she was asking for?

"Surely, you want more then fries," I said. "What about a hamburger? Hell, we don't even need to get fast food. We could get Chinese or Mexican." I couldn't take her into a restaurant, but I could have Carter order something for me to pick up. Either way, I figured I'd need to let him know where Lexi and I ended up so someone knew.

"Can we get McDonald's?" she asked wistfully. "I like their chicken nuggets."

"McDonald's it is," I said, already scanning the roadside for signs. "But I'm in the mood for a feast. I say we got lots of food, so what else would you like? A shake? Hot fudge sundae?"

Her eyes widened, then her expression tightened as she became guarded. "You're not like Buddy or Savannah."

I held her gaze in the mirror for several seconds. "No, Lexi. I'm not. I will *never* hurt you. I believe in treating people with kindness."

I worried I'd gone too far, too fast. An older girl would probably have been more suspicious, but she must have believed me because her shoulders loosened.

"I like you, Amber."

I swallowed the lump in my throat and gave her bright smile. "I like you too, Lexi. A lot. Which is why we're gonna buy lots of food. Maybe one of everything."

She giggled, and I couldn't help thinking she should be laughing with friends her age, not in the backseat of a car driven by a woman she believed would drive her to her next sex act.

A few miles later, I pulled up to a McDonald's drive through. I didn't order everything, but I did buy enough food to feed ten people.

While we waited in line, I sent a few texts to James, letting him know that Lexi had confirmed Buddy worked for Knox, and that Nixon was Buddy's boss. I also told him someone named Savannah was another handler, and a girl named Maya had said she thought they'd be moving girls to Memphis soon. The more he knew, the easier it would be for him to tell if Buddy was telling him the truth.

When we reached the window and the cashier started handing in bag after bag, she said, "You must be feeding an army."

I shot a grin at Lexi, then said, "Something like that."

Lexi smiled shyly when I passed the bags back to her.

As I drove away from the window, Lexi pulled a carton from one of the bags, then started digging through the next one. "I'll just take some nuggets and some fries," she said quietly. "Then you can have the rest."

She probably thought this was a test.

"All I want is the quarter-pounder," I said, my stomach growling. I hadn't eaten much of our room service hours ago, and the smell of grease and salt was making me hungrier by the second.

She handed me the box, and I set it on my lap as I merged back onto the highway, trying to decide how far out of Little Rock to go. Close enough to get to James if he needed me, but far enough to feel safe.

I ended up taking a Benton exit, about thirty minutes out from Little Rock. Anything farther and we'd probably be pushing an hour.

When I pulled off the highway, Lexi froze with a chicken nugget halfway to her mouth. "Where are we goin'?"

"Remember?" I said gently, setting the now-empty burger box on the passenger seat. "It's not safe to go back yet. So, we're gonna stay in a motel until we hear the all clear."

"Oh," she said carefully, like she wasn't sure she should believe me.

As I pulled into the parking lot of a cheap motel, a new worry hit me. Did I bring her in when I booked the room? Or leave her in the car?

I didn't think she'd run. If she'd been scared enough to go with Buddy at the convenience store, I doubted she'd take off at some highway motel when she had no idea where we were.

Still, I decided to give her the choice. If she understood she had options, maybe she'd be more open when I told her the truth about who I was or, more accurately, who I wasn't.

I parked the car, turned off the engine, and turned in my seat to face her. "I need to go in and book a room." I paused, holding her gaze, grateful she wasn't as withdrawn as she'd been earlier. "What would you rather do? Come in with me or wait in the car?"

Her eyes went wide. "You're lettin' me pick?"

"Yeah," I said.

She looked confused, but I was relieved she didn't seem scared. "Is it okay if I come in with you?"

"You bet."

Worst-case, she'd tell someone she'd been trafficked and they'd call the police. But the far more likely outcome was that she'd stand quietly at my side.

And that's exactly what she did. I asked for a room with two beds for me and my daughter, using my card, then we drove down to the room and carried the food inside along with my backpack.

Lexi climbed onto the bed next to the bathroom, sitting cross-legged in the middle, and kept eating, now working on a hot fudge sundae.

"I need to make a call," I said. "I'm gonna be outside for a minute or two, but I'll be right back."

"Okay." She sounded happier than she had since I'd met her. "Can I watch TV?"

I'd considered taking the landline phone with me in case she decided to call one of Knox's people, but I didn't want to scare her. Besides, I could watch her through the window. "Go for it."

I opened the blinds, then stepped outside, glancing back. She was actually smiling as she flipped through the channels.

After I shut the door, I drew in a shaky breath, realizing my body was as tight as a piano wire.

I checked my phone, disappointed but not surprised that there was no response from James. He was probably busy. I sent him a text telling him that "we" were safe and to contact me when he could.

Next, I pulled up Carter's number and hit call. He answered on the first ring.

"Skeeter was hopin' you'd call," he said, sounding relieved.

"I'm guessing he let you know he captured one of Knox's men?"

"He said he *hoped* it was one of Knox's men," Carter said.

"The girl with me confirmed it," I said. "She said her handler answers to Nixon."

"That's good news," Carter said, sounding relieved. "A couple of men are headed to him as backup. They should reach him soon."

I breathed easier knowing he wasn't handling it alone.

"Skeeter said you were going to take the girl somewhere out of Little Rock."

"Yeah. We're at the Lucky Days Motel in Benton."

"Thanks for lettin' me know," he said. "Have you figured out what you're going to do with her?"

"Not yet." That was my next worry. "She's starting to trust me, so I'm hoping to find out more about her home life. Ideally, her family comes and gets her. But if they're trash…" I ran a hand over my head. "I don't know yet."

As a cop, I'd call child services and they'd put her in foster care. But there weren't a lot of great foster home options for a thirteen-year-old, and if they sent her to a bad one, it could possibly land her right back on the streets.

I needed to talk to her first.

After we ended the call, I went back inside.

Lexi had settled on SpongeBob, and my stomach dropped

when I thought about the situation I'd pulled her out of less than an hour ago.

Her gaze lifted to mine, apprehension filling her eyes. "Do we need to go back?"

I shook my head. "Nope. We're staying here for now."

She seemed to relax.

She trusted me. Would she trust me when she found out I'd lied?

I closed the blinds, then sat on the other bed, propping the pillows behind me and stretching my legs out.

"In the mess at the truck stop, I told you I'm pretty new," I said, trying to sound conversational. "How many girls do you have staying with you?"

She kept her gaze on the TV. "There's five girls in our house right now."

"It changes?"

"Once we had seven. And sometimes we only have three or four when girls move on."

"To places like Memphis?" I asked, keeping my tone light.

"And other places," she said, suddenly hesitant. "Maya says some girls get to have special assignments. She says they don't want to keep us in one place for too long."

I didn't want to ask too many questions at once and make her anxious or suspicious. Instead, I glanced at the food spread across her bed, and said, "You gonna eat that other fry?"

She stared at me, wide-eyed, her body going still.

"Don't get weird," I teased. I planted a foot on the carpet between our beds, then reached for the fry container. I leaned back on the bed and flashed her an exaggerated grin.

A slow smile tugged at her mouth. She glanced at the TV, then back to me. "Do you wanna watch something else?"

"Nope." I said insistently. "You watch whatever you want. I bet you don't get to pick very often."

She blinked, confused. "How'd you know?"

"Well…" I plucked a now cold fry from the carton. "I'm guessing you're the youngest in the house, and the older girls think they run everything."

Her face scrunched. "Yeah."

I felt relieved that she hadn't said anyone was younger than her.

"Which one of the girls is in charge when Buddy's gone?"

She looked surprise, then seemed to shake it off and gave her attention back to the TV. "Margo." She made a face. "She's mean. I hope she goes next."

I decided to just go for it. "How did you become one of Buddy's girls?"

She gave me a wary look. "I'm not supposed to talk about it."

"Okay." I kept my voice gentle. "Can you tell me how long you've been working with him?"

She bit her bottom lip. "I don't know. I started before Christmas."

Four months then. Four months too many.

She studied me, more curious than scared now. "Are you takin' over for Buddy."

"Sort of," I said.

"I hope so," she said with a sigh. "You're nice."

A lump filled my throat when I thought about what she'd probably been through.

"Where are you from, Lexi?" I asked.

She gave me an anxious look. "I'm not supposed to talk about that either."

"To outsiders," I coaxed. "Right? I'm part of the operation now."

She scooted back and leaned into the pillows, but she didn't answer right away. "Fayetteville."

"I've been to Fayetteville," I said, then lied, "I went to the college there."

Her eyes widened. "You went to college?" she asked in awe.

"Sure did."

"I used to want to go to college," she said in a small voice. "But Buddy says I'm too stupid."

I wanted to text James to cut off Buddy's balls.

"Buddy's full of shit," I said. "You can go to college if you want to."

"You can't if you don't go to school," she said.

She had a point. And it was an opening. "Did you like going to school?"

"I didn't think I did," she said softly. "But now I miss it."

"What do you miss the most?"

"My friends," she whispered.

"Do you ever talk to them?" I already knew the answer, but I hoped she'd keep confiding in me.

She gave a short, humorless laugh. "You must really be new. We can't talk to anyone from our past."

It was probably too soon to ask about her family, but the door was open now. "Do you miss your parents?"

She didn't answer. When I looked over, fresh tears were pooling in her eyes.

"It's okay to talk about them," I said gently.

She shook her head. "No. We're not supposed to talk about our families. Ever. We're supposed to forget about them."

"That has to be hard," I said.

"Yeah," she whispered.

"But you miss them, right?"

When she answered, her response was so quiet I almost missed it. "Yeah."

Relief stole my breath. She had a home she missed. Somewhere to go back to. Because I'd have taken her in myself before dumping her into the system. But my life wasn't exactly built for raising a thirteen-year-old girl who probably needed therapy and stability, not to mention that the big boss of the people who'd used her wanted to torture and kill me.

"Did you fight with your mom and dad a lot?" I asked, sliding down on the bed so I was lying down too, like we were just two people watching TV. "My mom hated me when I was your age. I couldn't wait to leave. I just didn't know I *could* when I was your age."

She was quiet for a long moment. "My mom and I fought a lot about my clothes." Her voice cracked.

"Did you run away?"

She slowly shook her head. "No, Mom was mad at me sometimes, but I never wanted to run away." She hiccupped a tiny sob. "I miss my mom. And my dad. I even miss Chloe."

"Is that your friend?" I asked.

She shook her head and swiped at her cheeks. "My little sister."

I wondered if it was smart to press any further. But this felt organic. Just part of a conversation. I only hoped she wouldn't think I was setting a trap.

"What if I told you that you could see them again?" I held my breath, bracing for her reaction.

She went rigid. "Buddy says I can't go back. That they don't want me. He says I disobeyed them, and I'm a stupid girl. They don't have time for stupid, disobedient girls."

"I'd bet you a hundred bucks Buddy's lying," I said. "Hell, I'd bet you even more than that."

She turned her head to look at me, terror in her eyes.

"There's only one way to find out." I lifted my brows. "We could call them right now." I slid my phone out and held it up. "We can ask."

She stared at the phone like it was a poisonous snake.

I sat up and turned to face her, my legs hanging over the side of the bed. "If you don't want to make the call, I can do it.

They don't even have to know you're here. I'll put it on speaker so you can hear what they say."

She looked horrified, slowly shaking her head.

"I know Buddy wouldn't let you call them," I said softly. "But I'm Amber. I'm going to do things differently than Buddy did."

Her breath hitched. "He said if I ever called them, he'd kill Chloe."

I schooled my face so Lexi wouldn't see my anger. The last thing I wanted was for her to think I was pissed at *her*. "Like I said, I'm in charge now."

"What if he comes back?" she whispered.

I could see the desperation and longing in her eyes. She wanted to go home. But Buddy had done everything in his power to make sure she never did.

I leaned forward, resting my forearms on my thighs, and held her gaze. "Lexi, Buddy is never, *ever*, coming back. He will never hurt you or anyone else ever again."

Understanding filled her eyes. Then hope rushed in behind it.

"If I call your parents, and they say they want you to come home—what do *you* want to do?" I asked gently. "Do you want to go home?"

She nodded slowly, tears streaming down her cheeks.

"Do you know their phone numbers? If you don't, I can find them."

"I know my mom's," she whispered.

I nodded, my heart racing. "What do you say? Do you want to call them or me?"

Her chest rose and fell a few times before she said, "You."

I understood. She'd been told her parents didn't want her. If it turned out to be true, she wanted the blow to land on me, not her. Even if she was listening.

I opened the keypad on my phone. "Okay," I said, knowing

I'd pick this decision apart later, wondering if I'd handled it right. "Give me her number, and I'll call."

Lexi sat up, shoving the half-empty containers to the other side of the bed, then swung her legs over the edge so she was facing me.

I waited. When she didn't speak for nearly a half minute, I said gently, "Be brave, Lexi. Let's call."

"Buddy says I'm not brave," she whispered. "He says I'm scared of my own shadow."

"Then let's show him he's wrong," I said, steady and sure. "Tell me her number."

Lexi's chest heaved. I reached over and took her hand.

"I'll be right here with you," I said softly. "And if they say they don't want you, we'll figure something else out."

Confusion filled her eyes. "Don't I need to go back to the house?"

I slowly shook my head. "No. Not if you don't want to. And wherever you go, I'll make sure it's with someone kind." I squeezed her hand. "Now be brave and tell me her number."

She held my gaze like she was trying to decide if she could trust me. Finally, she released my hand and whispered the number so quietly, I had to ask her to repeat it as I punched it in.

When I was ready to hit call, I gave her a reassuring smile. "What's your mom's name?"

"Anna."

I nodded, hit call, and prayed I was doing the right thing.

The phone rang several times. I was already mentally preparing myself to leave a voicemail—Lexi's mother might not answer an unrecognized number—so I was surprised when a woman picked up, distracted. "Hello?"

My heart slammed into my ribs. God, I hoped this wasn't a mistake. "Anna. I'm calling about your daughter, Lexi."

There was several seconds of silence before she bit out, "Is this some kind of sick *joke*?"

My stomach dropped. How could I have been so wrong?

Lexi scrambled off the bed and hurried to my side, whispering, "Emily. Tell her Emily."

Of course. Many trafficked girls were given new names.

"Emily," I corrected quickly. "Sorry, Lexi is the name they gave her." I swallowed hard. "Anna, I hate to ask you this, but… Emily needs to know that you want her to come home."

Lexi—Emily—pressed into my side and clutched my arm.

"Who are you?" Anna demanded. "How can you even ask me that? Are you trying to get a bigger reward?"

I glanced down at Emily and considered putting the phone on mute. But if her mother heard her fear—heard *her*—maybe Emily's voice could pull her mother back from the edge.

"Emily," I said, holding her gaze. "If your mom didn't want you to come home, she wouldn't offer a reward. I promise you, she wants you."

Anna broke. "Emily?" she sobbed. "Are you there?"

Emily's eyes grew huge, and she froze.

Then a man came on the line, his voice hard with panic and anger. "Why won't you assholes leave us alone? We've been through enough!"

I looked down at Emily. She still didn't move. She didn't believe it. Or maybe she was still stuck in her fear. She'd been through a lot tonight. This was probably too soon.

"I have Emily with me," I said, wishing I'd thought to ask Emily for her dad's name. "She's in the Little Rock area, and the people who had her convinced her that you and your wife don't want her back. She only needs to hear you say that you do."

The silence that greeted me was terrifying.

Then he spoke, and his voice broke. "Emily… are you really there?"

"It's okay," I whispered to her. "They love you. They really *do* want you to come home."

"Em," Anna said, breathless and desperate. "Please come home, baby. Please. I love you so much. Em… *please*."

Emily just stared at the phone.

"Emily," I said gently. "You have to say something. They need to know it's really you."

Her voice came out tiny. "Do you really want me to come home?"

Anna began sobbing in earnest, but her husband's suspicion surged right back. "Are you holding her for the reward?"

"I don't want your money," I said, keeping my voice level. "I just want to bring your daughter home. She said you're in Fayetteville?"

"Are you with the police?" he asked cautiously.

"No," I said. "I'm a PI, and I ran into your daughter tonight at a truck stop."

"At a truck stop?" Confusion edged his voice. "What would she be doing at a truck stop?"

"That's not important right now." I said, cutting him off before he could spiral. I didn't want to get into what Emily had been through on the phone. Especially not in front of her. "What matters is that your daughter wants to go home. Can you meet me halfway?" Under any other circumstances, I'd have driven her straight to Fayetteville myself. But that would put me a total of nearly three hours from Little Rock. Three hours round trip would be bad enough.

"Why don't you take her to the police?" he demanded.

Emily's grip tightened around my arm.

"No police," I said. "She's been conditioned to be terrified of them. Will you meet me or not?"

"What the hell are you doing, John?" Anna snapped, then her voice rose, sharp with purpose. "Where do we meet you? Just tell us where."

I exhaled with relief. "I need to figure out what's halfway between Fayetteville and Little Rock." Since I didn't have a smart phone, I'd have to find a map. Then I realized I didn't have to figure this out totally on my own. I could call Carter. "I'm going to hang up and start driving west on I-40. Once I pick a spot, I'll call you with the meeting location."

"This is a trick," the man muttered in the background.

"I assure you it's not," I said. "But I'm still working this case, and this is the safest way to get your daughter back to you." I hesitated, then went ahead and said it. "There's a good chance some members of the Little Rock police are involved in what Emily was mixed up in. And not in a good way."

Anna gasped. "No police," she said quickly. "I just want my baby."

I glance down at Emily. "Do you want to say something before we hang up?"

She looked up at me, eyes wide.

"You're brave, Emily," I said. "This was brave. You can do this."

She gave a slow nod, then turned to the phone. "I don't want to go to the police," she said softly. "They'll just send me back to Buddy." Her voice broke. "Mommy... I want to come home."

"I'm coming, baby," Anna said, breathless. "I love you, and once I have you in my arms, I'm never letting you out of my sight again. I'm grabbing my keys and leaving right now. I'm coming."

"Anna," her husband called out. "Wait. You can't just go meet some random woman who calls claiming to have our daughter!"

"That's Emily! I'm going!" she shouted. "With or without you!"

I looked over at Emily to see if she had anything else to say, but she shook her head.

"We're leaving now, Anna," I said into the phone. "I'll be in touch soon."

I ended the call and pulled Emily into a tight hug. "That was incredibly brave. I'm so proud of you."

She hugged me back for several seconds, then she tipped her chin up and gave me a shy smile. "You owe me a hundred dollars."

I grinned down at her. "After that? I'll give you two hundred."

Chapter 23

Once I knew she was okay, I told her I needed to make another call before we left.

She stared up, suddenly hesitant. "Are you really gonna take me to my mom?" She looked like she couldn't believe it was true. Then again, this was a lot for her to take in.

"Yes," I said earnestly. "I swear I am. But we're not on the right highway to meet her, and I don't have a smart phone to look it up. I'm going to ask my friend to give me directions." When she didn't look convinced, I said, "I swear to you, Emily. I'm taking you to your mom."

Her face softened. "Okay."

I hugged her again. "If you need to go to the bathroom, now would be a good time. As soon as I get off the phone, we're going."

Then I headed outside, called Carter, and filled him in on my latest development. "Can you figure out a good place to meet them?" I asked.

"Have them come to you," he said, sounding irritated. "You found their daughter. The least they can do is drive three hours to get her."

I heaved out a sigh. "If you're worried about me being too far from Little Rock, then find a place closer. Because I *am* meeting them somewhere on I-40, and I'm currently on I-30. I can figure it out myself, but I still have the cheap burner, and I'd rather take the time asking her questions about Knox's operation than spend it looking up directions."

"All the more reason not to meet her parents *anywhere* until you get all the information you can," he grumbled.

"Carter," I said in frustration. "I have a traumatized thirteen-year-old girl who has been abused in countless ways, and all she wants right now is her mother."

"Okay," he conceded, sounding contrite. "You're right. But this is an opportunity to get more information. You're letting emotion rule your decision-making."

Was I?

James said I was the heart of our team, but he'd pull me back if my heart ever got in the way. He wasn't here, though, so was I letting emotion overrule good judgment?

It didn't matter, I decided. I wasn't going to delay Emily's reunion with her mother over hopes she had useful information. She'd been through enough.

"No," I said firmly. "I'll get whatever I can from her on the drive. Go ahead and make the meeting location halfway, and that'll give me more time. Emily was at the lowest level of the operation, and she's only been there four months. She's not going to know much."

He didn't respond and I was sure he was about to berate me or tell me to figure it out on my own, but instead he laughed. "I knew you were perfect for Skeeter." Then he turned serious. "Fine. You're right. She probably doesn't know much. You should have plenty of time to talk it through in the car."

"Thanks." I paused, tense when I asked, "Have you heard from him?"

"Not yet."

"Do you know whether his backup has arrived?"

"I can confirm that they have," he said, sounding like an attorney and not a friend. His tone was ominous, but he'd tell me if James had run into trouble.

"If you hear anything, will you let me know?"

"I will if you'll do the same."

"Deal," I said. "And thanks."

Minutes later, Emily and I were in the car, only this time I insisted she sit in the front with me. She gave me a shy smile, and I reached over and squeezed her hand in reassurance.

I'd barely left the parking lot when Carter called and said he was texting me a location, along with directions. I pulled over before I got on the highway and called Anna to set the meeting, confirming we should be there in about an hour and a half.

Emily was quiet for the first fifteen minutes of the drive, and I let her sit in silence. I suspected she wouldn't fully believe she was going to be reunited with her mother until she saw Anna with her own eyes. What she'd been through over the last few hours, let alone the past four months, would be a lot for anyone, let alone a thirteen-year-old girl.

But once she realized we were really headed toward Fayetteville, she relaxed and seemed open to answering questions about her friends and her family. Then she began to open up about what she'd been through.

Buddy had found her online, sending her DMs on Instagram from the profile of a teen boy named Sebastion. He'd started out by telling her how pretty she was and convincing her that her mother was a horrible person who didn't understand her or care about her. He told Emily he was sixteen—still too old for her—but she was flattered by his attention. After a few months of messaging, he convinced her to meet him in person, telling her he'd pick her up after school in his car. He gave her his car's description and told her he'd park a block from the school so she wouldn't get in trouble. Then, to be extra safe—in case someone was watching and would tell her parents or the school—he told her to get in the backseat.

When she approached the car, she was hesitant to get in. The windows were tinted, and while she could see someone sitting in the front, she couldn't make out his features. But ultimately, she decided she really wanted to meet him and got in.

Only when she got in the car, she realized the man in the front didn't look anything like the photos of the boy she'd been talking too. She'd tried to leave, but the door was locked—child proofed. Buddy, who was behind the wheel, assured her that he was Sebastion's older brother and that Sebastian had to stay after school for a project. Sebastion hadn't wanted to cancel on her, so Buddy had agreed to pick her up. To make up for the change in plans, Sebastion had asked Buddy to pick up her favorite Boba drink.

Even though she'd felt uncomfortable, she'd taken his words at face value. Besides, how would a random man, driving the same car as Sebastion's, know her favorite drink? He pulled away from the curb, and she gulped it down.

The next thing she remembered was waking up in a bare bedroom, on a mattress on the floor.

I didn't ask her what they'd asked her to do or how they'd trained her to do it. I didn't want her reliving any of it with me. She needed to save that for a therapist. But I did ask her questions about the operations. How many girls had she seen? How many had been moved? How many handlers were there? What names had she heard? As expected, she didn't know much, but she'd seen Nixon a few days before. He'd come by the house and said he had a shipment coming in from Texas in five days, but the big boss was on edge and had considered cancelling it. She had no idea who the big boss was.

"Can you tell me what Nixon looks like?"

She bit her bottom lip. "He's tall and kinda scary lookin'."

"How so?"

"He's got big arm muscles and he has scary eyes. Mean."

I gave a slow nod. "What color are his hair and eyes?"

"He's got black hair." She touched her ear. "It's pretty short, like kind of shaved. And he had a beard that's kind of scruffy."

"And his eyes?"

"I didn't really pay attention." She shuddered. "I don't like to look at his eyes."

When she'd finished telling me everything she could remember, she looked over at me and asked quietly, "Are you really a PI?"

"Yeah, Emily. I am." I shot her a look. "Sorry I lied about who I was before, but I wanted to get you out of there, and it seemed like the best way at the time. I didn't think you'd come if I told you I was there to save you."

She nodded, glancing down at her hands in her lap. "You're right. I would have been too scared." She looked up again. "What are you investigating?"

I drew in a breath, wondering how much to tell her, then decided to go with the truth. "My partner and I are going to bring down the big boss."

"Nixon's boss?"

"Yep. And Nixon too."

"And Buddy?"

I gave her a half-smile. "He's already been captured."

"By the guy in Buddy's car?"

"Yeah."

She was silent again. "What happens to Maya and all the other girls?"

"They'll be free," I said.

"But Maya really doesn't have anywhere to go," she said softly. "Her stepdad kicked her out."

That's what I was afraid of. Those girls were living in hell, but some of their living situations before hadn't been much better. "I'm not going to tell you any more lies, Emily, so here's the truth." I glanced over at her. "I don't know what's going to happen to her. But it has to be better than what you girls lived through."

She turned to look out the window. "I don't know. She said at least Buddy gave her something to eat. She didn't always have that before."

My heart sank, but I didn't have an answer. And I'd promised I wouldn't lie. So I changed the subject.

"Your parents will probably want you to talk to the police," I said carefully.

She shook her head, panicking. "No!"

I covered her hand with my own. "Ordinarily, I'd tell you to talk to them, but in this case—"

She looked up at me with wide eyes. "Amber, the police really *are* bad. Buddy said Nixon and the big boss have policemen who work for them."

"I believe you," I said, "which is why I'm discussing it with you now. I think that's what your parents will want you to do, but I'm going to try to convince them not to. Okay?"

She nodded, still anxious but looking more appeased.

I glanced at her again. "Do you remember Buddy or Nixon talking about the police and using their names?"

She shook her head.

"Did you ever see any of the police? Did they come to the house?"

She started to shake her head, then stopped. "*Wait.* I saw a guy one time. Out at one of the truck stops when I first started. He stopped and talked to Buddy while I was working the trucks."

"Was he wearing a uniform?"

"No. He was wearing a suit. Maya was working the truck

stop with me. She told me he was a cop, and if I messed up, Buddy would let him take me."

Maya sounded like a first-class bitch, then again, she might have parroted what she'd been told.

But I was stuck on the fact the man was wearing a suit, which meant he was probably a detective. "Do you remember what he looked like?"

She shook her head. "It was dark and he was kind of far away. But I think he was tall and had dark hair."

"You didn't see his face?"

"No."

"Do you remember anything else about him?"

She shook her head. "I'm sorry."

"That's okay," I insisted. "You've told me more than enough. Thank you."

She was quiet for a moment. "Will they come find me when I go home?"

"No," I said firmly. "When my partner and I are done, there won't be anyone left to look for you." I noticed a sign announcing our exit a mile ahead. "We're almost to your mom. Are you nervous?"

She nodded. "What if she's mad at me for going to meet a boy after school?"

"Emily, I promise you—your mom will be so thankful you're home that she won't be mad." I gave her a long look. "But in the future, don't go off with random boys who DM you on Instagram."

Tears filled her eyes. "I won't. I learned my lesson."

I reached over and squeezed her hand again. "I know you did."

I turned off at the exit, and we pulled into a McDonald's parking lot. I started to park on the side of the building, but Emily sucked in her breath. "That's my mom's car." She pointed to a maroon SUV parked in the back row.

I drove toward it and parked two spaces down from the driver's side, leaving an empty spot between us.

The driver's door flew open, and a woman scrambled out of the vehicle. She wore jeans and a long-sleeved T-shirt under a chunky black cardigan. Her light brown hair was pulled into a messy bun. Her nose was red, but her face was pale.

Apprehension filled her eyes when she looked over at us, and I realized she couldn't see Emily in the car in the dark.

Emily was frozen in her seat, watching her.

"Do you want me to talk to her first?" I asked gently. It was probably a good idea to prepare her for what her daughter had been through.

She nodded once slowly.

"You stay in here as long as you need to, okay?"

I got out and a man walked around the back of the SUV, looking like he was spoiling for a fight. He was tall and bulky enough that he probably thought he could plow right through me.

He'd be in for a surprise.

He started to march forward, his gaze locked on the car like he was ready to rip the door off its hinges, but I stepped in front of him, blocking his path.

"Get the hell out of my way," he snarled.

"Mr. Harrison," I said in a firm voice. "You are *scaring* your daughter."

"You're keeping her from us!" he shouted.

"John!" Anna shouted at him. "Stop!"

"Why isn't she getting out of the car?" he demanded, shouting at his wife. "Is she even in there?"

"She's sitting in the front seat, free to get out when she's ready," I said. "It's not locked."

"Then why isn't she getting out?" he demanded.

I was having second thoughts leaving her with this asshole, but I reminded myself that his daughter had been missing for four months. Emotions were running high. But I also didn't want to deal with him right now.

I turned to Anna and closed the distance between us. "Anna, Emily's been through a lot. I mean a *lot*."

"She ran away with that boy," her father said. "We found her Instagram messages."

I turned to look at him, shaking my head in disgust. "Mr. Harrison, your daughter was kidnapped and trafficked to men at truck stops—"

Emily gasped, covering her mouth in horror.

I continued, "She was held against her will, and threatened so thoroughly she is terrified of just about anything that moves. They told her if she contacted you, they would kill her little sister. They also told her you didn't want her to come home. I guarantee you that your posturing isn't assuring her that you're happy to see her. If anything, it's going to convince her to stay inside the car."

He lost some of his bluster, but he was still pissed.

I turned back to Anna. "She's going to need help. She's definitely going to need therapy, probably lots of it, but right now what she needs most is you, your love and reassurance, and a safe, *calm* environment to heal."

She glared at her husband.

"Like I said, they convinced her you didn't want her," I continued, "but I got her permission to call you and prove to her they were wrong. She's still terrified you'll turn her away, though, so please, *please*, be gentle with her."

She nodded, clutching her hands against her stomach as tears filled her eyes.

I lowered my voice. "I know one of the first things you'll want to do is go to the police, but there are some cops in Little Rock involved in this. I just don't know who they are yet."

"How convenient," John said with a sneer.

Fury filled Anna's eyes. "John, shut the *fuck* up!"

"She can't handle that," I told her, pointing back at him. "She can't handle his anger, so if he's going to keep acting that way, *you* are going to have to protect her from it."

She nodded, a firm resolve filling her eyes. "She won't have to worry about him. I promise."

I breathed a sigh of relief. "I'm going to see if she's ready to get out yet."

She lifted her hands to under her chin. "Okay."

I gave her an encouraging smile. "But if she's not, don't take it personally, okay? She's terrified you'll reject her."

"Okay," she said solemnly. "I understand."

I walked over to the passenger door and partially opened the door, squatting so I was looking up at Emily, not down.

I reached over and placed my hand on her arm. "Are you ready to see your mom?"

She turned in her seat to face me. Tears swam in her eyes. "Does she still want me?"

I gave her an encouraging smile. "Yes. Very, very much."

Her eyes shifted over to her father, who was by the back bumper of their car, pacing. "But my dad's mad at me."

"No," I said. "He's not mad at you. He's upset that you got taken. Sometimes men can't handle their emotions, and it comes out as anger. That doesn't make it right, but it's just the way some guys are. But when you get old enough to have a boyfriend and maybe get married, you do *not* have to tolerate a guy who behaves like that, okay? You can find a guy who doesn't get angry under pressure."

She nodded.

I glanced back at her father, who had lost some of his temper, but I could see it was still simmering under the surface. "Is your dad usually an angry guy?"

She shrugged.

"I told your mom that he can't act like that around you. She said she won't let him."

"Thanks," she whispered.

"But if he doesn't behave, I want you to let me know, okay?"

Surprise filled her eyes, but she nodded.

I wasn't sure why I'd said that, but I felt responsible for her. She'd been through enough shit. She didn't need to deal with any more. I had no idea what I could possibly do, but I'd deal with that later.

I grabbed her hand and squeezed. "Are you ready for a hug from your mom?"

Tears spilled down her cheeks as she nodded.

"Okay," I said with a tight smile. "It's time to be brave again." I stood and opened the door farther so she could get out. Once her feet were on the ground, she hesitated, staring at her mother over the top of the car door.

Anna gasped when she saw her. Possibly because she wasn't sure she'd ever see her daughter again, or possibly because her daughter looked nothing like the girl who had gone to school last December and not come home. Probably both.

But it only took a second for Anna to get over her shock. She remained rooted in the middle of the parking space, giving Emily the chance to go to her. But then she flung her arms wide in welcome, tears streaming down her face.

That was all the encouragement Emily needed. She rushed to her mother, nearly knocking Anna down when she slammed into her. Anna wrapped her arms around Emily, and they both began to sob.

John watched them. The rest of his anger bled out of him, but he stayed in place.

I walked over to him, keeping my back to Anna and Emily, and lowered my voice. "I know you're upset, but what she needs from you right now is love and peace. You have every right to be pissed—especially after hearing about what she went through, but the people who did this to her won't get away with it. My partner and I are working on destroying the organization running this thing." I held his gaze. "The man who took her will *never* have the opportunity to get near her or any other girl ever again. As for the rest? We will *destroy* them. So put your energy into healing your daughter and not on vengeance."

He stared down at me and grimaced. "I was such an asshole."

I gave him a grim smile, but I was relieved he'd softened. "It was an odd phone call, but I had to convince her that you both wanted her home. Now just love her. That's what she needs."

I turned around and walked over to Emily.

When she saw me, she pulled away from her mother and turned to face me. "Are you leaving?"

"Yeah. You don't need me anymore. Now, I have to go save the other girls."

She threw her arms around me, hugging me tight. "Thank you."

My throat tightened and my eyes stung. "You're welcome." I squeezed her, then stepped back.

"Thank you," Anna said. "I can never repay you. The reward—"

"I don't want the reward," I said. "*Really*. I'd rather you give it to an organization that helps girls like your daughter."

She nodded. "Yeah. Okay."

I took a step back and looked down at Emily again. "If you ever need me, contact Carter Hale. He's an attorney in Jackson Creek, Tennessee. Tell him you need Harper, and he'll make sure I get the message."

She squinted up at me. "But your name is Amber."

"Just like yours was Lexi," I said.

Then I walked to my car and headed back to Little Rock.

Chapter 24

After I got back on the highway, I called Carter.

"You get the girl dropped off?"

"Yeah, now I'm headed back to Little Rock. Where's James?"

He hesitated. "Did you get anymore information?"

"Yeah," I filled him in on what she'd told me. "We need to figure out which cops are involved."

"Maybe you'll get lucky and find the accountant," he said. "He'll definitely have the names on the payroll."

"That would be ideal, but it seems like a reach. Still, I suspect we have hours at best before Knox figures out we've taken Buddy and Emily. Then we'll be back on the defensive."

"Skeeter's likely to get helpful information."

"Have you heard from him?" I asked.

"Not yet."

"Send me his location, and I'll see what he's found out."

He paused, then said, "I'm wondering if you two should move from the hotel and into a new safe house."

My back stiffened. "That's twice now I've asked for James's

location, and both times you changed the subject. Where is he, Carter?"

He took a beat. "He told me not to tell you."

"*Why?*"

"Probably not why you think."

"What do *you* think I'm thinking?"

"That he doesn't trust you."

Funny, that hadn't even occurred to me. "I know he trusts me, so why doesn't he want me to come find him?"

"I'm not sure if you noticed, Harper, but Skeeter's my boss. If he doesn't want to tell me things, I'm sure as hell not gonna push it."

"But you know where he is?"

"I do." He hesitated, before adding, "I'm guessing he doesn't want you involved in getting the information."

I let that sink in, not sure how to feel about it. Did he think I'd stop him? Would I? But the more likely answer was he didn't want me to get my hands dirty. He was protecting me. I wasn't sure whether to be grateful or annoyed.

But no matter the reason, I knew Carter wouldn't tell me, so arguing would be a waste of time.

"I think the hotel is safe for now," I said. "It's probably too soon for Knox to realize we've attacked his operation. I'll head back and wait there."

"I think you should go somewhere else until Skeeter's done. Maybe head east or north this time and wait for word from him."

"No," I said forcefully. "I'm going back to Little Rock, but if I get close to the hotel and think something's up, I'll leave and let you know."

"Are you going to let him know your plan?"

"Yeah, and I'll give him some highlights about what I learned from Emily."

"Sounds good," he said. "Hey, how are you doing with all this?"

"You'll have to be more specific," I said with a humorless laugh. "A lot has happened in the last three weeks."

"True. I'm talking about this mess with Knox, bein' on the run. What your dealin' with in Little Rock."

I considered his question. "Honestly, better than I expected."

"You sure?" he prodded.

"I'm fine," I said. "I'll let you know if I need anything else."

"Okay."

I started to hang up, then blurted out, "Hey, Carter. Do you have any information on Nixon?"

"You're not thinkin' about going after him by yourself, are you?"

"No. I don't have a death wish. I just want to compare it to the description Emily gave me."

"I don't have anything on him," he said. "But I'll see what I can find."

"Thanks."

I hung up, trying to decide what to do next. I knew I should probably go back to the hotel, but I was still wired from the last few hours, and I didn't feel like hiding in a fancy hotel room while James was working the case. Even if I didn't let myself dwell on how he was working it.

I could check in with my contacts. Cassandra had come through. It was still early enough that I could go by the Velvet Room and see if Dani had gotten a copy of the video yet.

I knew James wouldn't be happy with my decision, but I was still wearing my wig. There was little chance I'd be recognized.

Once I got back to Little Rock, I took the exit to the strip club. The parking lot had more cars tonight, which would probably work in my favor.

I walked inside and took a seat in the back, getting plenty of looks from the patrons once they realized I was sitting alone. I almost convinced myself to order a whiskey so I wouldn't stand out. Instead, I ordered a club soda, then sat back like I was there to enjoy the show.

I didn't recognize the girl dancing. The crowd was more subdued, but then she didn't seem to be putting her heart into her performance. Not that I blamed her.

I didn't see Dani working the floor, so she was either in a back room or had the night off. I decided to give it a half hour before I asked about her.

A couple of brave men tried to approach my table, but the dark stares I gave them were strong enough to send them back to their friends without a single word.

I checked my phone several times, telling myself I had no reason to worry. James would get back to me when he could.

After about twenty minutes, I started getting restless and bored. I was about to ask about Dani when I saw her walk out of the back, flipping her hair over her shoulder.

Several men in the room noticed and sat up in their seats.

I motioned my waitress over and told her I wanted to pay for a lap dance from Ruby.

If she was surprised, she didn't let on. She just headed over to the dancer and pointed to me.

Dani started sauntering my way. She stopped next to me, and leaned forward, enough that her cleavage was practically in front of my face. "I hear you requested me, sweetie." Then her gaze landed on my face. Her eyes filled with confusion, like she knew she'd seen me before but couldn't place me.

I stretched up to her ear. "Hi, Dani. I thought I'd stop by and check on your progress with the video."

She jerked back like I'd stabbed her with a hot poker, her eyes wide. "What the…?"

"I'm undercover," I said. "So? Any progress?"

Her face hardened. "I haven't had a chance yet."

"Time's tickin'," I said, loud enough she could hear me over the music. "It might get deleted soon."

"It's not exactly easy to get," she snapped, then her gaze landed on the empty chair next to me. "Did you kick Skeeter to the curb, or did he replace you?"

"He has other plans tonight." I lifted my chin to get a better look at her. "What did Razor tell you about him?"

"That he's ruthless."

I cocked my head. "You've dealt with ruthless men before. Why were you so scared of him?"

She jutted her head back with a defiant look. "Who said I was scared?"

"Don't waste my time bullshitting me, Dani."

She made a face and shook her head. "Razor seemed so dead set on killin' him, it kind of freaked me out."

"What freaked you out?" I asked. "That you were with a guy your client wants to murder, or that the man you fucked is so deadly?"

She shuddered. "Both."

Fair enough.

"Why are you workin' with that guy?" she asked with a frown. "He doesn't seem your type. At. All."

I shrugged. "They say opposites attract. So, about that video… are you really looking for it or are you just stringing me along?"

She shot me a glare. "Can you really get my charges dismissed, or are *you* stringin' me along?"

I leaned forward, holding her gaze. "I guarantee the charges will be dismissed." I hoped like hell I wasn't lying. "But tell me if I'm wasting my time thinking you'll come through."

She leaned closer. "How are you gonna get them dismissed? You're not a—" she stopped herself. "You're not in a position to help anymore."

"I still have friends in high places," I lied. "So what's it gonna be? Should I go find what I need somewhere else, or will you be able to get it?"

She stood up and shot me a look of disgust. "I was gonna look into it tonight after work. But if I get this, you *better* come through." Then she marched off toward a table of men.

I settled my bill and left, driving back to downtown. We'd taken the car from the hotel parking garage, but I parked down by Brass Magnolia, figuring I might as well drop in on Bobby and see if he'd come up with anything. I didn't expect any updates, but it beat going back to the hotel and losing my mind until James showed up.

I headed up to the counter, happy to see Bobby behind the bar. I was still wearing my wig, so he didn't recognize me when he walked over. "What can I get you?" he asked, setting a napkin in front of me.

This wig could come in handy.

"Hey, Bobby. I'll take a ginger ale."

His eyes narrowed as though he recognized my voice but couldn't figure out who I was.

I grinned. "Harper."

His eyes flew wide, and he took a step back. "Whoa."

"I know, right?"

"Girl," he said with a slow drawl, "you were born to be a blond."

I wasn't sure about that, but I'd take the anonymity. "I'm killing some time, so I thought I'd drop in for a drink."

He pulled a face. "I don't have anything for you."

"That's okay," I said. "I didn't think you did, but like I said, I'm killing time."

He filled a glass with ginger ale and set it in front of me.

I glanced around. "Not many customers."

He grinned. "It's almost closing time. You must have insomnia if you're killing time this late."

"Something like that."

He wandered off to check on a couple of other people at the bar, then came back a few minutes later, resting his elbow on the bar as he leaned forward.

"I talked to my cousins. They didn't mention anything related to what we talked about last night, but they did say there's something goin' down. A lot of people are on edge."

I gave a slow nod.

"They said there's a hit out on a guy who used to be a big name down in southern Arkansas a while back, but they don't know who, so I don't know if he's the guy you mentioned."

I took a sip of my drink. "He's not."

His brows shot up. "You know about it?"

"Maybe."

He narrowed his eyes. "Are you okay, Harper? Are you in trouble? The whole time I've known you, I've never seen you in disguise."

"I'm fine," I said good-naturedly. "And I'm trying the wig because a few people have recognized me since I've come back."

He relaxed, somewhat buying my excuse.

A man walked in and Bobby tracked him to the far end of the bar. "That guy's a regular. I gotta go take his order. I'll be back in a few minutes."

"I don't expect you to babysit me," I said. "Go do your job." I took another sip, then eyed the bottles behind the bar, experiencing a moment of shock when I realized I hadn't felt a craving for whiskey as soon as I walked into the place. I had a craving now, but it seemed like a win that I'd been here at least five minutes before thinking about it.

I glanced down the bar to check out the other patrons.

There was a middle-aged couple, their heads bent close together. A few stools away from them sat a couple of men in rich-looking suits, sipping what looked like whiskey or bourbon. Top shelf, probably. Then my gaze drifted to the guy at the end of the bar, and I froze.

I knew him.

Detective Brad Huffington with the Little Rock Police Department. He was one of Keith's good friends.

I had a moment of horror, fearing that he'd see me and say something, then I remembered I was currently unrecognizable.

Bobby poured his drink—definitely a high-dollar, top-shelf whiskey—when another man walked in through the door and headed straight for Brad.

My heart stuck in my chest, because I recognized him too.

Keith Kemper. My ex.

Keith sidled up to him and ordered a drink. Bobby poured him the top-shelf whiskey too, and I had to wonder why two Little Rock detectives would be getting expensive whiskey after midnight on a weeknight.

The men took their drinks to a booth across the room.

Bobby made his way back to me, checking on his other customers along the way.

When he leaned on the bar again, I said, "Do you know those guys?"

He looked surprised. "Yeah. Brad and Keith. They're regulars."

"Do they always get expensive whiskey?"

He looked surprised. "Yeah. I guess so."

"Do they always meet each other here, or do they come alone? Or with other people?"

"What's with the twenty questions, Harp—"

I pressed my finger against his lips, and I lowered my voice. "Call me Amber."

He made a face. "Seems like you're takin' this new persona a little too seriously."

I leaned closer. "That guy, Keith? He used to be my partner."

"An ex-boyfriend?"

"And my detective partner."

Panic washed over his face, and he lowered his face about a foot from mine and hissed, "He's a cop?"

"The other guy too. They're detectives. And friends."

He watched them for a few seconds before he tore his gaze away. "What do you think they're doin' here?"

"Could be two friends grabbing a drink together," I said, then I took a sip of my ginger ale, disappointed it wasn't whiskey.

"Do you believe that?" he asked skeptically.

"I don't know. Seems a little late for a friendly high-dollar drink." I took another sip. "Especially since Keith usually likes to go to bed by ten."

"He must have changed his schedule since you broke up, because over the past few months, I've seen them in here once or twice a week. And always around this time."

"Is it just them?" I asked. "Or does anyone else meet them?"

"Sometimes there are a few other guys with them. Not always the same guys at the same time though."

"Do you know any of their names?" I asked, shifting in my chair to get a surreptitious look at them. They were leaning across the table, in an intense conversation.

"Brad and Keith are the regulars, but I think one of them is named Roger."

Roger. I went through a mental list of detectives and landed on Roger Nelson. "Can I borrow your phone?"

He looked suspicious. "Why?"

"I don't have a smart phone, and I want to look someone up."

He reluctantly handed over his phone. I pulled up his browser and searched for Roger Nelson, then handed the phone back to him. "This him?"

Bobby took it and lifted it closer. "This guy looks a few years younger, but yeah. That's him."

I nodded, then heard a familiar voice behind me.

"You flirtin' with the customers, Bobby? That's not like you."

I tried not to tense up when Keith walked up to the bar and stood right next to me. Thankfully my hair was partially covering my cheek. Score one for long hair.

"She's an old family friend," Bobby said smoothly as he locked his screen and tucked his phone in his pants pocket. "You boys need a refill already?"

"Been a rough week," Keith said, resting a hand on the counter. He turned slightly toward me. "You gonna introduce me to your family friend?"

"Amber," I said, pitching up my voice slightly and adding a southern drawl. I kept my focus on the back wall as though I couldn't be bothered with him. "And I have a boyfriend, so you're wastin' our time."

Bobby chuckled. "I'll bring your drinks over to your table."

Keith stayed in place, and I could feel his gaze burning into me. "You sure you don't want some company? I love blonds with long hair." He picked up a strand and fingered it.

"Asshole," I said, keeping my drawl, but barely. I struggled to hide my shock. He was acting nothing like the man I'd known and dated. "If you don't get away from me in the next three seconds, I'll call the police."

"And what do you think they'll charge me with?" he asked with a laugh. He wrapped an arm around my shoulders. "It's not a crime to hit on a woman."

"Maybe it should be." Then, because my temper got the better of me, I elbowed him hard in the solar plexus.

He doubled over, and I was pleased to see I'd effectively knocked the wind out of him. I set a twenty on the counter and started to walk out the door, but then, because he was already bent over, and it was far too tempting, I planted my foot on his ass and shoved hard enough that he fell to his hands and knees.

"Put your hands on me again, and this will feel like foreplay."

Then I walked out the door, Keith still trying to catch his breath, while Bobby burst out laughing.

When the cool night air hit my face, I realized that had been incredibly stupid. Brad could have come over and arrested me for assault or at least made my life hell for a good fifteen to twenty minutes.

Actually, it was interesting that he hadn't. Was it because he didn't want anyone with the department to know about their late-night meetings at a high-end bar?

Or maybe my imagination was trying to find issues where there weren't any. Just because they were meeting for drinks didn't mean they were up to something nefarious, present behavior excluded. Cops met for drinks after work all the time. But this wasn't the bar they usually frequented. And I had never known him to go out this late. It was definitely suspicious.

I drove the car back to the hotel and parked in the garage, then took the elevator up to our room.

James still hadn't texted or called, and I told myself to stop worrying. Desperate for a distraction, I grabbed my laptop. Carter had emailed me an arrest report for Joshua Nixon with the message, "Could this be him?"

Joshua Nixon was thirty-five. His black hair was longer than Emily had described, but that didn't mean anything. His lower face was covered in stubble, and it grew in a scruffy pattern on his jaws. But it was the dark, deadly look in his eyes that convinced me this was the guy she'd met.

This particular arrest was for assault, but the charges had been dismissed after the victim, a nineteen-year-old woman, hadn't shown up to testify.

Was she a trafficking victim?

After I read the report, I decided it was possible. The assault had happened outside a fast-food restaurant. He'd started beating her up, and a few customers had intervened. He'd tried to drag her to the car, but a police cruiser had been driving by and stopped. Nixon was arrested and the victim was taken to the hospital.

If she'd been a trafficking victim, there were several reasons she might not have shown.

One, Nixon's one phone call could have been to someone in the organization to let them know she'd been taken to a hospital, then someone had shown up at the ER to bring her "home." Two, the police had put her in a domestic violence shelter, and she'd run, deciding her freedom was worth more to her than justice. Or three, they'd made sure she'd never testify against Nixon or anyone else by killing her.

I had a sinking feeling it was option three, but I hoped to God she'd run and was living a very different life.

I studied the man's photo again. He looked like an asshole who'd earned a hard-ass reputation. Based on the evil look in his eyes, I wasn't surprised he'd viciously beaten a woman in public. And if he beat a woman like that in public, he was capable of far worse in private.

Chapter 25

I took off my wig and pulled out all the pins, rubbing my fingertips over my scalp, then took my laptop to the bed, still dressed in case I needed to get to James in a hurry. I tried to stay up until he returned, but the last time I checked the clock, my drooping eyes read a little after four.

I woke to a brush of lips against my temple. When I opened my eyes, the sky was lightening in the windows and James was heading for the bathroom.

"Hey," I called after him. "How'd it go?"

He stopped and turned back to me, then sat on the edge of the bed. He looked exhausted. "Sorry. I didn't mean to wake you. I was just relieved you were here."

I squinted up at him in confusion. "You thought I'd take off?"

He leaned over and gave me a tender kiss. "I hadn't seen you in hours, and Knox wants to get his hands on you. I was furious with Carter for lettin' you come back here. He put you at risk of Knox findin' you."

I scooted upright, more awake. "It wasn't Carter's decision, James. I came back here on my own."

"You left Little Rock with the girl. You should have stayed put."

I shot him a scorching glare. "Why the hell would I stay out of Little Rock? We need to stay in town to bring down Knox and his operation."

"You were alone!" he said, temper riding his words. "Anything could have happened to you!"

"I was wearing my wig. No one knew who I was. Not even Keith when he walked into the Brass Magnolia."

He stared at me like I'd grown a second head, then he got off the bed. "You went to the Brass Magnolia?" he asked in a cold tone.

"I wasn't about to come back here and watch Netflix while you were interrogating Buddy." I paused. "Did you get anything useful from him?"

"That's not important right now," he said, fuming.

"It's the *only* thing that's important right now," I countered. "What did you find out?"

"Why did you go to the Brass Magnolia?" he shot back.

"The same reason I went to the Velvet Room. To check in with my contacts."

He looked stunned, then his voice rose. "You went to the *Velvet Room*?"

"Calm down, Malcolm," I snapped. "In case you've forgotten, I'm not some amateur sleuth. I used to be a fucking police detective!"

He turned away and began to pace.

"Why are you so upset?" I asked, getting to my feet. "You had a job and I had one too."

He spun around to face me. "Your job was to get the girl away from the situation. Not traipse all over Little Rock!"

"*Traipse?*" I demanded. "Are you fucking kidding me? You were doing something far more dangerous than I was!"

"I had backup!" he said, shaking his head. "I wasn't doing it alone! If Knox had found you…" His chest heaved.

I walked over to him, my anger softening as the reason for his reaction began to sink in. "You were scared something would happen to me."

Outrage washed over his face. "I thought I made that pretty damn clear."

"You weren't *worried*," I said more to myself as I reached him, putting my hands on his chest. "You were scared."

"Again," he growled. "I made that clear."

I looked up at him in disbelief.

Frustration flooded his eyes, but then he stiffened and it bled away. His hand sank into my hair at the nape of my neck, his fingers fisting around the strands. "Harper, why is it so damned hard for you to believe I care about you?"

"Because," I said, frustrated. "You're *you*."

His chest muscles tensed under my palms. "You think I'm incapable of caring about someone?"

"I *know* you care about people, even if you don't like people to realize it. It's just hard to believe you care that much about *me*."

"*Harper*." He shook his head. "If I'd known you were traipsin' around the city—"

"Again, I wasn't *traipsing*—"

"—I would have lost my fucking mind. It was bad enough when I thought you'd just come back to the hotel."

I searched his face. "You have to trust me, James."

"I do. But no matter how careful you were, there are a dozen ways he could have taken you."

"It's done," I said. "Now what did you find out?"

"Did Keith recognize you?"

I rolled my eyes. "I told you I was wearing my wig."

"So? I'd recognize that ass anywhere." His free hand grabbed a butt cheek and pulled my body flush to his.

"I was sitting on a barstool, so it's unlikely."

He made a face.

"Besides, he didn't recognize a side profile of my face, and he was about a foot from me. I doubted he'd recognize my ass."

"Jesus Christ," he groaned, leaning his head back and staring at the ceiling. Then he leveled his gaze on me. "Are you trying to give me a stroke?"

"I was fine. He didn't recognize me, even when he tried to hit on me."

His jaw clenched so hard, it was a wonder he didn't crack a tooth.

"Listen, that part's not important—"

"The fuck it's not," he growled.

"He was meeting another detective. Bobby says they come in around that time a lot lately, around the same time, and sometimes one or two other guys meet them."

"So?"

"So, what are they doing drinking twenty-dollar-a-pour whiskey, multiple times a week, around midnight? Keith was ordering his second drink within five minutes. He told Bobby he'd had a hard week."

"I don't want to talk about him," he grunted, his fingers on my butt digging in.

Heat washed through me, and I tried to focus. "Then let's talk about Buddy. What did you find out?"

"I'd rather show you how much I need you to be safe," he said before his mouth crashed into mine.

I lost myself in the kiss, pouring just as much of my fear and passion into him.

He backed me up then pushed me onto the bed, already working on the button of his jeans.

I knew he was exhausted, but he didn't act like it as he showed me how much he wanted me to stick around.

Afterward, I lay in his arms, and I realized he smelled like a different soap than the one we had in the hotel, and he'd been wearing a different shirt. "You took a shower before you came back."

"I couldn't walk into the hotel looking like I'd beaten the shit out of someone."

I'd noticed the scrapes and bruises on his knuckles. "You wore a different shirt back."

"I got a change of clothes."

I didn't want to focus on why. I'd have to at some point, but not now. "What did you find?"

"Buddy's a talker when he's given the right motivation," he said. "He doesn't deal with Knox. Nixon is his contact, but he knows Knox's name. His job is to handle the girls—recruitment, keeping them in line, making sure they bring in money. He was told if he did well, he'd move up to what Nixon does."

"Which is?"

"Nixon moves the girls from city to city. But he also moves more than just girls."

I looked up at him in confusion. "What does he move?"

"Still people, but think domestic help—nannies, housekeepers, gardeners."

"Immigrants?"

He nodded. "Desperate illegals. The people who buy them want cheap help and they're tired of the turnover. This way, they make sure they can keep them for as long as they want." He shifted slightly toward me. "Believe it or not, the domestic help is bringing them more money than the girls right now."

Fury ignited in my chest. "I bet. Rich assholes eager to be slave owners."

He grunted. "Sounds like Nixon has a big mouth, because there's a shipment from Texas coming tomorrow night. He even told Buddy they're using a warehouse in the commercial district. But supposedly Knox is gettin' nervous and might postpone it."

"Emily said Nixon came to the house and told Buddy the same thing," I said. "What about the house where Emily was staying? Did you get that address?"

"Yep. Already sent it to Carter so he can trace to the owner."

I glared at him. "I could have done that, James."

He pulled me closer. "I know, but I'd planned to keep you busy when I got back. So he got a head start." He gave me a slow kiss to prove his point.

I settled into him. "You know the house won't be registered to him."

"Maybe it's owned by one of his blind LLCs. If not, once we find out who owns it, there's a chance we can backtrack it to Knox."

I definitely planned to try.

"If we can intercept that truck and tie him to a house that holds the girls," I said, "would that be enough for your HSI contact?"

He studied me for a moment. "Maybe, but I want the accountant."

I gave a slow nod. "Have you heard anything from the people watching Natalie? Does she have anything?"

He shook his head. "They say they haven't heard her take any calls out of the ordinary. Of course, she could have emailed or texted."

"We can't hold out hope that she'll come through."

"No," he said, his tone heavy. "We'll need to figure out another way. I've been wracking my brain, but I haven't come up with anything yet." He paused. "Did you get any new information from your visit to the dancer?"

"She said she was going to get the video after work last night."

"Do you think she'll come through?"

I pushed out a sigh. "I think she'll *try*. She's legitimately concerned I won't be able to get her charges dropped." I held his gaze. "Are you sure you can do it?"

His gaze was steady. "If she comes through, and the guy in the footage is connected to someone in Knox's organization, then they'll be dropped."

I wanted to ask more, but he looked beyond exhausted. I lifted a hand to his face, my fingertip tracing the dark circle under his left eye. "You need sleep, James."

His gaze scanned over my face, settling on my lips. "I can sleep when this is over."

"Bullshit. Are you forgetting our conversation last night about how your concussion could make you a liability?"

Fire filled his eyes, and he held my gaze. "I was just fine last night."

"Maybe so, and I'm glad to hear it, but you still need rest. Even without a concussion."

I knew he wanted to protest, but instead, he tugged me tighter. "I'll take a nap. Then we'll figure out what to do next."

I planned to have him sleep longer than a nap but knew better than to tell him so. Instead, I snuggled into his side, his arm wrapped around me, and soon his breathing became slow and shallow. I drifted off to sleep soon afterward, wondering when I'd become a cuddler.

Chapter 26

I woke up around ten. James was still sound asleep, so I carefully slid out of bed and headed for the bathroom, taking my phone with me. I checked to see if I had any messages, hoping Dani had tried to contact me, but my only message was a text from Carter, sent around 5:30, letting me know James was headed back to the hotel.

I studied the text for a moment as it hit me that James had checked in with Carter but not me.

I wanted to be butt hurt over it, but they'd been working together for years. James and I had worked our first case together a little less than two months ago. Of course James would check in with him. They probably had a protocol.

I texted back:

James sent you the address for the girls' house. Can you send it to me, along with anything you found?

About a minute later, he sent back: *Sent in an email. Maybe you'll both let ME sleep now.*

As I left the bathroom, I cast a glance at James, grateful he was still asleep. We'd left the curtains open, and even though the windows faced north, I was worried the light would disturb him, but thankfully, he was turned toward the wall.

I sat on the sofa with the laptop and saw an email from Carter titled *Address*. Emily and the other girls had been kept at a house in Little Rock. The house had been purchased three years ago by Harlan Properties, LLC. Harlan Properties was owned by Miles P. Harlan.

It didn't come as a surprise that Knox didn't directly own the house. The question was whether this Miles Harlan, if, indeed, he existed, was clueless or complicit.

His name seemed familiar, but I couldn't place it. I hoped it would come to me as I continued my search.

It didn't take me long to discover Miles Harlan likely wasn't an upright citizen. He'd had numerous civil suits brought against him claiming deception and fraud, one of which was by an insurance company. But it was his criminal case that grabbed my attention.

Five years ago, the state of Arkansas had brought business fraud charges against Harlan Properties, LLC. But the charges had been dropped ten days later.

I pulled his arrest report and discovered he'd been investigated by the LRPD Financial Crimes division. The two investigating detectives were Mark Ellison and Roger Nelson.

The same Roger Nelson who had been at the Brass Magnolia last night.

Mark Ellison sounded familiar too, but I knew he hadn't been in the department when I'd left last fall. It only took a few keystrokes to discover Ellison had died of natural causes.

I nearly dropped my computer when I saw that he'd died five days after the charges against Miles Harlan were filed, and four days before they were dismissed. I could have attributed it to bad timing if I hadn't already suspected his partner was possibly dirty.

I blew up the photo in his obituary and realized I'd known

him. The face in the photograph was younger and thinner than the man I remembered, but I'd met him soon after joining the homicide unit. Keith had taken me to a bar Little Rock detectives often hung out at after hours to meet some of my fellow detectives. Ellison had been gruff, with a reputation for being a hardass that was backed up by his chain smoking and intense personality. A few months later, he hadn't shown up for his shift, and everyone had known something was wrong. Roger Nelson went to check on him and found him in his recliner, an ashtray full of cigarette butts and a half-finished bottle of beer on the table beside him. The coroner had attributed his death to natural causes. His obituary had asked for donations to the American Heart Association in lieu of flowers.

No one had thought his death might be suspicious. He'd lived his job, which some of the detectives had said was to blame for his three divorces. I hadn't thought much of it either, other than telling myself I exercised and didn't smoke, so I wouldn't end up like him.

Had Ellison been murdered because of his case against Miles Harlan? Based on what Natalie had told me, it was entirely possible.

I did a general internet search for Miles Harlan and discovered he'd been a witness to a murder on a weekday afternoon. The victim, Daniel Kincaid, had been shot in a parking lot.

Then I realized why I'd recognized Miles's name.

Keith and I had initially been assigned to Daniel's murder, and I'd interviewed the sole witness—Miles Harlan.

He'd stuck in my mind because he'd made a strange statement. It wasn't that he'd held back—in fact, he was more than eager to tell me what he'd seen. But I'd gotten an odd vibe, like he was trying to sell me a shitty used car. I'd mentioned my suspicions to Keith, suggesting we bring him into the station and question him further. But Keith had dismissed my concerns, saying he was a low-level commercial developer and that was just the way he talked.

And then the next day, the case had been reassigned to Brad and his partner at the time, and Keith and I had been given another case. They'd justified the transfer by saying Brad had worked a previous case connected to the victim. I'd thought it odd, but it wasn't unheard of for cases to be reassigned. But now…

Now I had to wonder if the real reason they'd taken me and Keith off the case was because they didn't want me digging.

I was lucky I hadn't ended up like Mark Ellison.

James stirred on the bed, and I looked over to see him watching me, his head still on his pillow.

"How long you been up?" he asked, still groggy.

"Not long," I said. "But long enough to find a new lead."

He perked up. "Did the dancer come through with the video?"

"No," I said with a frown.

"You look worried."

"She's irritated with me, so she may just be dragging her feet." I shrugged. "Or maybe the video was gone." I gave him a hopeful look. "But I found a new lead to chase."

He scooted up so his back was propped against the pillows. "Whatcha got?"

I walked over and sat on the edge of the bed while I told him about Miles Harlan, including the fact that the case he was connected to had been reassigned to Brad Huffington—one of the guys I'd seen in the bar last night—and his partner.

"You want to talk to Harlan?" he asked.

"Definitely. We know the girls and Buddy were tied to Knox. Is Harlan's business a front for Knox, or does Knox rent the place from Harlan? Either way, we need to find out." I took a breath. "And I found another connection between Harlan and the police." I told him about the fraud case and how one of the detectives had been found in his home by his partner, conveniently dead of natural causes. And that the charges were dropped the next week.

He frowned. "Ten to one, Harlan's wrapped up in this. There's no way he's an innocent. Even if we can't tie him concretely to Knox, we'll likely find something to link him to your cop buddies."

I cringed at him calling them my buddies. The fact that I'd spent five years as Keith's partner, and that he'd spent more nights in my bed than I could count, made me feel dirty and used.

I must have hid my internal war, because he didn't comment on it. He just asked, "How do you want to handle visiting him?"

"I think we should drop by his office, but not to interrogate him. We should make an appointment."

"And you think he's gonna answer our questions about Knox because we made an *appointment*?" he asked skeptically.

"No, because we're not going to use force to get what we want. We're going to use subterfuge."

A slow smile tugged on his mouth. "Go on."

I gave him a mischievous grin. "What do you think about doing a little undercover work?"

He looked amused. "What do you have in mind?"

"We go as a couple looking to have him develop our commercial space."

"It would get us in the door." He nodded. "Sounds good, but he's still not gonna give us the answers we're after. Not unless we use force or intimidation."

"Not necessarily," I said. "We know Knox is keeping girls at one or more of his houses. We need a paper trail."

"You want access to his files."

I nodded. "Which he likely keeps on his computer."

"Were you gonna steal it? We'll break cover once he realizes it's gone, which makes going undercover pointless."

"No," I said, holding his gaze. "You're gonna distract him while I copy his files to an external hard drive."

He studied me for a moment, then laughed. "You *do* realize it's not gonna be that easy."

"Of course it's not going to be easy, but I've met this guy before. He likes to impress. We'll have him take us to his office, get him to sign into his computer, then you'll find a way to get him out of the room so I can make the transfer. If we've got some big project he really wants, he'll do anything to impress you."

He rubbed his jaw, focusing on the wall behind me. "It might work."

"It could *definitely* work."

"One small problem," he said. "His sensitive files likely have passwords. If they're complicated, then they'll be hard to crack."

I considered it. "Not if he was sent the passwords via email."

"You're gonna copy his emails too?"

"I don't know," I said. "Maybe. I can search the files and open a few to see if they have passwords. If they do, then I'll look for emails that could have them. Like from attorneys or accountants."

He considered it for several seconds. "Even if we find out who he uses for an accountant, we can't assume it'll help us discover Knox's."

"I'm not delusional," I said. "But there might be some kind of paper trail tying Harlan to Knox. Right now, all we know is that girls were kept at a house he owned." I grimaced. "And I used past tense, because we both know they'll probably move them as soon as they realize Buddy's not coming back."

He nodded.

Then I asked what I'd been wanting to know but was hesitant to ask. "Where *is* Buddy right now?"

He eyed me cautiously. "You mean, *is he dead?*"

"If he is, I suppose that would partially answer my question."

He gave me a forced smile. "He's currently alive. In case I need more from him."

"You think he held back information?"

"No, I think he told me everything he knows, but when we learn something new, I might want to run it by him to verify."

"And then you'll…"

His face went blank. "He may have other purposes."

"Such as?"

"I may hand him over to the Feds. I'm currently keeping my options open."

"What would be the downside of turning him over? He's at a low enough level that he probably won't be able to hire a shark to get him off."

"He's a low-life scum," he said flatly. "He kidnapped girls and forced them into prostitution."

"So capital punishment?"

He narrowed his eyes. "You think he should be tossed in prison for a decade or so, then tossed back out to … what? Follow the straight and narrow? You, of all people, can't believe the myth that prison is for rehabilitation."

"I don't know," I admitted, my frustration rising. "I know one man I want dead, and I feel no remorse over it, but the others…" I drew in a breath. "We're playing God, James. Deciding who lives and dies. What gives us that right?" But I also couldn't deny that last night I wanted him dead too.

He held my gaze. "Years ago, I had to draw a line in the sand to figure out how I could make that decision. You need your own line. I suspect it won't be the same as mine, which is fine by me."

He was right, yet I wasn't sure where that line was for me. What boxes had to be checked to justify murder? What number on the scale of evil tipped me over to pulling a trigger?

"As for the shipment tonight," he said, "I say we work under the assumption that it will still take place. It's likely it will get postponed or moved, but we need to be prepared. So the real question is where the transfer is taking place. I have Carter doing a deep dive into properties Knox might own in the commercial district."

"Knox might not own it," I said. "If Harlan Properties isn't owned by Knox, then he rents the house Emily was kept in. He might rent the warehouses too."

He gave a nod. "Good point. If you can get Harlan's files, and if we can open them, we might find the address of the warehouse." He shifted on the bed. "But it's possible the transfer will take place somewhere out in the open. Likely an area without cameras."

I mulled over the fact that they were transferring people. "It sounds like Little Rock is a hub."

"It makes sense," he said. "Two major highways intersect here. They could come up from Texas, then head east on I-40 and maybe keep some goin' on I-30."

I nodded. "Have you been in contact with your handler? Have you told him about the shipment?"

He hesitated. "Not yet."

"Why? Because we don't have enough hard evidence to tie it to Knox?"

"That and I don't know if the delivery's still happenin'. If I tell them it's happening or possibly happening, and it doesn't … let's just say it won't be received well."

He had a point. "If they move the drop-off to another location, do you think it will be somewhere else in Little Rock or another city?"

He looked grim. "I got the impression it would be another

city, but Buddy hasn't exactly been kept in the loop about that part."

"This is bigger than Knox."

He held my gaze. "This is bigger than Knox," he confirmed. "But he's a key piece. He's doin' plenty of damage on his own."

"Is your assignment to bring him down or stop the whole damn thing?"

"If I bring Homeland Security the right information, then they'll be able to take down the whole damn thing themselves," he said.

I nodded. "Which is why we still need to find his accountant. Knox is either taking payments or receiving them—maybe both—and they should be in his books. Even if they aren't flat out labeled, 'human trafficking bill of sale.'"

"Exactly."

"So, if the shipment still happens tonight and we intervene, we might save fifty people. But if we wait and get his financial records, and they have a connection to more people involved on a higher level, we'll save hundreds. Possibly thousands."

"Yeah."

I closed my eyes. "This is hard."

"I know. But maybe we'll luck out and find a bread crumb to the accountant in Harlan's files."

I huffed a laugh. "That seems like a Hail Mary."

"The play wouldn't exist if it didn't work sometimes," he said with a coaxing look.

"I don't know much about football, but I know enough to know it's not an actual play," I groused. "Besides, when did you start falling for pipe dreams?"

He laughed. "Maybe you're rubbin' off on me." He leaned over and gave me a kiss, then got out of bed. "I'm gonna take a shower. Why don't you see if you can get us an appointment with your developer?"

"Yeah," I said, still lost in thought. "Okay."

He went into the bathroom, and I heard the shower turn on. I looked up Miles Harlan's business name and number on the internet, then called and told his receptionist I had a large commercial building and wanted to see what Miles could do for me.

"I can fit you in tomorrow," she said. "Say, three o'clock?"

Dammit. That was too late. "Sorry," I said sympathetically. "We've been talking to another developer, and we're supposed to give him an answer by six o'clock tonight. I decided to see if we could get another opinion before committing to a thirty-million-dollar contract." I cringed, hoping I'd thrown out a number big enough to get her attention, but not so big it sounded ridiculous. "I guess we'll just go with the other guy."

"Thirty million, you say?" The number had definitely gotten her attention.

"Yes, but I understand if Mr. Harlan is too busy," I said politely. "Thank you for your time."

"Wait," she said in a rush. "Let me talk to him. I think he might be able to fit you in today after all." Music filled my ear after she put me on hold.

Less than twenty seconds later, she was back. "I told Mr. Harlan about your situation, and he says he'll be happy to meet you at one here at his office. Does that work for you? Ms. —I'm sorry. I didn't get your name."

"Amber Beachum," I said, keeping my voice professional. "The meeting will be with me and my husband, Jeff. Tell Mr. Harlan that we look forward to meeting with him." I hung up, pleased with myself for coercing him to meet with us today.

I only hoped this plan wouldn't crash and burn.

Chapter 27

I was glad we'd done some shopping the day before. Since we were attending a business meeting, I put on a silky light blue blouse with a navy suit and low, black heels. I also wore the long, dark wig and some light makeup.

When I emerged from the bathroom, James grinned in appreciation. "Damn. You are a woman of many personas, Detective Adams."

"You clean up pretty well yourself." It was an understatement. He was wearing a white dress shirt with a light blue tie, gray dress pants, and black dress shoes. To top it off, he was wearing a pair of glasses, which somehow made him even more attractive. His hair, which was usually slightly unruly, had been tamed and slicked back. It was strange seeing him dressed up like this, but he wore it well.

"You like the businessman look?" he asked, then lifted the frame of his glasses slightly. "Do you buy that I'm a distinguished millionaire looking to diversify his portfolio with real estate?"

I'd given him a cocky grin. "Are you into role playing, Mr.

Malcolm?" But was it *really* a role when he likely was a million-aire who diversified his portfolio?

He eyed me up and down. "Not normally, but it wouldn't take much for you to coerce me."

I laughed, feeling lighter than I should, considering we were about to try to steal a businessman's computer files. So much could go wrong, but we'd come up with a semblance of a plan.

First, we needed Harlan to sign into his computer.

The next piece of the plan had to be left up to chance, which James detested. We'd wait for Harlan to brag about something he owned. It could be a fly-fishing tackle shadowbox or a taxidermized squirrel. Anything. The plan was for James to act like an asshole in the beginning, but then show interest in the man's pride and joy. Harlan—if it all went to plan—would be eager to show it off in the hopes of winning him over.

Once I was alone, I'd pull an external hard drive (which we planned to purchase on the way) out of my purse and attach it to the computer, then download as many files as I could before Harlan and James came back.

But that was phase two. Phase one was to see what we could get out of the receptionist before we even met with her boss. We both had roles to play—I was the talkative wife, and James would be the reluctant husband who had already decided on our developer and was only humoring me, albeit with an attitude.

James and I pulled into the parking lot of Harlan Commercial Properties about ten minutes early. Carter had arranged a luxury sedan to fit our roles, and I wasn't complaining after the last few rides we'd been stuck with.

When we walked into the lobby, the receptionist beamed at us. She had a friendly smile and wore a blouse, little makeup, and a simple hairstyle—not overly dressed for her public-facing job. The reception area looked like it had last been furnished in the nineties—everything was in jewel tones and very worn. Based on her appearance and the waiting room, Harlan Commercial Properties wasn't used to higher-end clients. I suspected she and Harlan saw us as big fish they were desperate to land.

"Mr. and Mrs. Beachum," she said sweetly from behind her desk. "My name's Beth, and I'm Mr. Harlan's right-hand person. He's wrapping up a call, but he'll be with you in about five minutes."

"Hmm," James said, walking over to a wall to look at a photograph of an office building.

She cast James a nervous look. "Can I get you water or coffee?"

James's unimpressed gaze landed on the Keurig on a credenza on the other side of the room, before he shifted back toward the photo, his upper lip curling with distaste.

"Nothing for either of us," I said, "but I was hoping you could tell me about Mr. Harlan's clients." I smiled. "We're new to Little Rock, and this will be the first of multiple buildings we plan to develop. We're trying to get a sense of the people Mr. Harlan typically works with."

Her eyes brightened. "I assure you, Mrs. Beachum," she said enthusiastically, "we're used to working with higher-budget projects."

"But what about lower-end projects?" I asked. "We plan to have a few of those as well. Will Mr. Harlan be open to working with those? Or does he only stick to seven-figure projects?"

"He's worked with a wide range of clients," she said confidently. "From rental properties, to small strip malls, to multi-story office buildings and warehouses. I'm sure he can handle any project you bring to him."

He'd worked with warehouses. I took that as an encouraging sign.

"I hope he doesn't take on *too* many clients," I said with a frown. "We've worked with developers who were spread too thin or handed us off to incompetent people."

"We do have another partner, Ryan Delaney, and he handles the smaller projects. *But,*" she quickly added, "if you decide to go with Mr. Harlan, I suspect he'd handle all of your projects himself."

"That's good to know," I said, then glanced over at James, who had moved on to a new photo. "Isn't it, Jeff?"

"I'm not sure why you're wasting time talking to the receptionist," he grumbled.

I had to stifle a snort. He was perfectly channeling arrogant, elitist condescension.

"Jeff," I scolded, then turned back to her. "I'm sorry for his boorish behavior. He thinks this meeting is a waste of time. He wants to sign with the Delgottos and be done with it."

We'd decided to toss out that firm's name because of their previous shady dealings with J.R. Simmons—which I'd known nothing about—but also because they were considered big fish in the Little Rock developer pool.

"I actually *do* know quite a bit about Harlan Properties," she said defensively as she eyed James. Then she turned back to me, her expression softening. "I've been here for eleven years, practically since Miles started the company. And he includes me in the loop on quite a few things."

"Oh, good," I said, sounding pleased. "Then you must know a lot about the history of Harlan Properties."

She nodded, with a proud gleam in her eyes. "I certainly do. Miles has helped turn a small business with two clients into a multi-million-dollar corporation with *many* clients."

"But not *too* many clients," I reminded her. If he was making that much money, I had to wonder why he didn't spend a few thousand to decorate his reception area. There was a good chance she was exaggerating. Or, if Knox provided a huge percentage of his business, he wouldn't need to worry about making a good impression.

"I assure you, Mrs. Beachum, Miles will give you his undivided attention."

"That is *so* good to hear." I turned back to James. "Jeff, Franklin never promised us his undivided attention."

"That's because Franklin has a much larger, more prestigious corporation to run," he sneered, sounding exactly like a snob born into old money.

"Don't listen to him," I said, waving my hand as I sat on a chair closer to the desk. Then I lowered my voice. "He's always like that."

"Oh." She frowned, her gaze on him.

"But once we sign, I'll be the one you and Mr. Harlan deal with. It's Jeff's money, so he makes a big fuss about signing, but once the ink on the contract is dry, it's all on me." I added a giggly laugh.

Her face brightened. "You seem like you'd be a delight to work with, Mrs. Beachum."

I pressed a hand to my chest, pretending to be flattered. "Beth," I gushed. "You are *so* sweet. I have such a good feeling about you and Mr. Harlan, and we haven't even met him yet."

James released a grunt from across the room.

I leaned in closer. "Since I feel so good about you, I feel comfortable bringing something up." I paused. "*Of course*, I did some research into Mr. Harlan's company. I'd be silly not to," I leaned in even closer, lowering my voice. "I confess that part of the reason Jeff is apprehensive about taking this meeting is because we saw that Mr. Harlan had fraud charges brought against him about five years back."

Her face paled. "Those charges were dropped within days," she said in a rush. "I promise you, Mr. Harlan was never guilty of *any* wrongdoing."

"Well," I said, making a face. "Jeff likes to say that where there's smoke, there's fire. But I told him that sometimes, where there's smoke, there's just a BBQ." I released a tiny laugh.

She gave a weak laugh too.

I continued, "But sometimes you're in the mood for BBQ." I paused and held her gaze, turning slightly serious. "And *sometimes* you're in the mood for a bonfire."

She studied me as though unsure of what to say.

"Do you think…" I asked, hesitating. "Do you think Mr. Harlan ever creates a bonfire?"

Her eyes grew wide. "I assure you, Mrs. Beecham, Miles is aboveboard. He does *everything* by the book."

"Yes," I said smoothly, "of course. And believe me, I'm *so* grateful for that. But sometimes you need a project to speed along a little faster than, say, a supervisor or inspector feels comfortable with." I paused. "Does Mr. Harlan know how to work out those situations in his client's favor?"

She cast a glance down the hall behind her, then looked back at me, her face going blank. "You'll have to speak to Mr. Harlan about that." She glanced at James. "Like your husband said, I'm just the receptionist, and I don't know anything." But she wasn't acting outraged, like I'd insulted her boss's good name or even her. She just didn't seem comfortable sharing sensitive information.

Like a smart employee.

"I told you this was a waste of time," James grumbled, then took a seat in a stained peach-colored wingback chair on the wall next to the door.

"Jeff," I scolded lightly. "She can't say *too* much. She has no idea who we are."

He gave me a cold, scathing look. "Exactly."

I wasn't sure how I was supposed to answer that, but then decided he'd thrown it out there without expecting a response —he was offering his interpretation of a rich person's ambiguous musings. He'd probably spent enough time with J.R. Simmons to pick up a few mannerisms.

But it served its purpose, because the receptionist looked even more uncomfortable.

James and I were on opposite sides of the room. I wondered if I should sit by him, but I suspected it only reinforced the impression of our divided stance on this visit.

"I'm so sorry if my questions seemed out of line," I said graciously. "We're just used to the way things are done in Louisville. Hopefully, Mr. Harlan will get us sorted out before we leave."

She nodded.

"But I do have one more question," I said. "We're in desperate need of a new accountant. I figure since you're Mr. Harlan's right-hand person, you'd likely know of some good ones."

She brightened up. "I can definitely help you with that. We use Henderson and Matthias."

I pulled a notebook out of my purse and wrote it down. "That's so helpful. Thank you, Beth." I shot a glance at James. "Much more helpful than Franklin Delgotto, Jeff."

He kept his gaze on his phone and said dryly, "It's not Delgotto's job to find our accountant, and the one she just told you likely won't be helpful. We need someone who's willing to be *creative*."

Beth stared at him with a look of indecision.

I grimaced. "We got into a little trouble a few years ago, so we found someone who helped us make one thing look like another." I gave her a knowing look. "You know how things are. Those fussy people who don't understand what it takes to run a business like to put their noses in the books. We had to find someone to help us … smooth things over." I smoothed out some imaginary wrinkles on my pant leg.

She started to say something, then stopped, indecision flickering on her face.

I considered pushing harder, but she looked like she was still wrestling with how much she should tell me.

So I picked up a three-year-old copy of *Newsweek* and flipped through it without reading, while James scrolled on his phone with a scowl that screamed *this is a waste of time.*

Beth looked like she might finally be ready to speak when a man stepped out from the hallway.

He looked pretty much the way I remembered him. There was a little more gray at his temples, but the used car salesman aura was still there. I couldn't help wondering how he got clients. He made me want to take a delousing shower, not sign a multi-million-dollar contract.

Then again, he was probably exactly what the people who hired him were looking for.

"Mr. and Mrs. Beachum," Harlan said, flashing a smile so wide it made him look like the Joker. "So sorry to keep you waiting. I hope Beth offered you beverages."

James shot a look of distaste at the Keurig on the counter across the room. "We prefer espresso to drip coffee." His upper lip curled. "If you can call that watered-down crap coffee."

I guess he wasn't wasting any time letting Harlan know he was an asshole.

I had to stifle a laugh at the flash of horror on Miles's face, but he quickly recovered. "We can send out for something, if you like."

"We won't be here that long," James said, looking down at him. Literally. Harlan was maybe five-eight, and that was with a generous tape measure.

Harlan plastered on his best salesman smile. "Well, hopefully that means it won't take me long to convince you to sign with me. Come on back to my office." Then he turned and headed down the hall.

James moved beside me, and I stage-whispered loud enough for the receptionist to hear, "Behave, Jeff."

He only hummed as we followed Harlan.

The narrow hallway looked in need of a fresh coat of paint, and the photos were of office buildings. Nothing personal. No awards or certificates. Nothing for James to insist on examining later.

We walked past a small kitchen, a door labeled *bathroom*, and a closed door with a plaque that read *Ryan Delaney*.

Harlan led us through a door at the end of the hall and into an office that was larger than I'd expected—spanning the full width of the building. The furnishings matched the vibe of the waiting room.

An L-shaped manufactured desk sat to the right of the door. It looked like he'd purchased it at an office supply store a decade ago. His chair was chrome with black vinyl that had faded with age. The two guest chairs were chrome too, with navy vinyl seats.

But on the other side of the room was a long rectangular table covered with blueprints.

James spun slowly, taking it all in with a look of disdain.

Harlan studied him for a beat, then his face brightened. "I'm so glad I could shuffle things around so we could talk about your project." He gestured to the chairs. "Please. Have a seat."

He walked around his desk, lowered himself into the chair, then folded his hands over a stack of papers. "Beth says you have a thirty-million-dollar project."

"Yes, that's right," I said with a warm smile. "We're looking to take over the property on Oak and Monroe. We've already met with Franklin Delgotto, and he won Jeff over. Isn't that right, Jeff?"

James shot me a glance that suggested I had the intelligence of a bean plant, then turned to Harlan. "Delgotto runs a much more professional outfit. It's obvious you couldn't develop a parking lot. This place is a dump."

"Don't let appearances deceive you, Jeff," Harlan said good-naturedly, leaning back in his chair and resting his folded hands on his stomach. "I prefer to put my money into my toys."

James gave him a sideways look. "So you're a child."

Harlan laughed. "No, although my ex-wife would likely disagree."

I offered a polite smile, but James looked unimpressed.

We could've pressed him on his toys—a possible excuse to get him and James out of the room—but it was too soon.

Harlan sat up, still smiling. I got the feeling he'd smile even if a rat was nibbling on his toes. "Tell me about your project."

Going off the script we'd created, I launched into a story about a mixed-use plan and sprinkled in some developer buzz words like cap rates, anchor tenants, and long-term returns.

Harlan listened intently, nodding along. When I finished, he nodded again. "I can do all that."

"Would you mind showing us?" I asked. "Do you have any graphics or graphs?"

He blinked, like I'd asked him to teach me how to knit.

"She's asking for a PowerPoint," James muttered, then turned to me. "Honestly, Amber."

I wasn't sure if he was aiming his disgust at me or Harlan, maybe both of us. But Harlan took the bait. "I can definitely show you a presentation."

He turned to his computer and typed in a password so ridiculously easy I almost laughed.

bigboy1—all lowercase

While Harlan pulled up a PowerPoint and turned the screen slightly to give us a better view, James shot me a questioning look.

I gave a slight nod. *Got it.*

Harlan started his presentation. After about five minutes, James cut him off, which to be honest, was four minutes and ten seconds longer than I'd expected.

"I've heard enough," he said, annoyed.

Harlan jolted in his seat. "I can give you the condensed version, if you prefer."

James leveled him with a look. "This is bullshit. Delgotto said it was impossible to give us everything we asked for, and your amateur slides aren't going to convince me that you can."

Harlan laughed. "I hate to speak ill of a competitor, but Franklin can be a little … old-fashioned in his thinking. I like to think outside of the box."

My face brightened. "Oh, I like the sound of that."

I snuck a glance at James, who was giving Harlan a steely gaze.

I turned back. "We like to think outside the box too." I let the words hang, then added, "We think creativity in *all* areas is underrated." I paused again. "We want to partner with someone who is open to new ideas—and willing to take risks."

Harlan stared at me for a beat. "What kind of risks are we talkin' about here, Amber?"

"I'm talking about greasing a few sticky wheels if the engine gets stalled on the tracks." I kept my tone casual, like I was talking about building permits, not bribing people.

He nodded slowly, as if weighing my statement. "Do you anticipate any engines getting stalled?"

James spoke up. "If you run enough engines, they're all bound to stall at one point or another."

Harlan nodded. "True. True."

"Delgotto understood what we meant," James said. "We didn't have to spell it out for him."

Harlan lifted his hands in defense and laughed, like this was all good-natured banter. "Now hold on there, Jeff. I never said I didn't get it. I just wanted to make sure we're all on the same page."

"I'm not sure we're even readin' the same book," James said, disgust drenching his words.

Indecision flickered over Harlan's face, quickly followed by determination. "I understand your concern, Jeff, but you have to understand mine. We've just met. I can't disclose my full repertoire of tricks for greasing those wheels to the wrong people."

"You're calling us the *wrong people*?" James stood. "Then I don't see any reason to waste any more of my time." He gave me a sharp look. "Amber."

"Wait!" Harlan called, panic cracking his voice as James headed for the door.

James stopped and turned back, his face a mask of cold contempt.

"We can discuss a few things," Harlan said quickly, "so you understand the scope of my services. But I value discretion on all sides."

James held there for a long moment, studying Harlan like an ant under a magnifying glass. Then he sat again, wearing a look of bored impatience.

Harlan turned to me, his eyes darting between us like he was scrambling for his next move and coming up empty.

He wasn't going to give us anything unless we proved we were just as dirty as we were hinting. I decided to take a chance and maybe get more out of him than we'd planned.

"Mr. Harlan," I said slowly, like I was talking to a preschooler.

"Miles," he said. "Please, call me Miles."

"Miles," I repeated. "There's a reason we came to you. We were told that you're willing to help with … sticky situations." I let that bait hang. "Especially since you've had a few sticky situations of your own."

His face went blank. "Where did you happen to hear that?" he asked carefully.

"We may be new to Little Rock," I said, "but we *do* have some friends in town. Friends of the family." I grimaced. "Friends of Jeff's father, originally, and now friends of ours. When we were asking for developer recommendations, your name came up."

Harlan looked intrigued. "May I ask who your family friend is?"

I made a show of hesitating. "He values his discretion, so I hate to use his name outright. But as I mentioned, his father and Jeff's father were close." I lowered my voice. "Until our friend's father met with an unfortunate end."

Harlan listened, not giving anything away.

"Our friend's mother still dabbles in the family business," I added, "but she leaves most of it to her son." I tilted my head. "I don't know how interested he is in development projects, per se, but he *does* have a penchant for warehouses." I shrugged. "He likes to use hard-to-trace corporations to purchase or lease them."

Harlan's face went slack for a second before he recovered. "I see."

"In any case," I went on, "rumor has it you did business with his father before his tragic and violent demise."

"Did you hear this from your family friend?" he asked, his voice measured.

"Heavens, no," I said with a small laugh. "He's much too discreet to share that kind of information. But I *did* hear it from someone close to the family, someone in a position to know."

He nodded slowly again, as though weighing his options. "Yes. If we're talking about the same family, then I have done business with both father and son, and I know exactly how much they value discretion." He added. "Religiously."

I refused to let myself get excited just yet.

Pushing out a relieved sigh, I pressed my hand on my chest. "Oh, that *is* good news."

I was about to ask a follow-up question, but James beat me to it.

"Amber, don't be a fool," he sneered. "We can't take his word. He's given us no proof he knows who you're even referring to. He's only agreeing with whatever you say."

"Jeff," Harlan said in a placating tone. "I'm sure you understand that some clients prefer to keep their names private. Just like I suspect you prefer a bit of anonymity yourself." His smile sharpened slightly. "Especially with … special, *creative* projects."

James was quiet for a moment. "Yes," he said at last. "You're correct." He sat up a little, "But I'd still like confirmation we're talking about the same family."

Harlan hesitated, "I'm not sure—"

"How about a compromise?" I said sweetly, glancing at James before turning back to Harlan. "What if you tell us the first letter of their last name? That can't be too damning. There could be thousands of names starting with the same letter."

Harlan pressed his lips together, then asked, "Jeff, will that appease you?"

James seemed to consider it, then gave a sharp nod.

Harlan drew in a breath, as if he needed to summon the courage. "K."

I beamed. "Oh. That is *most* fortunate."

Harlan sagged back in his chair with visible relief. "Since I've done work with your family friends, what do you say we get this contract signed?" He gestured to the PowerPoint slide on the screen. "I can whip up a contract in a matter of minutes."

"Not so fast," James said. "There's one more thing we need to discuss."

Harlan pasted on a polite smile. "Of course. What would you like to know?"

"What kind of car do you drive?"

Harlan blinked. "I'm sorry?"

"You said you spend your money on toys instead of your office." He tipped his chin to the worn desk. "So what's the toy? What do you drive?"

A smug grin spread across Harlan's face. "I've got a Maserati Ghibli at home, but my Porsche 911 Carrera S is here." He jerked his thumb toward the back of the building.

"I call bullshit," James said, his voice dripping contempt. "I didn't see a Porsche when we pulled in."

"That's because it's out back." Harlan stood, went to the window beside his desk, and lifted the blind.

Sure enough, a metallic-gray Porsche was angled across two spaces as if it owned the lot.

James rose and moved closer to the window. "Is it optioned with the Sport Chrono package?" For the first time since we'd walked in, he actually sounded interested.

Harlan took the bait hook, line, and sinker. His face lit up. "Sure is. Chrono, upgraded exhaust, full leather interior. She purrs." He turned back, animated. "You wanna see it?"

James glanced at me, his brow lifted in silent question.

I huffed out a laugh. "You men and your cars." I waved a hand toward the door. "Go drool over it. I have a few calls to make anyway."

"Wait until you feel the torque," Harlan said as he headed for the door.

I looked up at Harlan. "Miles, do you mind if I make my calls back here? I would prefer privacy."

"If one of those calls is to Franklin Delgotto, telling him you're goin' with me, you can have the office for the rest of the afternoon."

I grinned. "I won't need it that long. Maybe fifteen to twenty minutes?"

"Of course," he said quickly. "Take as long as you need. We'll probably be a while." Then he headed out the door.

James gave me a serious look before following Harlan down the hall.

I shut the door behind them, relieved to find a lock on the knob. The last thing I needed was Beth coming back and catching me messing with her boss's computer.

After I shut the blinds so Harlan couldn't peek in and see me on his computer, I pulled the hard drive from my purse and plugged it into the computer tower, which looked older than dirt. Apparently, Harlan didn't spend much money upgrading his technology either. If it had a slow processing speed, copying the files could drag on.

Dammit.

His stupid PowerPoint slide was still open, so I minimized the window. Ten folders were neatly lined up on the left side of the desktop, but the ones I cared about most were:

Harlan Development, LLC

Clients & Investors

Financials

Insurance & Claims

Since *Financials* was what we needed most, I right-clicked the folder, hit copy, then pasted it onto the external drive.

A progress window popped up.

Copying 1,274 items (842 MB)... Approximate time remaining: 4 minutes.

How long could James keep Harlan out there?

I moved to the window and parted the blinds just enough to peek out. Harlan had the hood up, gesturing like he was teaching a class.

I'd probably have plenty of time. The man looked like he could brag about his car for hours.

While the *Financial* folder copied, I opened it to see if anything was password protected. Inside were more folders:

Bank Statements

P&L & Balance Sheets

Loans & Notes

Insurance Payouts

Accountant Reports.

I opened *Accountant Reports* and found a PDF labeled *Forensic Review*—the month and year Harlan was charged with fraud.

To my surprise, it opened immediately. No password needed.

A title page filled the screen, all clean fonts and professional logos.

Prepared by: Victoria Ames, CPA, CFE,

Mid-South Advisory Partners, PLLC.

Date: Five years ago.

I skimmed until I hit a section where she outlined ways Kincaid could "clean up" his books, from reclassifying expenses to backdated invoices. Basically, how to cook the numbers until the charges went away.

If Victoria Ames was handing low-hanging fruit like Harlan a road map to make fraud disappear, was she doing the same for the likes of Knox?

Maybe. Maybe not. But she'd just moved to the top of my list.

When the financial file finished transferring, I clicked *Clients & Investors*, then copied and pasted it into the external drive. The progress bar estimated three minutes.

While it copied, I opened the folder and did a quick search for Knox. I wasn't surprised when nothing came up, so I tried something else—searching for the address of the house.

A folder popped up.

The folder's name was the address, and when I clicked on it, a neat stack of subfolders filled the screen:

- Lease – Harlan Properties, LLC to Blackstone Capital, LLC
- Addendum – Renewal / Occupancy
- Rent Ledger – 12 months
- Utilities – Setup Confirmations
- Maintenance – Work Orders
- Vendor Invoices – Locks / Blinds / HVAC
- Inspection Photos – Exterior / Interior
- Emails – Tenant Communication PDF

Was Blackstone Capital, LLC one of Knox's corporations … or had he used a go-between?

The folder finished copying, and I grabbed the two other folders I cared about. Both transferred in under five minutes.

While the files transferred, I checked on James and Harlan multiple times. Harlan was happily showing off features under the hood like he was unveiling a masterpiece. James played along, pretending to be impressed.

They were still occupied, so as the last folder finished transferring, I stared at the desktop and asked myself what else I could grab.

I hadn't found any password-protected files, but I could still grab his emails.

He used Outlook, so I tried to copy the mailbox over to the drive, but the progress bar estimated it would take thirty-two minutes.

That was way too long, so I stopped the transfer, then searched for Knox in the emails. A handful popped up, so I selected them and copied them to the external drive.

Then I searched for the house address in his inbox. Multiple emails showed up, so I repeated the process.

I spent another three minutes grabbing anything in Outlook that looked useful: emails involving Victoria Ames, Kincaid, and Blackstone Capital. I wanted to keep going, but as the last files were transferring, there was a knock at the door.

"Mrs. Beachum?" Beth called out. "How are you doing in there? Do you need anything?" The doorknob jiggled.

My pulse spiked.

"I'm busy!" I shouted, hoping like I sounded like an entitled rich woman instead of someone who was up to something. "I'm on the phone."

The knob jiggled again. "Can I get you anything?"

"I said I'm busy!"

The final email transferred and I decided I couldn't push my luck any farther.

I disconnected the hard drive, closed Outlook, then shut down all the folders I'd opened. I maximized the PowerPoint again—exactly the way Harlan had left it—then scanned the office to make sure nothing look disturbed.

I couldn't believe this had gone so well. It had been entirely too easy. But we weren't out of here yet. We still had to leave without raising Harlan's suspicions.

Then I realized Beth had just given me the perfect excuse.

I slid the hard drive back into my purse and stormed down the hall, stomping like I was one inconvenience away from suing someone.

I walked past Beth. Her startled gaze snapped to me. "Mrs. Beachum? Is everything okay?"

Ignoring her, I headed around the building and stopped at the corner like I owned the place. "Jeff," I said in a sharp, clipped tone. "We're leaving. Now."

Harlan was sitting in the driver's seat. He leaned around the open door, eyebrows lifted. "Amber, is everything okay?"

"No," I said, my nose lifted in the air. "It is *not*. I asked for privacy, and your assistant interrupted me." I held up two fingers. "*Twice.*"

I let the word hang there for a moment.

"If this is how you do business, Mr. Harlan, then your company isn't suitable for our needs." I gave James a pointed look. "Jeff. Let's go."

James's look of disgust was enough to make Harlan shrink back into the car, but as soon as James headed toward me, Harlan seemed to realize thirty million dollars was about to drive out of his parking lot. He hopped out of the car and hurried after us as we stormed toward our car.

"Wait!" he called, his voice full of panic. "I'm sure there was a misunderstanding! We can work this out!"

I just gave him a single disapproving look, then climbed into the passenger seat.

James slid behind the wheel, and as we pulled away, Harlan jogged behind us. He followed until we turned onto the street, still shouting.

As much as I'd tried to make our getaway look natural, it still might make us look suspicious. We'd brought up Knox. That alone might be enough to rattle him. Would he report back to Knox? Or would shame and fear of admitting to a potential mistake keep him quiet?

Chapter 28

"Did the receptionist really walk in on you?" James asked in a low tone.

"No. The door had a lock, but she tried to come in."

"Do you think she was suspicious?"

"No." I shook my head. "I think she was trying to be courteous. But it gave us a good excuse to leave. Hopefully, it didn't raise their suspicions."

"So you got the files?"

"Yeah. That's the good news. The better news is I already found the lease. Blackstone Capital is the tenant. We just need to tie it to Knox. The bad news is there are thousands of files to comb through."

His jaw tightened, and he kept tapping the steering wheel.

"Ever heard of Blackstone Capital?" I asked.

"No."

I wasn't surprised. It was a pretty generic name.

"Harlan also had a forensic accounting review when he was going through his fraud charges," I said. "He used a different accountant than the receptionist mentioned—Victoria Ames." I glanced at him. "She's worth looking into."

James stopped tapping. "Maybe we should pay another visit to Natalie."

"To see if she knows anything about Victoria?"

"It can't hurt."

I considered it. "Do you want to do that now?"

He lifted a shoulder in a lazy shrug. "We're already out."

"Do we want to show up looking like this?" I asked, flicking my gaze over him.

"Sure," he said. "It's not like I'll be dressin' like this again anytime soon."

I shot him a grin. "You really took one for the team by letting Harlan preen over his car for so long."

He gave me a wry look. "He's got such a hard-on for it, I suspect he'd fuck it if he could figure out how."

I laughed. "He *did* say he could be creative."

James's mouth twitched. "True."

I reached into the back, grabbed my laptop, and plugged in the external hard drive. When James gave me a questioning look, I said, "As much as there is to go through, I might as well start looking."

"Good point."

I started with a search for Blackstone Capital and came up with five current leases on houses, and about ten previous leases, although, who knew if Knox used more than one corporation to lease properties. If he were smart, he'd spread them out to reduce exposure.

Next, I searched for Blackstone Capital online but came up with nothing, which meant they didn't have a public presence.

Since we were headed to talk to Natalie, I searched the hard drive for Victoria Ames. Multiple files popped up and I'd just started skimming them when James pulled into the parking lot of Natalie's office.

I glanced up at the building, then gave him a pleading look. "There are two security people watching the office, right?"

His eyes narrowed. "Yeah…"

"You have history with Natalie," I said. "She's more likely to talk to you, so you don't need me in there." I lifted my laptop slightly. "Looking at these is a better use of my time. You can tell the security team to keep an eye on me while you're in there."

I expected him to put up a fight, but he pulled out his phone and made a call to Carter. After he gave a short explanation of why we were there, he said, "She's in a dark sedan in Natalie's parking lot. I want security to give her their undivided attention until I'm back in the car."

When he hung up, I asked, "Wouldn't it be faster if you contacted the guards yourself?"

"In this situation, it's better to have a middleman," he said. "I still don't feel comfortable leaving you out here."

"Don't be such a worrier," I said lightly. "The sooner you talk to her, the sooner you get back."

He gave me a long look before he got out and shut the door. He turned and stared at the sedan across the street, where two men sat in the front seat. Then he headed for the entrance and walked inside.

I kept working, skimming reports and spreadsheets, dumping anything suspicious into a folder labeled *Review Later*.

James had been inside less than five minutes when a name I wasn't expecting popped up in an email from Blackstone to Harlan.

Natalie Crowe.

My breath hitched. I stared at the screen, then lifted my gaze up to the building.

Was Natalie tied to Blackstone Capital?

It took seconds to confirm.

One of the emails had her full signature block at the bottom: Natalie Crowe, CPA—Blackstone Capital, LLC. And right above it was an attachment titled *RentLedger_12mo.xlsx*.

Natalie wasn't just aware of Blackstone's leases.

She managed them.

Natalie worked for Gerald Knox.

My chest tightened as I started scrolling. Dozens of emails from Natalie to Harlan Properties—rent ledgers, maintenance approvals, renewal addendums—all tied to Blackstone Capital.

Natalie had been lying to us.

My heart began to pound. Had James walked into a trap?

If she'd contacted Knox, it wouldn't have been done with a phone call the security team could overhear. She would have texted or emailed.

I yanked the hard drive free and slipped it into my jacket pocket. This thing was pure gold, and I wasn't letting it out of my sight.

I dropped the laptop onto my seat, scrambled out of the car, and rushed for the entrance. The receptionist looked up at me with a questioning expression, but I didn't waste time with explanations or permission. I went straight down the hall, and when I reached Natalie's office, I flung the door open.

James sat in a chair in front of her desk. Natalie was positioned behind it, posture stiff. They both looked up in surprise, but James's hand was already inside his jacket, possibly reaching for his gun.

Natalie recovered first. She offered me a warm smile. "Harper. Goodness. You know how to make an entrance." She gestured to me. "It took me a moment to recognize you since your hair's different. Skeeter said you weren't coming today."

I shut the door behind me and sat in the chair next to James. "I changed my mind."

"Unfortunately, I haven't had a chance to look up those LRPD names yet." Her voice softened into an apology. "I've been distracted by everything going on." She gave James a grateful look. "I was just thanking Skeeter for his protection."

I leaned back, letting the silence stretch long enough to make it uncomfortable.

I angled my head to the side. "How soon after we left yesterday did you notify Gerald Knox that we'd come by asking about him?"

James sat up slightly—alert and on edge.

Natalie's face went pale as all expression drained away. For a half second, she looked like she might actually crumble. Then she pasted on a weak smile. "What are you talking about? Why would I contact Gerald Knox? I'm trying my best to lay low, not draw his attention."

"You played it smart," I said. "You had about a thirty-minute window before your security arrived yesterday. Plenty of time to send a message."

Anger sparked in her eyes. "I don't like what you're insinuating, Harper."

"I'm sure you don't," I said coolly. "Because I just upset your cushy world." I held her gaze. "I know you're the accountant for Blackstone Capital."

She tried to look shocked, but it didn't land.

James stiffened. "You've been doin' Knox's books, Natalie?" he asked, his voice deceptively calm.

Her eyes flew wide. "Skeeter, I—"

"It's a yes or no question," he said with an edge.

Natalie's hand trembled on the desk. She didn't answer.

James leaned forward. "Let me make this real clear. You'll answer my questions, or I'll pull your security detail and let Knox know you've been chattin' with me."

"But I haven't told you anything," she whispered.

"You think that matters?"

Her throat bobbed. "I told him I was stringing you along," she blurted, her voice shaking.

"We'll make it convincing," I said. "I have the emails you

sent Miles Harlan. Enough to make Knox believe whatever we want him to believe."

Her eyes widened in horror. "Skeeter, no. *Please.*"

"Then let's try again." His voice stayed calm but sounded scarier than if he were yelling. "How long have you been workin' for Gerald Knox?"

She drew a shaky breath. "About four years."

James's jaw tightened. "From around the time J.R. was killed?"

She nodded. "He'd heard the Feds hadn't recovered all of J.R.'s money. I don't know how he'd heard, and he refused to tell me. But he said he was impressed and needed an accountant like me."

"And you said yes." James leaned back slightly, eyes never leaving her. "Blackstone Capital. Knox owns it?"

She nodded again, the gesture smaller this time.

"What's it for?" he asked.

Her gaze dropped to her desk. "His trafficking business." The words came out flat, like she was reading from a spreadsheet. "It pays for the residential leases and utility bills."

My stomach rolled. "Wow." I didn't hide my disgust. "You say that like you're talking about landscaping fees."

Natalie's chin lifted defensively. "It's not like I could stop them."

"Does that help you sleep better at night?" I asked sarcastically.

Her face flushed with embarrassment, but she didn't look at me.

James's gaze flicked to mine, checking if I wanted to continue. I leaned back in my chair and let him take point.

"How many other corporations does Knox own?" James asked.

She looked up, wary. "Why do you think he has more?"

"Because men like him always do." His tone sharpened.

"And you learned under J.R. Simmons. You'd think it was strange if he didn't have any. You'd suggest he get some."

Her hand trembled on the edge of her desk. "If I tell you, he'll kill me. You just compared him to J.R. We both know how men like him operate."

James leaned forward, quiet and deadly. "The way I see it, if you *don't* tell me, there's a good chance you'll end up the same way anyway." He held her gaze. "But if you *do* tell me what I need to know, I can help you. You're a survivor, Nat. So start survivin'. How many?"

She swallowed. Her gaze snapped to me, then back to him. "You swear you'll help me?"

"If you start bein' honest," he said. "Yes."

Her chair creaked as she shifted. "Six. Two are legitimate." She rushed to add, "I mean legit on paper and practice."

James didn't blink. "Go on."

"One's a trucking outfit. River City Logistics. They have real loads. Real drivers. DOT numbers."

"Maybe not so legit," I said. "It's perfect for moving things you don't want traced. Like people."

Her eyes widened. "I didn't know."

I gave a humorless scoff. "Right."

She flinched, then forced her attention to James. "The other legitimate company is a bar. It's cash-heavy, good for washing money through the books." Her gaze turned pleading. "You know that's normal in that world."

James's expression didn't waver. "Name the bar."

"The Gilded Anchor."

He gave a slight nod. "And the other four corporations?"

"One is Blackstone. I told you about that one. The second is a maintenance company for cleaning and repairs. It services his businesses, but it does work for other corporations too."

"Illegal businesses?" James asked.

"A few legit ones, for appearances," she said. "But yeah,

mostly illegal. He bills way above standard rates. That's how he moves money between his own companies."

"And the other two?" James asked.

"There's a staffing and security company. It employs the staff for his operation—the enforcers, the handlers, the people he doesn't want on the real payroll. They're all 'contract guards' and 'temp workers.'"

"Creative," James said, then tilted his head. "You designed it."

She didn't acknowledge the jab. "The last one's basically an investment and management shell. It collects consulting fees and profit distributions from the others and uses it to buy things … and friends."

"Friends," I said. "Like cops?"

She gave a sheepish nod.

"Thank you," James said slowly, as if filing every word away. "That'll help for when we read through the records ourselves."

Her eyes widened in alarm. "What records?"

He leveled a look at her. "Yours. We'll be making copies of everything related to Gerald Knox and Harlan Properties."

She shook her head, horror spreading across her face. "No! If I give them to you, he'll kill me."

"You should have thought about that before you started workin' for him," James said.

Her cheeks flushed red with anger. "Easy for you to say," she snapped. "You're an intimidating man. I'm not. When Knox came to me, he *told* me I was going to do his books. He didn't ask." She leaned forward, eyes blazing. "If I'd said no, he would've killed my kids. Then my husband. Slowly, *while I watched*." A vein throbbed in her temple. "And then he said he'd kill me." She pushed out a heavy breath. "*I didn't have a choice.*"

A wave of sympathy caught me by surprise. She could've gone to the police or the FBI, but there were no guarantees they would have protected her or her family. The Little Rock PD's resources were limited—not to mention she knew she couldn't trust them. And while the Feds would be better, she'd probably be looking at the witness protection program. Her family's lives would have been destroyed.

"Something I don't understand," James said, his gaze distant, like he was turning a puzzle over in his mind. "Why would Knox trust you when it was obvious you'd cooperated with the Feds?"

"I already told you," she snapped. "He threatened to kill my family if I betrayed him in any way." Contempt filled her eyes. "I worked with the Feds after J.R. was killed, and I don't trust them. *At. All.* If you hand this over to them, I might as well kill my family and then myself before Knox gets to us."

I barely restrained a gasp, but she was right about one thing. Knox would make her pay.

James blew out a slow breath, some of the tension bleeding from his shoulders. "Why didn't you tell me any of this when I stopped by yesterday?"

"Tell you I'm doing the books for the man you're looking for?" Her laugh was humorless. "That would've put me in the same danger. With even less hope for protection."

He sat back, resting his hand on his knee. "I can protect you. But it may not be the protection you want."

Her face drained. "What does that mean?"

"To be clear," he said evenly. "I'm taking those files. And I'll be handing them to the Feds."

She sucked in a breath, tears filling her eyes.

"You don't trust them," James continued, not softening. "And frankly, you shouldn't. I doubt you'd get the same deal you had before. So I'm giving you a way out. You may not like it, but unless you want to rot in prison, it's your best option."

She went still, then swallowed, "I'm listening."

"Once I'm satisfied that I've gotten everything I need,"

James said, "I'll have men escort you and your family to the airport."

Her eyes widened. "If my books convict Knox, nowhere will be safe."

"Not if he's no longer around to come after you," James said, his voice turning lethal.

"What does that mean?" she shot back. "You think he can't order hits from prison? You think prison stops men like him?"

"Natalie," James said, calm as ice. "Gerald Knox will never see the inside of a prison."

She leaned back, disbelief hardening her face. "You'll never be able to touch him."

"Trust me," he said. "I will." Then his eyes turned dark. "Have you already told him I'm here? Right now?"

"No," she said emphatically in a rush. "I always liked you, Skeeter. I don't want to be part of getting you killed." Her jaw tightened. "But if you walk out of here and decide you won't help me, I *will* notify him. I'll say you showed up unannounced, and I didn't have time to warn him until after you left."

"You have his direct number?" James asked.

She nodded.

"I'm gonna need it," he said. "Along with every piece of information you've got about him. And I mean *everything*. If you wrote it on a Post-It and put it in your drawer, I want it."

She stared at him, dismayed. "Do you realize how much information that is? I can't fit it onto a flash drive. And it's not safe to upload it to a cloud."

"That shouldn't be a problem," I said, pulling the hard drive from my jacket pocket and setting it on the desk.

Her gaze dropped to it, and she froze.

"I forgot the USB cord in the car," I said. "You got one?"

Her gaze snapped to James. "He's going to kill my kids. He's not joking."

"Show me the files," James said. "While they're transferring, I'll send people to collect your kids and your husband."

"How are you going to find Knox?" she asked. "Because his home address is a closely guarded secret. *I* don't even have it."

James frowned, impatient. "You don't have to worry about that. Just get on a plane and leave the country." His brow lifted. "You should have plenty of money to pay for it."

A guilty look flickered across her face, but she turned to her computer and started booting it up. "I don't know where to start."

"Start with the folder labeled Knox," he said.

She scoffed. "They're not that obvious."

"Then just start copying and pasting files," he said. "We'll sort out the order later."

She opened a folder and let him do a quick scan of the contents. Once James was satisfied, she handed me a cord.

I connected the hard drive to the computer, and she started the transfer.

She had more files than Harlan, but they were neatly organized, and most were for other clients. James watched the transfer, making her open files from time to time to ensure nothing was password-protected. Or if it was, that she unlocked it.

During the process, James had her call her family on speaker and tell them to grab their passports and pack everything they could into two suitcases each, including two bags for her. Hired security would pick them up soon, and they would meet her at the airport. Since they didn't ask why they were fleeing, they must have all been prepared to take this drastic measure.

We were about two-thirds of the way through the transfer when my phone vibrated with a text from Dani.

I've got the video. When will my charges be dropped?

I sent back:

You know how this works. I have to make sure it's usable, then I'll take care of the charges.

Another message came through immediately.

Then meet me before my shift starts at 5. Otherwise you'll have to wait until tomorrow

I showed James the texts.

He cast a glance at the computer, then turned back to me. "We should be done here soon. Tell her we can meet her at three."

I messaged Dani, and we agreed on a Starbucks in south Little Rock.

But as soon as I hit send, a thread of unease tightened in my chest.

Natalie's files were probably enough for James to give to his handler, so I suspected we didn't need Dani's video. Still, I'd learned not to build a case on a single piece of evidence. If the video showed Nixon—or anyone connected to Knox—it could lead us straight to Wilhemina. And what if we could link Wilhemina to Knox through the files too? The case against him would be even stronger.

The big question was—how were we going to follow through on our promise?

"Do you have a list of the names of the girls working at the club?" I asked Natalie. It was a long shot, but I figured it was worth checking. They assigned new names to the girls, but what if Wilhemina had kept her club name? Nova Lux was unique enough to stand out.

Natalie glanced back at me, startled.

"In your accounting," I pressed, keeping my voice calm. "Do you have any names?"

Her cheeks reddened.

"I take that as a yes," I said. "Pull it up."

She looked up at James like she needed permission. After

he gave a slight nod, she opened a spreadsheet and clicked on a tab. "Here."

"You lookin' for anything specific?" James asked.

"Yeah." I didn't elaborate as I started scanning the list.

Nausea rose when I spotted Lexi's name, and the names of the two other girls she'd mentioned. But I didn't see the name I was looking for.

"Are these all the women and girls Knox is using right now?"

"No." Natalie clicked on another file titled *The Gold List Club*.

"The Gold List Club," James said sharply. "What's that?"

She lifted her gaze to his. "Knox's private club. It's attached to his legit bar, but it's upstairs and has a private entrance. Members only."

"What is it?" he asked.

"A gambling and strip club without the city and state ordinances."

His jaw tightened. "So they can do whatever they want?"

Natalie's mouth twisted. "I don't know exactly what goes on there. The members are invited and sworn to secrecy." She hesitated. "The books call them waitresses, but I'm not naïve enough to think that's all they are. And I'm not stupid enough to ask."

"And you have a list of the waitresses?" James asked.

"Yeah." She opened another tab.

I leaned in closer and scanned the new list until I found the name I was looking for.

Nova Lux.

And her start date was one month ago.

I tapped a column. "It shows she was paid wages. Do you cut checks to them?"

She shook her head. "No, I report their wages and pay the payroll taxes, but the club manager pays them in cash."

I glanced at James. The grim look on his face confirmed exactly what I was thinking. If Wilhemina and the other girls were getting paid anything at all, it was a fraction of what they brought in. If that.

Nova Lux was a one-of-a-kind name. There was a good chance this woman was Wilhemina. It was further confirmation that meeting Dani was worth our time.

If it wasn't a set up.

"What about a list of club members?" James asked. "Do you have that?"

"No," Natalie said. "I know there are currently seventy-two members, and they pay a thousand dollars a month in membership dues. But they're assigned numbers. I don't have names to go with them."

"What does the membership buy them?" I asked.

She turned back to me. "Access. They still pay for drinks … and entertainment."

Knox was making a killing.

It didn't take much longer to finish the file transfer. By the time it was completed, James's men had picked up Natalie's family, and the security unit stationed outside her office escorted her to their car to drive her to the airport.

Once James and I were back in our car, I said, "Ten to one, Knox had one of his guys snatch Wilhemina for his exclusive club."

"Agreed."

"If we figure out who scouted her, we'll ID one more person in his organization."

"It'll give us further confirmation," he said. "But I suspect Natalie has a list of Knox's employees."

"This is huge," I said, the full weight of it hitting me all at once. "We could bring his whole operation down. And give the Feds enough to bring down the bigger one."

"Agreed," he said. "Let's get Dani's video, see what we've got, and then I'll contact my handler."

"Yeah," I said. "Sounds like a plan."

He shot me a sideways glance. "We wouldn't have had any of it if you hadn't found Natalie in Harlan's files. She was acting cagey when I walked into her office. I suspect she was getting ready to run on her own. And she would have taken everything with her."

"I wish I could say it was purposeful," I said. "I just happened to see her name in an email. I ran a search, and suddenly she was all over Blackstone Capital's paper trail." I turned toward him and narrowed my eyes. "She kept her involvement with Knox from you, and you let her get away with it."

His expression tightened. "You think I should have hurt her physically?"

"No," I said quickly. "That's not what I'm saying at all." I took a moment to collect my thoughts. "But she lied to you. It's not unreasonable that you could've let her face the consequences with Knox. Instead, you protected her."

He made a face. "Knox forced her to do his books. She was trapped, just like she was with Simmons. She knew there would be consequences if she told me she was working for him—from him and possibly from me." His eyes stayed on the road. "Besides, I wasn't exaggerating when I said I suspect the Feds won't cut her slack this time." He flicked a glance at me. "I wouldn't be surprised if Natalie's family vacation ends up in a non-extradition country."

Funny. When I wore a badge, I would've been furious if someone had let her walk.

Now, I wasn't sure letting her flee was the right thing to do, but I wasn't as bothered by it. She'd helped Knox do evil things. But I could also understand why she'd believed there was no way out.

What did that say about my moral compass?

I couldn't remember the precise moment I'd crossed the line. Maybe there'd been no line, and the change in me had come on gradually, like sliding down a slippery slope so slowly you don't realize you were falling.

Or maybe I'd just started seeing things from a different angle, and the black-and-white rules I'd lived by had turned to a dozen shades of gray.

Perhaps that's what I told myself so I could sleep at night.

One thing was certain: I wasn't letting Knox see the inside of a prison.

The question was how long I could pretend this was justice instead of revenge.

———————————————

Chapter 29

———————————————

Dani was seated at a two-top at Starbucks with a cup in front of her when James and I walked in at 2:55. We'd gotten here ten minutes early so we could search the area for any signs of a trap but came up with nothing.

She recognized James first, but it took her a few seconds to place me in my other wig. Her phone wasn't in sight.

I slid into the chair across from her. James pulled up a third.

"Okay," I said. "Let's see what you've got."

Contempt tightened her mouth. "I still don't see how you're gonna hold up your end of this deal."

"We will," James said. "You have my word."

I resisted the urge to shoot him a look. Promising was one thing. Offering his word was another level of accountability, whether Dani believed in honor or not.

To my surprise, she did. Her attention shifted to him. "What are you gonna do with this?"

"If you're worried it will lead back to you," he said evenly, "it won't. We'll never tell where we got it." His gaze held hers. "Will anyone at the club suspect you provided it?"

"No." She sounded exhausted. "Ronnie—the security guard—got so high he won't remember a thing."

James nodded once. "Show us."

She pulled out her phone and set it on the table, then tapped into her videos. At the bottom of the screen were four black-and-white thumbnails. She selected the first and hit play.

The footage was about an hour long. A man walked to a table and sat alone, watching the stage. The image was too grainy and washed out for me to catch his face clearly. Occasionally, he took sips of his drink.

James fast-forwarded. The man didn't move much. Then, toward the end of the video, he pulled out his phone and made a call.

James slowed it down, and we rewatched the call. It lasted six seconds. Maybe less. After he ended the call, he tossed cash on the table and stood.

When the clip ended, Dani tapped on the next video. Same guy, different angle. His face still wasn't clear, but we could make out his thick dark hair and glasses.

She opened the next clip. It showed him leaving the club, moving toward the entrance alcove. The video was short, maybe ten seconds, but as he passed closer to the camera, something in my chest went cold.

"I know him."

James turned toward me.

I didn't want to tell him who the man was in front of Dani, not if I wanted her to sleep tonight.

"There's one more?" I asked, keeping my voice steady.

She nodded and tapped the final file.

The man walked into the parking lot, got into a dark sedan, but stayed put. The video kept going, so James fast-forwarded for nearly an hour until the car door opened and he walked toward the back of the building, out of sight. About twenty seconds later, he was back in the frame, this time holding a woman's arm and leading her to his car. He opened the door to the backseat and shoved her in, then closed the door and got behind the wheel. Seconds later, he drove away. The license plate was blurry, but we could still make out the numbers and letters.

"Was that woman Wilhemina?" I asked.

She nodded, her gaze still on her phone. Her shoulders were hunched. She looked like she was folding in on herself.

This wasn't proof Wilhemina had been kidnapped, but it definitely linked her to the man.

I gave Dani a slow, solemn nod. "This is good. You've got a deal."

Given the identity of the man in the video, she wouldn't just get her charges dropped. Between this video and what we might find in the files, we had enough ammunition to blow up the Little Rock Police Department.

"Who is he?" she whispered. "I can tell he's somebody."

"He is," I said, leaning closer and lowering my voice. "I'm gonna be straight. I have to be careful about who I show this to. I don't want anyone tracing it back to you."

Her brow pinched. "Why are you telling me that?" Her voice shook. "You're scaring the shit out of me. Now I'm not sure I should give it to you at all."

"I can protect you," James said quietly. "I'll get your charges dropped and make sure you're protected." His gaze didn't waver. "Do you trust me?"

She stared at him, tears swimming in her eyes. "How can I? Razor says you're vicious. Maybe I should just forget about all of this."

"You could," I said quietly, "and honestly, I wouldn't blame you. This is scary." I held her gaze. "But this man kidnapped Wilhemina. Now she's being held prisoner to work at a private sex club." My voice dropped. "Who knows what they're doing to her there—or what they'll do when they're finished with her."

Dani sucked in a breath.

"And what if they decide they want you next?" I said. "You're beautiful, and you're talented. I'm honestly surprised they haven't tried to grab you already."

Her eyes flew wide.

"How about you take a vacation?" James said, like he was offering her a latte. "My attorney will make the arrangements for your trip and handle the charges. Once that's done, we'll give you some seed money to start over. How does that sound?"

"You're kiddin' right?" she whispered, like she wanted it to be true but didn't dare believe it. "Why would you do that?"

"This is serious," he said flatly. "You stuck your neck out. I reward loyalty."

"When should I go?" Her voice trembled. "I mean … if I do this."

"Tonight."

He picked up her phone and opened her contacts, tapping quickly. "This is my attorney, Carter Hale." He slid the phone closer to her. "After we transfer the videos, call Carter as you're leavin'. Then go home, pack what you can. By the time you finish, Carter will already have your flight booked." His eyes lifted to her. "Give him your legal name and birthdate and tell him where you want to go so he can book the ticket."

"Anywhere?" she asked, still skeptical.

"Anywhere in the U.S." He paused. "He'll book the hotel too."

"Why are you doin' this?" she asked.

James's expression didn't change. "Because this is important. And everyone deserves a fresh start. Do we have a deal?"

She hesitated, then nodded vigorously. "Yes."

"I'm gonna send these to my email." He waited for her to object.

"Yeah. Okay."

Once they were sent, he handed her the phone, "Not many people get a do-over. Don't waste yours."

He didn't wait for a response. He stood and headed for the exit.

I got up too, but Dani grabbed my wrist.

"Harper," she whispered. "Is he for real?"

"Yeah," I said softly. "He's for real."

Outside, James was already in the car, the engine running. I slid into the passenger seat.

"You were more than generous," I said as I buckled in. "Especially since I suspect you don't know who the guy in the video is."

He pulled out of the parking lot. "I didn't need to know. Your face told me he's someone important." His gaze flicked to mine. "Who is he?"

"Bill Thomsen." I paused. "A Little Rock detective in the Burglary division."

James's jaw tightened.

"Who are we going to take this to?" I asked. "I don't know who to trust in the Little Rock PD."

James was silent for several seconds. "I need you to trust me."

My breath caught. "What does that mean?"

"I need to meet my handler," he said. "Alone."

"I didn't expect to go with you," I said. "I'm more concerned about whether we can contact someone in the Pulaski County prosecutor's office, and if so, who we can trust. We have to be damn sure they don't try to bury this or leak it back to Knox."

"Agreed." His gaze stayed on the road. "I need to think on

it." He flashed me a tight smile. "But this might be one of those situations where it's better to ask forgiveness."

"Do you think this, added to what we got from Natalie, is enough to fulfill your obligation to your handler?" I asked. "Because this is huge."

His jaw tensed. "It seems like enough to me. But who knows with those fuckers."

"Do you want to include the files my mother saved up?"

He hesitated. "I'll let you make that call."

I drew in a breath, trying to settle my nerves. "If you hand it over, it implicates my father."

He didn't respond.

"I don't care about that," I said, mostly meaning it. "It's just…" I stopped to collect my thoughts, then turned to him. "My mother died for that information. I don't want it to be wasted. And it feels like it might become an afterthought compared to the other evidence we've gathered." I was surprised at the lump that formed in my throat.

"We wouldn't have even been looking at Knox if not for your mother's file. So, it wasn't for nothing." He glanced over at me. "Your mother made this possible. She helped save countless numbers of people."

Funny, I hadn't seen it that way.

"Include it," I said.

"You sure?"

"Yeah."

He flipped on his turn signal and turned a corner. "For now, I think we should go back to the hotel and start digging through the files we got today." He paused. "But first, we need a couple more hard drives. I'll have to turn this one over, so I want two copies for us. We'll keep one close. The other we'll stash somewhere safe. Like my office safe. Just a little insurance."

"Yeah." He was right. We needed our own copy, and a

backup made sense. "Will you ask your contact how they plan to handle the cop? I know I keep bringing it up, but this is important."

"I know," he said, giving me a reassuring glance. "I won't let it get swept under the rug."

"Thank you."

He gave me that same tight smile.

We stopped at an office supply store and bought two hard drives and cords, plus a stack of sticky notes and pens.

"I want to start building a case too," I said. "I know Homeland Security is going to take over, but this way we can hold the local authorities accountable."

"Good idea," he agreed.

Back at the hotel, we went up to the room. I set the laptop on the coffee table and connected the original hard drive. Then I connected the other two drives and began transferring the data. I'd just begun when something hit me.

"We only needed one more," I said, more to myself than James.

"What?" he asked absently from the edge of the bed, tapping on his phone.

"We only needed one extra hard drive," I said, louder. "We can transfer everything to the laptop. We can save the extra drive for later."

He looked up. "No, copy it to all of them. The more backups, the better."

Having four copies felt a little paranoid. Then again… maybe it wasn't paranoid enough. "Yeah. Okay."

He stood. "I'm gonna take a shower and wash this stuff out of my hair," he said, grabbing a change of clothes. "Let me know if you need me. I won't be long."

"Okay." I realized I was still wearing my wig, but I left it on and concentrated on the transfer.

About five minutes later, he emerged in jeans and a T-shirt, his phone in his hand. His hair was damp. "I got an update from Carter. He booked tickets for Dani to Hawaii and put her in the Hilton Waikiki."

"Wow," I said dryly. "That can't be cheap."

He flashed me a grin. "You jealous? You want to go to Hawaii? I wouldn't mind seein' you lyin' on the beach in a bikini."

I laughed. "Yeah, lying in the sun with a fruity drink sounds good." But the second the words left my mouth, I realized what I'd just said.

I'd never have an alcoholic drink again.

James being James, he knew exactly where my mind had gone. "There are plenty of fruity non-alcoholic drinks."

I made a face. "It's not a big deal."

He held my gaze. "It *is* a big deal. Drinkin's part of society. You and me—and everyone else—are gonna say things that involve alcohol without thinkin' about it. That doesn't mean you're slippin', and it doesn't mean you want a drink."

"I'm still trying to wrap my head around the idea that I'll never have one again."

"One day at a time."

"Yeah." I felt foolish for even talking about it while I was transferring files that could bring down a trafficking network. Or at least a hub of it.

"Carter also texted about Natalie and her family," he added. "They've boarded a plane to New York. He doesn't know where she's headed after that."

I still wasn't sure how to feel about that situation, but I could deal with that later.

I kept copying and pasting, grateful the transfer was moving faster on my laptop than it had on Harlan's ancient computer.

I was about eighty percent done when my phone rang.

James was sitting on the bed, tapping on his phone. He looked up, his expression turning serious.

I pulled it out of my pocket. The number didn't have a name. "Hello?"

"Harper?" Bobby hadn't called me before, but I recognized his voice immediately. The hair on the back of my neck stood on end.

"Yeah, Bobby. It's me. Is everything okay?"

"This may be nothing," he said, sounding nervous, "but it might be something. I figured I'd tell you and let you decide."

I put the phone on speaker and lifted my index finger to my lips, warning James with a look. "Yeah, Bobby. Let's hear it."

James slid off the bed and crossed the room, perching on the arm of the sofa.

Bobby continued. "I was at my grandma's house, doin' some odd jobs for her, and my cousins dropped by."

"Oh?"

"They said Grandma lets them store things in the shed behind her house, and they were there to pick some of them up." He paused. "Harper... they were guns. Big guns. Like semi-automatic."

James went still.

I kept my tone neutral. "I take it that's unusual for them."

"I can honestly say I've never seen them load a half dozen semi-automatic rifles in the back of their car, but I'm not at my grandma's house all the time, so I guess it's possible they move them in and out on a semi-regular basis."

"But you think there's something to this," I said.

"Yeah. I joked that they were preparing for a war, and they said I was close." He hesitated. "When I asked them what that meant, they said they'd been hired to help watch over a shipment exchange early tomorrow morning. I asked if that was common, and they said no, but if it goes well, they might be working for the king of Little Rock."

"Did they say who the king of Little Rock was?" I asked.

"No," he said, "And I figured I was pushing my luck to even ask." A strained laugh slipped out. "I just laughed it off and said we live in a republic—there are no kings. They laughed again and said that just shows how little I know. That there's a *whole underworld* I know nothing about."

I flicked my gaze to James, but his face was neutral.

"They've talked about their illegal activities before," Bobby said, "but this is the first time I've ever heard them talk about a king … or a war." He drew a breath. "I don't know if this has anything to do with what you're lookin' into, but I figured it wouldn't hurt to let you know."

"Good call," I said. "Thanks Bobby. I'll definitely check it out."

"Okay."

"And if you see them again soon, don't ask too many questions. Don't make them suspicious. The last thing I want is for you to get hurt."

"I left my grandma's, so I doubt I'll see them again today," he said. "But I'll be careful."

"Good. And thanks again."

"Sure, Harper. Be careful."

"You too." I hung up and looked up at James. "Thoughts?"

"A couple." He went quiet for a beat. "One, Knox has hired more men to look for us, but he wouldn't call it a war. There's just two of us."

"And all those semi-automatic weapons would be overkill," I said.

He gave me a dry look. "Not necessarily. I've got a reputation, so they might arm themselves to the teeth. And the way you took out his men last week…." He let the comment hang. "But I still don't think they'd call it a war. They'd call it a hunt. Or an ambush."

I made a face. "Maybe. What's your other thought?"

"That Knox's shipment is still comin' through sometime early tomorrow," he said, "and he's hired extra men to protect it."

"That's where my head's at too," I said. "But early morning could be any time from one a.m. to six."

He frowned. "Agreed."

"Even if you tell your handler within the next hour, we don't know *where* it's happening." My stomach tightened. "It could still be in the industrial area as a fuck you—Knox's way of saying *even if you know, you can't stop it*. And of course he'll be ready if we show up." I turned to face him. "But what if it's law enforcement who shows up?"

"Maybe he's countin' on his paid stooges in the department to make sure that doesn't happen."

"True." Because at this point, I was pretty sure at least four Little Rock detectives were dirty ... and I suspected there were more. Natalie had estimated Simmons had five to ten percent in his pocket.

"Makes me wonder what you did that made them so desperate to get you off the force," he said.

I grimaced. "We're gonna Scarlett O'Hara that one and worry about it tomorrow." Because I'd drive myself crazy thinking about it right now.

He grinned, then tipped his chin toward the laptop. "How close are you to having it all transferred?"

I checked the progress bar. "Transferring to both at the same time slowed it down some, but I'd say five minutes."

"Did you transfer the files from your mother's folder?"

"Not yet."

"If you're still open to it, transfer them too."

"Okay."

He gave a small nod and stood. "I'm gonna call my handler."

"Sounds good."

He started across the room. "I'll be right back."

He was out the door before I could respond, but I couldn't help wondering how the hallway was more private than our room.

It wasn't.

He didn't want me to hear his conversation, and I wasn't sure what to make of that.

Fear and distrust rose up, twisting together and then burrowing under my skin. James Malcolm used to be a crime boss. He hadn't gotten where he was by being honest.

Was he tricking me now?

But I thought about the way he held me. The way he'd tried to make me feel better about my mother's file. The way he hadn't brushed off my fruity-drink comment—he'd stopped and made sure I was okay. The way he'd freaked out when he realized I hadn't come back to the hotel after taking Emily to her parents.

He'd been scared.

He wouldn't double-cross someone he cared about that deeply.

Would he?

He came back in about ten minutes later, his expression grim enough that my stomach dropped.

"That bad?" I asked, my heart in my throat.

He crossed the room and pulled me into a hug.

"You're scaring me, James."

He kissed my forehead and leaned back to look me in the eyes. "It's fine. My handler's an asshole."

"What'd they say?"

"I'm meetin' them in a half hour."

"That quickly?" I stared at them. "Are they based in Little Rock?"

"Yeah." He pulled me in again, resting his chin on top of my head.

This wasn't like him. Something was wrong.

"What aren't you telling me?" I asked.

He gave a low chuckle. "So paranoid."

"Don't." I tipped my face up. "Something's wrong. Don't lie to me."

His chest rose with a deep breath. Then he looked down at me, and the defeat in his eyes made my blood run cold. "I don't think they're gonna set me free."

My heart dropped. "What? What more do they want? This is enough to bring down Knox—and give them leads on other hubs."

"I know," he said quietly. "But they have me by the balls."

"Can Carter do anything about it?"

He slowly shook his head. "No. I arranged this deal on my own. Carter's not a part of it."

"Not even after the fact?"

"No." His jaw tightened. "My handler made it clear from the jump—my attorney stays out of it. The second I bring him in, they send me back to prison, reinstate my old charges. And stack new ones on top."

Fury burned through me. "That's not right."

"And yet," he said, his voice flat. "It's how it is."

"So you're still meeting with him?"

He held my gaze. "I'm turning the information over and letting the chips fall where they may."

"I'm sorry."

He shrugged, but he didn't look away. "Do you have any idea how much I care about you?"

A soft smile tugged at my mouth. "I'm a little slow, but ... I think it's finally getting through." I swallowed. "And I hope you know how much I care about you too."

He kissed me, gentle and unhurried. "I do." The corners of his mouth tipped up. "You've given me hope, Harper. Thank you."

"You've done the same for me," I said. "We'll figure out a way to get you out of this. If you'll tell me more about the agreement—what they promised and what they're holding over you—I can help you pick it apart."

He kissed me again, then loosened his hold.

My arms stayed locked around him, like I could keep him with me by force of will.

"I have to go," he said quietly.

"Let me come as backup," I said. "Even if I'm not in the meeting."

He shook his head, slow and firm. "Wait here. I'll text you when I'm on my way back. Then we'll figure out what to do next."

"I *know* what our next move needs to be." I lifted my chin. "We have to find Knox. Before the Feds pick him up and he's safe behind bars."

He tilted his head. "I don't have to turn this in now. I can sit on it until we find him."

"No." I didn't let myself hesitate, even though part of me wanted to. "You turn it over now, and we hope they move fast enough to get those girls in the houses." My voice tightened. "I can't let them spend one more night being used like that."

"Okay." He tried to step back and released a low laugh, more resigned than amused. "You're gonna have to let me go." He glanced at the laptop. "Are the files done transferring?"

"Yeah." Reluctantly, I released him and leaned over to unplug one of the hard drives.

As I handed it to him, a new thought hit me. "Do you think Knox will be there for the shipment in the morning?"

He looked surprised. "I doubt he shows up to those things."

"Usually, sure." My pulse picked up. "But Bobby said the king of Little Rock hired extra guns. Wouldn't that mean he's worried?"

James scoffed. "I doubt he thinks I'd bring in law enforcement. He probably thinks I'm out for revenge after his mother nabbed me, or I'm trying to take over his empire." His eyes darkened. "Maybe both."

"But he's scared you'll show up," I pressed. "He thinks you'll try to stop him."

"And you," he said flatly. "You're the one who took out all his men." His mouth tightened. "If he's building an army, it's for both of us."

I felt a strange flicker of pride, but I shoved it down. "That's beside the point. What if we find out where it's happening and go?"

"And take on his army?" he asked, like I'd suggested the two of us invade a country.

"No. We sneak close enough to confirm Knox is there."

"That's insane, Harper."

"It's a good idea."

His jaw flexed. "And if he *is* there, what then?"

"If we get the opportunity, we take him out. If we don't, we follow him when he leaves."

His lips pressed tight. "So many things could go wrong."

"Then we call the state police and let them stop it."

He hesitated, releasing a sigh as he lifted the hard drive. "I'm not sayin' no. Just… I've got to deal with this first before I can think about the rest."

What was I thinking? He was right. The exchange was already contentious, and he hadn't even met with his handler yet. "You're right. Go. I'll start going through the files. We'll talk when you get back."

"Instead of jumpin' right on the files"—he tugged a strand of the wig I was still wearing— "why don't you go take this off and take a long, hot shower? It'll help clear your head."

"I'm fine."

"We've been pushin' hard all day. Take a break, then come back fresh." He tipped his head toward the sticky notes. "After that, you can start tacklin' what's in the files. I presume you're gonna stick those on a wall?" He glanced toward a large painting hung over a credenza next to the bathroom. "Want me to take that down so you can start postin' 'em up there? It seems like your best option."

I frowned. "Yeah, it has the most surface area." I shook my head. "But I can take it down."

"So, about that shower…" he said suggestively.

I didn't particularly feel the need to shower, but he had a point about taking a momentary break to clear my head. Then again, I often worked things through in the shower. Maybe I could figure out how to find Knox. "Yeah. Good idea."

He took my hand and led me to the bathroom before he pulled me flush against him and kissed me like he was leaving for war. "When I get back, I want to fuck the real you. No wig."

My stomach fluttered. "Fine. Maybe I'll be waiting naked in bed."

"Jesus, woman," he growled, grabbing my ass with his free hand and hauling me closer until I felt exactly how serious he was. "You keep talkin' like that, and I'm gonna tell my handler to go to hell so I can screw you in the shower."

I stepped back, forcing myself to be stern. "No. You need to go. You're already going to be late."

For a second, he looked like he wanted to argue. Then he gave me a gentle push into the bathroom. "Shut the door before I change my mind."

"Be safe, James," I said, worry stealing my breath.

"I will." His gaze held mine. "Don't leave the hotel room. I have enough to worry about."

"I won't."

He shut the door.

I pressed the small of my back against the counter and tried to rein in my mess of emotions. James would be fine. And if his handler wouldn't release him ... we'd figure out a way. I'd make sure of it.

I stripped off the wig and cap, yanked out the pins, and stepped into the shower. The warm water washed over my skin, and I shut my eyes, letting it soak in. James was right. I'd needed this.

My mind fixated on how to pin down Knox. If we could discover the location of the shipment, confirm he was there, and follow him back to where he disappeared to—

Wait, the question was how to find the location without tipping our hand.

Who would even know ahead of time?

Then it hit me...

Razor.

If Bobby's cousins had been hired to help with the shipment, then maybe Razor was part of it too. James had said he was a lush, and most lushes talked. If he was pre-gaming at his usual bar before the exchange, maybe I could get something useful out of him. And if the exchange was happening early tomorrow morning, we could find him tonight.

There were a lot of moving parts to my plan. A lot of ways it could fail. But once the Feds started issuing warrants, Knox and his people would scatter like cockroaches. This might be our only chance to get access to him.

I got out, dried off, and went into the room for a fresh pair of clothes—then my gaze snagged on the coffee table and I froze.

Only *one* hard drive sat plugged into my laptop.

The other two we'd bought less than two hours ago were both gone.

Had someone been in our room while I'd been in the shower? But why take one of the drives and leave the laptop and the original drive behind?

The answer hit me like a nail-studded two-by-four.

James had taken the two hard drives. He'd pushed me to take a shower so I wouldn't notice.

My pulse hammered as I stared at the empty space on the table.

Why did he need two … and what the hell was he doing with them?

Chapter 30

Two hours later, and a good thirty color-coded sticky notes pasted on the wall, James still hadn't returned.

Had he ditched me? Had his handler arrested him on the spot? Or had he gone somewhere he hadn't wanted me to know about? Why had he taken two hard drives?

I called Carter.

"Have you heard from James?" I asked the moment he answered, pacing the room.

"Isn't he with you?" he asked with an edge in his voice.

"I take that as a no." My throat tightened. "Did he tell you he was meeting his handler?"

"No." The word was clipped.

I stopped pacing and pressed the heel of my hand to my forehead. "He left two hours ago."

"Why the fuck did he go meet his handler?" Carter barked.

"Because of what we got from Natalie." I forced myself to breathe. "What matters is this: we copied everything tied to Knox onto an external hard drive. We made several copies, and James called his handler, then set up a meeting to hand it over."

"Why the fuck didn't he call me first?" he demanded.

"I don't know." My stomach clenched. "He stepped into the hallway to make the call. When he came back, he looked … defeated. He said he didn't think what we found would be enough to get him out of his arrangement." I swallowed. "I asked if you could talk to them, and he said if he involved you, they'd toss him back into prison."

"Tell me exactly what you collected," Carter said with a groan. "He told me Natalie was working for Knox and that she had a ton of incriminating evidence, but he wouldn't get into specifics. I told him we'd go through it all and figure out what to give them." He paused. "Did he take it all?"

My stomach sank. "I transferred everything over to the hard drives. Unless he removed some of it, yeah." I told him what I'd found in Harlan's and Natalie's files—Blackstone Capital, the leases, the police on the payroll, and finally the videos from Dani.

"He handed them the whole case on a silver fucking platter," Carter said, heat in his voice. "Why wouldn't it be enough?"

"I don't know," I said. "There has to be something else going on."

He groaned in frustration. "If he'd brought me into the loop in the beginning—when he cut the deal in prison—he wouldn't be in this situation."

"Why wouldn't he let you help set it up?" I asked.

"I don't know," he said bitterly. "He wouldn't let me do *anything* to try to get him out. He seemed resigned to staying in there. Then he got a key piece of information from the Hardshaw Group, and months later, he had a deal."

"Wait." I squeezed my eyes shut, trying to put this together. "Wouldn't he have handed the information over before the bust? Or right after?"

"He gave them *plenty* before the bust," Carter said, his

contempt thick. "But they were lookin' for reasons to lock him up. He delivered the downfall of an international cartel, and they still called the deal null because he wasn't physically present when the arrests went down."

"I know he missed the bust," I said slowly. "But where was he? Why wasn't he there if he knew how important it was?"

He didn't answer for several seconds. Finally, voice tight, he said, "That's not for me to say."

My temper snapped. "That's bullshit, Carter. I'm in the thick of this now."

"Only a handful of people know where he was, and it's not for me to tell you." Carter's voice went flat. "But the bottom line is, Skeeter deemed it more important. He never regretted his decision. So we have to stand by that."

What on earth could have been more important than meeting the requirements of his deal?

But Carter was right—it wouldn't help to focus on that now.

"Why did he hold that piece of information back?" I asked. "Was it leverage in case they screwed him?"

"No." Carter hesitated. "He didn't have it then. It came into his possession about ten months after the bust."

"From where?"

"From the daughter of one of the three men at the core of Hardshaw." He exhaled. "She visited Skeeter in prison and asked for his help in bringing down her father."

I had questions about the *why*, but not of them felt urgent at the moment. "How was he supposed to help form prison?"

"Randall Blakely's daughter—Carly—was hoping to get him to implicate himself on video," Carter said. "She figured if she looked like she knew more than she did, he'd start talking. Skeeter gave her that information, in exchange for something he wanted. A file her father had."

"Did it work?"

"Sort of." Carter sounded grim. "He implicated himself but was killed during the confrontation."

That was convenient.

"A few days after Blakely's death, Carly contacted me. She said she kept her word. She had the file. We deemed it too important to transmit electronically, so I went to Dallas to retrieve it."

"What was it?"

"Some kind of computer code. I have no idea what it did or what it was for. But once Skeeter had it, things changed." His tone changed. "He didn't seem as hopeless. And a few months later, he was released. All charges dropped." He paused, then sounded resigned. "But he traded one cage for another."

James had gotten some kind of code from the head of Hardshaw Group, and it had been important enough to get him a second deal. But he'd only been released conditionally— and now he had to bring in enough information for them to bring down a Little Rock human trafficking ring.

So why would they wait three years for him to come through? And once he delivered the information wrapped in a bow, why was it still not enough?

None of this made sense.

That had to be why they didn't want Carter anywhere near the agreement. No attorney in his right mind would let a client take a deal without clear, enforceable terms.

But James was no fool. So why had he cut Carter out of the loop?

"Okay," Carter said, sounding like he was trying to regroup. "Skeeter's been gone two hours. Maybe the handler drove in from Memphis or somewhere a couple of hours away. We need to account for travel time."

"No." My nerves pinged. "He said the meeting was in Little Rock, thirty minutes after his call. When I asked how it was happening so quickly, he said the handler was in town. The timing would have put the meeting at around five-thirty. The meeting shouldn't have taken this long. It should have been a simple handover."

"You said there's a lot of information. They may be taking their sweet time going through it. Have you tried calling him?"

"Of course," I snapped. "And texting. He hasn't answered." My chest tightened. "Can you see his location through his phone?"

"Give me a minute." I heard tapping on his end before he said, "He's turned off his phone. Let me look up his Google Maps timeline."

His phone was off? I tried not to panic. He might have turned it off before he met the handler, or the handler might have insisted on it.

"Okay," Carter said. "I see he was at the Morrison Hotel around five-twenty. Then it shows he was at a diner downtown."

"What's the name?"

"The Capital Café."

I knew the place. "That's a five-minute walk from here."

"That's not his last location," he said. "It shows he was parked on the street near the corner of Asher and University about a half hour later."

Why had he gone to a second location?

It had to have something to do with the second hard drive.

First, I needed to focus on where he'd gone, otherwise, Carter might sidetrack me after I told him about the other drive.

"Let me see what's around there." I pulled up maps on my computer and typed in the intersection. I searched the businesses near the location. "There's a dry cleaner, a comic book store, a vacuum repair shop, a pawn shop, and another diner."

Why would he go to any of those places, and what was he doing? "When was his phone turned off?"

"His location went dark about an hour and a half ago."

My mind raced. "There's a chance he met his handler at the diner and headed somewhere else afterward. Carter, when he left, he took a second hard drive."

"What second hard drive?" Carter asked, his voice rising.

"We had three hard drives—the original we copied the files onto, then two more. James said the second one was for his handler and the third was for us, to put in his safe. But right before he left, he insisted I take a break to clear my head. He suggested a shower would help. He made sure I was in the bathroom and shut the door." My pulse kicked up. "When I came out, the second hard drive was missing. He took two."

I drew a breath, trying to make it make sense. "Was he planning to turn the information over to someone else?"

"I don't know," Carter said slowly.

"I've been trying to figure it out for the last two hours," I admitted. "And I don't like any of the scenarios I've come up with." I swallowed. "Would he blackmail Knox?"

"No," Carter scoffed. "He doesn't need the money, and he'd *never* give Knox a way out."

"But he might use it as bait to lure Knox out." My voice turned brittle. "He might tell him that he has my mom's files too and offer some kind of exchange."

"Maybe…" Carter sounded distracted. "And I can see him leaving you behind to do it."

I could too. And that made my blood boil.

"It would explain why he turned off his phone," Carter said. "So I couldn't track him."

My pulse thudded. "If he went to meet Knox, Knox could have kidnapped him. Or worse." I felt sick. "We have to get a location for Knox. What haven't we thought of? There *has* to be a way to get it."

"Now hold on," he said in a rush. "We don't know what Skeeter was doing, Harper," he said in frustration. "For all we know, he took the hard drive to someone else."

I'd thought of that too, but who?

Then it hit me. "He promised to get the exotic dancer's charges dropped."

Carter went quiet for a half beat. "Yeah?"

"The Feds have influence," I said, thinking fast. "But they might not be able to make that happen. And James gave his word, so he'd want to make sure they got dropped. Right?"

"If he gave his word, then yeah. He'd make sure it happened."

"Okay." The pieces started snapping together. "What if he met with the handler, and they didn't agree or wouldn't make any promises? Or... he didn't trust the handler to follow through." I took a breath. "He'd go to someone who could make that happen. Right? Would he go to the Pulaski County prosecutor?"

Carter sucked in a breath. "Oh... *fuck*."

My panic spiked. "What? Would going to the prosector be bad?"

"No." His voice tightened. "He wouldn't go to the Pulaski prosecutor."

"But you know who he *would* go to," I said, then forced my voice down. "Who, Carter?"

He hesitated long enough that my stomach twisted. Finally, he exhaled. "Mason Deveraux."

"*Mason Deveraux?*" I asked in disbelief. "James said Deveraux hates him."

"He does."

"Then why would he go to him?"

"They have history," Carter sounded like he hated admitting it. "It's contentious, but Deveraux is fair—except for when it comes to Skeeter. He's his blind spot."

"And if Deveraux's generally fair," I reasoned. "Then James would expect him to drop Dani's charges in exchange for the information?"

"Charges and more." Carter's tone softened. "Deveraux's ambitious. It sounds like half of what's on that drive could make his career."

"But wouldn't James's handler lose his mind if he shared the information with someone else?"

"As big of a jackass as this person sounds?" Carter let out a humorous breath. "Yeah, probably. But this is all speculation, Harper. All of it. We don't know that he met anyone besides his handler. For all we know, the handler took him somewhere after they met at the diner and made him power down his phone."

"So why the two hard drives?" I demanded. "And why hide it from me?"

"I don't know."

I gripped the phone harder. "What are the odds he met with Deveraux? Your best guess?"

He paused a beat. "If he met with someone other than his handler—and that's a real possibility because of the dancer—then I'd put it at eighty to eighty-five percent."

"So, now we need to track down Mason Deveraux."

Carter burst out laughing.

"This isn't funny, Carter."

"I'll say." His laughter died. "What's your plan? Call him like a mom asking if her kid can get his late ass home for dinner?"

He had a point.

"You can't call Deveraux, Harper," Carter said, all business now. "And even if James met with him, Deveraux's never going to admit it. You'll only make things worse."

"I've got to do *something*, Carter."

"Yeah. You stay put and go through the files."

"That's what I've *been* doing."

"Then keep doing it. If he's not back by midnight, *then* we'll worry." His voice went cold. "And I'll start making calls at that point."

"To who?"

"People who'd know if the Feds arrested him." He paused. "Until then, we wait." I didn't answer fast enough, because he added, "Do not leave that hotel room, Harper. Promise me you won't go hunting for his car or his phone."

It wasn't hard to guess what I wanted to do. But Knox's people wouldn't kidnap him. And if they killed him, they wouldn't have bothered turning off his phone. The best use of my time was right here: digging through the files and taking notes.

"Fine," I said, letting every ounce of my irritation show. "But if you hear from him, you tell me. Not like this morning, when he contacted you and you kept it to yourself."

He was silent, then grudgingly said, "From here on out, you're in the loop."

"Thank you."

"Oh, one more thing before I go," he said absently. "Skeeter asked me to get you a new phone. It's at the front desk, but I don't want you leaving the room, so call down and ask them to bring it up."

"A new phone?" I asked in confusion. "Does he think this one is compromised?"

"No, it's a smartphone." He paused. "With location tracking."

I hesitated, my heart racing again. "When did he ask you to do that?"

"When he called asking me to send security to pick up Natalie's family."

Had he been planning to do something with a second hard

drive before we met Dani and saw the video? Did that mean he wasn't meeting with Mason Deveraux after all?

"He can see your location," Carter said, sounding grim. "And so can I."

"Okay," I said, feeling numb. "I'll call down. Thanks."

We hung up and I called down to the front desk and asked them to bring up my package. Ten minutes later, I had a new smartphone, which had already been set up and activated. Carter's and James's current numbers were listed in my contacts. I set up call forwarding on the number I'd been using in case my contacts called or texted.

I took a few moments to pace the room. I wanted to trust James, and I did, to an extent. But I wouldn't put it past him to try to confront Knox behind my back.

I sat down in front of the laptop and looked at the map of his phone's last location. None of the businesses on the corners grabbed my attention—he could have met someone at any of those places—so I expanded my search, gasping when I saw a bar two blocks away.

The Brick House.

The bar he'd told me that Razor frequented.

I cursed a blue streak, then called Carter.

"You heard something?" he asked.

"I know where he went."

"How? Where?"

I drew a breath to try to calm my nerves, but it did nothing to help. "I looked at the map again and zoomed out a bit. There's a bar two blocks from his vehicle. The Brick House."

"Is that supposed to mean something to me?" he asked dryly.

"Carter, that's the place where Razor hangs out."

"Oh, shit."

"Before he left, I suggested we try to find Razor and see if he knew the location of the shipment. He said he couldn't think about it right then, but we'd talk about it after he came back." My temper rose again, but this time the anger was wrapped in fear. "He went without me."

"We don't know that," he said, but he didn't sound convincing.

I walked over to my bags of clothes. "It's as good a place as any to start looking."

"You are not to leave that room," he growled.

"Try and stop me." I hung up and pulled out a pair of jeans, a black tank top with multiple strings crisscrossed across the back, and a black jacket. I quickly changed, ignoring the three times Carter called and his five texts telling me he was going to send security to keep me in the room.

I was pretty sure he was bluffing, but I wasn't going to press my luck. I texted back that he was right, and I was going to wait. I doubted he believed me, but it might buy me some time.

I applied some dark eye makeup, which took longer than I would have liked since I didn't have much experience. I stuffed my hair back in the wig cap, tugged on the blond wig, and applied red lipstick. When I looked up at my reflection, I barely recognized myself. This would work.

I strapped a gun to my ankle, then put another handgun and my shoulder holster in my backpack, along with an arsenal of bullets. If I found out Razor had done something to James, I would stop at nothing to find Knox and end him.

Chapter 31

Before I left the room, I put the tube of lipstick in my jacket pocket, then headed out the door. I exited through the back of the building, taking the car in the parking garage in case Knox had figured out we were staying here and was watching for our car. Based on the car keys James had left on the nightstand, I knew he'd taken the luxury car to the meeting.

Once I found the car, I drove toward the bar, ignoring the first two calls from Carter. As I neared the bar, I answered the third one.

"What the hell are you doing, Harper?" he demanded furiously.

"You know," I said in irritation. "I love how you and James conveniently forget I was a cop. I'm not some simpleton playing amateur sleuth. I know what I'm doing."

"And I sure as hell bet you had backup," Carter shot back. "Right now you have none."

"I can handle myself," I said through gritted teeth. "I'm in disguise. No one will know it's me. If James is in there I doubt he'd even recognize me."

"I wouldn't count on that," he grumbled, then he snapped, "*Fine.* If you're gonna insist on doing this, you need to check in and let me know what's goin' on." He added, "So when you disappear and Skeeter gets back and needs to look for you, at least I'll have a few clues for him to follow."

"Very funny," I scoffed.

"Actually, it's not funny at all. I want to make it clear that I told you not to do this."

"You've made that very clear."

"I recorded that so I can prove it to Skeeter later when he threatens to fire me."

"That's not gonna happen, Carter," I said, some of my frustration fading. "And I'll check in with you."

"Thank you." He paused. "I guess it goes without saying: be careful."

I released a dry laugh. "Got it."

I hung up and pulled into a parking spot on the street, a half block between the bar and the last known location of James's phone. I considered bringing the backpack in but decided it would look suspicious. The gun at my ankle would have to do.

I headed down the sidewalk, scanning the windows of the businesses as I made my way to the intersection. Most businesses were closed, but the few that were open were small, the interiors lit enough for me to see he wasn't inside.

I wasn't sure whether to be relieved or concerned when I spotted his car twenty feet ahead, parked against the curb. My heart began to race I approached it, scared I'd find him dead inside. I held my breath when I reached the passenger side window and peered inside, then closed my eyes as relief rushed through me. It was empty.

So where was he?

I slowly spun around, taking in the businesses around the

corner, trying to figure out if he could have had a destination other than the bar. But everything looked closed, even the diner.

Time to find Razor.

I sent a text to Carter, telling him I'd found the car, but there was no sign of James, and I was headed to the bar.

As I walked toward it, I worked on a plan to get information. Since I couldn't just walk up to Razor and ask him if he'd seen James, I was going to have to get him talking. That meant I had to gain his interest.

The bar was dimly lit when I walked in. I gave myself two seconds to let my eyes adjust and search for Razor. There were about twenty men and a handful of women in the room, most of them at the tables and booths. None of them looked like him.

I stifled my disappointment as I headed to the counter and hopped up on a stool, several feet away from two men, the only other customers sitting at the bar.

All the bottles on the wall in front of me made me realize this was a moment of truth.

I'd known I'd have to face this issue, but now it was staring me square in the face. I couldn't order ginger ale or club soda. I needed to fit in, and that would post a neon sign over my head.

Dammit.

What did this mean for my sobriety? I was surprised at the sting of tears, but I blinked them away. I had to focus on finding James.

A bartender who looked like a linebacker with a big bushy beard headed over to me. "What're you havin'?"

I scanned the shelf behind him, then came to a decision. "A finger of McClellan." I reasoned if I was drinking expensive Scottish whisky, it made sense that I'd drink it slowly.

He cocked an eyebrow. "The good stuff, huh?"

"That and a bottle of water."

He gave me a curt nod and walked away.

I sat back in my stool, slowly scanning the room like I was a woman on the hunt for a man. I was halfway around the room when I spotted Razor in a booth talking to a man sitting across from him. I didn't recognize the guy, but I pulled out my phone and set it on the counter. I needed to get a photo of him.

The bartender returned with my drinks, sliding the whisky onto a napkin and setting the unopened water bottle next to it. "Ain't seen you in here before," he said, giving me a slow once-over.

"That's because I'm new to Little Rock," I said, shooting him a *don't fuck with me* glare.

"Where'd you move from?" he asked, still studying me.

"Memphis."

"What made you move to Little Rock?"

My expression hardened. "What is this? Twenty questions? What the fuck does it matter where I moved from?" I nodded to the glass. "I'm here to enjoy a good whisky and check out the local men."

The sharpness was deliberate. Meek women didn't pop into biker bars alone. I had to prove I belonged here or possibly be harassed. Or worse.

It must have worked because he lifted a hand in surrender as a grin spread across his face. "Fair enough. Enjoy Scotland's finest." His gaze flicked to the glass as though he was waiting for me to prove my point.

Steeling my back, I reached for the glass. I was terrified to take a sip. If I started, I wasn't sure I could stop. But if I got shit faced, I wouldn't have the wits to find James.

I lifted the glass up anyway, letting a small sip of the amber liquid pass over my lips. The rush hit hard, warm and familiar. I lowered the glass, trying to make it look natural while I clutched the tumbler like it was either armor or a snake waiting to bite.

He seemed satisfied and sauntered to the other end of the bar.

I needed to take a photo of the guy with Razor, but I couldn't just snap one. A selfie would be the best way to get it, especially since they were directly behind me, but I doubted selfies were the norm here. Then I remembered the tube of red lipstick in my jacket pocket.

I slipped it out, then opened my camera phone to selfie mode and held it up to reapply my lipstick, making sure I had a good glimpse at the two men in the booth in the upper corner of the frame. It was dark enough it took a moment to snap the photo.

The man with Razor glanced up and his face darkened. He leaned over the table and said something to Razor. I lowered my phone to my lap and quickly sent the image to Carter in a text. Then, to be safe, I deleted the image and put the phone to sleep, all while acting like I'd just finished primping.

"Did you take a photo of me?" a gruff voice said to my left.

I picked up my glass and slowly turned to face the man, not surprised it was Razor. I looked him up and down. "Why would I take a photo of *you*?" I asked in a condescending tone.

"Give me your phone."

I shot him a stern look. "Like hell I will."

His face reddened. "Give. Me. Your. Phone.

I set my glass down. "Fuck you, asshole. But if you're so damned paranoid, I'll prove to you I didn't take your damned photo."

I opened the phone and started to pull up the photo library, realizing I'd just screwed up again. This was a new phone with a new account. There wouldn't be any images.

Only there were multiple photos of the girls James had on his phone.

I doubted that was much better. Still, I made a show of lifting my phone and quickly shuffling through the images, hoping he wouldn't realize what he was looking at. I lowered my phone, put it to sleep, then set in on the bar face down while giving him a patronizing smile. "*Happy?*" I snapped.

"Then what the fuck were you doin'?"

"Using my camera as a mirror to put on lipstick," I said, pulling out my tube and showing him. "So, I can look good for big, burly men." I made an expression of disgust. "But not for assholes like you."

I turned away from him, pretending I didn't give a shit that he was towering over me. After a couple of seconds, he said in a softer tone. "Let me buy you a drink to make up for accusing you."

"Fuck off," I said, keeping my gaze on the bottles on the wall behind the bar. "I can buy my own drinks." Then to prove my point, I lifted my glass and took another sip, ignoring the blissful feeling of the smooth fire coating my tongue.

I wasn't sure what my plan was here. I needed to chill, or I might piss him off and either get kicked out or have the shit beat out of me, a definite possibility given his previous domestic violence charges. Or he might see me as a challenge and hang around to wear me down. I figured it could go either way. But I was counting on the fact that the bartender recognized me as a newcomer, and Razor might appreciate a fresh prospect to screw.

He slid onto the stool next to me and leaned close. "I said I was sorry. You had your phone up. What else was I supposed to think?"

I glanced over at him with a dry look. "What are you, famous? You think I'm paparazzi?

He laughed. "Nothin' like that." He flashed a toothy grin. "What can I do? I can't have a pretty thing like you pissed off at me."

"Tell you what," I said. holding my glass from the top between my thumb and index finger. "You can try to convince me you're not an asshole while I finish my drink, and if you've convinced me, then I'll let you get the next one."

"Oh, I *am* an asshole, sweetheart," he said with a dry laugh. "But I can-*not* be an asshole to you."

"Charming," I sneered, then took another tiny sip, letting the glass stay on my bottom lip long enough for it look like I'd drunk more.

"You haven't been here before," he said as he flagged the bartender.

"Are you here twenty-four/seven?" I asked with plenty of attitude. "Otherwise, how could you know?"

"I'm here quite a bit, and I'd *definitely* remember you." He grinned. "Why don't you tell me a little bit about yourself."

I turned slightly to face him. "If this is your way of tryin' to win me over, it's not workin' out for you so far."

"I thought women liked to talk about themselves."

I took another sip while I gave him an annoyed glare. When I lowered the glass, I said, "How does asking me to talk about myself win me over? You should be telling me about *you*."

The bartender stopped in front of us and waited.

"I'll have what she's havin'," Razor said, not taking his eyes off me.

"She's havin' a McClellan, so you might want to rethink that," the bartender said with a laugh.

Razor's eyebrows shot up and he made a face. "Then give me my usual."

The bartender walked away without a word.

"So… you're a high-dollar bitch," he said, but there was an air of appreciation in it.

I jiggled my glass, letting the liquid slosh around a bit.

"Tick-tock. So far I've learned you're a cheap asshole." I grimaced. "Not winnin' me over." Then I took another sip.

I still wasn't sure this was the right course of action, but undercover work wasn't my forte. As a cop, I'd always been direct and blunt. I hadn't ever needed to wiggle my way into a suspect's world, although I was smart enough to know it usually took days, weeks, or even months. It sure didn't happen with a single encounter.

Not to mention I was going to end up drunk if I kept playing this game.

That meant I needed to speed things along. The only way Razor was going to tell me what I needed to know was if I spoke his language. Force.

Thankfully, Razor seemed to like my *hard-to-get* game.

"What do you want to know?" he asked with a grin.

"What do you do? What are your hobbies?" I narrowed my gaze. "Are you married?"

"I work in security," he said, resting a forearm on the counter. "I like to drink. And I don't believe in tyin' myself down."

I resisted the urge to groan in frustration. This shithead wasn't giving me much to work with. Maybe I should try another tactic.

I rolled my eyes. "Boring." Then I turned away from him and faced the wall, dismissing him.

The bartender set a tumbler on the counter, and Razor motioned to him. "She just called me borin'. Can you believe that?" He released a hearty laugh.

The bartender didn't respond, just walked away.

Razor leaned closer to me and lowered his voice, making it sound menacing. "I'm the *farthest* thing from borin', sweetheart."

"Talk is cheap."

"Want me to prove it to you?"

I turned my head slightly to glance at him and lifted a disinterested brow. "How do you plan on doin' *that*?"

He studied me for a long moment, drained his entire glass, then hopped off his stool. "Watch this."

My gaze followed him as he headed over to a table with three men. He stopped next to the table, towering over a man whose back was to me. The man froze, then looked up at Razor.

"Get outta here," Razor grunted, glaring down at the guy.

"What the hell, Razor?" the guy shouted.

"I said get the fuck out of here, or I'll beat your ass out of here."

The man stood and turned to face Razor. He was several inches shorter, so he lifted his chin to stare up at him. For a moment, I thought he was going to challenge Razor, but then he took a step back.

"I was leaving anyway," he spat, before turning to head toward the exit.

"Chicken shit," Razor said with a laugh. He took a step and reached out to grab the guy's shoulder and jerk him backward before spinning him around. Razor pulled back his arm and uppercut him under the chin.

The man crumpled to the ground and his friends jumped up and ran around their table. No one else moved, not even the bartender. They flicked a glance to Razor and the guy, then turned back to their conversations.

Keeping a cautious glance on Razor, who was laughing, the guys hooked their hands under their friend's upper arms and dragged him, unconscious, out the door.

As soon as the door closed behind them, Razor turned toward me, grinning like the Cheshire Cat. "Still think I'm borin'?"

This man was unhinged. If I were smart, I'd walk out as

soon as it was safe to do so. But that would mean leaving without answers, and I wasn't willing to do that.

I had to be more careful with my plan.

I took a breath to calm my nerves. I could do this.

He stalked back over to me. "You gonna talk to me now?"

I gave him a haughty look. "Am I supposed to be impressed that you sucker-punched that guy?"

He leaned in, his face inches from mine, the smell of onions and whiskey hitting me full force. "Maybe."

Run.

But I was committed to this. I had to find James, because I refused to believe he was dead. Still, would Razor really be here right now if James had come to see him?

And yet…

James's car was down the street. He'd been in this area, so it stood to reason he'd come into this bar. If so, Razor would've seen him. And Razor—or someone else—would have taken James somewhere.

That meant I had to get Razor out of this bar.

I tipped my head up to face him, letting a seductive smile spread across my face. "What do you say we get out of here?"

His eyes lit up. "What do you have in mind?"

"My apartment's near here." I paused and hoped I looked sincere. "Want to come over for a drink?"

His grin spread. "Let's go."

After I grabbed two twenties from my pocket and tossed then onto the counter to cover my drink, I slid off the stool and headed for the door. A second later, I felt his meaty hand grab my upper arm and pull me to a stop. Was he planning to punch me too? I prepared myself to react, but he rested his arm over my shoulders.

"Slow down there," he drawled in my ear. "What's the hurry?"

"Maybe I'm eager to get you home."

We walked out into the cool night air and he steered me toward a pickup truck—the same model I'd found in my search.

He opened the passenger door and waited for me to get in. I suspected it was to make sure I didn't change my mind rather than as a chivalrous act. He tried to lean in and kiss me, but I arched back and teased. "So impatient. Trust me, it'll be worth the wait."

He gave me a leering grin, then walked around the front of the truck. I hurried up and reached for the gun at my ankle, then tucked it between my leg and the car door. Razor got in the truck and started the engine. "Okay, where to?"

"When you get to the street, turn right."

He did as instructed and started driving west. "How far down do I go?"

"I don't know," I said as I lifted the gun and pointed it at him. "Where do I find Gerald Knox?"

He swiveled his head and stared at me, his mouth hanging open. Then he turned back to face the road and hit the brakes hard, nearly rear-ending the car stopped at a stop sign in front of us.

"You're the bitch who's been hangin' out with Malcolm," he said, his voice gruff.

"That's me," I said brightly. "Speaking of Malcolm, where is he?" My heart pounded in my chest as I waited for the answer.

"How would I know?"

"He came into the bar earlier."

"Not that I saw," he said with a sneer. "Haven't seen him since before Christmas. If he came into the bar, he was talkin' to someone else."

Was he telling the truth?

I got the impression he was. So where was James? Had someone gotten him before he made it into the bar?

"Why're you so hot to see Knox?" he asked with a short laugh. "You honestly think he's got him? Trust me, Knox just wants him dead."

I didn't want to think about that possibility right now. "Fine, let's move on to part two: where's the shipment coming in tonight?"

"I don't know what you're talkin' about," he said in a smug tone.

"That's a load of bullshit," I said, holding up the gun a little higher. "Try again."

He laughed. "What? You plannin' to shoot me while I'm drivin'?"

"Yeah," I said, watching him carefully. I wouldn't put it past him to grab the gun or hit me like he had the guy in the bar. "I will if necessary."

"I call bullshit," he said, a slow grin spreading across his face. He'd just barely started to reach his right hand toward me when I pointed the gun at his left thigh and pulled the trigger.

The gun blast was deafening, muffling his shout of pain and anger. A dark stain began to spread across his upper thigh.

"You fuckin' shot me!" he shouted, turning toward me, disbelief on his face.

The truck drifted toward the center line, and he snapped his eyes back onto the road, white-knuckling the steering wheel.

"Reach for me again and I'll give you another one. Now keep driving."

"You stupid bitch!" he shouted.

"Where's the shipment coming in?" I repeated, my ears still ringing.

"How the hell would I know?" he screamed, pressing a hand to his left thigh.

"You expect me to believe you won't be part of it?"

"Lady, I don't work for Knox!"

I didn't buy it. He seemed to know what I was talking

about. When I'd asked, he hadn't asked *what* the shipment was. He'd just claimed to not know any details.

"Why do you care about the shipment?" he spat.

"Don't worry about that. You worry about bleeding to death or getting a matching hole in your other leg. Where and when is the shipment coming in?"

He slowly shook his head. "If I tell you that, I'm as good as dead."

"So tell me where Gerald Knox is."

"I don't know! Knox keeps his home a secret."

"Then who gives you orders or assignments?"

"No one gives me orders," he said through gritted teeth.

"You're bleeding quite a lot," I said nonchalantly, pointing my gun to the spreading stain on his jeans. "Maybe you should tell me something I want to know so you can get that looked at."

"I can't go to a hospital!" he shouted.

"Then you're in a world of shit," I mused. "If you don't give me something useful, I might get impatient."

He glanced at me again, hate filling his eyes. "Knox wants you."

"So I've heard," I said. "But talk is cheap and I have no idea how to find him. Maybe you should take me to someone who *does* know."

"And tell 'em *what?*" he demanded. "That you want his address?"

"This really shouldn't be this hard," I said, irritation slipping into my voice. "If you can't help me, then I might as well kill you and find someone who will."

He gritted his teeth while his one-handed grip on the steering wheel tightened.

"When and where is the shipment coming in?" I asked again.

"The industrial park," he grunted. "Four a.m."

"And Knox?"

"He's gonna be there," he said, starting to pant. "Just show up at the industrial park and introduce yourself."

"Maybe I will," I said. "But where will he be before then?"

"The fuck I know."

"Try again."

"He's not my boss!" he shouted, leaning over the steering wheel. "I don't know!"

"Who *would* know?" I asked. "Who tells you what you need to know?"

He was silent for several seconds, and he looked like he was struggling to make a decision before he said, "Nixon."

"And where would Nixon be right now?"

"Gettin' ready for the shipment." He was starting to breathe heavier.

"Pull over in that parking lot over there," I said, motioning to an empty gravel lot ahead. "Then shut off the engine."

He gave me a cautious look. I expected him to keep driving, but he turned in once we reached it. He pulled into the middle of the lot, put the truck in park, and turned it off.

"What now?" he sneered. "You gonna kill me?"

"No, you're gonna call Nixon."

"The hell I will."

"Then I guess I *will* kill you."

"All right!" he shouted, then reached for his pocket.

"If you pull out anything resembling a weapon, you'll have a hole in your chest next," I said coldly.

He slowly pulled out his phone.

"Good, now grab your car keys too."

He set his phone on the seat and pulled a key fob out of his pocket. I grabbed it and stuffed it into my jacket pocket.

"Now get your phone and hold it so I can see who you're calling," I said.

He typed in his passcode to open the phone, and I made

note of the numbers. He pulled up his contacts, and the name Nixon appeared on the screen.

"Okay," I said, "Now call him and put it on speaker. You're gonna find out two things. Where Knox is right now. And if someone found me, what Knox wants them to do with me."

He shook his head, his jaw clenched tight. "He's never gonna tell me the first part."

"You better hope you're wrong," I said flatly. "And if you tell him I'm with you, I *will* kill you." I narrowed my eyes. "Now call."

Razor looked like he wanted to strangle me, but he was also starting to fade. If he didn't make this call soon, I wasn't sure he'd be able to. I also couldn't help wondering what to do with him. Drop him off at a hospital? If I did that, I doubted he'd tell them I'd shot him, and the gun couldn't be traced to me.

The phone rang and a man answered in a rough tone. "This better be important, Razor. I'm dealing with a mountain of shit."

Razor's dark gaze lifted to me. "Just checkin' if I need to be there sooner than two."

"Why would you need to be here sooner than two?" he demanded.

"I don't know, man," Razor said, lifting his right hand to scrub over his face. "I know Knox is on edge."

"Of course he's on edge. We think Malcolm got one of our handlers and the girl he had with him."

Razor's jaw clenched and he swallowed hard. "So I heard. What about the woman Knox is after?"

"What about her?" Nixon barked.

"Is she helpin' Malcolm?"

"Probably. She wiped out an entire team last week."

Apprehension washed over Razor's face. "If someone found her, what would he want done with her?"

There was a moment of silence. "*Did someone find her?*"

Razor lifted his gaze to me, and I nodded once.

"Yeah," he said, his voice starting to fade. "She walked into The Brick House."

"No shit? Keep her there and I'll send someone to get her."

"Fuck that," Razor growled. "I'm not lettin' you get the credit. If I turn her in, maybe Knox'll take me seriously. Where do you want me to bring her?"

"You're presumin' she'll go with you."

"I've already got her in my truck."

There were another few seconds of silence. "Bring her to the warehouse."

I shook my head.

"No way. I'm bringing her directly to Knox."

"That's not happenin'," Nixon said with a short laugh.

"Then I guess he won't be gettin' her."

"Knox isn't gonna be happy if you show up on his doorstep."

"Then I guess he doesn't want her very bad."

I hoped Nixon gave him something quick because Razor was starting to slump in his seat.

"Fine," Nixon said. "He's probably at his house, 351 Overton Road, but if you tell him you got it from me, I'll kill you myself. Now I've got to go."

Nixon hung up and Razor tried to glare at me, but he was too weak to make it look effective.

"Where's your gun?" I asked.

"Don't have one," he said through gritted teeth.

"I call bullshit," I said, my gaze flicking to his waistband. "I can shove you out of the truck and pat you down, or you can just tell me and save us both the trouble."

His jaw worked, and I thought he was going to pick the hard way, then he said. "Behind my back."

"Both hands on the steering wheel," I said.

"I'm gonna bleed to death if I let go of my leg."

"Then the sooner you lean forward so I can take your gun, the less chance you have of bleeding to death."

Cursing under his breath, he grabbed the steering wheel and leaned forward. I reached over and hiked up his T-shirt, exposing the butt of a gun sticking out of the back of his jeans. I quickly snatched the gun and sat back against the passenger door. After I stuffed it into my jacket pocket, I snatched his phone off the seat.

"Okay," I said. "You can put pressure back on your leg."

He released the steering wheel and pressed both hands to his leg. "I hope Knox gives you a slow and painful death."

"He'll have to stand in line," I said as I checked his phone screen. It hadn't locked yet, so I called 911 and told the operator a man had been shot in the leg and needed medical assistance. After I gave her a rough address, I hung up.

"Help is on the way," I said, opening the door.

"What am I supposed to tell them?" he asked in dismay.

"An *interesting* guy like you'll think of something." I got out and shut the door. After I threw the key fob into a patch of weeds behind a dumpster, I hurried down the street back toward my car.

It was time to pay Gerald Knox a visit. But first, I had to check in with Carter.

"I have an address for Knox," I said when Carter answered. "351 Overton Road."

"Do I want to know how you got that?" he asked in a weary tone.

"I shot Razor in the leg to get him to talk."

"I didn't say I *wanted* to know," he groused.

"We both know you did," I said as I continued to walk the six blocks. "Have you heard from James?"

"No," he said, turning serious. "Did you find out anything?"

"No. Razor said he hadn't been in, and I believe him. If he had, I don't think Razor would have been there shooting the shit with a guy at the bar." Then I added. "Do you know who the man in the photo is?"

"The blurry photo of you putting on lipstick?" he asked wryly.

"The photo of Razor and a guy in a booth. The other was an excuse to get the photo. I take it you don't know?" I could hear sirens in the distance, so I picked up my pace.

"No, but I can do some digging. Is he important?"

"I don't know. I guess that's not important right now. The shipment's going down at four in the morning in the industrial park. Some of the hired help is showing up at two."

"Okay," he said, sounding like he was preparing to negotiate a hostage takeover. "You got two great pieces of information. Now you need to go back to the hotel and wait for Skeeter."

"No, I'm going to confront Knox."

"Are you out of your mind?" he shouted in my ear. "You can't face him alone, and there's little chance Knox has Skeeter. Knox wants him dead."

I wanted to argue with him. But I believed Razor hadn't seen him, which meant James hadn't gone to the bar. And deep down, I know Carter was right. Knox didn't have James. Confronting Knox alone would be foolish.

So where was James? Had he been surveilling the bar? Had he left his car parked two blocks away and gone to another location? Or had he met someone in one of the buildings around the intersection?

But one thing was clear—James likely hadn't been taken by Knox's men, which meant my best course of action was to go back to the hotel and wait.

"Okay," I said. "I'm heading there now. I'll let you know when I'm back in the room."

I hung up and continued walking, trying to put more distance between me and the scene behind me.

I was almost to my car when a figure darted out from behind a car parked on the street. They tackled me to the pavement, face first, and lay on top of me to pin me in place.

Caught by surprise, it took a second to realize what happened and react. I tried to rise up and shove them off me, but I felt a sharp sting in my neck. Then everything faded to black.

Chapter 32

I woke to a pounding headache. My eyes were still closed, and at first, I thought I was waking up with a massive hangover. Only I wasn't lying on a bed—I was sitting up, and I couldn't move my arms and legs.

Where was I?

I tried to open my eyes, but they were too heavy, and when I got them open to slits, I saw a dimly lit room. Everything was gray.

I stopped trying to pry my eyes open. I could go back to sleep and wake up later.

Only my shoulders were restrained, and my palms and knees stung.

I worked harder to open my eyes. I could make out a figure in a chair about three feet in front of me, but then my eyelids sank shut again.

"Time to wake up, Harper," a man said in a soothing tone. "I've got a busy night ahead of me, so I don't have much time."

Who was that? My brain was still sluggish, and I wondered

if that was why I couldn't place him. But I had to know him, right? Otherwise, why would he be sitting in front of me while I was sleeping?

The ache in my shoulders was becoming unbearable. I released a low groan and tried to move them, but they were stuck.

I forced my eyes open again, getting a better glimpse of the man in the chair. He was wearing dress pants and a button-down shirt with a tie. He looked to be in his forties, with thin, dark-blond hair trimmed short. He was sitting in a chair, turned slightly to the side as he watched me like I was a still life he wanted to draw.

I tried to move my hands again and realized they were tied behind my back. I no longer had my jacket, and my wig had been removed, my real hair brushing my shoulders. My feet were bare, and my jeans, which had concealed my gun, were torn up to my calf.

Panic swept through me and I jerked harder on my hands and legs, but my arms didn't budge, and my legs were tied to the chair as well. Terror burned off my grogginess.

"I'm sure it's disconcerting waking up to find yourself in this position," he said in a dull tone.

"Who are you?" I demanded, but I already knew. I also knew I was screwed.

If I'd met him out in the world, I would have taken his smile for a friendly gesture. But I was tied to a chair in the center of a concrete room of about ten feet by ten feet. His smile was pure evil.

"I think you know who I am. I hear you've been looking for me."

I tried to shrug, but my bound arms made it impossible. "Who knew the big bad Gerald Knox was really a scared little boy who hides in the dark?"

He laughed and shook his head. "You're one to talk. Didn't you run off to Lone County to hide and lick your wounds?"

"Been stalking me?" I asked in defiance.

"If you wish to call it that." He shifted in his seat. "Where's my accountant, Harper?" His voice was icy.

"How the hell would I know? I'm not your assistant."

"You and Malcolm paid her a visit, and now she's gone." He leaned closer. "What did you do with her?"

"I didn't do *anything* with her," I said in a flippant tone. "Maybe she was tired of working for you and quit."

He lifted his hand and slapped me hard enough across the cheek to make my teeth rattle.

"What?" I asked with a small laugh. "Does it hurt your feelings when someone doesn't want to work for you?"

He slapped me again, this time a backhand to my other cheek, but I didn't regret provoking him, because his violence meant I was getting under his skin.

"I heard you had a mouth on you," he said, all politeness gone. "Back when you worked with him before."

My brain still wasn't operating at one hundred percent, but even if it had been, I wouldn't have had a clue who he was talking about. Keith? One of my uniformed partners?

I couldn't imagine any of them telling anyone I was mouthy, because I'd been known for quietly observing.

"Bottom line," I said, tasting metal in my mouth. "I don't know where your accountant is."

"What about my handler?" he asked, his voice tight with unrestrained anger. "And my girl?"

"That *child* was not *your* girl," I spat. "And she's somewhere you'll never get to her again."

"And my handler?"

"I have no idea," I said truthfully. "And frankly, I don't give a fuck."

His palm cracked across my face, this time making my ears

ring. It took me a second to push the fuzziness in my head away.

"I've heard you're big on demanding respect," he sneered. "But it's *your* turn to learn some."

Again, I wasn't sure what he was talking about, and I had no idea why he would say that.

"Where's Malcolm?" he demanded.

"Handing over enough evidence to put you away for life."

He hit me again, and I struggled to keep my head upright because it was too early to start fading. I needed to stay focused. My time with Knox was just beginning.

He grabbed my face in his hand, his thumb and index finger pinching my stinging cheeks, and leaned over me, his face inches from mine. His eyes were dark with hatred. "Where's Malcolm?"

"I have no fucking idea," I said. "And that's the God's honest truth."

He studied me a few seconds longer, then shoved my face away. My chair rocked as he took a step back. "Not to worry. We'll find him soon enough." He flashed me a smile. "We don't need him for our talk."

I remained silent, running through my options but coming up short. My hands were bound behind me, my legs tied to the chair. I wasn't getting out of here, and the man in front of me would make sure I didn't. My only hope was that Carter could still see my location and would send help. Because, while I'd given him Knox's address, I doubted his home had a concrete dungeon. Of course, Carter might send his men to the wrong place. I had no idea when they'd stripped off my jacket or taken my phone.

"Where's your mother's file?" he asked.

"Somewhere *you* won't get it," I said with a bitter laugh.

Another slap.

"Let's try that again," he said. "Where is the——"

"You're wasting your time and breath," I said through gritted teeth. "I'm never going to tell you."

He punched me in the stomach this time, knocking the wind out of me. I wasn't sure why it caught me by surprise. I expected it to get a lot worse.

I wasn't wrong. Several minutes later, I still hadn't told him, and my left eye was swollen and my stomach ached.

Knox was getting frustrated and apparently worn out, based on his heavy breathing. He stepped away from me, beginning to pace as he rubbed his raw and swollen knuckles.

He stopped and turned to face me. "Where have you been the last few years?"

I was pretty sure I was concussed, because his question didn't make any sense. "I was in the Little Rock Police Department," I said, surprised to hear it come out slurred.

His eyes narrowed. "How did you coordinate your role as the Lady in Black while working for the police?"

"What are you talking about?" I said, shaking my head slightly and regretting it.

He took a step closer. "You're not her, are you?"

"I have no idea what you're talking about."

His eyes widened slightly. "You don't know about the Lady in Black?"

My vision was fuzzy, so I closed my eyes for a second and opened them, hoping it would clear. I was getting under his skin, and right now, that was my only defense. "What is that? An urban legend? Is she like Batman?"

A door on the far wall opened and Nicole Knox walked in, wearing a light blue tweed jacket and skirt with a white blouse. Her right arm was in a sling, but a black handbag hung from the crook of her left arm. Her two-inch heels click-clacked on the concrete floor.

Her sharp gaze landed on me. Hatred oozed from her.

I was in real trouble now.

"Did you find out where she's keeping the file?" Nicole asked her son.

"No," he said, breathless with frustration. "She won't say."

"You didn't try hard enough," she said.

"Look at her," he said, flinging a hand toward me. "She's not cooperating."

A slow, evil smile spread across Nicole's face. "She will once we give her the right motivation. Did you find Malcolm yet?"

"No."

Nicole frowned. "Your father would have found him a week ago."

"Thank you for the reminder, Mother," he said, his words tight.

Nicole strode toward me. "Not so tough now, are you, Ms. Adams?"

I looked up at her, refusing to show any sign of anger or fear. "I'm not scared of you."

"You should be." She slipped her handbag down her arm so she could reach inside with her left hand and pulled out a small handgun. Then she set her purse on the empty chair. "Maybe I should shoot you in the arm. You know the saying, 'an eye for an eye.'"

The look in her eyes told me she'd do it in a heartbeat. But I suspected she wouldn't stop with one shot. I also suspected she wouldn't be calling 911.

"I don't seem to be in a position to negotiate," I said. No sense pretending otherwise.

"Not true," Nicole said, bending at the waist to look me in the eye. "All you have to do is answer my questions."

"I'm not going to tell you where my mother's file is," I said, holding her gaze in defiance. "She died to keep it from you. It would be like spitting on her grave."

Nicole laughed. "She wouldn't have suffered to protect you."

Her words sank into my skin like a knife. "You didn't know my mother."

"Didn't I?" Her thin brow lifted. "She was my friend for a month. She told me things."

A chill went through me. "I don't give a shit what she told you. I'm still not giving you the file."

"You were a disappointment to both of your parents. Your mother told me in the strictest of confidence that she wished you had been kidnapped and murdered, not your sister."

While my mother had never outright said this, I'd still known. So why did it hurt so much hearing this sociopath say it?

"Old news," I said, trying to sound bored, but my lips and cheeks were swollen enough to make it sound like I had a mouth stuffed with cotton. "If you're trying to break me, that's not going to do it."

"Your father hated bringing you back to Lone Creek two months ago."

I'd figured that out days ago, so that shouldn't have hurt either.

A soft smile lifted her lips. "If you don't give me the file, I'll kill him too."

"You really suck at motivational speeches," I said. "You should have held back the part about him not wanting me to come home before you threatened to kill him."

"But you're so desperate for him to love you, you'll save him anyway," she said, "even though you know he wouldn't do the same for you."

"Do you know how to use YouTube, Nicole?" I prodded. "Because if you can figure it out, you need to binge some Brené Brown videos."

"You think you're so cute," she said in a mock cheery tone. She set her gun on the chair and pulled a leather belt out of her purse. Then, as if remembering her son was behind her, she turned and said, "Don't you have business to attend to?"

His body stiffened. "I'm doing it."

"Hardly," she scoffed, folding the belt in half and clutching it near the end by the buckle. "You failed here, and you're in danger of the exchange being interrupted. What are you doing to prevent that from happening?"

"We've beefed up security," Knox said defensively. "He's one man and we've already captured her." He flung his hand toward me. "We're *fine*."

Had he forgotten I'd told him James was turning over evidence on his illegal activities?

She glared at him for several seconds before she said in a chilly tone, "If this gets screwed up, it will be on *your* head, Gerry."

Then it hit me. Gerald Knox wasn't running the family business. Nicole was.

I started to laugh.

Nicole swung around to face me, her lips pursed in disapproval. "And what do you think is so funny?"

I slowly shook my head, ignoring the sharp stabs of pain in my neck and head. "You. Him." I nodded toward Gerald. "The world thinks he's in charge, yet it's really you. But you're a woman, and the big bad men won't respect you, so you need to use your son like a puppet."

Fury filled her eyes and she slapped my bare upper right arm with the belt.

Fire spread across my skin, but I grinned up at her. "Oh, the truth hurts."

She took a step closer, leaning over me. "Not as much as this belt will hurt *you*." Then, to prove her point, she hit me in multiple places on my body, her strikes becoming more forceful with each hit.

Stings screamed for attention all over my body—my arms,

my upper back, my legs, even one on my cheek. Tears filled my eyes, but I refused to give this woman the satisfaction of seeing me cry.

"Okay, Harper," she said in her mock polite tone. "Let's try again, shall we?"

"You're wasting your time," I forced out, trying to ignore the pain. "I will never, ever tell you where the file is."

"Oh, you underestimate me, my dear," she said with a gentle laugh.

I suspected she was right, but I wasn't about to admit it.

She swung back to the chair and set her purse and the gun on the floor, then scooted closer to me, so there were only inches between our knees when she sat facing me.

"I was gentle with your mother," she said with a kind expression. "She refused to talk, but I knew the papers were in a safe deposit box. I merely had to access them. Your name was on the box, so if I couldn't get them myself, I knew I could get them from *you*."

She paused and gave me an encouraging nod while still smiling sweetly, the image of a stereotypical, cookie-baking grandma. Which only made her more terrifying.

"But you, my dear, are the end of the line for getting access," she said primly. "And I *will* get those papers. If I have to keep you in this room for months and punish you multiple times a day, you will eventually tell me." She lifted a hand and gently caressed the burning welt from the belt on my cheek, intensifying the pain. "I promise you," she whispered tenderly. "It will become so much worse."

Panic and terror stole my breath. I believed every word she said, and I knew she'd take great pleasure in every ounce of pain she doled out.

A knowing smile lit up her face. She'd seen my fear and she reveled in it.

Hopelessness swept over me, suffocating me.

The light in her eyes showed me she saw that too.

She brushed a thumb over the welt on my cheek, pressing down to make sure it hurt. "I'm quite creative, Harper, and truth be told, it's been a while since I've been able to play." Her sweet smile was back. "I've missed it."

She wasn't angry. She was enjoying herself.

I didn't answer, because I wasn't sure what to say. Goading Gerald had frustrated him. Goading Nicole would only feed her hunger to hurt me.

But Nicole was already hungry. And she told me so over the next hour—maybe longer—with every crack of the belt, then jabs with a cattle prod a guard brought in. I lost track of time. I didn't know how long she kept at it, but eventually I lost consciousness.

I jerked awake when a large splash of freezing cold water hit my face.

I blinked, panic surging through me, which only intensified when I took in my surroundings.

Gerald was gone. Nicole was standing in front of me, flecks of blood dotting her white sling. A small table was against the far wall, and two guards were moving toward me.

"You had a little nap," Nicole said. "It's time to play again."

One guard moved behind me and cut the zip ties holding my bound wrists. The other guard squatted in front of me, using a long-bladed pocketknife to cut the zip ties on my legs. I considered trying to fight him, but I didn't think I had the strength to overpower him, let alone run.

I was going to die here.

Would James be disappointed that my lessons with Tex had been for nothing? Would he be disappointed that I couldn't find it in me to fight back?

The guards must have been given orders before they woke

me, because the guy in front of me tied my wrists together in front of me with a thin nylon cord.

A renewed sense of hope swept away my hopelessness. I could work with this. With my hands in front of me, I could open doors or even put up a fight.

But then they hauled me to my feet, and the guard behind me grabbed the bottom of my tank top and ripped the fabric upward, leaving my back bare. Next, something cold and metallic traced between my shoulder blades, cutting through the band of my bra.

As he worked, the man in front of me was unfastening my jeans and tugging them down.

A new panic swamped my head. I tried to pull away, but the man behind me wrapped an arm around my stomach as he used his other hand to cut my shirt and bra at my shoulders.

I began to thrash, trying to pull free, but the man behind me held me tightly to his chest as the guard in front of me knelt and tugged off my jeans and underwear. The man behind me lifted my feet off the ground as the other one pulled my jeans and panties free.

I tried to kick him, but he just laughed and batted my legs away.

Then the guard in front lifted my bound arms over my head, and for the first time, I saw a giant meat hook hanging from a chain in the ceiling.

I kicked furiously, but they easily lifted me up and hung my cord from the hook, my feet over a foot off the floor. The strain on my shoulders was unbearable, especially after having my arms tied behind me, and I cried out in pain before I could stop myself.

Nicole moved in front of me, her gaze lowering over my naked body, then back up to my face, sadistic pleasure in her eyes. She held a riding crop in her hands. "You're not as young as I prefer, but one makes do with what one has."

It took a second for the meaning of her words to sink in.

She pressed the tip of the crop to the bottom of my chin. "We're going to have so much fun."

"Go to hell, you evil bitch," I spat.

Her brow lifted in amusement. "That was very naughty, Harper. It's time you learned to obey, and lucky for you, I'm just the one to teach you."

And then she began.

Chapter 33

James

It was just past two in the morning when I walked out the back of the dry-cleaning business. I was hungry, exhausted, and pissed beyond words. My head pounded, and everything in me was desperate to get back to Harper. She had to be wondering what had taken so long.

My fucking handler had insisted I sit there while they went through the files, claiming they had to make sure they had enough information to get a search warrant for Natalie's computer. They'd known within fifteen minutes—and I was pretty sure they were making arrangements for other agents to bust the shipment—but they took great pleasure in keeping me there for eight hours, loving every minute of my annoyance. Finally, they told me I could leave but insisted I wouldn't be released from our agreement until the entire trafficking network had been taken down.

It had taken everything in me not to strangle the life out of them, but I'd walked away, mostly because Harper needed me, whether she knew it or not. If I killed my handler, I'd be living on borrowed time before I was arrested and imprisoned for life. I had to stay out until I helped Harper get the justice she deserved. I couldn't do that from behind bars.

When I reached my car, I got inside and opened the glove compartment, pulled out my phone and turned it on.

It exploded with text after text, as well as calls from Harper's burner cell and Carter's number.

I called Harper first, but it went to voicemail, so I called Carter next.

"Where the fuck have you been?" he demanded, sounding more furious than I'd ever heard him.

While my instinct was to bite his head off, I knew there was a reason he was reacting like this. Carter was panicked.

"With my handler. What happened?"

"Harper's missing."

My stomach felt like a twenty-pound weight had been dropped into it. My hand tightened on the phone until my knuckles ached. "What do you mean she's missing?"

"She went looking for you, and the last I heard, she'd shot Razor and left him in a parking lot. She was heading back to her car to go back to the hotel, but then her phone stopped sending a GPS signal about half a block from the bar."

I forced myself to concentrate on his words and shove my emotions down. "Why was she with Razor?"

He started from the beginning, with Harper calling him worried because I hadn't returned after two hours. They'd tracked my phone to a location two blocks from Razor's hangout. She'd reasoned that I'd gone after Razor without her and had gone to find me.

"I told her to stay at the hotel!" I shouted, punching the steering wheel with enough force to put a dent in it. "Why didn't you force her to stay?"

"I told her to stay!" he shouted back. "But it didn't help

that you took two hard drives and made a twenty-minute stop at a diner downtown before heading to your second location. She thought the first stop was with your handler and the second was to take on Knox yourself."

Nausea roiled in my gut. I wanted to be pissed at her, but I could understand how she'd think that. While she'd started to trust me, I hadn't proven she could trust me completely.

"You met with Deveraux first," he said, leaving no doubt about his disapproval.

"What difference does it make?"

"Oh, I don't know," he drawled. "Maybe if Harper had known you were visiting him first and your handler second, she wouldn't have assumed you were going after Razor even though you parked your car *two fucking blocks away!*"

I ran my hand over my head, my panic rising. He was right, but I didn't see the point in admitting it right now.

"She found your car," he continued, calmer, "and when she saw no sign of you, she headed into the bar. Razor was there and she got him into his truck and questioned him. She got Knox's home address and found out the exchange is happening at four this morning."

"And then she shot him?" I asked, trying to focus and not panic.

"I'm not sure of the order of things, but yes, she shot him in the leg and called 911 to get him. She told me she was going back to the hotel." He paused. "When her phone signal went out, I sent someone over to the bar to check it out." His voice went tight. "Her car's still there, and someone said they saw a man tackle a woman on the sidewalk. Two other men loaded her limp body into the trunk of a car and drove away. The guy I sent found her broken phone in the gutter of the street near her car."

I closed my eyes. I couldn't let emotion take over. I had to reason this through. "What's Knox's address?"

"You don't think he'd be stupid enough to take her there, do you?" Carter said in disbelief.

"It's the first place to look. We both know he wants her."

"And if she's not there, you'll let Knox know you're looking for her, and he could move her somewhere else before you can find out where she is."

He was right, but I was trying to put myself in Gerald Knox's head. He thought he was untouchable. I could see him taking her to his home to make it more convenient for him to torture her.

"He took her to his house."

"Skeeter…"

"Even if she's not there, now's a good time to go look. Knox is bound to be nervous. I'll show up at the shipment exchange, especially since he took Harper. He's going to be there in person to make sure I don't interfere."

He was silent for a second. "Okay. Do you want me to assemble a team? It'll take a couple hours."

I glanced at the clock on my dash. 2:13. Knox would be at the drop by four, likely sooner, so his house should be empty. Waiting for a team was safer, but I wasn't leaving her in Knox's hands a minute longer than necessary.

"You can start putting one together, but I'm headed to his house to scope it out."

"Wait for the team, Skeeter," he pleaded.

"I'm just checking it out."

"We both know that's not true," he said, sounding exhausted. "But think about this—what good are you to her if you get killed before you even reach her?"

"You underestimate my determination," I grunted.

"And you're one man," Carter said, "who's not as young as he used to be and is still recuperating from a concussion."

I wanted to tell him he was full of shit, but he wasn't

wrong. Still, my imagination was running wild with what Knox and his people could be doing to her.

"What time did her phone go dark?"

He hesitated before answering. "8:36."

I quickly did the calculation. She'd been with Knox for nearly six hours. A hell of a lot could happen in six hours.

"Send me the address."

"Don't do anything stupid, Skeeter," he said. "For the first time in a long time, you have something to live for. Don't throw it away now."

"I don't intend to," I said. "Send me the address."

Chapter 34

Every part of me hurt, but thankfully, I wasn't hanging from the ceiling anymore. Nicole had ordered her two minions to unhook me and dump me naked on the concrete floor.

She'd left at some point, muttering something about her son being pathetic. Did it have something to do with the shipment? Had James shown up to interrupt it?

I had no idea how long I'd been here or what time it was.

I only knew Nicole was going to kill me. I just didn't know how long it would be until she did it. From her earlier statements, it could be a long, long time.

My body was covered with whip marks and burns from the cattle prod. My left eye had swollen shut. She'd asked me countless times where the files were, and every time I'd refused to answer her. But instead of getting frustrated, she'd seemed pleased to have an excuse to inflict more pain.

I drifted off but woke up when I heard the door open. Nicole entered the room and shut it behind her, standing in front of it as she studied me with a smile.

She wasn't afraid of me. Not like this.

"Where's Gerry?" I asked, still lying on the floor.

She chuckled as she moved closer. I saw a flash of something shiny and realized she was holding a knife.

"Do you prefer him to me?" she asked. "Sorry, but he's busy making sure your boyfriend doesn't interfere with an important drop."

It had to be after midnight. Maybe closer to two.

"You say that so easily," I said, my cheek on the cold concrete. "Like you're not discussing the sale of human beings." It wasn't lost on me that she was in here alone, and my only binding was the rope on my wrists. But I couldn't even pick my head up off the floor, let alone overpower her and escape.

"The world doesn't run on fairness, Harper," she said, sitting on the chair which had been moved to the corner. "The world runs on power—he who holds the power makes the rules."

"But not *she*," I scoffed. "That has to piss you off. Letting the world think your son is the brains when we both know it's you."

Her eyes narrowed. "You don't know what you're talking about."

"But I do," I said. *Keep her talking*. "I was smarter than my partner on the force, but he always took credit for my discoveries. Men think they're entitled to power. When we're the ones who help them hold onto it."

The expression on her face changed, as though I'd struck a nerve.

"I bet your husband did the same thing," I continued. "Is that why you befriended my mother to get the files? Gerry wasn't smart enough to handle it."

She pushed out a sigh. "You always want your children to have it better than you. Easier. But sometimes we don't expect *enough* of them."

"And I bet your husband was the one who picked my dad

to be his attorney, so you were cleaning up the mess he'd created."

Her brow lifted. "Exactly."

"Which is why you need the files. The men fucked up and now you have to do the clean-up. You need to know what my mother had so you can be prepared in case the wrong people get their hands on it. Like the police."

She didn't respond, but suddenly she looked exhausted. It was the middle of the night and beating me for hours must have sapped her physical strength.

If she was tired, maybe I could rally and use her exhaustion against her. I just needed to keep her talking so she didn't call her minions in to hang me from the ceiling again.

"Maybe we can make some kind of compromise," I said.

Surprise filled her eyes.

I gathered my strength and pushed myself upright. Moving slowly was a good idea. Any sudden moves might make her think I was a threat. Not that I was capable of sudden moves right now. I barely had the energy to sit upright.

"How about we make a deal?" I suggested. "For every piece of information I tell you about what's in my mother's files, you can share something with me." When she hesitated, I added, "What can it hurt? We both know the only way I'm leaving this room is after I'm dead."

"It's a shame," she said, and a regretful look crossed her eyes. "Under different circumstances, I think you and I could have been friends."

I bit my tongue to keep from saying I didn't befriend masochistic kidnappers who sold and abused children. It wasn't lost on me how vulnerable I was. My legs were pressed together, bent at the knees and to the side, but I was still naked. I kept my back as straight as possible, not attempting to cover my breasts. Nicole had seen plenty of them over the past few hours.

"I guess I should start," I said with a hesitant smile. "Is there anything you're particularly concerned about, or should I pick something at random?"

Her eyes narrowed, like she couldn't believe I was playing games. "Tell me something random."

"Okay," I said, trying to keep my gaze off the knife she was twirling in her hand. "You weren't the only person in my mother's files. You and your family only make up about forty percent."

Her mouth dropped open. "You're lying."

"Why would I lie?" I asked with a small laugh. "You thought you were my father's only criminal clients?"

"I knew about J.R.," she said. Confusion covered her face. Then, as if grabbing for something she understood, she added, "Speaking of J.R., were you the infamous Lady in Black?" She shook her head. "I don't see how. I know you were working for the Little Rock police up until last fall, but Gerry was so sure you were her."

There was that name again. "We've already determined you're the brains of the family," I said. "I'm not the Lady in Black. I've never heard of her until tonight."

She took delight in that piece of information. "Oh, interesting indeed. So you replaced her?"

"Why would you think I'm her replacement?"

"Because you're working with Skeeter Malcolm," she said, like I was a fool. When she saw my confusion, she laughed. "You didn't know?"

"What he did in the past is his business," I said, but my mind was racing over who the Lady in Black could have been and why Malcolm would have used a woman to—

I was an idiot. I knew exactly who the Lady in Black must have been.

And Nicole could tell I'd put it together. "You know who

she is," she said, leaning forward, excitement giving her a burst of energy.

"How would I know who she is?" I scoffed. "I've never been to Fenton County."

She tilted her head. "I never said she was from Fenton County."

Shit. "Of course she was from Fenton County. If she worked with James, then she had to be there."

"Hmm…" she said skeptically. "I don't believe you." She stood and took a step forward, her knife pointed toward me. "You know who she is."

I kept my gaze glued to the blade in her hand. "How would I know that when I'd never heard her name before tonight?"

She took another step, her eyes lighting with excitement. "But you know anyway." She leaned closer to me. "And you're going to tell me."

Funny. I was probably about to die protecting Rose Gardner's secret identity. Because while I'd never met the woman, and I undoubtedly felt threatened by her past relationship with James, I would never let this woman get within fifty miles of Rose and her children.

How ironic that neither she nor James would ever know.

Nicole turned toward the door, and I could tell she was about to call for the guards to come string me up again. If they did that, the session would end with me covered in countless cuts, either dead or wishing I was. No, I wouldn't let that happen. If I was going to die anyway, I'd rather do it trying to save myself.

So, I leapt up at her. I was still too weak to get to my full height, but I reached her waist and managed to pull her to the floor.

She hit the ground hard. She regained her senses seconds later, though, and was about to shout when I covered her mouth with my hand.

She hadn't lost the knife in the fall, and without hesitation, she stabbed me in the side.

I gasped, and a triumphant look filled her eyes.

A sharp pain filled the side of my chest, and I nearly collapsed on top of her.

She pulled out the blade, whipping her arm back and then swinging down to stab me again.

Somehow, I found the strength to push her arm hard with my free hand before the blade made contact, but the arc of her interrupted swing brought the tip dangerously close to my cheek.

My other hand was still covering her mouth, and she tried to bite my palm. I drove my chest hard against her sling, hoping to inflict pain where I'd shot her last week.

I knew I should have an escape plan, but the only thought in my head was that this woman was going to kill me, and I needed to disarm her in any way I could.

I shifted my hand to her wrist and slammed it onto the concrete floor. But she still didn't release the knife.

I heard shouting outside the door—muffled and urgent—followed by multiple gunshots.

Nicole's eyes flicked to the door. The sounds outside the room gave her a burst of energy. She bucked me off her and onto my back. Within seconds, she was looming over me with the knife, her eyes wide with fury. She brought the knife down in a stabbing motion over my left breast, but I grabbed her forearm with both hands and tried to hold her off.

"I'm going to kill you, Harper Adams," she sneered. "But not before you tell me who the Lady in Black was."

"Go to hell," I grunted, my side sticky with blood. I was already weak, but my body was turning cold, and I could tell I was already going into shock. I didn't think I could hold her off much longer.

"I can make this easy for you," she said with a saccharine smile. "Just one name and then your suffering will be over."

"I'll never tell you," I said through gritted teeth, "just like I'll never tell you where my mother's files are."

The shouting was right outside the door now, quickly followed by a round of gunshots. I couldn't let myself believe that James or anyone else had come to save me. I had to focus on not letting her kill me.

But my arms were beginning to shake, and her knife blade was inches from my upper chest. I wasn't sure how much longer I could hold on.

Then the door burst open and Nicole flinched, panic filling her eyes as a shadow filled the doorway. "If you shoot me, you'll kill her too!"

I didn't understand what she was saying, because I didn't have a gun, but then a pair of boots and jean-clad legs appeared to the left in my blurred vision.

"Good thing I don't need a gun for this," James said, then kicked the toe of his boot into her ribs and sent her several feet from me.

Nicole screamed as she landed on her injured arm, but James was already kneeling beside me. My eyes lifted to his, and I wasn't surprised to see the horror in them.

His gaze swept over my welts and blood, then landed on the pool of blood next to my left side. His eyes lifted to mine in question.

"She stabbed me." I gave him a shaky half-smile. "I didn't get a chance to use anything Tex showed me."

He pressed his hand to my side with his bare hand, trying to apply pressure.

"James," I said, barely above a whisper. "I'm sorry I left. I thought…"

His jaw clenched. "Save your sorries. There's nothing to be

sorry for. I'm gonna to get you out of here, but I don't want to hurt you."

"Just help me sit up."

He hesitated like he didn't think that was the best idea, but then he scooped his arm under my upper back and lifted me to a sitting position.

Nicole was still lying on the floor, moaning. The knife lay on the floor between us.

I reached for it as Nicole lunged for it too, a wild, feral look in her eyes.

A gunshot rang out and blood flowed from a wound in her upper right arm, but it didn't stop her. She grabbed the hilt of the knife.

James shot her again, but she lifted the knife, tip pointing down. When she lunged for me, I used all my weight to push her onto her back and grab her knife hand, twisting her wrist away from me. But my forward momentum not only pointed the knife toward her chest but drove the blade in.

Shock filled her eyes and her face instantly lost color.

"Meet you in hell," she spat at me.

"Looks like you're getting there first," I whispered, struggling to breathe.

James pulled me off her and tried to get me to lie down again, but I pushed his arm away and scrambled to my feet. "No. Get me out of here."

I grabbed at his clothes, and he wrapped an arm around my back to pull me upright. "You need to be lying down, Harper. You're hemorrhaging."

"No," I said forcefully. "I'm not dying in this room." I tried to take a step, but my legs gave out and my body crumpled.

He scooped me into his arms and held me close. "You're not gonna die, Harper," he said, his voice tight as he carried me out of the room and down a dark hall. "You're too damn stubborn."

"Yeah," I said, then coughed, pain filling my entire chest. "It'll take more than that bitch to kill me," I said, but the words felt loose and I wasn't sure I'd even said them. My peripheral vision had turned dark.

"Damn straight."

We were bouncing, and I had the vague idea that we were going up stairs.

"Stay with me, Harper," he said in a pleading tone that caught me by surprise.

"You came for me," I said in awe, my cheek resting against his chest.

"You thought I wouldn't?" he scoffed, but he didn't sound pissed. "I'll *always* come for you."

I wanted to promise him the same, but I wasn't sure I'd be around to hold up my end of the deal. Then cold air hit my body, and I began to shiver uncontrollably. But the dark sky was above me, which meant we'd made it outside. I forced my gaze up to James's face. "Thank you for not letting me die in there."

He glanced down at me, fear in his eyes. "You're not gonna die," he ordered.

A smile lifted the corners of my mouth. "I'm trying."

"Do more than try." Then he put me in the backseat of a car. Seconds later, something soft was pressed against my side. "Just hold on, Harper," he pleaded again. "Just hold on."

I wanted to hold on, but this was too much. Everything faded to black.

Chapter 35

When I woke, pain radiated everywhere. I let out a loud moan and within seconds, James was standing over me, worry on his face.

"It's okay. You're safe."

I glanced around and realized I was in a hospital room. It took me a few moments to remember what had happened, and I panicked. I tried to sit up, but James held my shoulders down.

"Harper," he said, gently. "You're safe."

"They'll find me here. They'll kill me."

"Who?"

"Keith. Brad Huffington." I continued to fight against him, sending a shooting pain through my side. "The Little Rock police. They'll figure out we know they're involved and kill me."

He leaned in closer. "Do you think I'd let that happen? You're safe. They think your name is Amber Beachum."

I stared up at him in confusion. "But I was stabbed. There would be a police report. Someone will want to interview me."

"The Feds took over the case." When I still looked confused, he said. "I called my handler. They took care of it. I checked you in as Amber Beachum, and they told the LRPD they're in charge of your case and the LRPD isn't to get anywhere near you."

"Why would they do that?"

"Because I asked them to. And they owe me."

I closed my eyes. "What did it cost you?"

"Nothin'," he said, placing a kiss on my forehead. "Now stop worrying. I didn't go to all that trouble of gettin' you out of there to just let you die in a hospital."

I looked up at him, tears swimming in my eyes as everything came rushing back.

He softly cupped my cheek. "It's over. Nicole is dead. So is Gerald Knox." He made a look of disgust. "And I had nothin' to do with his death. The state police and the Feds took him out when they surrounded Knox and his men during the exchange."

I let that sink in for barely a second before I asked. "What about the girls?" My stomach twisted with anxiety.

"Safe."

"And Wilhemina? Do we know about her?"

"At Knox's private club. I guess the women lived there so they never left the premises."

He looked into my eyes. "Sorry about Knox. I know you wanted to kill him."

"Turns out Nicole was the mastermind," I said, closing my eyes. "She just let her husband and son take the credit."

We were both silent for a long moment before I said, "I think she hurt girls in that room."

He didn't say anything, just waited to see if I'd continue.

"She said she hadn't *played* in a long time. Then she said she was used to girls younger than me." I opened my eyes. "She was a sadistic… evil…"

"She's dead. You killed her."

I slowly nodded, letting that sink in.

"And if you hadn't killed her, I would have done it myself," he said, fury in his eyes. "For what she dared to do to you."

Images of what she'd done flashed in my head, making me shudder.

"You're safe," he said, stroking the top of my head. "I promise."

I looked up at him, hating to bring this up now, but it was important for him to know. "Knox thought I was someone called the Lady in Black."

Surprise and worry flashed in his eyes.

"Then he realized it wasn't me. Nicole said she knew it wasn't me, because it would have been impossible for me to get to Fenton County with my LRPD schedule."

His stared at me in disbelief.

I gave him a soft smile. "Nicole realized I'd figured out who the Lady in Black was. I denied it, but she saw the moment I put it together. She planned to slash me with her knife until I gave her a name." I grabbed his forearm. "I didn't tell her, James. And I never would have. I was prepared to die to keep her safe."

"You couldn't know who she was," he whispered.

"I know," I whispered back. "I know."

For the first time since I'd met him, he looked like he wasn't sure what to do.

"I will never tell, James," I said, tightening my grip on his arm. "I'm not even saying her name now. But I know her identity, just like I know she's the woman you loved." I hesitated, wondering if I should confess the next part, but I was going all in. I whispered, "Just like I know she's the mother of your daughter."

Pure panic filled his eyes, and he started to take a step back, breaking free of my hold.

"No one told me," I insisted, finding the strength to sit up, worried he was going to leave. Pain shot through my side, stealing my breath, but I ignored it. "I figured it out a couple of nights ago when you told me you'd loved someone." I grimaced. "I told you I'm a good detective."

He didn't say anything.

"It doesn't change anything," I pleaded. "It doesn't change how I feel about you. And I know why you don't want anyone to know. I swear to you, James, I'll keep your secrets. I *will* protect them."

He was silent for several seconds, then he sat on the edge of the bed and wrapped his arms carefully around me. "Thank you."

I rested my head on his shoulder, tears burning my eyes.

His hand stroked the back of my head. "How'd you figure out the last one?" he asked.

"The photo on your mantel," I said, still leaning into him. "And the timing. And you said she made a decision that you couldn't live with. That seemed like it fit the bill."

He remained silent, but his arms tightened slightly, yet stayed loose enough to not hurt me.

"I have questions," I said, leaning back slightly to look into his eyes, "but I'm not going to pry. You can tell me when you're ready." I gave him a half-smile. "And when we're somewhere more private."

He placed a tender kiss on my lips. "Thank you."

"I guess the Feds are going to be all over the LRPD's involvement in Knox's finances."

He held my gaze. "They don't know about the police involvement. I took that part out of what I gave them."

I stared at him in confusion. "Why would you do that?"

"To give us a chance to bring them down ourselves. But I only bought us a month before they start investigating the LR police. I'll need to get an extension so you have time to heal."

"If you didn't tell the Feds, then who are you getting an extension from?"

He held my gaze. "It's how I got Dani's charges dropped."

I sucked in a breath, then instantly regretted it. "You went to Mason Deveraux."

He gave a curt nod. "I did. I gave him all of it, but I asked him to give us a chance to dig into the cops."

"Why would you do that?"

"Because you need to find out what you were on to that scared them enough to discredit you and destroy your career. And I'm going to help you do it."

I started to tell him he didn't have to help me, but he'd already told me he would.

I could still hear Nicole's voice in my head, telling me my mother wished I'd been kidnapped and murdered instead of my sister. And that my father hadn't wanted me to come home. I still believed something in me made me unlovable, so my brain grabbed the only explanation that felt safe…

What James felt for me was lust. If he wanted to help me, he was probably getting something out of it too.

It was easier to believe that then to think someone could really love me. Believing that was much too dangerous.

I also recognized it was fear talking. Fear of rejection, like I'd been rejected before. Fear of being hurt. I knew deep down I wasn't unlovable.

But it was one thing to know something and another to truly believe it.

"Okay," I finally said. "We can start in a couple of weeks."

"No," he said sternly. "They're not going anywhere and they have no idea we're onto them. We're going to take two months."

"Two months?" I asked in disbelief. "What are we going to do for two months?"

"I was thinkin'," he said in a husky voice as his lips hovered inches over mine. "Maybe it's time to take a vacation. I can't remember the last time I took one. If ever."

"So we'll start when you get back from vacation?"

He chuckled against my lips. "Like hell I'm leavin' you behind. You're comin' with me."

It took a second for that to sink in. Part of me thought I should protest, but I couldn't figure out why. "Where are we going?"

"Maybe somewhere warm with a beach. But if there's somewhere else you want to go, we can go there instead."

The urge to protest was strong, but for once, I was going to accept something good. "Okay," I said. "A beach sounds great. But no crowds if possible. I don't know if I can handle a lot of people right now."

He kissed me tenderly, then lifted his head. "I'll take care of everything."

I drifted off to sleep soon afterward, and when I woke, I saw Louise walking into the room.

James rose from his chair and dipped his chin. "Deputy. I'll let you two have some time together."

Louise watched him walk out of the room and turned back to me.

"How did you know I was here?" I asked, starting to panic. If Louise knew, then the LRPD could find out.

"Malcolm called me," she said. "He told me you were here under an alias, but he wouldn't tell me how you got injured."

"Huh." I was genuinely shocked James had called her, but then I wasn't. He knew she'd worry about me.

"I heard there was a human trafficking ring takedown early this morning," she said. "They're saying it was massive."

"You don't say," I murmured weakly.

"What a coincidence you got stabbed and beaten early this morning."

I grimaced. "Little Rock isn't as small as people think."

"I know you can't confide in me for some reason," she said. "Which has to do with your alias, but I'm not stupid enough to believe you weren't part of it." She paused. "You and Malcolm."

"We might know a little bit about it," I admitted, then I added, "We're going after the LRPD next. But James won't consider it for a couple of months." When she looked surprised, I added, "Because of this stupid stab wound."

"I still want to be a part of it," she said.

I nodded. "As long as you agree to work with James."

She hesitated, then made a face. "I'm going to have to defer to your judgment on that one."

"Thanks."

"So…" she said, "You and Malcolm?"

"Me and Malcolm. He's not who I expected."

She gave me a tight smile. "I hope you know what you're doing."

I had no idea what I was doing, but being with James felt more right than anything ever had. I was going to enjoy it while I could.

Read a bonus chapter of when James met Mason Devereaux.
(Rose Gardner fans will want to read this!)
http://subscribepage.io/udlpED

About the Author

Denise Grover Swank was born in Kansas City, Missouri and lived in the area until she was nineteen. Then she became a nomad, living in five cities, four states and ten houses over the course of ten years before she moved back to her roots. She speaks English and smattering of Spanish and Chinese which she learned through an intensive Nick Jr. immersion period. Her hobbies include witty Facebook comments (in own her mind) and dancing in her kitchen with her children. (Quite badly if you believe her offspring.) Hidden talents include the gift of justification and the ability to drink massive amounts of caffeine and still fall asleep within two minutes. Her lack of the sense of smell allows her to perform many unspeakable tasks. She has six children and hasn't lost her sanity. Or so she leads you to believe.

denisegroverswank.com